DISSENT

The Heretics Saga: Book 2

C. A. CAMPBELL

To those who dare to dissent.
You are the spark that will
set the world on fire.

Trigger Warnings

THE HERETICS SAGA is entirely a work of fiction. However, it is set in a dark, troublesome world that sometimes parallels the reality experienced by many readers. As such, some content may be triggering for some audiences. Please review the list below before reading:

- **Themes of racism, prejudice, homophobia, and violence/crimes against religious, BIPOC and LGBTQIA+ communities.** As the author, I have sought to display all of these things in a negative light and taken steps to ensure sensitivity. However, it may still be troubling to some readers.
- **Physical, emotional and sexual abuse - including abuse against children.** These scenes are vague and brief, but may still be triggering to those with past experiences.
- **Mental health concerns, including post-traumatic stress disorder, suicidal ideation, and illusions to self-harm.**
- **Scenes of a moderate sexual nature.**
- **Violence, death, torture, and battle scenes.**

If any reader (particularly from the above communities), believes some content is potentially harmful or if this trigger warning list is incomplete, please reach out to me so I can make a correction. My contact information can be found at the back of this novel in the 'About the Author'.

Part One
Codename Princess

"Can you remember who you were,
before the world told you
who you should be?"

— Charles Bukowski

ONE

Chin up. Show them what you're made of.

As the towering double doors slammed shut behind her with the boom of a jail cell, Shiloh Haven lifted her chin and forced her feet to move steadily across the marble floor. Each step echoed in the quiet chamber. In the center of the room, she stopped and pressed her hands to her sides so they wouldn't shake. Hewn from the same white marble as the floor, five judges' seats towered high above her head. White—this chamber was all so blindingly white and fiercely cold. But not as cold as the eyes of the five members of the United Council as they gazed down upon her from their seats—five deadly monarchs on their thrones.

"Are you Shiloh Haven?" Councilor Beck asked from the center seat, her voice ricocheting against the stone and settling in Shiloh's bones.

Yes, your majesty. Shiloh swallowed the distaste on her tongue. Officially, the United Council ruled as equals, but like everything else in Arcadia, it was a lie.

"*Beck is the leader,*" Jake had whispered as he prepped Shiloh before she'd even left the hospital. He'd clasped her hand tightly, his lips tickling her ear as he spoke. "*She can twist and pull the strings of the other Councilors to make them dance, if she chooses—the ultimate puppet master over the would-be puppeteers."*

Shiloh forced her voice to be soft. Simpering. Like the good little girl she used to be. "Yes, Councilor Beck."

Councilor Beck leaned her slender frame over the top of her bench, her red Arcadian-issued blouse flowing against the stone like spilled blood. The strands of her age-defying gold hair ended just below her shoulders, not even a millimeter longer or shorter than the Codex demanded. The curves of Beck's face bespoke of a kindly grandmother, but her narrowed eyes, which studied Shiloh closely, mirrored something more serpentine.

For a moment, Shiloh's mind trailed back to the last time she saw Beck: rising to her feet, giving the unshakeable command that ended Hope's life. There'd been no mercy in Beck's voice as she ordered the death of a child.

Shiloh's fingers began to curl, but she forced herself to breathe —*in and out*—and relaxed her hands before they became fists. She made her face stay blank, poised, and trustworthy, so Beck couldn't read the fire that blazed within her.

Finally, Councilor Beck settled back into her bench, her face unreadable. "Thank you for being here, Ms. Haven. I trust you are feeling well enough to proceed."

It had been mere hours since Shiloh had left the hospital, where she'd spent two weeks after being shot and nearly killed. Upon discharge, she'd been ushered to the airport Minneopolis to board a plane to Chicago, the capital of Arcadia, with Jake and his family. If Shiloh breathed deeply enough, pain still roared from her once-collapsed lung and from her newly healed bones. Beneath the long white sleeves of her Arcadian-approved shirt, the bruises Silas had left lingered in splotches of purple and green—ghosts which demanded remembrance.

Still, Shiloh bowed her head in response. "Of course. It's my pleasure to serve the Council."

Shiloh took the beat of silence that followed to survey the

others in the room, recalling what else Jake had told her. Councilor Maxwell Smith sat to Beck's right, his face pale and rumpled, his hands curled like claws over the arms of his chair. Like Beck, he'd sat on the original council that had formed Arcadia.

"Old as stone," Jake had said, *"and as unforgiving."*

To Beck's left, Charles Bennett slumped in his chair, plump-bodied and dull-eyed. Bored. He'd been elected to fill his brother's place after the original Councilor had died in a car accident—and by *elected*, Shiloh knew he'd been selected by the others on the Council. No vote in Arcadia truly mattered. She'd always suspected the farce, and Jake had confirmed it.

"He's not power hungry," Jake had said of Bennett, *"but he's obedient. He'll do whatever is asked of him... no matter how savage."*

Behind Shiloh's right shoulder, Serenity Jameson shifted in her seat, crossing and uncrossing her legs. She'd taken over for her mother when the former Councilor died from cancer only five years ago. As such, Jameson was the youngest.

"She's the kindest, but also the weakest. The most easily manipulated."

And lastly, just beyond Shiloh's left shoulder, was the face she knew the best.

Councilor Osgood looked just like his son, down to the same bronze eyes, but Shiloh tasted only hate—sharp and acrid—on her tongue when she looked at the Councilor. He had sent Silas after Shiloh, knowing the tactics Silas would use to control her. Yet Osgood was the only reason Shiloh hadn't bled to death in Jake's arms after Silas shot her. Shiloh felt no gratitude, though. The Councilor's actions had been for Jake. Otherwise, Osgood would have left her to die in the snow.

Councilor Osgood leveled his gaze at Shiloh for only a heart-beat before turning away. But a message had passed through that brief, hard look.

Stick to the lie.

He and his assistant, Hazel, had prepared her for this, starting over a week ago when he'd shown up unannounced in her hospital room and explained in no uncertain terms that, if she wanted to avoid a prison camp, she would do exactly as he commanded. Osgood might always suspect his son and his son's girlfriend of committing heresy, but it was absolutely critical that the rest of the Council did not. So, Osgood supplied pieces to fill in the holes where he questioned Jake and Shiloh's story and prepped her for the role of a lifetime.

On the flight to Chicago, he'd made Shiloh repeat the story over and over until her tongue felt raw. Hazel gave her a fresh, starkly white Arcadian uniform and painted blush on her pale cheeks—making her look perfect, innocent, like a virginal sacrifice.

In the chamber, Smith's voice rumbled like rocks colliding, "Miss Haven, do you recognize the importance of this hearing?"

"Yes, sir," Shiloh said.

"And do you swear to be honest and truthful?"

"Yes, sir."

"Then let's begin."

Shiloh inhaled through her nose and exhaled slowly through her mouth. She wished she wasn't alone in here, but no one could accompany those who entered the Councilors' chamber. What happened in the chamber stayed in the chamber.

"Close your eyes."

The memory of Jake's words sounded like an echo in Shiloh's chest. He'd whispered them into her ear only minutes ago as they waited in a nearby room for it to be her turn to testify against Silas Petrovic.

When she'd closed her eyes, he'd laced his fingers through hers. *"I'm right here."* His thumb trailed across the top of her knuckles, starting a fire that climbed up the length of her arm and settled somewhere deep in her belly. *"If you're afraid in there, just close your eyes and know I'm always right here."*

Shiloh pressed her eyes closed for a second, and she swore Jake was right there. She could almost feel his fingers cradling hers.

And his love gave her courage.

The onslaught of questions began, Beck and Smith firing them at Shiloh like enemy soldiers surrounding her on all sides.

Calm. Docile. Unwavering.

Shiloh forced herself to be all these things as she led them through the neat version of events. How Silas had wanted her to gain Nicolette's trust, and of course, Shiloh was so, so willing to betray the heretic for the sake of Arcadia. But then Silas had pulled her into another plot—to help him get Jake arrested so he could take Councilor Osgood's place on the Council. And how could Shiloh let that happen? So, she'd confessed everything to Jake... to his father... even though she knew Silas would try to kill her. And he had. He'd almost succeeded.

No, Shiloh had never known about the heretic's escape plan.

No, Shiloh had never worn an audio recorder for Silas, no matter what he said. She certainly didn't know that it—and all the recordings—had been destroyed by Councilor Osgood, long before it could reach the Council.

Yes, Shiloh was a loyal citizen to Arcadia. Always, *always* loyal.

Councilor Beck leaned forward, placing her chin in her hand as she looked down at Shiloh. Long, carefully manicured nails curled onto her cheeks like talons. "You were certainly brave to risk so much."

"Yes." Councilor Osgood spoke for the first time. Through the entire interrogation, he sat stiff and tense, tapping his fingers on the edge of his chair, his face shadowed. "I am incredibly grateful to Ms. Haven for uncovering this treasonous plot."

"As are we all," Jameson said, her smile seeming sincere.

"I only have one more question, Ms. Haven," Beck said.

Shiloh swallowed, her mouth parched. "Yes, Councilor?"

Beck's lips curled up in a smile, ribbons on a bomb disguised as a gift. "You're certain—*absolutely certain*—that Jacob Osgood had nothing to do with that heretic escaping?"

Shiloh's heart froze in her chest. Councilor Osgood stopped

his tapping, glancing toward Beck and then toward Shiloh. His gaze drove a single command into her back.

Lie.

As though the Councilor could read Shiloh's thoughts, Beck added, "I want to remind you that there are grave punishments for lying in this chamber."

Imprisonment. Torture. Death.

Shiloh had already faced all that. For Jake, she had walked through fire, taken on Elite, faced certain death. For Jake, she could do anything.

She could burn this world to the ground.

After all, that was her new Rule #1. One of the few rules she would ever follow again.

Fight for the ones you love.

No matter the cost.

Shiloh tilted her head up and met Councilor Beck's eyes. Unblinking. Unafraid. Chin held high. "Absolutely nothing at all."

Two

"Jake, please sit down."

Jacob Osgood barely heard his mother's plea as he paced across the carpet of the small room where they'd been forced to wait. An hour had passed since Shiloh disappeared into the United Council's chamber, and each passing second stoked the tension beneath Jake's skin until it raged, a volcano about to erupt. Only three options would relieve the growing pressure: scream, pace, or put his fist through the wall.

So, he paced.

"Jake." The stiff, fake leather of the couch creaked as Mom rose. She stepped into Jake's path and, when he tried to step around her, she rested her hands on his shoulders. "She's going to be fine."

Was she?

If anyone could stand in that chamber—beneath the eyes of the Council—and lie her way out of this, it was probably Shiloh. Granted, Jake had given testimony too, but he was an Osgood. Each Councilor had known him since he was an infant. They *liked* him, considered him family. He'd known just how to act, how to move to the invisible strings the Councilors like to pull—a familiar puppet dance. He knew just how to charm Serenity Jameson, and tease Bennett out of his boredom, and even impress the sourness off Smith's face. In the end, only Madison Beck's gaze had marked him with anything close to suspicion.

But Shiloh was different. She was a Haven. Her surname condemned her.

They'd be merciless.

As though sensing his uncertainty, Mom added, "She's smart. She survived Silas for months. She can survive the Council for an hour."

At the sound of Silas's name on his mother's lips, Jake's jaw tightened. He glared hard at the wall just past Mom's shoulder. There, the white Arcadian emblem stood out against the navy wall. A question Jake hadn't dared ask his mom haunted him. He could tell himself he hadn't asked it because he and his mother hadn't been alone since everything had happened with Silas. Jake had either been at Shiloh's side or there had been others around. Despite Jake believing Silas would be a big scandal, the Council had buried the whole thing and forbidden anyone to speak about it outside this trial.

But now, Jake realized he hadn't asked because he feared the answer his mother might give. His father's betrayal hurt the way touching a hot oven hurt. Painful but expected. But his mother's betrayal would strike him like a knife slammed between his shoulder blades.

Finally, Jake lifted his gaze to his mother's. Her eyes were identical to her brother's—a stunning, crystal blue. "Did you know?"

"Did I know what?" she asked, her voice gentle.

He opened his mouth to speak, but he couldn't find the words, so she continued for him. "Did I know Silas was the commander of the Elite? Yes. Did I know what cruelty he wrought on those he saw as his enemies? Yes. But I didn't—I swear to you—*I didn't* know what was happening with Shiloh. He was only supposed to be looking out for you. Protecting you. I never thought—"

Her voice cracked, shattered like porcelain against cement, and her eyes fell shut. Jake noticed it then. Behind the makeup Mom had painted on like an impenetrable mask, lines embedded beneath her eyelids and across her brows that spoke of worry... and, worse...

Grief.

But when her eyes opened again, they crackled with something completely different. Rage. "But I *never* thought he'd hurt *you*."

Something burned at the back of Jake's throat. But no—*No!* He refused to feel anything toward Silas but hate. He tightened his hands into fists, glared down at the ground. *No... no...*

Mom brushed back the hair that had fallen into Jake's eyes, a gesture that made him feel like a little boy. "If I'd known," she said, "I would have done anything in my power to protect her."

Jake swallowed, once, twice, until the emotions choking him dislodged. "Do you promise?"

His mom drew a finger across her chest, forming an X. Something she hadn't done in years, but it still meant something. A promise she refused to break. "Cross my heart."

Mom opened her arms to pull Jake toward her, but the door opened with a groan. Jake flung himself around.

He caught only a glimpse of dark hair before he launched forward. He pulled Shiloh into his arms before the door even closed behind her. Her soft frame fit against him like a second piece. Her breath warmed his skin as she buried her face into his neck. And finally, *finally,* the pressure loosened in his chest, and he felt like he could breathe.

"Are you okay?" Jake murmured against her ear.

Shiloh nodded, but her hands fisted into the fabric at the back of his shirt. Of course, she wasn't okay. He'd seen it these last weeks, the way she'd woken so many times in the hospital: a gasp on her lips, her eyes searching the darkness for a threat. "It's okay," he'd whispered, even though he knew it wasn't, stroking her sweat-damp hair away from her face until she fell back asleep.

He'd never told her he had nightmares of his own. If he closed his eyes now, he'd see it: bruises all over her body. Silas's hand wrapped around her throat. Deep red blossoming over her white school shirt. The car racing through the snow as she grew lighter and lighter in his arms.

In Jake's nightmares, they never made it to the ambulance in time. He lost Shiloh over and over and over again.

Jake held her tighter and inhaled slowly, breathing her in. She smelled like fragrance-free hospital soap: a fresh, unimposing scent that further soothed the smoldering volcano in his chest.

She's here. She's right here.

I didn't lose her.

I won't lose her.

Shiloh stepped back first, looking toward Mom.

"How did it go?" Mom asked.

"It went all right," Shiloh said,

"But—" Jake began, hearing the hesitance in Shiloh's voice.

Mom shook her head, gaze shifting around her. Like the walls might have had ears. And maybe they did. The conversation he and his mother had before was deeply personal, but it spoke poorly of Silas. Speaking ill of the Councilors was a much deadlier game.

Shiloh tucked a strand of her hair behind her ear. "What do we do now?"

"Now, we wait," Mom said.

And so, they waited. Jake and Shiloh nestled close on one couch, while Mom sat on the other. Shiloh's eyes never left the door, despite Jake's efforts to distract her: his whispering, his good-natured teasing. She clung to his hand, and Jake doubted she even noticed how her fingernails dug into his palm. It didn't matter. Nothing mattered.

Except her.

Silas *had* to be found guilty. Jake's father had compiled too much evidence against him. Even if Shiloh and Jake's words were in doubt, Samuel Osgood was unquestionable. Jake refused to believe in a different outcome, refused to believe in any reality where he lost Shiloh.

It was days later, surely—maybe even decades—when the door opened again.

Mom stood so quickly she swayed in her high heels. Jake released Shiloh's hand, only to wrap an arm around her waist, pulling her close. Shadows played across Dad's face as he closed the door behind him. His gaze darted around the room, never focusing on anyone for long.

"Sam," Mom murmured, closing the distance between the two of them and grabbing Dad's hand.

He met her eyes and sighed, then swept his gaze toward Jake and Shiloh. He said it quickly, like pulling off a bandage. Or maybe, creating a wound with one quick stab.

"Silas will be executed tomorrow morning."

Beside Jake, Shiloh let out a breath, her shoulders slumping in relief. Jake tried to feel that same relief, and he *did*. But he also felt...

He felt...

Froq, how was he supposed to feel about *this*?

Mom gulped a breath. "That's... good," she said, and it almost sounded convincing. But there, beneath the mask of makeup— beneath the small curve of lips she tried to pass off as a smile— lingered something else.

Silas was her *brother*. The brother who had betrayed her husband and son, but her *brother* he remained. He would die tomorrow. Her brother. *Jake's* uncle.

No, Jake thought, *he's a monster. Nothing but a monster. He cannot be both things.*

Can he?

No, and yet...

And yet...

A picture of Silas formed in Jake's head. And, for the first time in weeks, it wasn't the image of Silas holding a gun to Shiloh's head. Now, the memory was of Silas as he'd been before: two years ago on a family summer trip, elbowing Jake in the side, laughing at something one of Jake's little cousins had said as they all roasted marshmallows over a fire.

From somewhere far off, Dad's voice broke through. "Aubrey and the kids are visiting him now."

Froq. Cameron... Chloe... Charlotte...

A sound broke from Jake's lips as though a punch had landed in his gut. Shiloh glanced at him, worry pinching her brow together. His cousins would be devastated. Because Silas was their father. A father who loved them.

I thought he loved me, too.

Why? Why didn't he love me?

Stop it! Jake's head shouted back against the onslaught of memories that threatened to turn his mind into a battleground. *Silas is a monster!* Even now, Silas was locked in a cage deep below the Unity Center. *He's a monster. Monster, monster, monster.*

Maybe, if Jake saw Silas in that cage—looked at the hands that had wrapped around the throat of the girl Jake loved, looked into his uncle's eyes, and found the darkness that had surely always been there—maybe then Jake would know for sure.

"Can I see him?" Jake blurted.

Shiloh inhaled sharply. Mom and Dad looked at him with wide eyes.

"Can I see him?" Jake repeated, steadying his voice.

"Jake," Shiloh said, his name a soft protest. He didn't look at her, afraid of what she would see on his face.

Mom glanced at his father, who hesitated, working his jaw back and forth.

"Are you sure?" Dad asked.

No, Jake wasn't. Not at all.

But he nodded, anyway.

THREE

Nicolette Howell landed hard in the snow. The chill stabbed her face. But just as quickly as she had fallen, she shoved herself up. She spat the snow from her mouth and lifted her fists to fight.

"Again," Nic told the tall boy in front of her.

The boy's name was Luca. *Just* Luca, with no last name—or that was what he'd said when he introduced himself three weeks ago, back when Nic first met him and the other members of the Sparrows, the faction of ROGUE Nic's mom and Paul had joined.

Luca arched a single eyebrow. "Think third time is the charm or something?"

"Again!" Nic growled.

"Easy, Nic," Paul said from where he stood, just outside the circle he'd drawn in the snow to mark the edge of the training ring. He crossed his arms over his long, thick coat. "Don't let your emotions get the best of you."

Paul glanced at the children who stood at his side. The two oldest Qadir children, Eris and Amir, and Becca Singer, too, hovered outside the ring, watching the duel intently. At eleven, nine, and seven respectively, they were old enough to be training, and like Nic, they all had been training since they could remember. Before Paul had come to the Sparrows last summer, Brooks—the Sparrows' formidable leader—had trained them on her own, but Paul had eagerly jumped in.

Paul wielded a harmony of patience and firmness; Brooks preferred relentlessness. They balanced each other well. But today, Brooks was doing... some leader-thing that was apparently too important for anyone to tell Nic about it. So, today, Paul handled the training alone.

"Did you hear that?" Paul asked the children. "Do not let your emotions cloud your abilities. You must be calm." He tapped his temple. "Focused."

The children nodded eagerly.

Nic took a steadying breath, trying to calm her racing heart. Paul was right. Adrenaline could make you strong, or it could make you blind. Nic couldn't give Luca the least advantage. Luca was five years older than her, towered even higher than Paul, and though his build was lean, he was strong. He knew just how to look intimidating, with the broody look that never left his face, the way his green eyes flashed against his light-brown skin, and the fact that he'd already thrown her into the snow twice today. She couldn't afford the smallest of weaknesses.

"Again," she repeated, forcing her voice to be level.

Luca looked at Paul. After studying Nic for a long moment, Paul nodded. Luca shrugged but assumed the fighting position once more. His booted feet slipped apart in the snow, pushing up the sleeves of his cracked leather jacket.

"You got him this time, Nic!" Ali cheered from his place on the other side of Paul.

"Whose side are you on, bro?" Luca snapped, never taking his eyes from Nic.

Ali smiled sheepishly.

Though brothers, Luca and Ali were opposites. Grim and Chuckles were their codenames, and it had taken Nic approximately three minutes after meeting them to figure out which was which. Where Luca was dark and broody, Ali was light. *Too* light. Obnoxiously light. Even though he was Nic's own age, he reminded Nic of a five-year-old on Christmas morning.

As Luca moved in a circle, Nic slid her feet carefully through the snow, so she never turned her back or side to him. They continued their spiral for a full minute, both waiting for the other to make a move. On the sidelines, Paul explained to the children what they were doing right, why they were doing it, and what they could do better.

Nic tried to tune him out. Her breath came faster; her heart raced in her chest. Nic eyed Luca's hands and his long fingers that could wrap around her throat so, so easily.

And Nic's vision faded from present to past.

A door opened. An Elite stood in the doorway, his prod crackling at his side.

Nic blinked hard to clear her vision and pulled her fists tighter, trying to cling to reality.

Not now.

The flashbacks had been coming more frequently. As though, instead of fading, the memories of the cage she'd been locked in last summer strengthened with time. But Nic couldn't lose touch with reality now.

Please, not now.

Her vision cleared to take in the landscape. The massive lodge stood at the top of the slope they practiced on. With its carved, gleaming wood and walls of glass, it must have been magnificent once, but now it bore the scars of time and disuse: broken glass sealed with tarps, crumbling beams. But it was Nic's home now, at least for the time being. She *wasn't* in the cage.

Luca hadn't budged from his position, waiting for Nic's first move. He was patient, this one. He would see her slightest flinch, anticipate her action, and avoid it.

Unless he can't see.

Nic glanced at the snow beneath her. She'd always been taught that there was no such thing as fighting *fair*. There was just fighting or dying.

Nic lunged forward a step. Luca shifted in anticipation of her move, but she kicked through the snow, launching a white cloud into his face. He flung his hands up to protect his eyes, and Nic barreled her shoulder into his gut. Luca fell, but as he did, he latched his arm around her, pulling her with him. They landed in a heap of grappling hands and kicking legs. When Luca tried to pin her hands, Nic drove both feet into his abdomen and flung him face-first into the snow. He pushed to his hands and knees. Nic dove onto his back and wrapped her arm around his throat.

They jerked her wrists behind her back and bound them together. The electric handcuffs blazed against her skin.

Not now*!*

Luca seized Nic's arm, pulled it away from his windpipe, and stood with a force that flung Nic over his shoulder. She landed on the ground, her breath slamming from her lungs. Luca's foot hovered over her throat, not touching her, but Nic felt it still, crushing her windpipe.

Just like Silas had crushed it.

Fingers dug into her windpipe, a gloved hand that squeezed and squeezed and wouldn't let go.

I can't breathe.

Somewhere, from a distance, Paul spoke, narrating to the children what exactly Nic had done wrong. But Nic couldn't hear it, couldn't see anything but her own gasping face reflected in an Elite's helmet.

I can't breathe.

Nic rolled to her knees. She clawed the collar of her coat away from her throat. But the choking hand remained.

I can't breathe.

"Nic."

Her heart slammed against her ribcage; her lungs blazed with the need for air. At any moment, her chest would rip open. At any moment, the fingers wrapped around her throat would steal the last of her air.

She was going to die.

Sometimes, in this cage, she wanted to die.

"Nic!"

A hand, a real hand, touched her arm. Nic flinched away. The illusion shattered. She gasped for air again and, this time, it coated her lungs like a balm. Her heart slowed. Paul kneeled before her, his face drawn with concern.

"Are you okay?" he demanded. "Are you hurt?"

Nic shook her head. Behind Paul, everyone else watched her too. The weight of the five gazes hammered into her. Judging her. Or worse, *pitying* her. Seeing the weakness within her.

Nic gritted her teeth and jumped up. She swayed on unsteady knees but forced her legs not to buckle. "I'm fine. I can go again."

Paul stood. "I think we're done for the day," he said, reaching for her shoulder.

Nic shied away from his touch. "I said I can go again!" she yelled, advancing toward Luca.

Luca retreated a few steps and held up his hands.

"Nic, that's enough," Paul said from behind her, his tone now low. A warning.

The three youngest children watched with gaping mouths. Even Ali had lost his smile. The pity on his face made a scream build up in Nic's chest. She had to make them see she was fine, that she wasn't something to pity. That she was *strong*.

"Fight me." Nic took another step toward Luca.

Luca shook his head. "You've had enough."

"*Fight me!*"

When Luca still didn't assume a fighter's stance, she shoved him in the chest. He didn't even try to defend himself.

"I'm not weak!" she screamed.

Paul seized Nic's arm and spun her to face him. "I said enough, Nicolette!"

Nic's skin felt like it might detach from her bones; her chest was still ripping open. She flicked her gaze from Paul to Luca, to Ali, to the three children, all staring at her like she might have lost her mind.

"Fine!" Nic snapped, whirling around and storming back up the hill toward the lodge. Her cheeks burned from the wind and the cold, and she ground her fists together until her fingers dug into her palm, even through her gloves.

"Nic, wait!"

Nic picked up speed at the sound of Paul's voice, but he caught up anyway. He stepped in front of her. She expected his jaw to be locked in frustration and anger—she hadn't been acting like a very good soldier, had she? But instead, deep lines formed across his forehead. Concern.

That was even worse.

"Are you okay?" Paul asked.

"I said I was!" Nic tried to step around him, but he shifted to block her escape.

"I don't believe you."

Nic clutched her arms to her belly, a shield, and looked toward the distance. To the side of the lodge, in another hundred yards, the lodge's hill sloped down and disappeared into a hazy fog. Silhouettes of old ski lifts towered in the grey sky like looming giants.

"Well, I *am* fine," Nic said.

I'm fine. I'm fine. I'm fine.

At least, she was *supposed* to be fine. She'd escaped the Elite. She'd protected ROGUE. Reese Andreou—Stefani's mother and an ally to ROGUE—had passed word through the network that the rest of the plan had gone well. Silas was arrested for treason, and her friends were safe. They'd *won*. Nic should be *fine*. Her bad dreams, her jumpiness, were supposed to go away.

But they hadn't. As soon as she'd found her way back to ROGUE—to her mother and Paul, everything had gotten worse. Panic lived like a parasite in her bloodstream. Nic often woke from nightmares with a scream lodged in her chest and cold sweat on her back. Perhaps before she'd been so focused on survival, she'd buried what had happened to her. But now, it clawed its way to the surface, making her feel like she'd just left the cage. Like all the bruises still lingered on her skin.

"Your mom and I..." Paul said with a deep sigh, scrubbing a hand across his gray-dusted beard. "We're worried about you. We know something is wrong, but you won't talk to us."

I don't want to talk, she almost shouted. *I want to forget that this ever happened to me.*

Nic needed to bury it down. She'd been trying these last weeks, pushing the memories, the panic—even the sadness of missing her friends—down deep inside until she felt like she was coming apart at the seams. But she had to keep it together. She couldn't let them see. They already treated her like a baby.

She saw them, Paul and Mom and sometimes Brooks, whispering together with the same fierceness with which The Family had plotted the bombing of the Cleansing. Something was going on; they were planning something again. Nic would sometimes catch a few stray words, one they'd said frequently. *Codename Princess.* But anytime Nic drew close, they'd stop talking, and when she asked, Paul and Mom said what they'd said her whole life.

"Nothing."

"This isn't your concern."

Good to see that, after so much time had passed, they still didn't trust Nic. She couldn't let them see her falling apart, or they never would.

"Well," Nic said, after far too long of a pause. "There's nothing to be worried about."

"Nic," Paul protested.

But Nic wasn't listening anymore.

She moved to step around his right side, and when Paul shifted to block her, she darted to the left and slipped around him. She bolted into a run, not back toward the lodge, but around the side of it. The snow rose to her knees, but she was fast. She could outrun him. Flee into the pines at the west side of the lodge if she must, if it'd get him to *leave her alone*. She glanced behind her only after she'd rounded the corner of the lodge.

He hadn't followed.

Nic stopped on the very edge of the slope. It plunged downward into the gray haze so thick it was impossible to see into the distance. The first of the poles for the ski lift towered above her head. The snapped lines dangled toward the ground like broken limbs. Quiet. It was so quiet out here, the whistle of wind the only sound.

In the stillness, Nic's panic screamed beneath her skin. She wanted to claw it out. To bleed it out. Anything. She just wanted it to stop.

Do you hear that, God?! she shouted out the prayer in her head. *I want it to stop. Make it stop!*

She waited for it. The peace she'd felt before, when she first returned to ROGUE, but just like all the times she'd called out before, it didn't come. She was on her own.

She was all alone.

Nic wished she could talk to her friends. She missed them with an ache that went deeper than she could have imagined. Val and Stefani. Shiloh. And Jake.

Jake...

Nic lifted a gloved hand to her frozen lips, remembering the warmth of that stolen kiss. A small spark of joy in the darkness that had overtaken her life.

Something moved in the fog before her.

Nic stiffened and dropped her hand to her side, to where her gun hung in its holster beneath her coat. A shadow took shape in the haze, perhaps thirty yards away—a shape distinctly human. Someone was coming. They moved silently, even in the deep snow, like they'd been trained in deadly stealth.

Nic slipped her hand under her coat and drew her gun.

When the person stepped from the fog, Nic lifted the gun and aimed it at their chest. They froze, a single hand lifting upward in surrender. The fur-lined hood concealed their face in shadows. But they were not a member of the Sparrows; Nic was certain of that.

Before Nic could demand who the stranger was, they spoke, "What has two eyes but cannot see?"

A member of ROGUE then.

"My enemies when I come for them," Nic replied. She lowered the gun, pointing it toward the ground, but didn't put it back in its holster.

"Hello, Nicolette," the stranger said.

Nic's grip tightened on her gun. "Who are you?" she demanded.

The stranger lifted a hand to their hood, and Nic tracked their every move. Pushing down the hood. Lowering the scarf from her nose.

Nic *did* know her. Nic recognized the scattering of freckles across her pale, sharp cheekbones. The tight curls cut close to her head, dark but dusted with grey. She realized what she should have noticed sooner—that the woman had only ever lifted *one* hand because the other sleeve of her coat was empty.

And for the second time today, Nic couldn't breathe.

"Sawyer," Nic managed.

"It's good to see you, Nic," the woman said. She did not smile. Sawyer never smiled.

Nic wished she could repeat the warm greeting. There was a time when Sawyer's appearance would have thrilled her, but dread drilled into her chest. The last time Nic had seen Sawyer, she'd come to The Family with plans to bomb the Cleansing. And now, she was back.

Sawyer Ardelean, the leader of ROGUE, was here.

Everything was about to change.

FOUR

Even though Jake had toured and explored the Unity Center at least a hundred times, he'd never seen the Vault: the dungeon deep beneath the Unity Center, holding the most dangerous criminals when they came for their trials. When Jake was younger, he'd imagined it medieval, a gloomy space decorated in darkness and cobwebs.

But instead of a drawbridge, Jake and his father—along with a small army of guards—stepped into an elevator. After Dad put in a specific pin required to access the floor, the elevator descended downward—down, down, down for what felt like ages until it finally jerked to a halt. Jake, Dad, and their guards stepped out into a short stone hallway that ended in a set of metal doors. The doors slid open, allowing entry into a small chamber containing only two Elite and a long desk full of monitors. Each screen featured a different angle of the same sight: Silas in his jail cell.

In the cage, Silas cradled Jake's youngest cousin, Charlotte, on his lap, while Aubrey kneeled beside the single, hard metal chair he sat upon. Jake's throat tightened, and he swiftly looked away, but his rebellious gaze crept up to the monitor once more. When an Elite left his desk and came in to break the family apart, Charlotte wailed and clung to her daddy—the sound of her sobs not carried over the monitor. Jake closed his eyes, trying to fill his head with the memory of the bruises on Shiloh's skin, a reminder of who Silas really was.

The wall on the far side of the room parted with the whine of metal. Aubrey and Charlotte walked into the room, and the door boomed shut behind them, turning back into a solid wall.

Charlotte clutched her mother's hand, looking desolate, even her drooping pigtails looking forlorn. But when she spotted Jake, a smile split her ruddy cheeks.

"Jake!" Charlotte shot toward him, but Aubrey seized her wrist and yanked her back to her side. Aubrey shot Jake a look that could have fileted him open before she hurried into the hallway. Charlotte sobbed once more, every wail echoing in Jake's chest until the doors snapped shut behind them.

She blames me, Jake realized. *And soon all my cousins will, too. I'm going to lose them all.*

The ground ripped open beneath his feet, and he was falling, falling. A hand alighted on his shoulder, squeezing firmly, bringing him back to solid ground. Dad stood at his side, and, for once, Jake was grateful for his presence.

"You still want to do this?" Dad asked softly.

Jake glanced at his feet, at the cement beneath his shoes that was, in fact, still there. "Yes."

"All right. Then remember"—Dad's fingers ground into Jake's shoulder as he leaned close—"don't say anything stupid."

And, just like that, Jake's gratitude toward his father vanished.

Jake gritted his teeth to keep from snarling something back, and then he stepped toward the wall, which parted once more. The wall slammed shut behind him, trapping him in a small room— four walls and no door—and plunging him into darkness. Then the Elites at the control panel opened the next door and then the next. Altogether, Jake crossed through five chambers, one gate never opening until the other closed.

At last, he stepped through one more wall, and Silas appeared framed in a large window. Silas slumped in his chair, head bent forward. Only he and his metal chair broke the cage's endless circle of white.

Did Nic's cage look like this?

Sparks shot through Jake's chest. Ah, yes, there it was. The fury and hate he should be feeling.

Silas looked up, and a smile split across his face. "Jake, my boy!" he said in a jovial tone. "To what do I owe this pleasure?"

Jake clenched and unclenched his fists, finding nothing to say.

"Well?" Silas rose to his feet and approached Jake. The tether around his ankle stopped him just shy of the window, the anchor to it blinking from the leg of the chair.

At last, truth tumbled out.

"I wanted to see you one more time," Jake said, "to figure out who they're putting to death tomorrow. A man or a monster?"

Silas chuckled deep in his throat and spread his arms wide apart. "Take a good look, Jake. What do you see?"

The possibilities clattered in Jake's head. *Uncle. Elite. Father. Torturer. Brother. Murderer. Man. Monster.*

Which one is he really?

"Well," Silas pressed, when Jake hesitated too long.

"A monster," Jake said, his voice more certain than he felt. "Definitely."

Silas faked a grimace and fanned a hand over his heart, if monsters had such things. "That hurts. I'm still the uncle you've always known and loved."

"The uncle I knew wouldn't have tried to put me in prison," Jake growled. "The uncle I knew wouldn't have tortured the girl I love. Why—" That word broke through the fierceness of his tone, choking him. He cleared his throat, gritted his teeth until his jaw ached. "Why did you do this?"

Why did you do this to me?

Silas crossed his arms over his chest and cocked his head. "Why did I do what? Become an Elite?"

Jake began to nod, then stopped. No, Jake couldn't take that bait. Being an Elite in Arcadia was a high honor. A good citizen would never ask that.

Instead, Jake asked, "Why did you betray my father?"

Why did you betray me?

Silas shook his head. "That is just a misunderstanding. A manipulation by an overimaginative girl."

Fine. Jake shouldn't have expected Silas to answer that question. He wasn't stupid enough to confess to his treason. Jake had to come at it a different way.

"Why do you hate heretics so much?" Jake asked, choosing each word carefully. "Most people fear heresy, or dislike it, but you... It goes deeper with you." *So deep that, when you thought I was a heretic, you stopped loving me.* "It's personal, isn't it?"

Silas considered Jake for a long moment before responding. "Heresy is..." Silas began, then he stopped. Shook his head.

"Is *what*?" Jake snapped. "Is dangerous?"

"No, it's *disgusting*," Silas said coolly, his tone emotionless, but something flickered behind his eyes, some true feeling behind his mask. "Heresy is a plague. A disgusting disease that infects everything it's touched. You were lucky enough to be born into a world without heresy. You never knew the way cruelty could be hidden behind a smile and a cross."

"Cruelty?" Jake repeated, the word tasting sour with irony. "You'd know a few things about that, wouldn't you?"

Silas rolled his eyes. "If you've come here seeking remorse, I'm afraid you'll go away dissatisfied."

"I don't need remorse," Jake said, his pulse beating against his ears like a war drum. "I'll take justice."

"Justice?" Silas scoffed. "My execution? A high price, don't you think? For a few bruises on a Haven girl."

An image flashed: Silas's hand curving around Shiloh's throat, his gun digging into her temple. Jake slammed his fist against the glass. The window rattled like an enraged snake. "You're just angry she beat you at your sick game."

"Oh, how cute. You actually think this game is over." In a flash, Silas's smile disappeared, and his palms landed on the glass so hard it trembled again. He leaned close, his face morphing to let out the monster within. "It's far, *far* from over."

🔥

Breathe in... breathe out...

The air in the room smelled stale as Shiloh forced herself to breathe slowly. It had only been minutes since Jake walked out of the room, leaving her sitting on this inflexible, leather couch. It was already too long.

"He'll be fine," Mrs. Osgood said from her place on the couch facing Shiloh, the woman's voice poised and sure, her chin cocked confidently. But her fingernails tapped, tapped, tapped on the arm of the chair—betraying a nervousness not reflected in her tone. "Samuel will not let Silas anywhere near Jake. They'll talk through a window. That's all. You don't need to be worried."

"I'm not worried," Shiloh lied.

Mrs. Osgood tilted her head, unconvinced.

Okay, Shiloh wasn't worried that Silas could *physically* hurt Jake. But a different worry slithered in Shiloh's gut. She'd seen Jake's expression when Councilor Osgood had announced the judgment. Yes, there *was* relief—the same profound relief Shiloh felt.

But there was also devastation.

Shiloh wasn't worried about Jake facing Silas now; she was worried about what happened *after*. Shiloh didn't know how to do this: how to bear the fire of hatred within her and yet still find the goodness to comfort Jake for his loss. Perhaps if she was a kinder, more compassionate person, she could do it, but she knew herself better. When tomorrow came and Silas took a bullet to his brain, there'd be no sympathy, no sorrow.

Her only regret would be that she couldn't pull the trigger herself.

Shiloh took another breath. "Mrs. Osgood—"

"Reagan," Jake's mother corrected, as she had many times before, each time she'd visited Shiloh in the hospital. Mrs. Osgood had never stayed long—just long enough to exchange the bouquet of flowers beside Shiloh's bed with a fresh one, long before the previous even withered. Shiloh suspected not much could earn the Councilor's wife's esteem, but nearly dying to save her son and her husband had to be it.

"Reagan," Shiloh began again, the name still feeling awkward on her tongue, "do you think—" She paused, struggling to find the words.

Reagan met her gaze patiently. But Shiloh never had the chance to work out exactly what she wanted to say, because the door flung open with a suddenness that made Shiloh's heart leap into her throat.

Madison Beck strode as though she owned the room—like she owned the entire world—moving to stand between the couches before Reagan could even rise to her feet. A single female hovered behind Beck, dressed in Codex-compliant clothes, much like Shiloh wore. But the stiffness in her spine, her shifting gaze, and the gun on her hip gave her away as a bodyguard.

"Madison," Reagan greeted as she rose, a brightness in her voice that didn't quite match the tension in her shoulders.

"Reagan," Beck replied with the same feigned excitement, reaching forward to embrace Reagan's shoulders with her hands. The two exchanged kisses in the air near each other's cheeks. To Shiloh, who rose carefully to her feet, it looked like two actresses portraying their roles so well that the audience could almost believe they weren't watching an act.

Almost.

Beck kept one of Reagan's hands clasped between both of her own. "How are you, my dear? Such a hard time, with the loss of your brother."

There was a test within the words. And Reagan knew which words would pass it. Her smile never faltering, she said, "Anyone who would betray the council is no brother of mine."

Beck's smile curved like a sickle, then she released Reagan as though the touch had scalded Beck. Her eyes darted toward Shiloh like an arrow sinking into a target. Shiloh fought the urge to flinch.

"Miss Haven," Beck said, her smile not nearly as warm now.

"Hello, Councilor Beck," Shiloh replied. She forced her chin high and her face blank, even as a spark flared in her guts as Beck's words echoed in her memory. Words that ended Hope's life.

"Elite #767, do your duty."

"I wanted to show you around the Unity Center," Beck said. It wasn't an offer or a request. Her want was a demand.

"Certainly," Reagan answered for Shiloh quickly. "We can—"

Beck held up a finger, and Reagan's words halted in her throat. "Not you. Just Miss Haven."

Shiloh felt Reagan's gaze flick to her like a hand of concern set on her shoulder. But Shiloh didn't look away from Beck. In the Councilor's Chamber, Beck's eyes had seemed dark, but here, Shiloh realized they were not the deep black of her own eyes. They were lighter, a shade Shiloh couldn't quite place. A chill of warning swept down her spine. She'd been staring too long for a meek Haven girl.

Shiloh dropped her gaze to her feet.

"Madison, surely you're busy," Reagan protested sweetly, her smile widening so much her teeth flashed between her red lips, turning into something between a grimace and a snarl. "I can show her around."

"Nonsense. I insist." Beck swept back to the door. When Shiloh didn't follow, she called back over her shoulder, "Miss Haven!"

The words were a command, a snap of the fingers at a well-trained dog. *Heel.*

And so Shiloh took a step forward.

Reagan's hand landed on Shiloh's elbow. Shiloh paused, but only for the space of three heartbeats—long enough for Reagan to drop her lips close to Shiloh's ear and whisper two words.

"Be. Careful."

Just as quickly, Reagan released her, and Shiloh followed Beck out into the hallway. Beck's guard fell into their wake. The door closed behind the three of them with an echoing boom.

Like a gunshot.

Like a bomb.

FIVE

It's far, far from over.

A chill swept through Jake's chest and settled all the way at the base of his spine. Silas's face was so close to Jake's own that, even through the window that separated them, Jake could almost see his own reflection in the pupils of Silas's eyes. The same eyes Jake knew so well, his mother's eyes, his uncle's eyes. But these eyes seemed completely new. His uncle's eyes had been warm as a summer day.

These were cold as ice.

"Tell me, boy," Silas continued. "Do you really think your daddy saved your girlfriend's life because he didn't want your poor little heart to be broken? He did it for the same reason I didn't kill that traitorous bitch months ago. Shiloh has always been more valuable to us alive."

"What are you talking about?" Jake snarled.

"You'll see." Silas leaned back on his heels. "But here's one last piece of advice, my dear nephew. Say goodbye to your girl... while you still have the chance."

Jake could feel it in his arms—a haunting memory, the subject of his every nightmare. Shiloh, broken and bloody, her weight growing heavier and heavier as she slipped away. And he couldn't... couldn't...

Jake forced words out of his tight throat—managed to turn them into a roar. "You're *lying*!"

A slow smile curled across Silas's face. "Oh, but am I?"

In his mind, Jake lunged through the wall and seized Silas's throat to wipe away the smirk on his face, just like he'd watched Silas do to Shiloh. This was what Jake had wanted, right? Proof of the monster? But monsters were creatures of fear, and now Jake was infected with it. Fear pounded in his ears, slammed in his chest, screamed from every cell of his being.

"Never," Jake swore. "You will *never* hurt her again!"

Silas's smile only widened.

Behind Jake, the wall flung open, and a bodyguard appeared. "Councilor Osgood says it's time to go."

Jake flung himself toward the exit, setting his spine rigid and his feet steady so it wouldn't look like he was fleeing. "I'll see you at your execution," Jake called over his shoulder.

And Silas murmured one last thing back.

As Jake left the Vault behind, Silas's last words reverberated through Jake's mind, through his very bones, until his very soul trembled.

"Too bad I won't be there."

&

The chime of the elevator's arrival broke the stormy silence between Shiloh and Beck. The silver doors slid open. Beck gestured for her to enter first. Shiloh stepped into the amber sunlight that poured into the glass elevator. Beyond a thick pane of glass, the setting sun lined the Chicago skyline in shades of orange. Shiloh set her back against the far wall. To her relief, Beck stood near the opposite wall. The guard swept in just before the doors closed, her hand resting on her gun.

"What floor?" the automatic voice of the elevator chimed.

"Lobby," Beck replied.

The elevator descended. As it moved between the floors, the amber light moved, too, shifting between patterns of light and dark. Shadows fell over Beck's face, only a single stroke of light highlighting a different feature every few seconds. Her taut lips. Her creased forehead.

Her eyes.

Eyes that now stared at Shiloh harder than they had before, unblinking, unyielding.

Shiloh shifted her gaze toward the red hologram before the door, counting down the floors.

11...

10...

Not close enough.

9...

Shiloh glanced back to Beck and jumped. The Councilor had closed the distance between them without a sound, and she now stood only inches away. Shiloh pedaled backward, but her back slammed into the handrail on the wall. Trapped.

Shiloh's heart hammered; her brain whispered a warning, *Run.* Something deep within her recognized the threat before her, the same as she would recognize a venomous snake raised to strike. Beck loomed close—so close she could do anything. So close she could pull out a knife and slit Shiloh's throat. Judging by the disinterested look on the bodyguard's face, she wouldn't raise a finger to help Shiloh.

Beck kept her hands at her side as she searched Shiloh's face. It reminded Shiloh of Mother, her Haven caretaker, searching a Haven girl over as though seeking the smallest imperfection for which to punish her... and delighting when she found it. At last, Beck settled on Shiloh's eyes.

Green, Shiloh decided. Beck's eyes were green, but not like the green velvet of grass. No, these were darker, fiercer. Like the color the sky turned before a tornado.

Ding!

"You have arrived at the lobby," the elevator announced.

Beck stepped back at last, her heels silent on the metal floor. She made a sound deep in her throat, one that either indicated interest or disappointment. The doors of the elevator opened with a sigh, letting in the rumble of noise from the great crowd beyond. The lobby bustled with life, a sea of people dressed all the same in their Arcadian-compliant uniforms: a bland, unknowable white. They roamed around massive, granite pillars that stretched toward a great domed ceiling far above their heads. In the center of the dome, a hologram of moments in Arcadian history was suspended. Currently, a much younger Madison Beck signed the Treaty of the Sundering. Somewhere, above the din of the crowd, Shiloh could hear a voice narrating, over and over.

"Welcome to the Unity Center, celebrating the great nation of Arcadia and its united people."

As Shiloh and Beck stepped out of the elevator, Beck's red shirt stood out like a drop of blood in snow. The crowd parted around them, casting glances over their shoulders, bowing their heads in respect. A group of preteens, here on some school field trip, passed by and bent their heads together, whispering, "Sweet Arcadia, is that Councilor Beck?"

But no one dared approach Beck.

A second later, another announcement sang out: a reminder that Councilors may be seen around the building but should not be approached without expressed permission.

Beck led Shiloh toward the center of the lobby. Shiloh knew what she'd find there. She'd seen it in pictures and videos, even in movies. The Equality Fountain was far grander in person. Streams of water poured down from the domed glass ceiling into a deep, tiled basin that rose to Shiloh's waist. Water and light—in varying shades of blue, red, and white—arched in numerous directions and shapes, but not enough to obscure the hexagon column of mirrors at the heart of the fountain. The mirrors captured the reflection of the faces gathered around the fountain's edge.

All are equal, read an engraving around the bronze base of the mirrored column, *when all are the same.*

Beck paused behind the crowd who had formed a line at the fountain. The group wore uniforms similar to the one Shiloh wore at Ardency, the same as the Codex uniform but with a black jacket and tie. One by one, the students, who were barely younger than her, selected a pre-Sundering coin from one of the small, golden buckets set on the edge of the fountain and held the penny lovingly in the palms of their hands.

"I wish to be more obedient," said one girl, before flicking the coin into the water, where it sank to join the coins resting on the bottom.

"I wish to serve Arcadia better," said another boy.

And on... and on...

Shiloh's stomach churned. Had she been like this once? So conditioned to do whatever it took to survive that she'd been as groveling as these children? How thick of a wall had Shiloh built around the pain and the rage that she'd managed the masquerade? Thick enough she couldn't feel it... couldn't feel *anything*. And then the wall had cracked, little by little. When Hope was arrested and then executed. When Jake had slipped behind the walls and started chipping Shiloh apart from the inside out. When Silas had hammered at her wounds without knowing what he was doing. With every little cruelty, with every loss of freedom, with every chain Arcadia wrapped around her wrists, the wall had cracked a little more. Inch by inch by inch, until the wall crumbled to ashes at her feet.

Whatever the case, she wasn't that good girl anymore. And now...

Now she felt *everything*.

"Go ahead," Beck said, breaking into Shiloh's thoughts. Beck swept her hand toward the fountain. "Make a wish."

A frazzled-looking professor had ushered away the students, leaving nothing between Shiloh and the fountain. She took a step forward. The spray cast from the arches of water moistened the bridge of her nose. Her reflection in the mirrored pillar glared back.

Shiloh forced her face to soften as she picked up the bucket of coins. Silver dimes and copper pennies clustered together, as worthless as pebbles.

"Jacob Osgood is a handsome boy, isn't he?" Beck murmured, as her reflection appeared behind Shiloh's in the mirror.

Shiloh nodded slowly, another alarm bell sounding in her head. Where was Beck going with this?

"Do you love him?" Beck asked flatly.

"Yes," Shiloh replied, without hesitation.

"I hope you two enjoy your time together while it lasts," Beck said, adjusting the cuffs of her blood-red shirt. "I'm sure you know it will not last long."

The words formed a dagger meant to slip between Shiloh's defenses. Shiloh said nothing, not taking the bait. This speech was nothing she hadn't heard before.

"Young Jacob Osgood has long since been spoken for."

Shiloh nearly dropped the bucket, tightening her hold a moment before it slipped from her fingers. Of all the things she'd thought Beck might say, Shiloh hadn't expected that. Shiloh quickly schooled her face back into blankness, but it was too late. Whatever expression had crossed Shiloh's face, Beck had already seen it. A smile coiled on Beck's lips as she realized that, this time, the dagger of her words had driven into Shiloh's chest.

"Jacob's future match was decided by the Marriage Board years ago," Beck went on, still smiling. "Set in stone, as it were."

Shiloh took a breath, refusing to let any more emotion show—

to give Beck any more satisfaction. Shiloh forced herself to move, to select a penny, to put the bucket back down.

"Do you want to guess who?" Beck asked.

Shiloh shook her head.

"Come on now. Surely, you can figure it out. You're a smart girl."

Shiloh's heart fell out of and then back into rhythm. Those words—*You're a smart girl*. Those were Silas's words. He'd said them so many times she could hear their echo now, laying over Beck's words. Matching up entirely.

Except Beck didn't know Shiloh the way Silas did. Maybe, Beck called her smart because of Shiloh's statistics, her perfect GPA, or maybe...maybe Silas had told Beck about her. That possibility shot shivers down Shiloh's spine. It spoke of a closeness between Beck and Silas that disconcerted Shiloh. Perhaps Silas had told Beck his side of the story.

Perhaps Beck had believed him.

Beck tapped her foot. "I'm growing impatient, Miss Haven. I want you to guess."

Shiloh turned the penny she'd chosen around in her fingers, pretending to be thinking, but Beck was right. Shiloh was smart. "Your granddaughter."

Beck's sickening smile flashed in the mirror. "Ah, yes, Katerina. Don't you think they will make a beautiful couple?"

Shiloh pictured the young woman, a couple years older than her, whom she'd seen on the dance floor at the Yuletide Eve Ball. Shiloh had never met Katerina Beck, but recognized her all the same, thanks to the Council-approved news coverage that turned the Councilor's families into celebrities.

Katerina was gorgeous. Opulent. The kind of beautiful that belonged to royalty in fairytales. The same kind of beautiful that Jake was. Shiloh had to admit Jake and Katerina would be a matching set, from their stunningly good looks to the rich, powerful blood that ran in their veins. They made far more sense than Shiloh and Jake ever had.

But the defiant part of Shiloh's heart growled back. *No.*

Shiloh fastened her lips together to keep from saying it.

No. No. NO!

"Don't be upset, Miss Haven." Beck stepped forward until their elbows hovered side by side. "The greatest love stories are doomed from the start."

"I'm not upset," Shiloh said calmly.

I'm furious.

Shiloh glanced at the mirror to ensure her wrath didn't show on her face, adjusting the emotionless mask she wore. Beck caught her eyes in the mirror and let her own placid mask drop. Whatever bit of kindness Beck had been parading fell away, leaving behind only hardness. Her green eyes turned cold as an unrelenting winter storm.

"Listen, girl." Beck hissed the words so low that, if she had not been so close, the words would have been lost beneath the rumble of the water, the thunder of the crowd, the roar of Shiloh's heart in her ears. "You will go back to school and complete the track that *we* chose for you. You will happily go to the college that *we* picked for you. You will end things with the Osgood boy and marry whomever *we* decide. You will be exactly what *we* want you to be. If you express even the slightest dissent, I swear with the very breath I breathe, I will make sure that what happened to your Haven sister at the Cleansing happens to you."

Shiloh's heart continued to pound in her ears, but she didn't feel fear. She felt *rage*. Burning hot like a fire within her. She looked at the mirror, at the reflection of Madison Beck and Shiloh Haven side by side. She wondered if Madison Beck saw what she did.

Enemies.

"Did you hear me?" Beck hissed.

Shiloh nodded. "I heard you."

Not "*I understand*". Not "*Of course, Councilor*". Not "*My duty is to serve*". These were all the things Shiloh *should* have said, but she didn't. She couldn't force them off her tongue. What game was she playing here?

But that was just it. Shiloh *wasn't* playing. For the first time, she wasn't playing their game.

"Aren't you going to make a wish?" Beck said, pressing the words through her grinding teeth.

Beck was offering Shiloh one more chance to get it right. She could toss the penny in and wish to be a better, more loyal citizen. It'd be nothing more than a lie. And if she didn't, she would only bring wrath and suspicion upon herself. Shiloh looked down at the penny in her palm and then around her—at the fountain, the domed ceiling, the tall pillar. This rich splendor. This shiny red skin on a rotten apple. She thought of Nic and ROGUE, out there somewhere, preparing to fight once more. And Shiloh knew what she'd wish for.

She flicked the coin off her thumb and watched it arch into the air, plunk into the water, and sink to the bottom to rest.

I wish to see this place turned to ash.

"Well," Beck asked, "what did you wish for?"

"Isn't it like birthday wishes?" Shiloh asked, turning to face Beck. "If you tell what you wished for, it won't come true."

Beck's lips curled, not into a smile but a snarl. Like the bomb fuse had finally worn down.

"Shiloh!"

The familiar voice felt like a breath of fresh air, and Shiloh turned as Jake broke from the crowd. Worry lined his face, but he carefully replaced it with a wide, carefree smile when he glanced to Madison Beck.

"Here you are," Jake said, laying a hand on Shiloh's shoulder. *I'm here*, the touch said. *I've got you.* He looked at Beck, giving her his winning grin. "Councilor, good to see you. How are you?"

Beck plastered on her own tight smile. "I'm fine. Thank you for asking. If you'll excuse me, I was just about to leave."

"Of course," Jake said.

Beck looked at Shiloh one last time in the same searching, deep way Beck had looked at her in the elevator. Like she could see something Shiloh couldn't. Then she nodded, like she had decided something. "Goodbye, Miss Haven."

Before Shiloh could reply, Madison Beck turned and disappeared into the crowd, her guard following close behind.

Jake's arm slipped around Shiloh's waist, pulling her against him. Shiloh leaned into him for support. She felt drained, stretched out, like a rung-out dishcloth.

Jake searched Shiloh's face. "What did she want?"

Shiloh turned all that had just happened over in her head, analyzing Beck's every word, every action. "I think she wanted to test me."

"And did you pass?"

Shiloh shook her head. "No, I don't think I did."

SIX

Brooks stepped out of the haze and paused at Sawyer's side, her feet noiseless in the snow. The leader of the Sparrows only came up to Sawyer's chest, even shorter than Nic, but she was not a woman Nic dared underestimate. Nic had seen Brooks spar against Paul, who doubled her in size. She'd tossed him into the snow like it was easy.

Nic glanced between Brooks and Sawyer. So that was where the leader had gone. Important business, indeed.

"Well," Brooks said, her deep voice muffled behind the scarf pulled over her nose, "let's not just stand here freezing our asses off."

She marched toward the lodge. Sawyer inclined her pointed chin as if to say, *After you.* Nic followed in the footprints Brooks left in the snow. Nic's breath, visible as puffs in the cold air, quickened as the same question pounded in her head like a drum.

Why?
Why?
Why is she here?

Nic grasped the porch railing as she stepped over the broken, icy steps. Brooks opened the door, and it groaned on ancient hinges. The sound of chaos met Nic's ears as she entered the lodge: the murmur of voices, the laughter of a child, the sounds of the Sparrows.

The Sparrows gathered in the lobby before the great stone hearth. With the tarps covering the shattered windows, the fireplace gave off the only light and the only warmth. Its flames cast shadows throughout the room, which should have felt gloomy. But the Sparrows bolstered with a life that made the air feel warm and bright. They sat on the moth-eaten upholstery of the abandoned couches, or the few old dining room chairs that hadn't broken over the years, huddled close in layers and blankets to keep warm, bent in conversation.

There was Charlie, crouched near the fire, tending to something cooking in a cast-iron pot hung above the flames. He laughed at something Ali was doing, which—given the pack of cards in his hands—was likely some lame magic trick.

There was Fatima Qadir, her hijab framing her beautiful face, as she worked a needle through a hole in a shirt with skillful fingers, tilting her head toward Wallace, who sat next to her. The elderly man waved his hands in the air, and Fatima smiled kindly like he wasn't telling a story she'd likely heard a dozen times. Nic had only been here three weeks, and she'd already heard the same stories of Wallace's pre-Sundering life at least twice.

There was Mick, Charlie's husband, whose fierce, scarred face seemed out of place, considering he currently cradled the slumbering Ezra Singer, who wasn't even two years old yet. Becca Singer now sat next to Mick, clutching a book and scowling as Mick corrected the pronunciation of a word she'd just read.

There was Yousef Qadir off to the side, chasing his two eldest children around the room as they squealed with laughter. Naia, his youngest, giggled from her perch on his shoulders.

And, of course, there was Mom and Paul, standing nearby,

whispering as they so frequently did. Mom clutched the top of a nearby dining chair. By the look on her face, Nic guessed Paul had just informed her mother of Nic's episode.

Fantastic.

Amir broke away from his father and tore closer to the door. Brooks caught his neck in the crook of her elbow and mussed his hair with a fist. He wheezed with laughter and called out, "Mercy! Mercy!"

Brooks released him, and he scampered behind the sofa, where his mother sat, to shield himself. This action drew attention to the door. They had no doubt heard the door, registered Brooks and Nic entering, but now they noticed the two were not alone. Luca looked up first and jerked out of his slumped position as he spotted Sawyer. Then, one by one, they all turned to notice. The conversation died in their throats, plunging them into silence. Even Yousef stopped and pulled Naia from his shoulders.

Nic studied her mother and Paul. Paul's lips lifted in a smile, and Mom let out a breath. They looked happy to see their old friend, relieved even. But they didn't appear surprised.

They knew, Nic thought. *They knew Sawyer was coming.*

Yet another thing they didn't deem Nic important enough to be informed.

"Well, I'll be damned," Wallace broke the silence. He'd twisted his head, cocking it awkwardly to point his one good eye toward the door. He swayed a little as he stood and then found his footing. He maneuvered the couches and approached with an outstretched hand. "Sawyer Ardelean. How the hell are ya?"

"I'm well, Wallace," Sawyer said, lifting her lone hand. But Wallace had offered the wrong hand. He swiftly changed and clasped Sawyer's hand in a warm shake. If the error bothered Sawyer, her face—always emotionless as stone—didn't crack.

And so it went, with Sawyer making the rounds to greet the people she led. She allowed Amelia to hug her and greeted Paul warmly—her lips twitching in the closest Sawyer ever came to a smile. She complimented Yousef and Fatima on their beautiful children. Sawyer even bent down to Becca's level and told the little girl how sorry Sawyer was about Becca's daddy. Told Becca he'd been a really good man. The best.

Becca's eyes welled before she threw down her book and stormed out of the room, toward the steps that led to the upstairs rooms. Nic had never asked what led the Singer children to be orphans, but whatever had caused that wound, it still bled. Nic's heart twisted for the girl. She knew that pain all too well.

"I'm sorry," Sawyer sighed, watching the girl go.

Charlie squeezed her shoulder in understanding before hurrying after Becca.

Sawyer finished her rounds by talking to the brothers: Luca and Ali. Ali grinned and bounced between two feet, excited to see her. Even Luca smiled, which was probably the first genuine smile Nic had seen from him. This was why Sawyer was the leader, Nic supposed. Because everyone in ROGUE loved her. Because she, despite her cool exterior, would have walked through hellfire and brimstone for all of them.

But she would also demand much. Maybe *too* much.

Nic winced at her own thought. *What's wrong with me?*

Once upon a time, Nic wanted to give it all for ROGUE. She still did, didn't she? Wasn't she still willing to sacrifice anything to ensure Arcadia's downfall? Wasn't that the purpose of ROGUE? Of Sawyer? *Of Nic?*

Then why was Nic's heart beating loud enough she feared the entire world might hear?

Thump, thump, thump.

A hand rested on Nic's shoulder. She jumped at the sudden touch.

"Are you all right?" Mom asked. Paul stood beside her now, looking at her with the same concerned expression.

Thump, thump, thump.

"I'm fine," Nic snapped. She was about to demand answers from them when Sawyer left the fire and approached their group.

Mom and Paul turned to face Sawyer. Brooks stepped close too. Brooks had taken off her hood and scarf, revealing her long dark braids. That was all Nic could see now—the back of their heads—as the four formed a square that excluded Nic.

Thump, thump, thump.

Sawyer lowered her voice. "Is there somewhere we can go to talk?"

Brooks nodded and gestured to the side of the room, where an old check-in counter stood, its rich red wood dimmed with dust. Beyond was a room that had once been an old office. They were going to leave, Nic realized, without giving her any answers—leave her wondering if Sawyer brought another mission that would result in Nic returning to that white, white cage.

They started to turn.

Thump, thump, thump.

"What are you *doing here*?" The words almost snarled from Nic's lips, and they all froze and turned back to her.

"Nicolette!" Mom hissed in her *you've-crossed-a-line-young-lady* tone. Mom opened her mouth to say more, but Sawyer held up her hand.

Sawyer cocked her head at Nic, studying her closely.

"Why are you here?" Nic repeated.

"Actually," Sawyer said at last, "I ultimately came to talk to you."

"Me?" *Thump. Thump. Thump.* "About what?"

"About someone you met while you were"—Sawyer paused—"*away*."

Nic shook her head. "I'm not going to tell you anything about Jake. I know he's the Councilor's son, but he's my friend, and I don't know—"

"I couldn't care less about the Osgood boy," Sawyer interrupted.

Nic's brow furrowed. "Then who?"

Sawyer took a step closer and lowered her voice. "I came to talk to you about Shiloh."

SEVEN

Val Haven had always found fire to be beautiful. She studied the crackling forge as she used tongs to extend a piece of metal into the heart of the flame. What some might see as a flickering mass of red heat, Val saw as a variant of hues, each one hotter, fiercer than the next: red, orange, yellow, white, and blue. It was a masterpiece.

When the metal rod turned red, Val pulled it out with the tongs and moved it to the anvil. She lifted the hammer but paused a moment to close her eyes and envision what she wanted to turn the metal into. When she had the image in her head, she brought the hammer down. Metal clanged against metal. A thrill fluttered through her chest as it bent beneath her blows.

For as long as she could remember, Val had always loved art, picking up the broken crayons at the Haven and drawing on whatever scrap of paper she could scrounge up. Maybe she'd loved it before then, but her memories before the Haven were dim as night—as they were supposed to be. *Rule #2: We don't remember the past... and all that ordure.* It was still a surprise the school allowed her access to the forgery or to the art studios. Future laborers like her certainly didn't need to know artwork, and the school certainly didn't waste time giving her classes. But some school counselor must have taken pity on Val—or realized she might be more manageable if she had a healthy outlet for her aggression—because they'd allowed her access to the art studios and to the forgery in her free time. In her gratitude, Val resisted the sometimes-overwhelming urge to burn the whole mother-froqing place down.

Playing with fire had always been her favorite form of art—the heating, pounding, and cooling. Val got lost in it, making it easy to miss the buzz of her tracker, warning that her curfew was in an hour. Even easy to miss the sound of the door opening and closing. But it was impossible to miss *her*. It had always been impossible. Stefani's presence brushed across Val's skin like a physical touch, sending goosebumps down her spine.

Val set down the hammer, laid the bending metal on the table, and lifted the safety visor from her face. Stefani practically floated around the cramped space, weaving between tables and metal equipment. Val watched every movement, her breath getting lost somewhere in her chest. Froq, Val could never get used to how beautiful Stefani was. She was art in motion—the one thing Val could never capture correctly in any medium, no matter how hard she tried.

"How's it coming?" Stefani asked, folding her arms on the metal table and leaning over so she could gaze down on the mess of metal Val had made. She picked up one of the finished pieces: a daisy whose petals were made from the thinnest metal Val had ever managed. The playful smile on Stefani's face softened into admiration. "It's beautiful, Val."

"It's not finished." Val pulled her gloves off and began to clean up, tucking all the random pieces into the bin which held her works in progress... some she'd started and would never finish. She would finish the flowers, though. She needed to form a few more buds, and then she'd work on the stems, twirling them together and binding them with a delicate copper bow. In the end, it'd be a bouquet of wildflowers she'd give Stefani at her graduation. That day—which loomed over Val like a dark cloud—marked the last time she would ever see Stefani. After that, Stefani would be sent away to some far-off college, while Val was stuck here. First to finish school, and then to work in some local, brutal factory.

Metal flowers could never wither, even if their love had always been destined to die. Beautiful things didn't survive in cages.

She grabbed the piece from Stefani's hands and tossed it into the bin. Val winced as it clattered, thrown harder than she had meant. Great. Now she'd have to remake it.

"You okay?" Stefani asked.

Val bobbed her head in a nod, knowing Stefani could see straight through her. She'd always been able to. Luckily, she didn't press.

"Jakey-boy texted me," Stefani said, and Val stiffened as it came rushing back, what Val had locked herself in this forge to forget. Shiloh. The trial.

"And?" Val asked.

"He wants to see if we can talk."

They had news then.

"Call him!" Val demanded. *And he better, by the mother-froqing Council, have Shiloh with him.*

"We should go to my room first," Stefani said.

Without even stopping to pull on her coat, Val grabbed Stefani's wrist and pulled her outside. In two minutes, they were alone in Stefani's room. In the female Legacy dorm, reserved only for children of the wealthy and powerful, Stefani didn't have a roommate.

Stefani reached into her coat pocket, but the movement seemed to take forever.

"Come on," Val insisted.

"Okay, okay," Stefani said, yanking the phone from her pocket and unfolding the small square of glass. "Bossy."

Val glared.

Stefani reached across the distance between them and coiled a piece of Val's dark hair around her pale finger, tugging just slightly. Just the way Val liked it. "It's a good thing I like it when you're bossy."

Stefani's voice was low. Sexy. It drew Val's gaze to her lips, which Stefani had painted a shade of pink that was now Val's new favorite color. The color of bubblegum. The color Stefani flushed all over when Val touched her just the right way. Heat roared through Val's body, and she ached to taste Stefani's mouth, to taste every part of her, knowing every inch of her would be as sweet as it looked.

But Shiloh...

Val shook her head, forcing herself to focus. "Call. Him," she growled through her teeth.

Stefani giggled, but finally tapped on her phone. The hologram appeared from the screen of her phone, merely a beam of light in the dimness of the room. It hummed as it rang, and then Jacob Osgood appeared as though he'd just stepped in front of them. Just him. No Shiloh.

Val crossed her arms over her chest and gave Osgood her best glare.

She was decidedly *not* a fan of Osgood. Never had been. In the week prior to Nic's first escape attempt, Val had started to admit—very grudgingly—that maybe Osgood did genuinely care for Shiloh. But then, when the truth came out about Silas, Osgood had tossed her aside like yesterday's trash.

Even though Shiloh seemed to have been quick to forgive him for that, Val had no intention of being so merciful.

But Stefani greeted him cheerfully. "Jakey-boy!"

Traitor.

"Hey, Stef," Jake said quickly, his voice nearly drowned out by the background noise. Cars honked and revved. Wind wailed. And the beat of wings—perhaps drone wings—hitting the air. Around him, the hologram showed distant skyscrapers, dimly lit, with little square windows.

"Where are you?" Stefani asked.

"We escaped to the roof of my dad's Chicago condo," Jake said, and then rotated his phone so that Shiloh appeared in view.

Val's shoulder relaxed a fraction. Deep in her bones, Val could still feel the terror of the night Nic escaped, and Shiloh nearly died. The terror, *and* the guilt. Val had kept Shiloh at arm's length, blaming her for things that weren't her fault, shoving Shiloh away because that was how Val survived—by pushing away anything that could hurt. But if Val had lost Shiloh too, when they'd barely made amends, Val would never have forgiven herself.

And the possibility of losing Shiloh wasn't over yet.

"What happened?" Val demanded.

For a moment, it looked as though the signal on the phone had grown weak, and the hologram had frozen—Osgood and Shiloh remained so still.

Then Osgood said, with no emotion, "Silas will be executed tomorrow morning."

Never before did Val want to cheer at the news of someone's death, but she almost pumped a fist in the air. "Good froqing riddance."

Stefani's smile—which sometimes seemed a permanent feature —dimmed a little. "You guys okay?"

"Why wouldn't I be?" Osgood said, with too much effort. "It's what he deserves."

Froq. Was that compassion stirring in Val's chest? No froqing way! But then, as a Haven girl, she understood what it was like to be told people you loved deserved to die. But in Osgood's case, it was actually the truth.

Val shoved the feeling down and looked to Shiloh as she laid her head against Osgood's shoulder, her face placid. But Val wasn't fooled by the mask. Stefani smoothly transitioned to catching them up on the rumors of what exactly had happened to Jacob Osgood's girlfriend to land her in the hospital. The latest was that Harper Martinez had pushed her down a flight of stairs out of jealousy.

Stefani's voice faded to the background as Val met Shiloh's gaze through the hologram, like it was only them, standing together in the Haven, not wanting Mother to hear.

"You okay?" Val asked noiselessly, only moving her lips.

Shiloh's eyes closed for a second, then reopened. "Yes," she mouthed back.

"Liar."

Shiloh's lips twitched, an almost-smile. And, whether or not she was okay, she and Val would be together again soon and they'd figure it out. They were Haven girls. And Haven girls looked after each other. That was the one rule Val would never break.

⚶

Sawyer led Nic into the small, cramped office. Nic's mom and Paul had tried to follow, but Sawyer insisted she speak to Nic alone, and they *never* questioned Sawyer. In the room, a desk sat against one wall, covered with a decade's worth of dust broken only by a few handprints.

When Sawyer closed the door behind them, it plunged the room into darkness. The single window had been covered by a blanket. Sawyer moved to where a lantern and a book of matches sat on the desk, left likely for the purpose of private meetings. No one else used this room. Sawyer used the edge of the lantern to secure the matchbook, then struck a match. A warm, flickering glow spread through the room.

Sawyer swung around to face Nic and leaned back against the desk. "So…"

"So," Nic repeated, crossing her arms over her chest. She kept her voice calm, even though her blood pounded in her ears.

Mom and Paul had acted weird when Nic had first told them about Shiloh Haven. What had Paul said? *"Reminds me of someone I knew, but they died a long time ago."* The question was who, and what had led them to tell Sawyer about her?

"First off, Nic," Sawyer began, "I should tell you that... I know what happened to you."

Sawyer's dark eyes pierced into Nic like they could see her soul. Nic swiftly looked away. She wanted to tell Sawyer to stop, to shut up. *No one* knew what had happened to her; not really. Nic had never talked about it.

There weren't words for such things.

But Nic bit her tongue, and Sawyer continued, "Nic, I cannot express how deeply sorry I am... or how grateful I am to you. I can only imagine what the Elite did to you. I know that must have been..." She stopped, glancing down at the empty sleeve at her side. She let out a breath. "There are no words for what it must have been. Few people could have withstood what you went through without breaking. Thank you for your bravery and loyalty to ROGUE."

The seams within Nic's soul strained to contain the building pressure. Being a brave soldier of ROGUE was all Nic wanted to be. A year ago, Sawyer's words would have made her do cartwheels. Now, she wanted to talk about anything, *anyone* else. "You said—" Nic's voice croaked, and she cleared her throat. "You said you wanted to talk about Shiloh?"

Sawyer nodded.

"Why?"

"Because I think she might be someone... someone important."

"Who?" Nic asked.

Sawyer shook her head. "We're not certain it is her. Your mother and Paul only suspected and alerted me. I don't want to tell you my suspicions and cloud your judgment, but I am hoping you can give me more information."

"What kind of information?"

Sawyer reached into one of the side pockets of her cargo pants and drew out a folded piece of paper. She held it out to Nic. "Is this her?"

Nic unfolded the paper. It was a print of what looked to be a magazine that must have covered the Osgoods' Yuletide Eve Ball. Shiloh stood next to Jake, her arm slipped through his, looking exquisite in the gorgeous black dress she'd worn. Nic studied Jake the longest, at how perfectly handsome he'd looked in his suit, and the way he looked down at Shiloh. Like he loved her. Like she was *everything*.

A pang went off in Nic's chest. She thought about how she'd kissed Jake goodbye; how Jake hadn't kissed her back. Yes, things between Jake and Shiloh had been strained when Shiloh left, but looking at that picture, Nic had no doubt they'd find their way through the troubled water, if they hadn't already.

And Nic was stupidly, stupidly jealous.

"Well?" Sawyer asked when Nic had stared at the picture for too long. "Is that Shiloh?"

"Yes," Nic said, handing it back.

It was Sawyer's turn to stare at the picture for a long moment, her face as smooth and unreadable as stone. She made a sound deep in her throat as she set it down on the desk beside her. "How old is she again?"

"Almost eighteen."

"And do you know her birthdate?"

"March... I think."

Sawyer shook her head. "No, that's not right," she murmured, more to herself than anything, looking at the floor. "But they could have changed that detail easily enough."

"They?" Nic asked.

But Sawyer ignored the question. "Did she talk to you about her life before the Haven?"

Nic scoffed. "No, never. That would have violated Rule #2."

"Rule #2?"

"The Haven girls live by strict rules to survive. Rule #2 was 'Don't remember the past'. I don't know if she doesn't remember or if she just doesn't talk about it, at least not to me."

A shadow crossed Sawyer's face, her hand strangling the edge of the desk. "Shiloh's Haven was truly that awful?"

"Aren't all Havens?" Nic asked.

Sawyer blinked past Nic's shoulder for a long moment before looking back. "Did she at least tell you how old she was when she came to the Haven?"

Nic began to shake her head, but Sawyer took a step toward her. "Think, Nic. Please. It's vital that I know this."

Nic let her mind shuffle through her memories of Shiloh: all the tutoring sessions, the conversations they had. But it wasn't Shiloh she remembered speaking it; it was Val. When Nic had first come to the Haven, it was Val who had explained how odd it had been that Nic was so old. Val had been four when she'd come to the Haven, and Shiloh had been six.

"I think she was six," Nic said.

"Six." Sawyer leaned heavily against the desk. "Are you sure? Are you absolutely sure?"

"No," Nic admitted, "but I think that's right."

Sawyer gazed down at Shiloh's picture on the desk. Nic shifted her weight from foot to foot, fighting the urge to demand what this was all about.

"One more question," Sawyer said, looking up. "I can't tell in the picture. What color are her eyes?"

Nic frowned. It was an odd question. "They're dark, like..." She searched around the room, trying to describe the exact shade of darkness in Shiloh's eyes—like shadows and the dark of the night. But finally, Nic looked back to Sawyer, whose own eyes gleamed in the lamplight. The resemblance took her breath away. "Like... like *yours*."

And Sawyer—the leader of all ROGUE—whom Nic had never once seen smile, threw her hand over her lips and *laughed*.

"She's alive. Oh my god, she's *alive*!"

Eight

Getting Stefani to stop talking was a feat equal to running a triathlon blindfolded. After several failed attempts to end the conversation politely, Jake hung the phone up midway through the third ongoing rumor regarding Shiloh's disappearance from school—which was, apparently, that Jake had murdered her. He shoved his phone back into his pocket and turned to face Shiloh.

The lights of the city danced across her pale face. He drank her in: the slant of her chin, the curve of her lips, the lines of her body. His fingers ached to touch her.

Say goodbye to your girl.

The memory of Silas's voice echoed in his head. It knocked the breath from him, and Jake pressed his hands into the terrace that surrounded the roof to steady himself. Despite the biting winter chill that hung over the capital in February, the air on the roof was warm. The forcefield that domed over the roof kept it pleasant year-round, allowing the lush flowers to grow and create a paradise for his father to escape to whenever he stayed in the capital on business, which was often. But right now, the garden didn't feel like paradise. It felt too hot, plastering Jake's shirt to his back with a layer of sweat.

Forget what Silas said, Jake told himself for the millionth time. *He's lying.*

As long as Silas was in the cage, Shiloh was safe and, despite what Silas said, escaping from the Vault was impossible. Jake's father had reassured him of this when he had told Dad what Silas said.

"He was only trying to mess with your head. There is no escaping the Vault."

But still, everything inside Jake trembled.

But what if—

"What did he say to you?" Shiloh asked.

Jake jerked his head toward her. She was studying him with those endless dark eyes. "What?"

"Silas," Shiloh said, and there was no missing the way she flinched when she said his name. "What did he say to you? You've been acting strange since you came back from seeing him."

"It's noth—" Jake started, but she cut him off with a shake of her head.

"Please don't lie to me, Jake. There's been enough lies between us."

Jake glanced out at the city, trying to buy time. Whereas most cities in Arcadia had areas that were crumbling to the ground, Chicago shone. Colored lights bathed the skyscrapers. Hover crafts buzzed below and above them, public transportation for people and packages, filling the air with the constant familiar hum. From one angle, Jake could glimpse Lake Michigan's dark waters stretching out, and from another, he could see the light beams coming off the Unity Center; all various colors, moving and dancing in their own show.

It was beautiful, extraordinary.

And it was a den of vipers.

Shiloh slid her fingers into his. "Jake."

"My dad wants me to come here this summer," Jake said. He knew he was changing the subject, buying time until he figured out exactly what he should tell her. "He wants me to apply to be a summer intern for one of the Councilors."

This was what his father had pestered him about as they had ridden the elevator back up, Jake's insides still shaking from all Silas had said.

The Councilors each chose an intern during the summer, a college student who would wait on them hand and foot in what was supposed to be a position of honor. Jake would be eighteen by summer, so his father had reasoned it was time. And besides: *"It will show where your loyalties truly lie."*

"Summer?" Shiloh repeated.

And, surely, she was thinking what Jake had thought. That their time together was on a clock that *tick, tick, ticked* beneath his skin. It was February, three months until graduation, six months before they'd be sent to different colleges. If he left at the beginning of summer, it'd steal so many of their precious days.

Jake gritted his teeth. "I told him no."

"He has your whole life planned for you, doesn't he?" Shiloh said, not really a question.

Jake grunted, because of course, his father had it all figured out: A summer internship, four years of college, maybe a State Advocate seat, a marriage to someone other than Shiloh, and... one day... a Councilor's throne. Everything destined for him, and nothing he wanted.

Jake laced his fingers through Shiloh's own and pulled her away from the roof's edge, tired of the sight. He led her through the boxes of flowers. They both knew he was still stalling, but she leaned into his side and let him. It had been so long since they'd been alone like this.

"Do you ever think about what you'd do if your life wasn't already decided for you?" Jake asked. "If you didn't have to become an engineer, what would you be?"

Shiloh cocked an eyebrow as though surprised by the question. Jake wondered why he hadn't asked her sooner. But Shiloh had been so smart, so naturally gifted, engineering actually seemed fitted to her.

"I don't know," Shiloh said at last. "I guess I never thought about it. Before you, I didn't see the point of wanting things I can't have. What about you?"

Unlike Shiloh, Jake had the luxury of dreaming, even if it could only be a dream. "I'd be a lawyer like my mom was before my father became Councilor. I'd help people get justice."

Shiloh squeezed his hand. "You'd be good at it."

Jake's smile wobbled on his lips. He steered them toward the center of the rooftop garden, where a red wooden gazebo had been built. There were cameras all over this rooftop, which caught footage but not sound, where the security guards could be watching them even now. But the gauzy curtains surrounding the gazebo would grant them privacy.

As they climbed the steps into the gazebo, another question crossed Jake's mind. "Would you have children?"

Children weren't options, not in Arcadia. Not when the population had dwindled after the Sundering and the Great Excision, which had left anyone who hadn't fallen in line dead or in prison camps. Having children was an expectation.

She paused on the gazebo's step and met his gaze steadily, as though, of this, she was far more certain. "No. I wouldn't."

"Oh." Jake wasn't sure what else to say, wasn't sure what to feel. He bought time as they moved to the lounge chairs in the middle of the gazebo. The curtains blocked out much of the light from the garden and the city, casting Shiloh in shadow, even though they sat side by side on one of the chairs.

They were seventeen years old, with mountains of obstacles before them. Children should be the farthest thing from Jake's mind. But if he let himself dream of a life of his making, twenty years from now, there were children there.

"Why not?" Jake asked softly.

She glanced around her and then lowered her voice, so Jake had to lean closer to hear. "How could I have a child and risk they'll be put in a Haven one day?"

Jake winced. "Fair. That's... fair." He steadied himself with a breath. "And if it wasn't a risk? If we lived in a different world?"

Shiloh shook her head. "We don't live in a different world, Jake."

"Yet," Jake whispered, an oath behind the words. Not yet, but soon. He wouldn't rest until the world was different, until Havens no longer existed. And maybe... maybe Shiloh still wouldn't want to have children in a world like that, and if that was the case, he'd cross that bridge when they came to it, but at least the decision would not be one made out of fear.

Shiloh studied his eyes for a moment, then nodded. "Yet," she agreed.

Jake reached forward to brush a strand of hair behind her ear. The softness of her skin enchanted him, swept away all thoughts of anything but how good she felt beneath his fingertips. He trailed his fingers across the stubborn line of her chin and across her bottom lip. She was soft as silk. A familiar burn erupted in his blood, an explosion of want. No, *need*. He desperately *needed* her.

If I don't kiss her right now, I'm going to die.

It was an insane, irrational thought, but nothing had ever felt more true. Jake leaned toward her... and she pressed a finger to his lips.

"Jake," Shiloh said firmly, "we still need to talk."

Jake groaned. "I don't want to talk."

She slid away from him and put a crackle of ice into her tone, a sign she was done playing his distraction game. "What did Silas say?"

Jake sighed, letting his head fall into his hand. "It doesn't matter, Shiloh. He said whatever it took to get under my skin. He said... he said..." Jake yanked at the roots of his hair until it hurt and used the last of his will to spit out the words that haunted him. "He said I should say goodbye to you while I still had the chance."

&

Shiloh sucked a breath in through her teeth. She could almost hear the words in Silas's dark tone: *Say goodbye.* Something inside her shivered. But Silas couldn't hurt her anymore. He was locked in the most inescapable cell in all of Arcadia. She shouldn't fear him.

Breathe in. Breathe out.

"What else did he say?" Shiloh asked.

Again, Jake tugged at his hair. She caught his hand with both of her own and pulled it away from his head, cradling it close to her chest.

"He said that the games aren't over," Jake managed between his gritted teeth.

This time, all of Shiloh shivered. She tried to fight it, but it shuddered through her all the same. Jake's hands slid up her arms, the comforted becoming the comforter.

"Shi, he's just trying to froq with our heads. He'll be dead tomorrow."

Shiloh nodded, but she wasn't so sure. Yes, Silas loved to torment her. But he'd never, not once, lacked the power to back up his mind games. What did Silas know that Shiloh didn't? Was there a hand he'd held back?

And if the game wasn't over, what was the next move?

"Shiloh, look at me."

Shiloh hadn't realized she'd been staring past Jake at one of the gauzy curtains that concealed the gazebo. She forced her eyes to focus on his. He laid a hand on her cheek, keeping her locked in place, letting his warmth seep into her skin.

"He's never going to hurt you again," Jake said. "I promise."

"Okay," Shiloh said, but she didn't feel at peace. And she

wouldn't—not until she saw a bullet go through Silas's skull. Tomorrow couldn't come soon enough.

Silence fell between them, nothing but the steady electronic hum of the city, of the drones whizzing by somewhere above the roof of the gazebo.

"Your turn," Jake said at last, playing with the ends of her hair. "What did Beck say?"

Shiloh hesitated, but of course, Jake deserved to know. "She wanted me to know that you are already spoken for."

Jake's frown dug deep furrows into his brow. "What do you mean, *spoken for*?"

"I mean that the marriage board has already decided your marriage. Or rather, your father and Councilor Beck have already arranged it."

Jake let out a humorless laugh. "What? My father wouldn't..." His voice trailed off, the laugh dying on his tongue. Because they both knew his father *would*.

Jake's jaw tightened. In the darkness, his eyes had turned to a molten black, the only light in them was the flame of his rage.

"Who?" he demanded. Then, "Froq, don't tell me." He burst to his feet, paced a few feet away, turned back around. "Katerina."

Shiloh nodded, rose to her feet, and took a step toward him.

Jake's hands tightened into fists at his side. He glared somewhere over Shiloh's right shoulder. "My father and Beck have always pushed Katerina and me toward each other, but I thought they were trying to create something that just isn't there. She and I have only ever been civil... and awkward. To have something set in stone—" He stopped, his voice turning into a sound like a roar deep in his throat.

Shiloh wrapped her arms around her chest, feeling suddenly cold despite the climate-controlled air. She wasn't sure what brought her to say it, but the words left her lips, anyway, "She's beautiful, Jake."

"So what?"

"And, well, I'm n—"

"Don't," Jake growled, holding up a finger in warning. "Don't you *dare* finish that sentence."

The fury in his tone made Shiloh seal her lips together, not daring to make another sound.

He took a breath, visibly cooling the fire within him. "Maybe you're right," Jake said, with a shrug of his shoulder. "Katerina Beck is beautiful." He approached Shiloh slowly and stopped when only inches separated them. "She may be the brightest star in the night sky."

Shiloh's stomach twisted.

"But you, Shiloh..." He framed her face between both of his hands and tilted her neck back, forcing her to look deep into his warm eyes. Into the fire that burned for her there. "You are an *entire* universe."

Shiloh's breath got lost somewhere in her chest. There was no air. There was only him—his scent, his eyes, the blazing warmth of his touch—filling every part of her.

Him, him, him.

His nose brushed against hers, his lips so close they teased hers as he whispered, "And I don't care what anyone says. I'm going to love you. Deeply. Defiantly. Not for as long as they let me, but for always. I'm going to love you forever."

"Forever is a long time," Shiloh breathed unsteadily.

"I froqing hope so." Jake chuckled, the sound vibrating from his chest to hers. He trailed his lips across her jaw, toward her ear. His teeth nipped gently at her earlobe, sending a flare of heat through her chest and down to her core, coiling and pulling taut with want.

"I'm going to burn the world down for you, Shiloh."

"I think," Shiloh said, through ragged breaths, sliding her fingers into Jake's hair to steer him back toward her lips, "I'm quite done with talking."

"Thank froq!"

They collided like two stones striking together, sparks flying wherever they touched. It had always been an inferno between them—fire meeting gasoline—hotter and brighter and realer than anything she'd known. But *this* felt hotter still, like all the things that had tried to tear them apart in the last weeks—Silas, death, the Council—had instead only made their fire burn brighter.

Shiloh's legs met the back of the lounge chair, and she pulled him down with her. The weight of him pressing her down into the cushion intoxicated her. It had been so long, too long, since they had been alone like this, free to touch each other exactly as they wanted. No, they'd *never* been alone like this. She'd never been free. There had always been Silas, listening in, hovering like a shadow in the corner of her mind.

But they'd survived that. They'd defied everything. They defied it still.

Their love *was* defiance.

Each touch, each kiss, each bite and lick and gasp sparked with rebellion. And it was *not* enough. Shiloh wanted to burn with it, to go up in the flames he ignited within her body. So, when his hand hesitated on the buttons of her shirt, she curled her legs around his waist and hissed hot against his ear, "Don't stop."

He pulled back just enough to study her eyes, his deep gaze as languid as the sweep of his tongue against her skin. She felt it in every part of her, delicious and sweet.

His fingers undid a button, still watching her face.

She repeated the command between gasps, "Don't–"

And another button.

"–stop."

His lips trailed after his fingers, leaving kisses down the rise and fall of her chest. His thumbs brushed against her hipbones as his mouth found its way to her stomach. Shiloh's back arched toward him. *More, more, more,* her heart raged.

"Are you sure?" he asked, pulling away once more.

She wanted to scream at him in frustration, to laugh at his stupidity, but she calmed when she looked up at him.

He offered a gift. One last chance to turn back. Maybe, once, Shiloh would have done it. She might have been afraid to fall off this ledge; to break this one last physical barrier between them. She might have shaken as she remembered the taunting of froqing Harper Martinez and felt the insecurity of not measuring up to all of Jake's past.

But Jake was looking at her, the way he'd always looked at her: like she was all he could see.

And she didn't want to stop. She wanted to fall.

No, she wanted to froqing *leap*.

"Are you absolutely sure?" Jake repeated, his hands clinging to her hips, his voice thick with the effort to restrain himself. "Nothing happens here unless you tell me it's what you want."

"Silly boy," Shiloh said softly, reaching down to brush aside that same stubborn strand of hair that always fell on his forehead. "Haven't you figured it out by now? *All* I want is you."

He grinned against her skin, his fingers curling around the waistband of her pants, and—

BOOM!

The sound of crashing metal startled them apart. Her heart pounding for an entirely new reason, Shiloh launched upward and looked around, but could not see through the curtains. Feet pounded on the rooftop, storming toward them.

"Mr. Osgood!" a deep voice roared.

Jake rushed to the entrance of the gazebo. Shiloh fumbled with the buttons of her shirt.

"Guards," Jake said, only a second before they entered.

Two of them, nervous energy clinging to their skin. One seized Jake's arm and hauled him out of the gazebo, while the other started toward Shiloh. She'd only done up half her shirt when the guard yanked her up and dragged her out toward the rooftop door, which had been flung open, colliding with the wall—the noise that had startled Jake and Shiloh apart.

"What is going on?" Jake demanded. He dragged his feet, casting glances over his shoulder at Shiloh.

"We have to go," was the only explanation his guard gave, guiding him toward the stairs that led to the roof. "It isn't safe here."

"Not safe here?" Jake asked. "This is my father's condo. How is it not safe?" He tried to plant his feet, but the guard propelled him forward with a hand on his shoulder.

"Just move!"

At the bottom of the stairs, Jake resisted again, but only long enough to reach behind him and grab Shiloh's hand. They clung to each other as the guards stood on either side of them, pulling and shoving in the direction they needed to go. They rushed through the hallway, avoiding the elevator in the lobby and instead taking a side door onto stairs that led down all twenty floors. On the long descent, Jake demanded twice more to know what was happening, but the guards gave no answers.

By the time they reached the bottom, Shiloh and Jake panted for breath. They burst through one more door, and a gust of cold air stabbed Shiloh's face for only a second before she reached the wide-open door of a car. One last shove sent Jake and Shiloh sprawling onto the backseat. The door slammed shut, and the car lurched forward with a squeal of tires.

"Buckle up," commanded a familiar voice.

Shiloh straightened herself to find Mrs. Osgood—Reagan—on the backseat that faced Shiloh. Reagan looked poised; despite the fact she wore rosy satin pajamas instead of her normal uniform. But the way she strangled her phone in her hands showed that she wasn't nearly as calm as she seemed.

"Mom, what the froq is going on?" Jake demanded.

The car screeched around a corner. Shiloh slid across the seat and collided with Jake.

"I said buckle up," Reagan snapped.

Shiloh fumbled with the seatbelt latch, but on the third try, it snapped into place. She looked back at Jake's mother. Her eyes dipped down to where the front of Shiloh's shirt still gaped, her bra peeking through. Reagan looked away swiftly. Shiloh clutched at her collar, her cheeks flaming.

Beside her, Jake secured his seatbelt and gave his mom a pointed look. "*Now* will you tell me what's going on?"

Reagan glanced down at her phone and then back up, and fear flashed like lightning across her face.

Shiloh's hand, still clasping her collar, shook. Her heart screamed into her ears—*Please no, please no, please no*—as though, somehow, she already knew. Silas had said the game wasn't over, and here was his next move.

And then Reagan spoke: "Silas has escaped the Vault."

NINE

"Who's alive?" Nic demanded. "I don't understand."

Sawyer sobered up, planting her usual solemn expression in place. She'd probably tell Nic that it was nothing for her to worry about. None of her business. Just like Mom and Paul and everyone else in ROGUE.

"I deserve to know," Nic said, before Sawyer could say any of those things.

"Yes, you do."

Nic's mouth hung open, prepared to argue. She snapped it closed.

"But," Sawyer added, "I'm surprised you don't remember."

"Remember?"

Sawyer nodded. "Do you remember Alec and Elaine?"

"Of course, I do."

Nic had only been three when Alec and Elaine died, but she felt like she knew them deeply. Everyone still talked about them, told stories like they were heroes of old. Or some people—like Mom and Paul—talked about them like they were old friends whom they really, really missed.

Sawyer paused. "And do you remember their daughter?"

Now *that* Nic remembered. According to Mom, Alec and Elaine's daughter and Nic had been like sisters, despite the age gap between them. Nic had been too young to remember all that, but Nic did have one exquisitely clear memory—of that night. That horrible wretched night when ROGUE had been defeated. When so many of its leaders had been executed. When Alec and Elaine and their daughter had died.

Nic's eyes closed, and the memory flickered in the darkness behind her eyelids. She would have been only three at the time, but the fear had etched the night into her core. Even now, the taste of terror scolded her tongue, acidic and bitter.

At the time, Nic had understood only that she had to run. The bad men had been attacking them, and now Mom, Dad, and Paul had to escape—to get Nic and Alec and Elaine's daughter to safety. What followed came in flashes.

Running through the dark forest. Nic's dad holding her tight against his chest. Alec and Elaine's daughter clinging to Paul's shoulders. And then... gunshots. Mom yelling at Nic to run. Alec and Elaine's daughter, Nic's friend, taking her hand, yanking her away from the sound of bullets.

The two girls found a tree, a small hollow in the trunk only big enough for Nic to fit. "Stay here until your mommy and daddy come," Alec and Elaine's daughter said. "Don't come out. No matter what, okay?"

So, Nic stayed, even when her friend left, even when she heard the screams and the explosion and the gunshots. She clamped her hands over her ears and buried her face in her knees as the darkness enclosed around her.

The first rays of the sun had peeked over the horizon when Paul found Nic in the tree. Mom's hug was so tight, Nic could feel it in her bones even now. But Alec and Elaine's daughter had never been found.

She'd died that night.

Nic opened her eyes, taking a moment to remind herself she

was still standing in the old office. Sawyer watched her steadily. Sawyer had been lucky not to be executed that night with everyone else. She'd only survived because she'd run, and the exploding handcuff the Elite had put on her wrist detonated with such force that the Elite had assumed she was dead. Nic could still smell her blood, hear her moans when Mom, Dad, and Paul had found Sawyer lying broken on the forest floor.

Nic shook off the dregs of the memory, trying to think clearly. Why had Sawyer brought up Alec and Elaine's daughter? What did a long dead girl have to do with—

Nic's hand flew to her mouth as the truth slammed into her like a bullet. "Oh my God!"

Oh.

My.

GOD!

How had Nic not seen it months ago?

Shiloh came to the Haven when she was six, the same age Alec and Elaine's daughter had been when she died.

Their daughter... whose body had never been found.

A girl whose codename had been Princess, just like Mom and Paul had been whispering, but whose real name had been... *Shiloh*.

Sawyer gave another smile. "You connected the dots, I see."

Nic lowered her hand. "You think Shiloh is Alec and Elaine's daughter?"

"Yes."

Nic stared at Sawyer. The leader of ROGUE. The sister of Elaine Ardelean Sanders. "But that... that would make her your... your..."

Sawyer's smile widened. "My niece. She's my niece. And she's *alive!*"

TEN

Jake's blood roared in his ears. *Escaped. Escaped. Escaped.*

"That's not—" The words caught in his dry throat, and he had to swallow multiple times before he could force them out. "That's not possible. No one can escape the Vault."

"But he did," Jake's mother said, flatly.

"But *how*?"

"I'm not sure." Mom looked away when she said it, toward the window. The opaque glass reflected her face, which was masked to reveal nothing.

Still, Jake could feel it. *She knows something she isn't saying.*

A suspicion crawled like a spider down Jake's spine. With the guards, the cameras, the series of doors, someone couldn't get *out* of the Vault, but *someone else* could come in and get them out.

But then, if Silas had help from someone that powerful, he could be anywhere... do anything...

Say goodbye to your girl.

Jake turned sharply toward Shiloh. She sat with her eyes closed, her face expressionless. But one hand clenched her collar, and the other coiled so tightly around her knee that her knuckles paled.

Her chest heaved as she breathed in and out, in and out, fighting to stay calm. Jake pried her hand away from her knee and laced his fingers through hers.

It's okay, he wanted to promise. But it wasn't. Nothing was okay. No one was safe as long as Silas was free.

The car took another series of turns, trying to shake anyone who may or may not be following them. Tires squealed to the time of Jake's heart.

"Where are we going?" Jake asked.

"We couldn't stay in the condo," Mom explained. "Silas... well, Silas has been there. We're being moved so he can't find us. Your father is arranging the details."

"And where *is* Dad?"

Mom glanced down at her phone. "I'm not sure. I suspect he's been secured at a different location."

Of course. Separating the Councilor from his family. Silas could only go after one person at a time. It didn't matter, so long as the guards got Shiloh somewhere safe.

Silence fell, heavy and thick. After a small eternity, the car finally stopped.

The guards ushered the three of them out of the car and into the dark alley between two towering skyscrapers. Jake grabbed Shiloh's hand and didn't release it, not as they entered the building from a side door, as they piled into a service elevator, or even when they stepped onto the ornate carpet on the hallway of the twenty-fifth floor. A dozen doors lined either side of the long hallway.

Jake's stomach clenched. Surely, this wasn't where they were staying.

Shiloh pulled at his hand, and he leaned close. "Jake," Shiloh hissed into his ear, "why are we at a hotel? This isn't—"

"Ms. Haven," said the head-guard in the lead—a white-haired man who only went by his surname, Rakes—as he brought them to a halt and opened a door. "I'm sure this will be sufficient."

Shiloh hesitated before disentangling her hand from Jake's and stepping into her room. When Jake followed Shiloh, Rakes held up a hand. "You'll be staying with your mother. It's better if we all stay... in designated locations."

Again, separating the "royal" family from the "peasant" in case the guards had to choose whom to protect. Jake's fingers curled, and he opened his mouth.

"It's fine," Shiloh interrupted from the door. "I'll be fine."

No, it *wasn't* fine, but before Jake could argue, she closed the door.

"Mom, why are we here?" Jake demanded, when they were in their own room, a suite with a separate bedroom and a couch in the main area made out into a bed. "Why aren't we getting on a plane and getting Shiloh the froq out of this city?"

Mom scanned her phone, the one she'd clung to this entire time, as though it might hold answers. "I'll be honest, son. I don't know. But I trust your father. If he says this is what's best to keep us safe, it is."

Her words didn't begin to ease Jake's fears. Instead, Silas's words in the cage haunted him.

Say goodbye to your girl.

"Mom?"

"Hmmm," Mom said. She tapped a fingernail on her bottom lip, still studying her phone. Jake fought against the urge to throw the phone off the twenty-fifth-floor balcony outside their suite.

"Promise me something."

As though recognizing his solemn tone, Mom lowered her phone, giving him her full attention. "What?"

"Promise me you'll protect Shiloh."

"Of *course*, we're going to protect her," Mom said swiftly, waving her hand like it was a silly question.

"Silas said something..."

"It doesn't matter," Mom insisted fiercely. "I'm *not* going to let anything happen to her."

"You promise?"

Mom stepped closer and drew an 'X' across her chest. "I cross my heart and hope to die."

🔥

From Shiloh's viewpoint in her hotel room, she watched the air-traffic race by on the backdrop of brightly lit skyscrapers. She must now be on the opposite side of the city from the condo, because she could no longer see the waters of Lake Michigan or the Unity Center. But they hadn't gone far enough.

Silas was out there... somewhere.

Taking a breath, Shiloh pulled the heavy, velvet curtain closed, concealing the door and the wall of glass that led out to the balcony. She returned to the platform bed and pulled her knees to her chest, covering them with her frayed, standard-issue pajama top. The heat of the fireplace nipped at her cheeks. The crackling flame blazed so close to the bed that, had the fire not been a hologram, it would have lit it into cinders.

She watched the dance of the flames, as though the hypnotic shades might hold more answers than the colors of the city had.

Think, Shiloh. You have to think.

A sudden burst of—not fear—rage broke through Shiloh's chest. This wasn't fair! Shiloh had won—she had *froqing* won. But now, the game was beginning all over again. If she wanted to survive—to keep Jake safe—she had to stay one step ahead of whatever Silas planned next.

How do you play chess when you can't even see the board?

TAP! TAP! TAP!

Shiloh jerked her head upright, her heart slamming against her sternum. She searched around the room to locate the sound. Nothing seemed out of place, but the shadows cast by the fire—the only light in the room—seemed to grow larger and darker.

TAP! TAP! TAP!

She placed the noise at last: a knock against the wall of glass.

She jumped from the bed and spun to face the curtains that covered the balcony. Her heart pounded out a warning.

Someone was outside.

What should she do? Should she yell for the guards who were still in the hallway?

But then... Silas wouldn't have knocked. If he was this close, he'd already be in the room. Then who? Or what?

Another round of tapping came, and Shiloh approached the door slowly. By the time she reached the windows, she barely breathed. She grabbed the edge of the curtain, parting it only a fraction of an inch, just enough to peek out.

Then she growled, threw the curtain aside, and ripped the balcony door open. "Jacob Osgood, I'm going to kill you," she snarled, keeping her voice low so it wouldn't carry to the door.

Jake slipped past her to get inside. He jumped from foot to foot, running his hands up and down his bare biceps like he could erase his goosebumps. "You almost did. You took so long to answer I almost froze to death."

She slapped his shoulder. Probably harder than she meant to. "You scared the froqing ordure out of me!"

"Shh." He covered her lips with his hand, glancing behind him at the door to the hallway, where the guards were stationed. When the door didn't pop open, he slipped his hand down to her shoulders, looking a little contrite. "I'm sorry. I didn't mean to scare you."

Shiloh puffed out a breath, the tension in her muscles softening at his touch. "How did you even get here?"

Jake shrugged. "I jumped."

"Jumped?" Shiloh glanced at the balcony. Earlier, she'd noticed the balconies between rooms were next to each other, but a four-foot gap stretched between them. If he'd missed the jump, he'd have fallen several hundred feet to the unforgiving concrete.

Shiloh shook her head. "You're insane."

Jake's mouth lifted into a crooked smile. "Yes, but you love me."

Arcadia be froqed, I do love you.

His smile fell quickly. "I had to see you… to make sure you're okay."

Swallowing, Shiloh looked away from the worry written on Jake's face, sweeping her hair behind an ear just to make her hand busy. "I'm not okay," she admitted. "I'm terrified."

He reached forward, and she thrust herself toward him. He pulled her close, wrapping her in the shelter of his arms.

"Hey, hey, hey," Jake whispered soothingly, his lips brushing the top of her head. "I'm not going to let anything happen to you. I promise."

But how could he possibly keep that promise?

"He was right, Jake. The games aren't over." Shiloh stepped out of Jake's arms so she could study his face. "Did Silas say anything else to you? Anything at all? Even something small might help me figure out what he's planning next."

Jake thrust his hand into his hair and made a fist. "Yes," he admitted with a sigh. "There was more."

Shiloh crossed her arms over her chest in a shield and waited.

"He said that the reason he didn't kill you, the reason my father decided to save you, was because you are more valuable to Arcadia alive. And I don't even know what that means."

A whisper of a memory echoed in Shiloh's brain.

The daughter of our greatest enemies.

"I think I might know," Shiloh said softly. She sank onto the side of the bed. "With everything that happened, I never got the chance to tell you." Keeping her voice in a whisper, she informed him of everything she'd heard at the Yuletide Eve ball, when Silas and Jake's father had met in his office. Everything she'd heard about Alec and Elaine Sanders.

When Shiloh was done, Jake, who'd sat down on the bed beside her, stared into the fire, the light casting a lacework pattern across his face and the skin of his arms bare in his t-shirt. She wanted to trace the pattern with her fingertips and then her lips. Distract herself from her own head by memorizing the taut lines of his muscles.

"So do you think... your parents were connected to ROGUE somehow?" Jake asked.

"It seems the most likely conclusion," Shiloh replied.

"And you don't remember anything about them?"

Shiloh shook her head automatically and then paused. Not remembering was an ingrained instinct; how she'd protected herself in the Haven, where the smallest mention of her parents would lead to pain. But she did remember flashes. Gunshots and screams the night before she went to the Haven. A man's voice, singing softly. A woman who smelled like pine needles. Beyond that, a thick curtain, an impenetrable fog lingered around her past. Shiloh let her mind nudge against it, carefully, like touching a bruise.

Suddenly, she was six-years-old again, Aunt Morgan's nails digging into her wrist as she yanked Shiloh's forearm beneath the faucet of scalding water. She'd caught Shiloh crying, and when Aunt Morgan had asked what was wrong, little Shiloh had stupidly told her she missed Mommy.

"We don't miss heretics," Aunt Morgan had said, the water blistering Shiloh's skin. She'd held her there, until Shiloh had screamed, *"I don't miss Mommy! I hate her!"*

Shiloh jerked, shaking her head to loosen the memory. Jake frowned at her, concerned.

"No," Shiloh said, "I don't remember. But whoever they are... I think it's why Silas chose me to spy on Nic. Because he wanted the satisfaction of controlling me. Of breaking me."

"But he didn't," Jake said. He took her hands between both of his, his thumbs caressing circles up and down her wrists, sending goosebumps racing all the way to her shoulders. "He couldn't."

Shiloh wished she felt the confidence Jake's voice held, but all she felt was cold. She couldn't see Silas's next move. If she couldn't see it, how could she stop him?

When Shiloh didn't respond, two warm hands landed on her hips. Jake pulled her into his lap, her knees on either side of him. "Listen to me." He slid his fingers into her hair, tilting her head back gently until she looked at him. "You're not alone anymore. Whatever you face, we face it together. You and me. Always."

Shiloh let her forehead fall against his. *Together.* The word spun like magic in her veins. Alone was all she'd known before Jake, and alone was what she'd chosen when she faced Silas before. But Jake was here, even after everything. And whatever darkness awaited her tomorrow, she could face it with him.

They stayed like that as the seconds turned to minutes, their foreheads together, their breaths rising and falling as one. And, slowly, the cold that had settled into Shiloh's bones faded before the strength of his arms, the warmth of his skin, and the fire of his love.

Like fire was to ice.

Like summer was to winter.

So was Jake to Shiloh.

Shiloh lowered her mouth to his, and she could taste the heat of the flame they'd found in the gazebo. It would have been so easy to push him back into the bed, to resume where they'd been when they were so rudely interrupted. But a cough from the hallway—so loud it sounded like it came right next to them—ruined the moment.

"Froq," Jake swore, his hands fisting the fabric of her shirt in frustration. "We're never alone, are we?"

"I could be quiet," Shiloh offered.

Jake buried his face in her neck and let out a tortured groan. "But I don't want you to be quiet."

Shiloh flushed with warmth all over, and she felt him grin against her skin, proud of himself, of the effect he had on her. His hands slipped beneath her shirt, trailing over the bare skin of her back.

Wherever he touched, heat pricked to the surface, stoking that fire deep in her belly, the one that was almost painful with want.

"When we finally have sex for the first time," Jake whispered into her ear, "I don't want you to hold back. I don't want to spend it worrying we're about to get interrupted again. I want all of you. I want it to be perfect."

"It *will* be," Shiloh said, so breathless she had to stop herself from panting. "Besides, I don't exactly have a lot to compare it to."

He pulled back, a question wrinkling between his eyebrows. "I thought you'd—"

"I have." She cut him off.

Shiloh didn't often think about the one boy she'd dated; what she'd felt then was a mere matchstick compared to the inferno Jake lit beneath her skin. That boy had been little more than curiosity, an expectation. And the handful of times she'd had sex with him... well, they simply weren't worth remembering.

"But, well," Shiloh went on, "it was never very—" She stopped.

"Very what?" Jake asked.

Shiloh squirmed, and he latched his hands over her hips to still her, wincing. "It was never very... good. Um, at least... for me."

Jake's brow continued to wrinkle for a moment, and then his lips parted in a small 'O'. Shiloh squirmed again, and his thumbs clamped down on her hipbones. She realized why this time—the objective data that she was not the only one with a heat blazing beneath her skin.

"Well," Jake said, his voice thick, his eyes turning to liquid gold. "I can fix that for you."

Shiloh's heart stuttered; the heat beneath her skin flared hotter. She glanced at the door. "I thought you said we couldn't—"

"I know what I said." His fingertips traced up her spine and around her ribcage, his touch feather-light. A torture. A paradise.

"But I have lots of other ideas. I've had a long time to think about all the things I want to do to you. A whole list."

Shiloh's heart threatened to stand completely still as his fingers continued their path, down, down, his palm pausing on her stomach. When she realized what he meant, her heart restarted with a jolt, pounded against her sternum.

Oh froq...

Jake kissed a path across her jaw, nuzzled the space beneath her ear. "Let me touch you," he begged. "*Please.*"

His pleading—like he might die if she refused him—rendered her speechless. She could only nod.

Shiloh thought she knew something of fire, but when Jacob Osgood touched her—really touched her—it turned out she still had much to learn. Jake's eyes never left her face, utterly captivated, as he coaxed the flames to grow. His other hand clasped her hip and steadied her as she rocked against him, finding a new, intoxicating rhythm. Her existence succumbed to only sensation. Nerves sang. Muscles quaked. Sparks flashed before her eyes. She clawed at his shoulders, his back, desperately trying to cling to something. Anything. Because she was falling. Or maybe, she was flying.

She was flying and falling and *burning, burning, burning...*

A cry rose up in her throat, threatening to break her oath of silence. Jake covered her lips with his, inhaling her, devouring her. This kiss was her undoing. The flames within her exploded, blinded her eyes, raged at her very core. Hotter and hotter and hotter, until...

She *ignited*.

After, she thought she'd surely been left in ashes, utterly destroyed. But he kissed her slowly, bringing her back to her senses.

"Froq, Shi..." Jake said against her lips, panting almost as hard as she was.

"Froq," she agreed, barely managing a whisper.

He pulled her down amongst the blankets and pillows. Shiloh nuzzled close to him, resting her head on his chest. She slipped her hand beneath his shirt, traced her fingertips across the lines of his chest—hard and soft all at once. His eyes closed. A satisfied noise resounded deep in his throat, akin to cat purring. Shiloh smiled in pride and swept her hand downward, but he caught her wrist before she could explore farther.

"No," he said, wincing as though the word hurt him.

Shiloh stilled her fingers but asked, "Why not?"

"Because..." He sucked a breath in, still not opening his eyes, like he was trying to remain in control. "Because you aren't obligated to return the favor."

"I don't feel obligated." Shiloh brought her lips close to Jake's ear, dropping her voice low. "I *want* to touch you."

Another noise in Jake's throat. This one almost a whimper. "Then because I could *not* be quiet. It's been too long, and I want you too much. If you touch me, I will *completely* lose my mind."

Shiloh shivered. It was a heady feeling to be so wanted by someone so gorgeous, so passionate, so good. He could have anyone, and yet he wanted *her*. It didn't just make her feel desirable —it made her feel powerful.

"Soon," he promised, bending his head down to kiss her.

His tongue traced the lines of Shiloh's lips, swept within. The taste of him caused the embers of want to flare back to life. How was it possible to have been so satisfied and still want him so much, so soon? Shiloh tangled her fingers into his hair and kissed him back, dragging his bottom lip between her teeth. He groaned and wrenched himself away.

"All right," Shiloh agreed reluctantly, taking a breath to cool her skin. "But remember what you said, about that list of things you want to do to me?"

Jake arched an eyebrow.

"I want to do them all. Every single one."

There it was again—that molten gold spark in his eyes. But

then he closed them and threw his head back into the pillow, moaning as though the words had been physically painful. "Froqing ordure, Shiloh, are you *trying* to kill me? I'm gonna have a froqing heart attack. *Froq.*"

Shiloh laughed, resting her head back on his chest. How easily he'd made her forget about the world outside this bed, the fears that lingered at the cusp of her mind, that threatened to return as a silence fell between them. His arms formed a shelter, a protection, a home away from all that would hurt her.

"You'll stay with me?" Shiloh asked, locking her fingers into his shirt like a vice to hold him in place. "For the whole night?"

He brushed a kiss against her temple. Somehow, that brief caress still rattled her soul. "Shi, I'll stay with you until I draw my last breath."

As sleep tugged at her, another laugh left her lips. "You're so, so cheesy."

As soon as the door to the office opened, Nic's mother, Paul, and Brooks looked up expectantly from where they had waited, leaning against the old front counter.

"It's her," Sawyer said, keeping her voice low so as not to alert the other Sparrows who ate a late dinner around the fireplace.

Mom looked toward Nic, who nodded. "I really think it is, Mom. I don't know why I didn't see it before."

Or why Mom and Paul hadn't just openly asked her about it before alerting Sawyer. Perhaps they didn't want to bias her assessment, or maybe they were just used to keeping everything from Nic. It was hard to say.

Mom and Paul exchanged a look before breaking out into grins. Mom's turned into a delighted giggle she hid behind a hand. Brooks shook her head and swore beneath her breath, stunned, but in a good way.

"Now," Sawyer said, "we have to figure out a way to get her out."

"Out?" Nic repeated. "What do you mean?"

"She can't stay within Arcadia's reach," Sawyer said. "It's not safe for her. If the United Council kept her alive this long, it's for a reason. It's only a matter of time before they use her to threaten me."

Nic's mouth went dry. To love something was to fear losing it. Which was a weapon Nic knew Arcadia wouldn't hesitate to use.

*

Jake stroked Shiloh's hair as she rested her head on his chest, listening to her breath as it slowed, until it became a lullaby of a steady rhythm. It took much longer for his own breath to slow, for his pulse to return to a normal speed. The fire that had raged within him took even longer to subside. Every time it cooled, Jake thought of it again—the feel of her, the way she'd moved against him, the way she'd whimpered against his kiss as she came apart at his touch, the promises she'd left him with.

Froq, just when he thought he couldn't want her more...

At last, his body calmed, but in its place came reality, the fear that Silas had infected Jake with.

She's right here, Jake told himself, drawing comfort in the weight of her against his chest, the feel of her hair cascading between his fingertips. *She's safe.*

Yes, out there was Silas. Out there was a scheme unfolding. But Shiloh was here, and she was safe. A half dozen guards stood right outside her door. Nothing could touch her tonight. And whatever tomorrow brought, they'd face it together.

Jake brushed a kiss against her forehead. Her brow furrowed in her sleep and then relaxed as a faint smile twitched on her lips. Jake smiled back, whispered "I love you." And then he gave a verbal command to the fire that plunged them into darkness.

As he drifted off, Jake let the lullaby of her breath lull him to sleep. Tonight, nightmares could have no power. Whatever he dreamed, he'd wake to find her in his arms, and all would be fine. Sleep finally claimed him, pulling him into a dark, dreamless embrace.

And then a scream erupted in the night, shattering his illusion of peace. "*JAKE!*"

Jake's eyes flung open as Shiloh was ripped from his arms, a hand wrapped around her ankle.

ELEVEN

"Shiloh!" Jake lunged for her hand but missed as she disappeared into the shadows at the end of the bed. Shiloh screamed again, but the sound cut off swiftly. As Jake's vision adjusted to the dark, a figure took shape, a tall form swathed in thin black metal and a reflective face shield.

An Elite.

Jake's heart raged in his chest. "Silas!"

One of Silas's arms wrapped around Shiloh's waist, and the other clamped over her mouth. Shiloh fought, slamming her elbows into the metal of the suit, her legs kicking through the air as Silas dragged her toward the balcony door.

Jake launched himself from the bed after him. "Guards!" he yelled, but he didn't slow, charging toward Silas.

Something slammed into Jake's side and sent him sprawling, the weight of another person slamming on top of him. He swung blindly, grappling with fists he couldn't see. The figure blending with the black of night. Hard metal fingertips caught Jake's wrists and pinned them to the ground by his head. A knee propelled into his chest. A reflective mask appeared, inches from Jake's face. Close enough that, even in the dark, Jake could see his own reflection in the second Elite's helmet.

"Stay down, boy," the Elite hissed, the voice distinctly feminine, even muffled through the helmet. Then she jerked her head toward the balcony. "Get the girl out," she commanded the other Elite.

"No!" Jake roared. He kicked and fought, but her hands pinned him to the ground like he was a weakling. A little boy. Nothing.

He couldn't see anything but the Elite's dark visor, his own terrified face looking back at him. But he heard Shiloh's muffled scream, the balcony door sliding open, the tirade of the city, the beat of a glider flying too close.

"Guards!" Jake roared again.

"Don't you get it?" the Elite said, a laugh behind her voice. "They aren't coming to help you."

"Let's go!" barked the other Elite from the doorway.

That's not... that's not Silas's voice.

"Stay down," the female Elite said, shoving off Jake and rising to her feet. "If you know what's good for you."

She sauntered toward where the other Elite stood at the balcony door, Shiloh pinned to his body. Jake glimpsed Shiloh's eyes in the city's lights, bright with fear. Jake jumped to his feet and ran one step toward the Elite before she spun around, snatched her gun from her belt, and fired.

The explosion splintered his ears only a second before it slammed into his body. Then he was falling... falling...

The last thing he heard was Shiloh screaming his name.

❦

The explosion of the gunshot reverberated into Shiloh's bones, shattering them, ripping her apart by the seams. From the city lights behind her, she saw Jake collapse. His name screamed from her throat, muffled behind the Elite's metal glove. She screamed again and again, flinging elbows and kicking her feet, trying to get free, to get to Jake.

No... no... no... Jake... NO... he can't be...

He can't be...

"Relax, girl!" snapped the other Elite, sliding her gun back into its holster. "I only tranqed him."

The chaos in Shiloh's body quieted. Tranqed? Then he wasn't dead. Shiloh squinted, trying to make out the rise and fall of his chest. But the Elite who was holding her spun her toward the door and shoved her outside with such force that she stumbled across the length of the balcony, catching herself on the metal railing.

The balcony's frozen cement burned her bare feet, and the wind stabbed the exposed flesh on her arms, whipping her hair about her face. Below the balcony, a flat, square aircraft hovered, beating the air. A metal ladder stretched from the glider to where it hooked on the balcony railing.

"Now be a good girl," the Elite behind her said, "and climb down the ladder, or I'll have to throw you down."

Shiloh's fingers tightened on the metal railing as the words echoed in her head. *Good girl. Good girl.*

No.

No!

She was *no one*'s good girl anymore. Not Silas's, and certainly not this man's, whoever he was. Because he was *not* Silas. Whoever was doing this, it wasn't Silas.

You're more useful to Arcadia alive.

And if that was the truth, then the Elite couldn't kill her.

Shiloh glanced around. On the streets far below, cars weaved between the buildings like marching insects. The female Elite, who stood in the balcony doorway, barred Shiloh's escape back into the room. To the left was the balcony to the suite next door, where Reagan slept. A gap stretched between; only a few feet, but it felt like a million miles.

But Jake had jumped it.

The male Elite swung over the rail and grasped the ladder. He moved down a rung before he reached for Shiloh. "Come on."

Shiloh didn't budge.

The female Elite shoved her shoulder. "Move!"

Shiloh lunged forward, grasped the ladder, and ripped it free from the rail. The male yelled out as the ladder fell through the air. Shiloh slammed her weight into the female, causing her to stumble back. Then Shiloh bolted toward the end of her balcony. She clambered onto the metal railing, and as the female Elite lunged for her ankle, Shiloh jumped.

Time seemed to slow as her feet left the metal railing, nothing but hundreds of feet of air beneath her. Gravity pulled her down too soon. Instead of clearing the railing of the other balcony, she crashed into the side of it. She cried out, grappled desperately as she fell, and seized the base of the metal bars. Her arms jerked against her weight, pain searing through her newly healed clavicle, but she only tightened her grip.

"Froqing blight!" roared the female Elite from above. "#280, get your sorry endsphere up and move the craft."

Shiloh heard the aircraft rev and knew the Elite was piloting closer. She kicked, trying to find purchase with her feet, meeting only air. She moved one hand up the bar, but as soon as she released, her other hand nearly gave way.

"Help!" Shiloh screamed. "Mrs. Osgood! Reagan! *Help!*"

Hands latched around her wrists. She looked up, fearing she'd find a dark mask. But instead, Councilor Osgood loomed above her.

He hauled her over the rail, stronger than he looked. He steadied her feet on solid ground, hands still locked around her wrists.

Shiloh glanced behind her. The female Elite still stood on the other balcony as the male Elite piloted the aircraft closer.

"Councilor Osgood, they're coming," Shiloh said. "Please call your guards. We need—"

She stopped, caught on the word *guards*. The same guards who hadn't responded to Jake's screams for help. The guards who were supposed to keep Shiloh safe... unless *someone* had changed the orders.

Councilor Osgood stared down at her with a cold, unmoving gaze. Shiloh's pounding heart slowed to a steady, angry beat as the truth settled into her bones.

"*You* did this," Shiloh growled through her teeth. She jerked back, but Osgood tightened his hold on her wrists.

His eyes narrowed and hardened. Shiloh's hair lashed around her face as the hovercraft drew level with the balcony. Her last hope of escape snuffed out like a candle as the Elite joined them on the balcony, and she saw only one course of action.

Show them what you're made of.

Shiloh lifted her chin and squared her shoulders, meeting Samuel Osgood's glare with her own. "Jake will never forgive you for this. Never."

Councilor Osgood shoved her backward into the arms of the Elite. "Just tranquilize her already. I said I wanted this done quietly."

One of the Elite's hands clamped around Shiloh's arm, and the other drove the hard steel of a gun into her back. But Shiloh kept her eyes fixed on Osgood, and before the gun fired and took her into unconsciousness, she gave him one more warning.

"*Jake* will never forgive you for this, but *I'll* be the one to make you pay for it."

TWELVE

The darkness coiled around Jake like thick chains and anchors, dragging him down, down, down. He fought against it and drowned in it. Wrestled to the surface and found himself at the bottom again. In the deep waters, screams and flickers of Shiloh's terrified eyes tormented him. He opened his mouth to call her name, but it filled with only water.

In the distance, someone spoke. "Jake, honey, come on. Wake up!"

All at once, the darkness splintered. Jake rocketed upward. "Shiloh!"

A hand grasped his shoulder. "Jake, it's okay."

Jake sat on the floor of Shiloh's hotel room where he'd fallen after the gunshot. Dressed in her satin pajamas, Mom kneeled beside him, her expression drawn taut, even as she ran a soothing hand down his back. But the rest of the room was empty.

"Where is she?" Jake demanded. "Where's Shiloh?"

Mom's mouth twisted, but she didn't speak.

Jake surged to his feet. The world tilted on its side, and he stumbled, catching himself with a shoulder on the wall. An invisible knife pierced between his eyebrows.

Mom stood. "You have to stay calm. You were hit with a tranquilizer bullet. Rakes gave you something to speed along the effects, but—"

Jake gritted his teeth. "Where. Is. She?"

Mom exhaled in defeat. "We don't know."

No!

The word screeched in one continuous note through his head, his chest, his entire being. Jake wanted to scream with it, to fall to his knees and sob, to slam his fist into something. Or *someone*.

"I promise we have every Protector in the city looking for her," Mom said, "and — *Jake!*"

But Jake was already halfway to the door. He flung it out of his way and stepped into the congestion of bodyguards and Protectors that clogged the hallway. He homed in on the first bodyguard he saw, one who'd been stationed at Shiloh's door.

"Where the froq were you?" Jake snarled when he was inches from the man's face. "I screamed for you!"

The bodyguard didn't flinch, and Jake's fist shook with the restraint not to throw a punch. He spun on the other guards who had now stopped their conversations to stare at him.

"Did you all go froqing deaf? This entire building had to have heard her scream!"

"Jake."

The familiar voice settled into the base of Jake's spine, a dagger slipping in between his vertebrae.

"Dad?" Jake turned to find his father standing in the doorway of the suite Jake and Mom had been given. "What are you doing here?"

How long had Jake been out? Minutes? Hours? From what Mom had said, it probably hadn't been that long. So how had Dad gotten here so quickly from whatever hole he'd been hidden in?

Do you think your dad really saved her life because he cared about your broken heart?

The guards who didn't respond... the *two* Elite...

Suspicion settled into Jake's gut like a fist, the steam in his blood turning to a full boil.

"I came back just after midnight," Dad said. "I'm so sorry this happened, son."

You're a froqing liar!

Dad nodded into the room. "Come inside. We can talk privately."

Jake hesitated, but if his dad was involved, Shiloh's fate might depend on how Jake handled the next few moments. Silas was right. The game wasn't over. Shiloh had played it in secret and on her own for months to save Jake's life. Now, it was Jake's turn.

Come on, puppet. You know this tune. Dance to it.

Jake took a breath and then stepped around Dad into the room. Mom, who'd followed Jake into the hall, entered as well, and Dad shut the door behind them. Besides the three of them, the suite was empty.

"You should sit," Dad said. "You look pale."

Jake collapsed onto the end of the sofa bed. Mom perched on the arm of the other sofa, smoothing out her satin pants, and Dad sat beside her, his back stiff.

"Are you hurt?" Dad asked.

Jake shook his head. "I don't understand how this happened. Why didn't the guards help us?"

Jake held his breath, hoping Dad might have some believable answer... something other than confirming what Jake feared. But Dad's eyes flicked to the left, not looking at Jake as he responded, "I'm not sure, but I'm going to get to the bottom of it, I assure you."

Jake's fingers strangled the blanket beneath him until his knuckles paled, but he forced himself to relax. *Think. Play this right.*

"I swear to you, we are tearing this city apart trying to find her and Silas," Dad said.

Promises, promises, promises. How many do you plan to break today, father of mine?

"He had help," Jake said, deciding playing dumb was his best move. "He wasn't alone. He could be *anywhere*." At least, Jake didn't have to fake the franticness in his voice. That was real.

Dad stretched across the distance and laid a hand on Jake's knee. "It's going to be okay."

Jake glared down at the hand, fighting the urge to whip away in disgust. From her perch on the couch, Mom's gaze flicked from Dad beside her to the glass wall of windows leading to the balcony. Had she known this would happen? Had she known when she'd crossed her heart only hours before? Dad's betrayal was unsurprising, but Mom's? Jake's eyes stung at the thought, and he swallowed back the pain, broken glass in his throat.

"What can I do?" Jake asked. He pulled his phone from his pocket, spinning it between his hands. "There has to be some way I can help."

"The best way you can help is to go where you're safe," Dad said. "I'm sending both you and your mom home as soon as possible."

"But—"

Dad held up a hand. "The less people I need focused on keeping you safe, the more people I can devote to finding Shiloh."

The thought of flying back to Minnesota while Shiloh was here in Chicago made Jake want to vomit. But this was a game, Jake reminded himself. And Shiloh's life depended on how he played it.

"Okay," Jake said with a sigh. "But I want updates." He tucked his phone into one hand and set it down on the bed. "Every hour."

Dad nodded. "Every hour."

Jake pushed a button on his phone and slipped it beneath the blankets to hide the blinking light. "And you're sure there's nothing I can do?"

"Why don't you go take a shower?" Mom replied. "It may clear your head. You might remember something that'll help."

Jake knew this tactic. Mom hadn't gotten any less obvious over the years. She was trying to get him out of the room so she could talk to Dad in private.

Perfect.

Hesitating long enough to be convincing, Jake grabbed his bag —the one the guards had brought later in the evening and set by the door—and trudged into the bathroom. He twisted on the shower, the water raining down onto the stone. But he didn't climb in. Leaning his back against the wall, he slid down to the cool tile and spoke a command to the thin metal on his wrist—the watch connected to his phone. The hologram popped up, capturing the image on his phone's camera. It showed only the pattern of the comforter above it, but it picked up sound just fine.

For the longest moment, the only sound was the distant cascade of the shower. Then Mom spoke. Her voice was quiet, but poison dripped from every word. "I'm giving you ten seconds to explain to me what is really going on, or I'm going to get *very* angry."

Jake let out a breath. His mom hadn't known.

"Reagan," Dad said.

"One," Mom began.

"I can't—"

"Two."

"Silas—"

"Fuck you!"

Jake jumped. Mom *never* swore.

"This *wasn't* Silas!" Mom went on. "I saw you, Sam. Out there on the balcony. Shiloh was screaming my name, and so I ran out and I saw *you*. You *gave* her to them!"

Jake's head fell back against the tile, a groan echoing deep in his chest. He remembered that day, standing in the snow, when Dad held Jake as his world fell apart and promised—*froqing promised!* —to save Shiloh. And all of it had been part of some sick game.

Of course, it had. Jake had been a fool to believe otherwise.

"You're going to tell me why," Mom said. "And, because you lied to me, I'm only counting to five now. Three."

Footsteps pounded as Dad must have stood and paced. "Reagan, you have to trust that I have my reasons."

"Four."

"Damn it, Reagan!"

"Five."

"Shiloh is Alec and Elaine Sanders's daughter!"

Mom gasped. "*What?*"

Dad paused, took a breath, and said, more steadily, "She's Shiloh *Sanders*."

The name pounded like a heartbeat in Jake's ears. *Shiloh Sanders. Shiloh Sanders. Shiloh Sanders.*

Who are you really, Shiloh?

"That's not possible," Mom said. "You ordered all of them dead. I heard you tell Silas that night."

The realization of each word stabbed into Jake's chest. Silas. Dead. The Sanders.

Oh froq...

No, no, no.

Please tell me Silas didn't kill Shiloh's parents...

Jake shook the thoughts away. He would have to deal with them later. Right now, he had to listen.

"You only heard part of it," Dad said. "I was... weaker then. I told Silas to spare the girl and ensure that no one ever knew she was still alive."

Silence hovered for a moment. Steam from the shower formed a thick cloud around Jake.

"That wasn't weakness," Mom said, her voice gentler now. "That was *mercy*."

Dad grunted.

"Have you known who she was this whole time?" Mom asked. "And you never told me?"

"No. Only since Yuletide. When Silas told me."

Another long silence rained. Liquid poured, and a glass clinked: Mom fixing herself a drink at the bar. Jake held his breath, hoping they'd say more.

"And so you're using her as bait?" Mom asked.

Dad hesitated, then finally, "Yes."

Ice chimed in a glass. Another sip. Another layer of disgust added to Mom's voice. "And so that's why you really saved her after Silas shot her?"

"No!" More footsteps and pacing. "I didn't even think about that at the time. I just saw Jake in pain, and I had to do something."

I don't believe you, Jake thought. It was a pretty story, nothing more.

Mom groaned. "And *this* isn't going to cause Jake pain?"

"Don't look at me like that," Dad said.

"Like what?"

"Like I'm some kind of monster."

Something slammed, echoing over the pound of the shower. "Then stop acting like a monster!"

Jake buried his face in his knees, his chest cracking open.

"I promised Jake I'd protect her, Samuel!" Mom's voice thickened, like she might cry. "I *fucking* promised! She's just a girl—a girl who's never had anyone to protect her. I am begging you. Don't do this!"

"I don't have a choice. Silas told Beck. She demanded this happen, and with the suspicion this family is under, I'm not in a position to refuse."

"Beck?" Mom snorted, saying the name like it tasted foul on her tongue. "That bitch."

Dad lowered his voice so far that Jake had to strain to hear it. "Don't say things like that."

Mom ignored him. "She's the one who helped Silas escape, isn't she?"

After a long pause, Dad whispered. "Probably. She wouldn't want to lose her lapdog."

Before Jake could process this new information, Mom asked a question that made everything go still—his head, his heart, his very breath.

"And how far are you going to take this, Sam? If ROGUE doesn't give you what you want? What are you going to do with Shiloh then?"

The stillness stretched on forever until Jake thought he might never breathe again. Then Dad spoke, his deep voice rumbling from the darkness within, where the monster not only lived—it *thrived*. "Reagan, don't ask me questions you don't want the answer to."

Red flashed before Jake's vision. It took everything within him to remain sitting on that floor when he wanted to draw a sword and slay a monster. He knew he should stop listening—any more might send him over the edge, but he couldn't bring himself to end the camera.

"You think Jake won't figure this out?" Mom asked.

"I didn't think he'd be in her room," Dad said defensively.

"Then you're an idiot. And you clearly don't know our son at all. Of course, he'd be in her room. He's going to figure it out, Sam. He's already committed one act of heresy for a girl he barely knew. What do you think he's going to do now?"

"I'm not talking about this anymore." Dad's feet sounded on the floor, carrying him farther away from the recorder. "I have work to do." The door slammed. And then silence.

Jake stopped the video and climbed to his feet, using the vanity counter to steady his legs. He wiped away the fog on the mirror, and his father's eyes looked back at him.

What do you think he's going to do? his mom had said, and Jake knew the answer.

I'm going to burn this froqing world down.

THIRTEEN

"YOU HAVE TEN MINUTES TO REPORT TO ROOM Q35 FOR ENGLISH II," Val's tracker wailed on her wrist. "PLEASE HEAD TOWARD YOUR DESIGNATED LOCATION."

"Oh, shut up," Val groaned, not bothering to pull herself away from Stefani's lips to do so.

Stefani giggled, the sound vibrating against Val's chest as their bodies entwined together on Stefani's bed. "Are you sure" — Stefani lowered her face onto Val's neck, nuzzling, kissing, nipping — "you want to be late again?"

Val wasn't sure of froqing anything right now, except that Stefani's lips felt like heaven on Val's skin, and her body like paradise beneath Val's fingers, and she smelled like a froqing tropical forest, and whatever she was doing with her fingers should absolutely never end. But froq, if the tracker kept going off while Val was still in Stefani's room, someone was going to get suspicious.

But, peace and harmony, why did it have to be *so* froqing good? Granted, she was the only girl Val had really kissed. But ever since the first time Stefani had kissed her, Val had been lost in her touch, her taste, never wanting to be found.

"THIS IS YOUR FIVE-MINUTE WARNING!"

"Froq!" Val forced herself to untangle her legs from Stefani and rolled off the bed. "Froq, froq, froq!"

Val shoved her shirt back into her trousers, tried to smooth her hair, and grabbed her coat at the end of the bed—all while not allowing herself to look at Stefani. One look and Val might lose her will. Only at the door did Val glance back to find Stefani at the end of the bed, looking into her compact mirror, reapplying her bright pink lipstick.

Val groaned. "Please tell me I don't have lipstick on my face."

Stefani grinned and snapped her mirror closed. "You don't."

Val let out a breath and jerked the door open. Stefani grabbed her coat and scarf and darted after her, pulling them on as she went. Their trackers gave the three-minute warning as they rushed through the empty common area of Stefani's dorm.

Almost to the door, Val reached for Stefani's hand, but she snatched it back just in time. What was she thinking? Trying to hold hands while walking across campus? *Impossible!*

Val jerked the front door open, the biting chill easing the burn in her cheeks. An alarm split through the air, blaring from both her coat pocket and from Stefani's silver backpack.

"Mandatory broadcast," the tablets snarled. "All citizens must watch."

Val rolled her eyes as she pulled the tablet from her pocket, but a second later, a chill chased down her spine, even as Stefani closed the door. From the way Stefani's ever-present smile faded, she'd figured it out, too.

Mandatory viewings generally featured United Councilors giving a speech about peace and unity, or some other ordure that made Val want to scratch her ears out. But sometimes... on bad days, it was the public execution of heretics.

Silas.

Stefani and Val returned to the common area and sat on the nearest couch. Stefani unfolded her tablet and set it on the table before them, as a hologram shot up. Their trackers now silent, the Arcadian anthem boomed from the screen loud enough to rattle Val's ears.

The execution chamber in the Unity Center appeared: a white circular room with only a single structure. The giant pillar rose in the center, climbing twenty feet into the air, halfway to the towering domed ceiling. Stairs spiraled around it—one last, long climb for the damned. A small crowd gathered at its base, the camera panning over them briefly.

"Do you see Shiloh?" Val asked, unable to locate Shiloh's head of dark hair in the crowd.

Stefani squinted. "No. I don't see any of the Osgoods either. Or Silas's family."

Val scowled. "That seems too... merciful for Arcadia." Murdering innocent people in front of their families—who didn't even dare cry or show emotion—was what Arcadia got off on. Granted, Silas was far from innocent, but still...

Stefani swirled a strand of hair around her finger. On the screen, the Arcadian anthem ended, and the room entered a thick silence. The camera swung toward the door as the soon-to-be-dead mongrel entered the room. He slumped against two Elite as they dragged him up the aisle, like he was so wounded, he could barely move his feet.

Good, Val thought. *I hope they beat Silas as badly as he beat Shiloh.* They certainly wouldn't have beaten Silas the way he'd had Nic beaten. That would have taken days. Weeks.

Entering from another door in the chamber, the executioner—shrouded completely in white—met Silas at the stairs but ascended first. The Elite almost carried Silas up the steps, his feet dragging until they forced him onto his knees at the top. An electric tether launched from the pillar's stage and latched to Silas's handcuffs with a snap that echoed in the death chamber. And then, at last,

Silas was abandoned on the tower with the executioner, head bent low.

"Something's wrong," Stefani murmured.

"What do you mean?" Val asked.

"I don't think that's Silas."

Val's stomach turned inside-out. "What the froq are you talking about? Why wouldn't it be Silas?"

"There's been no news coverage of his crimes," Stefani said. "They've kept it hidden. Why would they broadcast his execution?"

"I don't know. To show that even Osgoods aren't untouchable?"

Stefani shook her head, as a voice—the voice of Councilor Beck—boomed from off-camera.

"Justus King," she said. So not Silas then. "You have been convicted of heresy for aiding the enemies of the Councilors. Do you have any last words?"

The hooded man began to speak, but what he said was nonsensical—words out of order, sentence structure broken and backward. But Stefani squawked and slapped Val's shoulder.

"Give me your tablet!"

"Wha—"

"Your tablet!" Stefani shoved her hand into Val's coat pocket and yanked out the tablet. She thrust it open and began writing furiously.

"Stefani, what—"

"*Shh!*"

Val looked over Stefani's shoulder, but before she could begin to read, the man's voice stopped. Within a second, the gun exploded. Val whipped her head back in time to see Justus King's chains release and his body tumble from the tower. The man slammed into the marble floor with a sickening thud. A river of blood poured across the perfect white. He was dead.

Broken.

Just like Hope.

"Long live Arcadia!" Councilor Beck's voice echoed in the chamber.

Val closed her eyes against the burn and dug her nails into the couch. She wouldn't cry. She refused.

When her emotions stopped betraying her, she peered over Stefani's shoulder once more. Stefani had scrawled the man's nonsense words down and now wrote translation above it, her tongue caught between her teeth as she thought hard.

Val tried again. "Stef—"

"It's a message," Stefani said, not looking up.

"To?"

Stefani lifted her eyes and gave Val *that look*. Anger erupted in Val's chest. Arcadia was sending a message to ROGUE, and they'd murdered an innocent man—a member or at least an ally of ROGUE—to do so.

Froq Arcadia. Froq it in the endsphere with a hot iron.

Both Val's and Stefani's trackers went off as soon as the broadcast died. "RETURN TO DESIGNATED LOCATION WITHIN TEN MINUTES."

Stefani and Val ignored these orders and the ensuing nine- and eight-minute warnings. Finally, Stefani dropped the stylus with a gasp. It bounced on the tablet screen and rolled to the floor.

"What does it say?" Val asked.

Stefani pushed the tablet into Val's lap to show the text:

Shepherd and Wildfire's daughter is alive. Scalpel will turn herself over in 48 hours or Princess will be executed. Time starts when the trigger is pulled.

Val shook her head. "I don't understand. Who's Princess?"

"I'll have to explain later," Stefani said, rising from the sofa. But worry was still sketched in every line of her face.

Cold. Val was cold all over, even before she tucked her tablet into her pocket and followed Stefani outside into the deep snow. Val had never minded Minnesotan winters, no matter how brutal. The blanket of white seemed to equalize everything by painting it the same color, and Val preferred grey skies to sunlight. But now she shivered at the colorless world.

Something was wrong. Val could feel it, like claws sinking into her chest.

"Have you heard from Jake or Shiloh today?" Val asked.

"No."

"Stef." Val caught Stefani's arm and pulled her around. Stefani tucked her head, trying to hide her face in her scarf, but her eyes gave her away. She was scared. Stefani was *never* scared.

Val thrust out her hand. "Let me call him."

Stefani hesitated, looking around, but they were still alone.

"THIS IS YOUR FIVE-MINUTE WARNING," the trackers wailed.

With a sigh, Stefani handed Val her phone, pausing only to find Osgood's contact and dial. Val pressed the thin glass to her ear, listening to it ring... and ring... and ring...

"Come on, you prig," Val growled. "Pick up the froqing phone."

Finally, the ringing stopped, but the hologram mode didn't activate.

"I can't talk right now," Osgood said, his voice so quiet she barely heard it.

"Where's Shiloh?" Val demanded.

Silence. Val swore he wasn't even breathing.

"Osgood, you tell me what's going on! Right now! Or, so help me, I will skin you alive and turn your endsphere into a handbag."

A beat. A deep breath. Then: "I'm about to get on a plane back to Minnesota. I'll call as soon as I can."

"Please." Val meant her voice to be a dragon's roar, but it broke, shattered, crumbled into shards at her feet. "Please, just tell me. Is Shiloh safe?"

Osgood made a sound, like someone had wrapped a noose around his neck and pulled. No... like he was about to sob. Val clutched Stefani's arm so her knees wouldn't buckle.

Don't you dare say no. Don't you dare... don't you dare...

"No," Osgood said.

And the phone went dead.

❧

38 HOURS REMAINING...

Shiloh paced once more around the circle of white, trailing her hands up and down the walls, attempting to find a seam, a nick, anything. She'd woken in this place—this cage of white and round walls with only a metal chair chained into the middle of the floor. She'd seen no one in the hours she'd been here.

There had to be a way to escape. Shiloh just had to find it. She laid two hands against the wall, leaning onto her tiptoes to do so, and then the wall disappeared. Or seemed to. Though she felt it smooth beneath her palms, it grew transparent, and a masked face appeared behind it.

"Hello there, Haven girl," said the Elite, her voice trilling with a hint of laughter.

Shiloh whipped back her arms and folded them over her chest. "What do you want from me?"

The Elite said nothing.

Shiloh tilted up her chin. "Whatever it is you want, I'm not going to give it to you."

"Then it's a good thing" –the Elite stepped closer to the window— "we don't want anything from *you*."

Caution fluttered in Shiloh's stomach. "Then what do you want?"

For a long moment, the Elite only stared, the weight of her unseen gaze heavy enough that Shiloh curled her fingers to keep from shifting nervously. She forced herself to look back where the Elite's eyes should have been, meeting them steadily, even though all Shiloh saw was her own reflection. Who was this woman, anyway? This #111, as the white numbers on her suit identified her? Another high-ranking officer in the Elite? Or just some lowly page to run the king's errands?

"Silas was right about you," #111 said after a moment. And there was something about the way she said 'Silas', a tone of affection that made Shiloh nearly gag. "For someone supposedly so smart, you're utterly clueless."

#111 clearly didn't plan on divulging any useful information. She'd only come here to gawk at Shiloh like a zoo animal in a cage. If Shiloh kept giving her attention, #111 would start banging on the glass just to see her response. Shiloh turned away, paced to the chair, and sat. She turned her head toward the far wall so she wouldn't even give the Elite the satisfaction of her attention.

#111 banged on the glass, anyway. "I'd enjoy your next forty-eight hours." She paused and then said in a witch's cackle, "Actually, it's thirty-eight hours now."

A shiver raced across Shiloh's arms, her hair standing on end, but she continued to glare at the far wall. *Don't ask... don't...*

"Aren't you going to ask why?"

No.

"Because ROGUE isn't going to give us what we want," #111 continued. "And then do you know what will happen to you?"

Old Shiloh would have felt the room spin, would have been trapped in her own terror, like she had been when Silas had first escaped. But now a deadly calm came over her. She knew what Arcadia would threaten to do—and perhaps this time they actually would do it. But if they did, she wasn't going to let them have the satisfaction of her fear.

So instead, Shiloh rolled her eyes toward the ceiling. "You'll kill me? Honestly, you all need to get better threats. That one's getting old."

Shiloh wished she could have seen the Elite's expression, but #111's growl of frustration tasted sweeter than ice cream. Shiloh feasted on it. Relished it.

"Thirty-eight hours, girl," the Elite said, slamming her hand against the window. The clang of metal and glass echoed through the chamber. In her hand had been a timer, which now stuck to the window. Its red numbers bled a glow into the cage, twisting the world into a pale pink.

"Thirty-eight hours," the Elite repeated, the same numbers as the timer, rapidly counting down. "And then I'll take great pleasure in putting a bullet in your little heretic head."

Shiloh lifted her chin higher. "I look forward to it."

FOURTEEN

Nic bolted upright, the mattress wailing beneath her, a scream lingering in her throat. The unzipped sleeping bag clung to her body, plastered with a thick layer of sweat. She looked around frantically, expecting to see the white walls of the cage, but instead, she saw the old hotel room she shared with her mother, the fire in the hearth now burned to embers and ashes.

Slowly, Nic's nightmare loosened its hold. The hand unwrapped from her throat. The burn of the electrical impulses of the Elite's prod faded from her nerves. But her throat remained raw, as though she'd been screaming for hours.

Nic glanced over to Mom's side of the bed, but it was empty. She was probably at guard duty, which was a relief. Nic tried so hard not to wake Mom with her nightmares. Mom would only ask questions or offer sympathy, trying to soothe Nic like a baby scared of the monster beneath the bed. It made everything worse.

Nic's throat blazed even hotter, and she stood to grab her

thermos of water from the mantel. Only a few drops teased her dry lips.

More. She needed more.

Tucking the thermos beneath her arm, she padded into the darkness of the hallway and past the closed doors where the other family units of the Sparrows slept. The floorboards—cold as ice on her bare feet—creaked beneath her, and the wind wailed outside, but otherwise, silence permeated the lodge. Though when Nic made it halfway down the steps, a yell shattered the silence.

"God fucking dammit!"

The pre-Sundering curse words made Nic jump. Those swear words were more common in ROGUE than the ones the teens who'd grown up in Ardency used, but Nic had never heard Sawyer Ardelean swear. She was always in control.

Her pulse unsteady, Nic crept down a few more steps so she could see into the lobby through the stair posts. She lowered herself down, hiding in the shadows of the banister.

A few adults gathered on the couches: Sawyer, Mom, Paul, Brooks, Mick, and Yousef. The flickering light cast shadows on their faces, frozen in stoic or anguished or furious expressions.

Something bad was happening.

"Sawyer," Mom said softly, "I'm so sorry."

Sawyer shook her head. "No. This can't happen. I can't find out she's alive after all these years, only for them to take her from me again."

Nic covered her lips with her hand to silence her gasp. *Shiloh. Oh, God, what happened?*

Hours ago, Sawyer had been asking Nic to share everything she could about her long-lost niece, plotting ways to get Shiloh out of Arcadia, but something had changed. Something terrible.

We're too late.

Mom reached a hand to Sawyer's shoulder, but Sawyer burst to her feet and paced before the fire. Mom's face contorted, glancing to Paul beside her, whose expression was hard and unreadable. Paul caught Mom's hand in his, entwining their fingers together. It wasn't the first time Nic had seen them hold hands, but this time seemed different from those previous fleeting moments.

This time, they lingered, their eyes locking, Mom's body leaned closer to Paul's. But then, maybe Nic imagined it, because just as quickly Mom jerked back and yanked her hand from his grasp. Paul looked away from her, his face disappearing into shadow.

Everyone remained silent, giving Sawyer time as she paced back and forth before the hearth. Nic shivered in the cold, too far away from the fire to feel its warmth.

Finally, Sawyer stopped pacing and turned. "I'll do it."

The room filled with the sound of gasping and curses, like they'd all been struck in the stomach.

"What?" Brooks snapped. She jumped up from where she'd sat cross-legged on the floor.

"I'll trade my life for hers," Sawyer said.

"You can't do that," Mick said, clutching the radio in his hand.

"The hell I can't," Sawyer snapped back.

Brooks shook her head. "You're the leader of ROGUE. We nearly lost everything when your sister died. We can't lose you. Not now. You've worked so hard to get us ready to fight again, and we are so close."

"You heard them," Sawyer said, thrusting a finger toward the radio in Mick's hand. "Forty-eight hours to turn myself in, or they'll kill her."

Nic grasped the banisters to keep from tumbling down the stairs at this blow. *No, no, no.*

"I understand that this is a terrible situation," Brooks said, her voice softening, if only a little. "But you can't give Arcadia what they want."

"I will never be able to live with myself if I don't," Sawyer said. She looked to Mom and Paul, searching for help.

Paul ran a hand over his beard and sighed deeply. "We have no guarantee sacrificing you will even save Shiloh. We've been offered this deal before by Osgood. It didn't... end well for us."

Sawyer's face darkened, nearly lost in the shadow of the room. Probably thinking of that night long ago when she lost so much. A deal had been made, and a deal had been broken.

And almost everyone ended up dead.

"My heart mourns for you," Yousef said softly, "but I agree with the others. It is not a chance we can take... or a price we can afford to pay."

Nic looked at her mother between the railing, the only one who had yet to answer. Sawyer had known Mom since before Mom was Nic's age, and now the two old friends stared at one another for a long moment. Then Mom dropped her head toward the ground.

"I'm sorry, Sawyer. Truly."

Sawyer growled, "I don't need anyone's permission."

"Sawyer," Brooks said, gritting her teeth, "if I have to tranquilize your ass and keep you locked up for the next two days, I'll do it."

"You wouldn't dare," Sawyer said.

"She would," Mick said, rising to his feet, his hand falling to the gun on his hip. "And so would I."

Sawyer glanced between the two of them, a dangerous animal about to strike. But then she realized she'd been cornered, and she swore again, a sound of wretched defeat.

Before Nic knew what she was doing, she leaped to her feet and stormed toward the group. "There has to be another option!"

Mom jumped. "Nicolette," she hissed.

All the adults swung toward Nic in surprise, except for Sawyer, who eyed her like she'd known she was there all along.

"It can't just be either Sawyer dies or Shiloh dies," Nic said, grinding her nails into her palms. "There has to be another option!"

"And what would you like us to do?" Mick asked, his tone condescending.

"Save her!" Nic snapped back, stepping toward them. "Rescue her! Send in soldiers to get her back."

Mom sighed as she stood and reached a hand toward Nic, her tone gentle and soft, but it felt no less condescending. "Nic, based on the information we have, we believe she is in the capital. We couldn't even reach the capital in time."

Nic's nails dug deeper. "There has to be another ROGUE faction closer!"

Mom rested a hand on Nic's shoulder. "I'm sorry, honey. It isn't possible."

Nic shrugged her away. "Mom, she saved my life. She risked *everything* for me. For months!"

Mom cringed. "I know."

"Unfortunately, they're right," Sawyer said with a bitter sigh. "Sending an army into the capital, or to wherever they have her hidden, is a death sentence that would only lose lives and time. Sacrificing myself is the only option."

"And that *isn't* an option," Brooks snapped. She laid a hand on the gun at her belt, a newer model with the tranquilizing ability. A threat without words.

Mick nodded slowly, and Yousef bowed his head as though already praying to Allah for Shiloh's lost soul. Sawyer turned away, resting her forehead on the hearth of the fireplace, her eyes falling closed.

"There has to be something," Nic tried again. "There has—"

The words cut off in her throat as if a hand had wrapped around her neck. Nic saw it, then. The tears on Sawyer's cheeks. The unbreakable leader, broken.

No, Nic's heart moaned. *Please, God, please...*

But God, as usual, was silent.

34 HOURS 19 MINUTES REMAINING ...

Jake clutched the phone tighter in his hand. "Pick up. Come on, Stef. Please, please, pick up!"

It was after midnight now. They'd been back in Minnesota for hours. He'd waited until he believed it was safe to call Stefani, after his Mom finally swallowed some sleeping pills and went to bed, and Anna—his housekeeper and childhood nanny—had retreated to the guesthouse. Still, Jake jammed himself into the far back of his closet, keeping his voice low so the guards outside this bedroom wouldn't hear him.

"Stefani, pick up the froqing pho—"

The hologram launched, showing Stefani's face, half-buried between the blankets and pillows. "Jakey boy?" she murmured sleepily, eyes still closed. Then, as she woke further, she flung her eyes wide and burst upward. "Holy ordure, Jake, what the froq is going on?"

"Shh, keep your voice down," Jake said.

She lowered it, purring low like a cat. "Val is about to have a mental breakdown."

Jake's heart sank into his gut, remembering the barely veiled panic in Val's voice. He'd hated himself for dismissing her on the phone, but Mom and his guards had surrounded him. Jake wasn't sure how she'd even put so much together after the execution. Watching the mandatory broadcast in the car on the way to the airport had stoked the flame brewing within Jake.

"That execution..." Stefani pushed her blue-streaked auburn hair away from her face. Her streaks had been green when Jake had last seen her. Had that really only been two days ago? It felt like an eternity. "That message." She took a breath. "Froq, please tell me it wasn't about Shiloh."

Jake ran a hand through his hair. "Froq, I wish I could. I have no idea what the message said, but... my dad had Shiloh kidnapped. Stef, they took her—" Jake's voice broke; his lungs ached. He fought to keep breathing. "They took her right out of my arms."

Stefani's face crumpled. She laid a hand over her lips, let it fall. "Jake, I'm so... I'm so sorry."

Jake swallowed hard, not trusting his voice.

Stefani dropped her voice even lower. "Is Shiloh really the daughter of Alec and Elaine Sanders?"

Jake nodded. He had no idea how Stefani could know... except that it must have been in the coded message.

"Well, froq me with a pinecone." She gave a low whistle, and a familiar gleam danced in her gaze, the one she wore when she smelled a story. "You and her. Who'd have thought? Even I couldn't imagine something that scandalous."

Jake gritted his teeth. "Stef, *focus!* Who the froq are the Sanders? Shiloh had no idea. The only reason she knew their names was because she overheard Silas at the Yuletide Eve Ball. The best she could figure was that they were important to ROGUE."

"Important to ROGUE?" Stefani jumped to her knees and jammed her face closer to the screen. "Jake, Shepherd and Wildfire —Alec and Elaine Sanders—weren't just important to ROGUE. They *created* ROGUE."

Jake nearly dropped the phone. "What?"

Stefani bobbed her head in a nod, hair bouncing around her head. "After the Sundering, they traveled across Arcadia, uniting the different factions of heretics, and they created the radios and the codes and everything else that enabled them to communicate. And then they led a rebellion that nearly ended Arcadia. But it was more than that. More than just being their leaders. People *loved* them. The way my mom and dad still talk about them—they were like some beloved king and queen. And ROGUE *loved* their daughter, too."

Stefani's fingers splayed across her chest, eyes shining bright in the dark. "Jake, if you're the Prince of Arcadia, then Shiloh is the long-lost Princess of ROGUE."

The world tipped to one side. Jake leaned his head against the wall, trying to steady himself. Stefani's words kept coming. Explaining that when Alec and Elaine had died, everyone had assumed Shiloh died with them. Including her aunt—codename Scalpel—the current leader of ROGUE.

"That's what they want, isn't it?" Jake asked, his voice feeling like it came from far away, like it wasn't even his own. "They want Scalpel to trade her life for Shiloh's."

Stefani sobered quickly, her shoulders slumping. "Yes."

Jake shook his head. "ROGUE can't do that."

Because losing another leader would surely ruin ROGUE, and ROGUE couldn't fall. It was the only hope for Arcadia to fall. Besides, there wasn't a guarantee Jake's father... or Beck... would even keep their word and allow Shiloh to go free once Scalpel surrendered herself.

"No. They can't." Stefani dropped her head toward her lap, nervously picking at her long nails. "Jake—"

She trailed off, and everything within Jake—his rushing blood, his twisting stomach—warned him that he didn't want to know what she was about to say. Her words would *break* him. Jake reached for something to hold onto, finding nothing but an old soccer cleat.

"Stefani, just tell me," Jake said.

She took a breath, her voice thick. "They're going to kill Shiloh. They gave ROGUE forty-eight hours after the execution to surrender, or they'll kill her."

And, surely, Jake had been dropped in a bath of boiling water. It scalded his skin and rushed down his throat until he was drowning. He'd known—of course, he'd known!—what his father would do if ROGUE didn't bend, but hearing it from the lips of a friend made it all the more real. The vision flashed before Jake: Shiloh broken and bleeding, going limp in his arms.

No, his heart moaned at the memory.

No!

NO!

Jake broke from the surface of the water—the fear—that threatened to suffocate him. Shook it off. Grasped for purchase onto something solid. He seized rage with one hand and determination with the other and refused to let go.

"I'm not going to let that happen," Jake growled.

Stefani gave him a sympathetic look. "Jake, listen—"

"No!" Jake jumped up, the hand that didn't hold the phone fisting in his hair. An idea settled into his head—one that was reckless and dangerous and could very likely end in his own execution. But he didn't care. It was Shiloh's only chance.

And she was worth dying for.

Jake met Stefani's eyes through the camera and spoke quietly, "I need you to get a message to ROGUE. Tell them I'm going to give them something else to trade for Shiloh. Something my dad would do anything to get back."

"And what's that?" Stefani asked.

"*Me.*"

Part Two
Sacrificial Lambs

Love will find a way
in paths where
Wolves fear to prey.

— Lord Byron

FIFTEEN

21 HOURS 12 MINUTES REMAINING....

Jake flung the strap of his bag over his shoulder, charged from his room, and descended the stairs of his house two at a time. A guard stalked quickly behind him, but he didn't look back as he angled from the foyer and toward the garage.

Rakes, who'd been stationed in the foyer, joined the guard who tailed Jake. "Mr. Osgood, where are you going?" Rakes asked.

"None of your froqing business," Jake muttered.

Passing by the numerous other pristine cars his family owned, Jake stopped before the newest addition. The sleek beauty gleamed, even in the dim light of the garage, painted a shade of red that whispered promises of parties and girls and driving way too fast—all the things Jake had been about before a bomb had literally blown up his life. The car had been a gift to Jake a few weeks ago to make it easier for him to commute between school and Shiloh in the hospital. In actuality, it was the most extravagant *I'm-sorry* gift Jake had received from his father. An *I'm-sorry-I-got-your-girlfriend-shot* gift.

What would his father buy this time? A whole froqing island?
I'm-sorry gifts aren't good enough anymore.

Jake slapped his palm onto the trunk, and it popped open with the recognition of his handprint. He threw the bag inside.

Rakes lifted his watch to his lips and murmured into it, "Get Mrs. Osgood. We have a problem."

Yep. That summed up Jake. He was a problem.

You have no froqing idea how much of a problem I'm about to be.

Jake jerked the car door open and slid into the driver's seat, but when he tried to slam it closed, Rakes caught the door. "Wait just a second, son."

"I'm not your son," Jake snapped. "And get your hands off my car."

The door into the garage opened. "Jake!"

Froq. Jake knew he would have barriers in his exit. He'd only hoped he could escape before Mom got there. Guards were much easier to shake than mothers.

Rakes stepped aside, and Mom replaced him, one hand resting on the car's roof. She stooped low to meet Jake's gaze.

"So... where are you going?" Mom asked, almost conversationally, like he might have been popping out to grab some milk at the grocery distribution.

"Back to school," Jake said.

Mom sighed, closing her eyes for a heartbeat. "Honey..."

Jake gripped the steering wheel with both hands, glaring out the windshield. "Mom, I am going insane just sitting here, getting texts every hour from Hazel telling me there's no new word. There's nothing I can do, so at least let me go back to school and my friends so I can have some sort of distraction. The guards can protect me there."

Mom's lips turned into a flat line. The silence stretched between them, and Jake gave her his best pleading look. Froq, he'd pout if he thought it'd help.

"Fine," she exhaled at last. "But some of the guards *are* going with you."

She gave the guard next to Rakes a pointed look, and his hand landed on the back seat's door handle.

"No!" Jake barked, loud enough his mom jumped.

She arched an eyebrow, the curve of it demanding: *Excuse me*?

"I mean, they can come," Jake added, "but have them follow me in their own car. I just want to be alone."

Mom hesitated for a long moment. "Okay." She leaned in and gave him a kiss on the cheek. She wore no lipstick—no mask of makeup at all, but Jake didn't have time to process what that meant. "Call me when you get there. And don't take the car out of autopilot."

Mom gave him one last worried look that almost made Jake feel guilty. Almost. And then she shut the door. Within ten minutes, the engine was growling as it pulled out of the driveway, the dark sedan holding the three guards trailing behind his car.

As soon as Jake reached the highway, he hit a button, and the car's navigation system purred, "Autopilot disengaged."

Jake stomped on the gas, and the car burst forward, propelling him back into his seat. He revved the engine until its roar matched the pounding of his heart. In the rearview mirror, the black car picked up speed, the guards staying a hundred yards behind. That was the best Jake could do.

The car's dashboard glowed with blue holograms, showing music options, news, and a clock he glanced at every few minutes. Forty-eight hours had bled out into less than twenty-one, and he could feel each second crawling by.

Let this work, he pleaded. *Please let this work.*

🔥

20 HOURS 3 MINUTES REMAINING...

Halfway between his home and Ardency, Jake and his guards were the only two vehicles he could see. People didn't often travel far from their homes. Why would they? Arcadia planted them where they needed to be. The only people who lived in this stretch of rural land were the laborers who tended the fields, fields which were now covered with snow as far as Jake could see.

Jake drummed his fingers against the steering wheel, music pounding from the radio. Each glance out his rearview mirror made his heart slam harder against his sternum. An old box truck crested a hill ahead of Jake. Rust stained the cab of the truck, and the side bore a plumbing service advertisement.

The truck approached at a speed that seemed impossible for such an old, crippled thing. Jake expected it to fly past, but then, with a squeal of brakes and rubber on asphalt, the truck whipped sideways, screeching to a halt less than twenty yards ahead.

"Froq!" Jake slammed both his feet down on the brake and jerked the wheel to the left. The car spun, wheels and brakes screaming, around and around until it jolted to a halt, only yards from crashing into the truck. Another cry of brakes filled the air as the guards' black sedan did the same dangerous spin.

Jake gasped for breath, clinging to the steering wheel. The truck's cab doors flew open, and the back door whirled up, launching out a stream of people. Hoods and scarves concealed their faces, and their hands clutched rifles they lifted with practiced ease. On the other side of Jake's car, the guards stumbled from their vehicle and trained their guns.

Froq, froq, froq.

Jake dove beneath the dash of the car a second before bullets rained like hail against his car. The passenger side windows splintered like spiderwebs, but not breaking. Not yet.

Jake pressed himself lower, flinging his arms over his head. Outside, a scream shrieked louder than the gunfire. Another bullet struck the passenger window, and it shattered. Glass exploded through the car. And then...

Everything went quiet. Jake's heart thundered at the back of his throat, the only sound in the unnerving silence.

"Grim, get Osgood!" a distinctly feminine voice ordered.

Jake reached for the door handle with a trembling hand, but before he touched it, the door ripped open. A tall, skinny figure towered over Jake, cat-green eyes glaring above the scarf that covered the rest of the rebel's face.

Grim seized Jake's arm and heaved him from the car. "Come on, rich boy."

Jake scrambled to keep his feet under him as Grim dragged him toward the truck bed, his hand tight enough to leave bruises on Jake's arm. It seemed ridiculous. Surely, Grim knew Jake was going willingly. As they walked, Jake craned his neck to see what had become of his guards. Three forms sprawled on the grey asphalt, utterly still. Tranqed? Shot? Some of the weapons the heretics carried were pre-Sundering, when guns had only one purpose: to kill.

If they're dead, then it's my... it's my fault.

Jake stumbled over his own feet, but Grim jerked him upright.

The other rebels jumped back into the truck before Jake as quickly as they'd come, only one headed in the direction of Jake's car. When everyone else had gotten in, Grim shoved Jake against the bumper.

"Get in!"

Jake hauled himself inside the bed of the box truck, landing on his knees. Grim vaulted in afterward and slammed down the rolling door, closing them into darkness. The truck careened forward, and Jake fell onto his hands. Besides Grim, two other people loomed above him. Their shadowed eyes trailed like claws down Jake's spine.

"Um..." Jake said, pasting on a cocky smile. "Nice to mee—"

A knee slammed into Jake's back, knocking him flat against the metal floor. Hands whipped his arms behind his back.

"What the froq are you doing?" Jake demanded, forcing himself not to fight back.

The knee dug deeper into his spine, and a rope coiled around his wrists, rough as stone as it pulled taut against his skin.

"Shut up, rich boy," Grim snarled. "Or I'll gag you, too."

Jake gulped, a chill racing all the way down his spine. Through Stefani and her parents, Jake had made the plan. ROGUE would pretend to kidnap him and then bargain his life for Shiloh's. So far, the plan was going as it should. Except for one tiny detail. As Grim yanked the blindfold tight against the back of Jake's head and his vision went dark, it became completely clear:

ROGUE wasn't *pretending*.

SIXTEEN

"**W**ant to see another magic trick?"

Nic swiveled her gaze from the steps leading to the bunker door to Ali. He sat beside her at the long metal table, which was the only piece of furniture in the front room of the bunker. From beneath the dark beanie that was pulled down to his eyebrows, Ali's dark eyes gleamed.

No, I do not want to see another magic trick. To be frank, Nic hadn't wanted to see the five before this. But she'd had nothing else to do while she waited for the return of Sawyer, Luca, Paul, and all the others who had gone on the mission. But Nic's mom, who sat on her other side, answered before Nic could work up the will to crush Ali—which admittedly, would be like kicking a puppy.

"Sure," Mom said.

Ali held up his palms to face Nic and Mom, twiddling his fingers. "Nothing in my hand. But wait... what's that behind your ear?" He swept a hand toward the side of Nic's head, and Nic jerked away instinctively. He never made contact with her; still when he pulled back, he held a Pre-Sundering penny between two fingers.

Mom clapped politely, and when Nic didn't follow, she sent her a stern look and mouthed, *"Be nice."*

Nic clapped too, and Ali beamed. It almost made Nic wish Mom had done as she originally wanted and left Nic with the Sparrows who had stayed behind at the lodge. As soon as the plan had formed, Nic had demanded to come, and Mom's answer had been, as usual, a resounding *no.* Sawyer had overridden her since Nic remained the only person Shiloh would know and trust if this plan went sideways.

As for Ali, Luca had insisted he come along. Apparently, the two brothers were never apart for long.

Ali flicked the penny from one palm to the other. "Wallace said there used to be this really old saying. Penny for your thoughts. So…" Ali gave a flourish of his hand before holding the penny out to Nic like a grand offering "Penny for your thoughts?"

Nic didn't take the coin. "What does that even mean?"

"It means 'What are you thinking?'," Mom explained.

Nic gnawed on the inside of her cheek. In the moments when Ali left her alone to think, there had only been one thought spinning around in her head since Minnesota—the codename for Reese Andreou, ally to ROGUE and State Advocate of Minnesota—had passed the message to Sawyer about Jake's plan. They had raced to put it in action, leaving the lodge for this bunker hidden deep beneath the Andreou's property.

Since then, her mind ran in an endless loop:

Shiloh in danger. Jake coming here. A kiss beside a snowy wood.

How would Jake react when he saw Nic again? Had she changed their friendship with that kiss or had she utterly destroyed it?

Of course, Nic would *not* be telling Ali—or Mom—what she was really thinking.

Nic looked around the room as though a better answer might

be hiding in the corner. Dark machines hummed softly in the shadows along one wall, creating interference so the bunker remained hidden by any ground-penetrating radar. A tunnel, which lead to other rooms and back exits, stretched off this main area. She should have hidden in there this whole time.

The construction of this bunker was new, completed within the last few weeks. Nic's mother had explained that it took years for the Andreous to construct it, only using people they trusted, and rotating them so no one person had the full plans of what they were working on. There seemed to be an apology in Mom's words as she explained. Perhaps, she had the same thought Nic had. That if this bunker had been completed seven months ago, Nic could have hidden here during the attack on the Cleansing. She never would have been captured. She never would have been held in the white, white cage.

Nic pressed her eyes closed at the thought.

Don't go there. Don't go there.

"Nic," Ali said. Nic opened her eyes to see him waving the penny in her face. "You okay?"

"Just hoping they all come back safe," Nic replied at last, her voice squeaking. She cleared her throat. "Those are my thoughts... what-what I've been thinking about."

Mom gave her a thin smile. "They'll be fine," she promised. But this entire time, Mom had been the one wringing her hands together in her lap, fidgeting with the silver ring she still wore on her left hand. The one Nic's father had given her.

Ali too glanced at the door, his grin faltering for only a beat before he turned back. "I've got one more trick. Wanna see it? I promise it's a good one."

Nic rolled her eyes to the ceiling. *Oh, good God, if you're still up there and listening, send me some mercy... please...*

A door creaked open. Footsteps sounded on the steps. Mom climbed to her feet, her fingers curling on the hilt of her gun. Nic held her breath as the feet drew nearer, and the first person appeared on the steps. Even with the scarf and hood in place, he was easily recognizable.

"Paul," Mom sighed with relief. She rushed forward a few steps before yanking herself to a halt.

More people followed—the lanky form of Luca and the short frame of Brooks, along with Yousef and Mick. Sawyer entered behind them. She held tight to the arm of another figure, pulling him out of the shadows and toward the center of the room. His hands were bound behind his back, and a tight blindfold dug into his eyes. But Nic knew him instantly.

"Jake," she breathed, stumbling out of her chair.

Jake froze and turned his head toward the sound of her voice. "Nic?"

Sawyer shoved Jake forward, past the table, and toward the darkened hallway that led deeper into the bunker. Nic hurried after them, but Paul caught her arm. "Hold on, Nic."

"What is she doing?" Nic demanded, watching as Jake was marched into the shadows like a prisoner of war. "He's on *our* side."

"I know," Paul said with a sigh. "But now he has to convince Sawyer he can be trusted." He shook his head. "And that isn't going to be easy."

&

19 HOURS 48 MINUTES REMAINING...

"Sit," the now-familiar feminine voice snapped, as the hand on Jake's arm pushed him into a chair. He'd gotten used to her demanding tone. She'd been issuing orders from the moment he'd been pulled from the truck and marched what was surely a couple of miles in knee-deep snow. Wherever they were now, her voice echoed, like the walls were too close together.

Someone pulled at the rope binding Jake's arms, but not to

free him. Instead, they tied him to the cold metal of a chair. The blindfold fell away. Jake blinked in the dim light that came from a single bulb above his head. The small room they'd taken him to held only two bunks mounted to each wall, like the army barracks he'd once toured as a boy. The woman stood over him. With her heavy coat, hood pulled up, and the dark cloth covering her nose-to-chin, he could only see her narrowed eyes.

"You know, when I volunteered to be kidnapped," Jake said, forcing a lightness into his tone, "I didn't think you'd take it so literally. I thought we had a deal."

"The last deal I made with an Osgood didn't go so well for me," she said, planting her hand on her hip. And only then did he notice how her other sleeve hung empty, no fingers peeking from the cuff. She must have seen his vision shift, because she said, "Yes, that's just *one* of the consequences."

The taste of bitterness and contempt singed Jake's tongue. At his dad, yes, but also at himself. Sometimes, it seemed impossible to hate his father without hating himself. Jake swallowed the taste down.

He asked, "You're Scalpel, aren't you?"

She hesitated and then dipped her chin in a small nod. Scalpel, the leader of ROGUE. Shiloh's aunt. Shiloh's only chance of survival.

"Look, I'm sorry for whatever it is that my dad did to you, okay?" Jake said. "Believe me, I am. But I am *not* my father."

Scalpel snorted. The noise echoed from behind Jake. Jake twisted toward the sound, finding three more rebels lingering in the shadows.

Jake gritted his teeth and forged ahead. "As much as I would like to, I don't have the time to prove it to you. *Shiloh* doesn't have the time. So, I suggest we focus on what we have in common."

"And what could you and I possibly have in common?" Scalpel asked.

"We *both* love Shiloh."

Scalpel flinched.

"We *both* want to save her. Don't we?"

"Of course, I do," she snapped.

"Then you *have* to trust me."

Scalpel looked Jake up and down. "Love, huh?" She drummed her fingers against the gun holstered on her hip. "You know we're going to have to make this look convincing, don't you? We can't exactly let you go back to your father... unscathed. He'd suspect you were a willing participant."

Jake hated to admit it to himself, but she was right. "What are you going to do? Chop off my finger and send it to him in a box?"

"You've been watching too many banned movies." Scalpel signaled to the three men in the corner. They stepped closer, towering above Jake.

One—the green-eyed giant, Grim—shook out his hands, and then curled them into fists. His eyes now squinted at the corners, like he couldn't contain a smile. A cat looking at its prey. Jake's stomach tossed as it became clear what exactly *convincing* would entail.

"Badger, Grim, like we discussed," Scalpel said, and another of the men stepped to Jake's other side. If he'd been standing, Badger would only have come to Jake's shoulder, but something about the white, jagged scar that traveled from his eyebrow to below the scarf covering his mouth told Jake his size was meant to lull people into a false sense of security.

"East," Sawyer said, "do you have the camera?"

The third man in front of Jake lifted an object—a box with a lens that Jake barely recognized as an ancient video camera.

"Ready?" Scalpel asked. "On the count of three. One."

"I guess I should say I'm sorry," Badger grunted, "in advance."

"Two."

"I'm not," said Grim, a smile in his voice.

"Three."

On cue, Grim slammed his fist into Jake's nose. Even though

Jake had expected it, he gasped as the impact slammed his head back. His hands strained against his bonds as instinct tried to lift his arms to shield the next blow. Badger's punch landed before Jake even caught his breath, with a force that made the chair wobble. Jake's vision flickered.

Before them, Scalpel spoke into the camera, "You took something of mine, Osgood. So, I took something of yours."

A fist landed in Jake's gut and another beneath his chin. Jake bit down on his tongue to resist crying out.

"If you want to see your son again," Sawyer continued, "you are to leave Shiloh at the location designated on the map included with this camera. She is to be left alone. You will allow us to leave freely and return to safety. Only then will we release him back to you. And if you don't—"

One more punch to the face. Jake's world dipped and spun, tinted with black. A warm, metallic taste burned his tongue. Blood.

"—I swear to you, there won't be enough pieces of your son left to bury."

Grim seized Jake's hair, ripping it back, forcing him to look up. "Had enough, rich boy?" he asked, voice low so the camera couldn't hear. "Surely, that girl isn't worth all this."

A fire flared in Jake's chest, and all he could see was *that girl*. Shiloh laughing at him, bent over a textbook, curled onto his chest, sighing against his lips, wearing the bruises she'd taken only for him.

And no, Jake hadn't had enough.

"Hit me again," Jake said.

Grim's eyes widened, then he wound back his arm. Jake braced himself.

"Grim, that's enough!" Scalpel ordered.

Grim's fist froze in the air, trembled with restraint, then fell. He stepped away from Jake. Scalpel had turned back to Jake, and the camera was now trained to the floor.

"Go on," Scalpel said to Grim. "Put the map and the camera in Osgood's car and set the autopilot to his home."

Grim took the camera from East, and he and Badger left the room. East stooped to look at Jake. The eyes beneath the hood were kind. "You okay, kid?"

Jake could barely see from one eye, and blood dripped from his nose. But Shiloh had a chance, and that gave him hope.

"Never better," Jake said.

East reached for Jake's bonds, but Scalpel barked, "Leave him."

"I think he's shown—" East began.

"I don't care," Scalpel said. "He's still an Osgood. He stays tied up."

East's gaze flicked from Scalpel to Jake, his hands hovering. "I can guard him in this room. I won't let him leave."

Scalpel hesitated.

"What do you think I'm going to do?" Jake asked. "Run?"

"You hadn't better," Scalpel said, her voice treacherous as splintering ice. "If you try, I shoot you. Nowhere vital, but somewhere it'll hurt." She looked at East. "He doesn't leave this room." And then she was gone.

19 HOURS 33 MINUTES REMAINING...

Nic paced the length of the room, scrutinizing the shadows of the hallway. She'd watched as Mick and Luca left first, Luca clutching an odd device, Mick rubbing his fists as though they ached. She thought she saw blood on his knuckles, but in the shadows of the room, she couldn't be sure. Luca paused only long enough to whisper to his brother, and then he and Mick left.

Now, as Nic paced, her mother and Paul watched her wearily from where they sat at the table like Nic was a bomb whose timer was about to go off. *Tick, tick, tick.*

Finally, Sawyer emerged from the darkness, but neither Jake nor Yousef followed.

Nic raced up to her. "Where's Jake?"

"Being held in the room," Sawyer replied. She side-stepped Nic and continued her path toward their bags, which leaned against the wall.

"Being held?" Nic repeated. Surely, she'd heard wrong. She glanced to Paul, who shook his head slowly, confirming that she'd heard correctly. Nic followed after Sawyer. "He's not a prisoner."

"Of course, he is."

The volume of Nic's voice climbed. "He's our ally. My *friend*."

Sawyer stopped to shuffle through her bag and didn't even acknowledge Nic with a glance. A scream of frustration built in Nic's lungs. The thought of Jake held in one of those tiny rooms like she'd been held in the...

Her brain stalled at the thought. Her breath quickened.

The door to the bright white cage sealed shut with a bang; she pounded on it with aching hands. "You can't keep me in here forever!"

But they could... of course, they could.

A hand touched her elbow. Nic jumped, swinging to face her mother.

"Nic," Mom began softly, gingerly, like handling an explosive, "let's just—"

Nic shrugged her off, brushed the memory away, and glared at the side of Sawyer's head. "If we hate him because of who we *think* he is, we're no better than Arcadia."

Sawyer's head snapped toward her, a crack of rage breaking through her stony face. Before she could say anything, Nic spun on her heel, grabbed her own pack out of the pile, and stormed back down the hallway, her boots echoing on the metal floor. No one followed.

She found Jake in the first room on the left. She slipped past the unlocked door. Yousef sat on one bunk, a silent guard. Jake sat on the bed across from him, holding a cloth to a bleeding nose.

Catching a glimpse of Jake's face, Nic inhaled sharply. "What happened?"

"This ol' thing?" Jake mumbled, gesturing to his face. His entire face swelled, red hot and puffy; his right eye couldn't even open. When he moved the cloth from his face, Nic could see that his nose lay at an odd angle. Blood smeared across one cheek. "It's nothing."

"*Nothing*?" Nic choked. "Jake, that isn't *nothing*."

Yousef shifted, the springs of the stiff mattress squawking beneath him.

"They had to make it look convincing." Jake forced a smile that looked painful as it parted his swollen cheeks. "All part of the plan. It looks worse than it is." Jake wiped at his face with the cloth again, only managing to smear it more.

Nic sighed. She hated this—the way even Jake fudged the truth, as though she was a fragile flower who wasn't strong enough to take it. She rifled through her bag, yanked out her first aid kit, and tore open more gauze.

"Here." Nic closed the distance and lifted the gauze to Jake's cheek, wiping away the blood. She didn't realize how intimate the gesture was, how much like a caress, until Jake jerked away from her touch.

Here was the answer to the questions she'd been pondering. Yes, Jake remembered that she'd kissed him, and yes, it had changed things.

She tried to read his expression. He seemed... concerned. But concerned about *what*? Concerned she might get the wrong idea? Concerned she might try to kiss him again? Concerned he'd break her heart?

Can he break my heart?

They stared at each other for a long moment, the awkwardness almost palpable.

Yousef cleared his throat and stood. "I'm going to be right outside the door."

Heat nipped at Nic's cheeks as Yousef stepped outside. Great. What was Yousef thinking? That there was something going on between them? Would he tell Nic's mom? Or Sawyer? God, Nic didn't know which would be worse.

The door clicked, and Nic realized how small the room was. The walls closed in around her, and she forced herself to breathe. Sweat beaded her neck as she looked back to Jake. He took the gauze from her fingers, careful not to let his skin brush hers. He swept the remaining blood away from his cheek.

"Nic," he said her name with a heavy sigh. "I know things weren't exactly great between Shiloh and me when you left because I'm an idiot. But she and I *are* together."

"I know that." Nic rolled her eyes. "I always knew it was a matter of time before you two worked things out."

Jake stuffed his hands into the pocket of his coat, which he still wore, even though the air down here was rather pleasant. He fiddled with something in his pocket. It crinkled, loud as thunder in the silence. Nic's gaze dropped momentarily to his lips, remembering how good they had felt. And also remembering, how he had not, even for a moment, kissed her back.

It didn't matter how Nic felt. Because Jake and Shiloh were indomitable. She wouldn't come between them, and she didn't want to.

Idiot, idiot, idiot.

"Look, Nic." Jake sighed. "About the k—"

"I'm sorry I kissed you," Nic blurted. He jerked away, as though startled, and her cheeks burned. But the words kept coming, spilling out of her mouth in her desperation to make things right. To save the friendship she couldn't bear to lose. "I don't know why I did it, except I thought that I'd never see you again... and I'd never kissed someone before... and Stefani..." She threw up her hands. "Well, I don't know, but I'm sorry. It didn't mean anything."

Jake studied her, and Nic was pretty sure her entire body blazed red from head to toe.

If the earth could just swallow me whole right now, that'd be great.

"So... you don't," he said carefully, like each word was fragile, "have a crush on me?"

"Of course not!"

Liar, her mind—or maybe her heart—accused. But it didn't matter. It was a lie she needed to cling to.

He let out a sigh, sliding a hand through his hair. "Okay. Good. That's a relief."

"So," she said, desperate to change the subject before she did something stupid. Like cry. "Tell me what happened during the escape."

Jake hesitated. He leaned back, sagging until his back met the wall behind the bunk. Nic crawled in beside him, keeping enough space between them that a whole other person could fit. Then Jake finally began, each word reluctant and painful: about Shiloh being shot, about saving her, about Silas's trial and the verdict.

"So, he's dead?" Nic asked, her heart fluttering. A world without Silas Petrovic, where she didn't have to fear his shadow. Maybe now the nightmares would—

"No," Jake interrupted. Her hope popped like a balloon. "He escaped."

"*Escaped?*"

Jake nodded and explained, about the Vault, about Silas's warning, about the escape.

"So, he's just out there," Nic managed. The air had grown thin; the shadows in the corners darkened. Like Silas might be lingering just out of sight, ready to pounce the moment she let down her guard. Nic dragged a breath in through her nose in an attempt to calm her rattling nerves. "Somewhere... Free."

Jake winced. "Yes."

And just like that, Nic was back in the cage, hands wrapped around her throat, hoping this time she would die because she couldn't endure anymore.

A hand fell on her shoulder, and Nic jerked away from the touch, her vision clearing to see Jake.

"Hey, you okay?" he asked.

"I'm fine," Nic said, but her hands formed fists, nails grinding into her palms. She would never be fine so long as Silas lived, so long as he could hunt her and find her.

A spark of anger lit up Nic's chest, and she clung to it, letting it blaze higher.

Good... let him find me. And when he does...

Her fingernails dug deeper into her skin, until they reopened the little cuts already there.

I'll kill him myself.

The door opened with a whine of stiff hinges, but it wasn't Yousef at the other side. Sawyer, her scarf pulled up to her nose, looked between Nic and Jake. She huffed a sigh, which reminded Nic of a small child preparing themselves to do something they didn't want to do.

Through ground teeth, Sawyer asked, "Osgood, are you hungry?"

Well, Nic thought, *maybe* someone's *finally listening to me.*

SEVENTEEN

11 HOURS 9 MINUTES REMAINING...

Each passing hour dragged like razor blades across Jake's skin.

Scalpel allowed Jake to join the rest of the group for a tense, meager dinner of deer jerky and a cold can of beans. Amelia and Paul had thanked him for the help he'd given Nic. They, along with East, gave polite conversation. A boy about Nic's age—whose codename was Chuckles—showed Jake a few magic tricks. The tricks were really quite terrible, but Jake was grateful for anyone who didn't look at him like he was a rabid dog about to strike.

Scalpel didn't speak to him, ignoring any questions he attempted to ask, watching his every move, keeping her scarf pulled over her face. And when Grim and Badger returned, they too watched him with unwavering steadiness. The ninth and final member of the group—a woman with rows of long braids Scalpel called AWOL—watched him, too. Her gaze flicked between Scalpel and Jake, the corner of her lips twirling with amusement as though she'd placed bets on which one would come out of the encounter alive.

After dinner, Scalpel had disappeared into another room. Jake had slunk off to his makeshift prison cell, away from all the eyes. Nic had joined him. They'd wasted a few hours playing cards, talking about nothing, but Jake remained distracted and tense. Shiloh consumed his every thought.

Are they hurting her?

Is she afraid?

Jake had only left this room a handful of times, wandering out to ask if there'd been any word. Amelia or Paul or East would only shake their heads sorrowfully.

Now, with eleven hours remaining, Jake laid back on one of the bunks with his head on his crumpled coat and a thin blanket Amelia had given him pulled over his shoulders. The bunks above him were filled with Chuckles's soft snores and East's sonorous ones. In the bunk across the room from Jake, Nic lay with her back against the wall. By how she shifted and occasionally groaned in her sleep, Jake doubted her slumber was peaceful. There was much to give her nightmares, and Jake wished he had the power to take it all away.

To make it all better.

And maybe... maybe he did...

He slipped his hand into the pocket of the coat, to the piece of paper he had printed out after he'd spoken to Stefani the night before. He'd kept it hidden this whole time, a little act of heresy tucked in his pocket.

Heresy?

More like treason.

He wasn't sure why he still hesitated to give it up—but Scalpel, the leader of ROGUE, had made it quite clear that she did not trust Jake. But he had to take a chance.

Jake slipped quietly out the door and back toward the first room of the bunker—the one that looked like a war room for the nation's highest commanders. He hoped to find Scalpel, and... sure enough... he did. At least, he assumed it was her. Her scarf now hung around her neck, revealing her face. She sat at the table with a few others, a lantern set in between them, casting a dim glow over all their faces.

Jake approached slowly.

"Los Monstruos, The Brigade, and Children of America are ready and fully willing to support a new war effort," Scalpel was saying, "but Gideon's Army and Imminent Reign are dragging their feet."

"Gideon's Army still waiting for a sign from Jesus?" Badger muttered under his breath.

Paul, who sat beside him, shook his head, but Scalpel continued like Badger had said nothing.

"And after what happened at the Cleansing, the Royals won't entertain a dis— Osgood." Scalpel stopped the conversation abruptly, her head snapping toward him. Everyone swiveled in their chairs to follow her gaze.

Scalpel didn't move to pull the scarf back over her face, and neither did anyone else. Jake didn't perceive it as a sign of trust, more so as no longer seeing the point of remaining concealed.

Paul, Amelia, and AWOL still sat around the table. Badger and Grim had returned, and they all had been joined by a face Jake knew well.

"Advocate Andreou," Jake said, not concealing his surprise. But perhaps he shouldn't have been. He had no idea where they even were, but he did know she'd pulled the strings to make this happen.

"Jake." She gave him a gracious smile, one she wore with a practiced perfection that made her plain face seem endearing and trustworthy. She'd worn it almost every time he'd seen her, in high society events or at the State Advocacy meetings he'd observed. A face you could trust. "You can call me Reese."

"Has there been word?" Jake asked. If anyone had been in contact with his father, it'd be her. Jake didn't know how deep the friendship between his father and Reese truly went—in the masquerade of Arcadia, it was hard to tell what was real affection and what was feigned. But he did know his father trusted Reese, and that was something.

"Your father has agreed to the terms," Reese replied. "Councilor Beck will be furious, but your father will have to deal with that later."

Relief made every muscle go slack. Jake sagged into an empty chair. "Oh thank—" He stopped, the expression 'Thank the Council' not feeling appropriate. "Thank *you*," he said instead, "for everything. And I'm sorry... for involving Stefani in this. I didn't have any other option."

Reese drummed her fingers on the metal table, the sound echoing. Like her daughter, Reese's nails were painted, but hers were a serious nude shade instead of the bright colors Stefani preferred. "Don't be sorry. You didn't force my daughter to do anything she wasn't willing to do. And Greyson and I would be hypocritical if we raised our children with our beliefs and then prevented them from acting on theirs. She can choose whatever rebellion she'd like."

Beside Reese, Amelia shifted in her chair and glanced at Paul.

"So, what happens now?" Jake asked, looking around the table.

Everyone's focus trained on him, the stranger in their midst. From where he sat, feet kicked up on the table, Grim glared at Jake. Badger spun a knife on the table in mindless circles.

"We'll do the trade in the morning," Scalpel said. "That's all you need to know."

Jake's mouth went dry as a thought occurred to him. "My father might try to set some kind of trap."

"Oh, we're counting on it," Scalpel said, and the corner of her lips twitched in a way that was as familiar as a lullaby, but not because Jake had seen Scalpel do it before.

Jake let himself study Scalpel's face for the first time, the lantern highlighting the sharp lines of her face. And her eyes. Jake stilled, his breath catching in surprise. Those were Shiloh's eyes.

The eyes narrowed. "Why are you looking at me like that?"

Jake shook his head. "Sorry. It's just... well, I can see the resemblance, between you and Shiloh. It's... uncanny."

Scalpel seemed to soften a little for a moment, but then her back snapped straight again. "You should go back to bed."

From the corner of his eye, Jake saw Grim mouth, "Run along, rich boy."

Jake gritted his jaw. Now or never. "I have something for you," Jake said to Scalpel.

A line deepened between Scalpel's eyebrows. "And what's that?"

"Truth." Jake pulled the piece of paper from his pocket and held it out.

She inspected it like it might have fangs and then snatched it from his fingers. When she unfolded it, a string of Pre-Sundering curse words hissed beneath her breath. She snapped her gaze to his, eyes crackling dangerously. "And why the fuck would you give me this?"

She still thought he had some ulterior motive.

"Because truth is the one thing the Council fears more than anything," Jake said. "In the right hands, it's the one weapon that could destroy them. And I hope those hands are yours."

"What is it?" said AWOL, standing so she could peer over Scalpel's shoulder. She let out her own string of curse words. "That's... that's..."

"Councilor Bennett and his husband," Jake finished for her.

The shock struck the table like lightning. Grim sat ramrod straight, his feet crashing to the floor. Badger slapped his hand down on the knife mid-spin. Paul murmured "Sweet Jesus" under his breath.

"I'm sorry," Amelia squeaked, trying to peer over Scalpel's shoulder. "Did you just say *husband*?"

Scalpel, whose eyes—dark and hard as onyx—didn't leave Jake, passed Amelia the picture. Amelia's jaw dropped. Paul and Mick leaned close to see. Only Reese didn't flinch. She looked curious, but not surprised.

"Explain," Scalpel commanded, leaning toward Jake. "Now."

"Charles Bennett was married before the Sundering," Jake said. "To a man. When he was *elected*'" —He made sure to stress the final word with a heavy dose of sarcasm— "the Council insisted that he keep it quiet. His husband has been posing as his bodyguard all this time." Watching from the corner as the man he loved fell in line, married a woman, and had kids. The men's love for each other lived in a handful of stolen moments, one of which Jake had captured.

Jake hadn't meant to stumble upon them, but at the Yuletide Eve Ball, when he'd been searching for Shiloh, he found them in one of the spare rooms. They'd probably locked the door, but Jake's handprint on the door would have caused it to unlock. It was his home, after all, and a random guest room he had permission to be in. They had been so caught up that they hadn't noticed when he cracked open the door, or when he slipped out his phone and captured a picture of them kissing. Jake hadn't been sure at the time why he'd done it. Or maybe he'd hoped all along he'd have a chance like this.

"I knew it," Reese said, glancing at the paper in her hand before passing it to Badger, who sat beside her. "I knew it, but I could never prove it."

"You're close to the Council," Jake acknowledged. "But I'm closer."

Reese leaned back in the chair, lifting her gaze to him as though seeing him for the first time. A glint appeared in her eyes, one that reminded Jake of the sparkle in Stefani's gaze when she was brewing mischief.

"Let me get this straight," Badger growled, drawing Jake's attention away from Reese. With his face uncovered, he looked even fiercer. Several other scars joining the long one Jake had glimpsed, as though some beast had clawed his skin. His hands tightened so hard on the picture that AWOL snatched it from his hands before he could crumple it. "When the Councilor kisses a man, it's all fine, but when I do it, I belong in a prison camp?"

Jake winced. An image filled his head: Stefani and Val exchanging a secret smile as they sat together in the cafeteria. Thunder roiled in Jake's gut.

"It's total ordure," Jake said, "or, as you'd probably say, *bullshit*."

"Bull-*fucking*-shit," Badger said, curling his fingers around the knife on the table.

"Why would the Council allow this?" Scalpel asked, as the picture returned to her. "Why elect Bennett knowing he's gay?"

"Because the bond between the Council families runs deep and strong," Jake said. "All the way back to my grandfather and the original Council. They don't want people who are perfect; they want people who are perfectly loyal to one another."

"And they are," Reese agreed. "But I think it's more than that. Councilor Beck likes people she can control. All she'd have to do is threaten to send Bennett's husband to a prison camp, and he'd fall right in line. Love makes you vulnerable."

Jake hadn't thought of it like that, but Reese was right. It was the same exact trick they'd tried with Shiloh, attempting to get Scalpel to surrender herself.

"I still don't understand why you would give this to me," Scalpel said. "This is beyond you trying to save Shiloh. This is... this is *treason*."

Jake smiled crookedly. "Total sedition, really."

"And what exactly do you want me to do with it?"

It was Paul who answered. "If we showed that to people, they'd be furious. They would question why they lost loved ones for things the Council does without consequence." He stroked a hand down his beard thoughtfully. "And questioning power... that's what begins a revolution."

"Exactly," Jake said, a thrill racing through his chest. "Truth is dangerous, didn't you know? Truth is what the Council fears the most."

Badger and AWOL looked at Jake as though they were seeing him for the first time. Paul and Amelia exchanged a hesitant smile, whole conversations seeming to pass between them. Grim—well, he still glared, hatred coming off him in waves, but Jake ignored him.

"Well, thank you for this," Scalpel said, folding the picture and sliding it into her vest pocket. "But, as I said, go back to bed."

Jake ground his teeth. No, froq that. He wasn't about to be dismissed. "I can get you more."

"More truth?" Paul asked.

Jake nodded.

Reese leaned forward, propping her elbows on the table and folding her hands together. Her eyes still held a glint. "Like what?"

"I know things," Jake said. "I've *always* known things, ever since I was a kid. My father thinks he hides things well, but—" Jake swallowed, for one moment feeling like the little boy who'd huddled in his bed, as voices floated through the floor vent, carrying truth that could give a grown man nightmares. "But I suppose the ones closest to the darkness see it best."

"*I* know things," Reese said, and then gestured around the table. "We *all* things. What we need is *evidence*."

"And I can get it," Jake said. "I'm the Prince of Arcadia." He didn't try to hide the note of distaste that crept into his tone at the title—the one Stefani frequently taunted him with. The one e-newspapers and e-magazines referred to him as when they published cute pieces about the son of a Councilor. But the point of the title remained. "I have been born and raised to become one of them. Which means... I'm the perfect weapon to use against them."

The members of ROGUE glanced around the table at each other. Reese smiled.

"Sawyer," Paul began looking to Scalpel, "maybe we should—"

"Why?" Scalpel—*Sawyer*—demanded before he could finish. "Why would you betray your father? Why would you be willing to risk this? You just said so yourself: you could be the next Councilor... the *most* powerful man in all of Arcadia."

Jake gritted his teeth and leaned over the table toward Sawyer, pressing his hands onto the table. "I know what you think of me, *Sawyer*. I know, when you see me, all you see is my father. But you're wrong about me. I don't want the Council seat or the power. I know what's required to have power in this country, and I *refuse* to become that sort of monster. And as for my father, *he* betrayed *me* when he decided to take the girl I love out of my arms."

"So that's your motivation?" Sawyer scoffed. "A girl? You do realize that, after tomorrow, you two will never see each other again."

Jake shook his head. "We'll find a way."

"No, you won't. Because after tomorrow, I won't *let* you come near her."

The words thundered through the room, echoing off the metal walls.

"W-what?" Jake choked. Surely, he'd been shot. He knew that white, hot pain of being shot in the gut, and surely, that was what had just happened.

Sawyer took a breath, and her voice became steady and unfeeling once more. "From what I've pieced together from Nic's story, you've done nothing but put Shiloh in danger from the moment you entered her life."

Jake opened his mouth, but he couldn't speak. Truth was a weapon, and it filleted him open.

"Even if your paths were to somehow cross again, I won't let Shiloh anywhere near you," Sawyer repeated.

"*Let* her?" Jake said. A spark of fury lit his blood, a shimmer swiftly beginning to rise. "Careful, Sawyer. You don't know your niece very well. She's dealt with Arcadia's chains all her life, and now that she's broken free of them, she won't submit to yours."

Sawyer's lips formed a thin line. Around the table, everyone shifted uncomfortably.

"I spent twelve years thinking Shiloh was dead," Sawyer said. "And I will protect her, no matter the cost."

"Protect her from *me*?" Jake repeated. "I *love* her!"

"And love is *fickle*. I'm supposed to trust *you*—" She let out a laugh—hollow and humorless. "Trust that your love for her is enough motivation to betray your family, to throw away all the power that is being offered to you—"

"Sawyer," Reese said, steel threaded within the softness of her tone.

Sawyer held up a finger, not even looking at the Advocate. "What happens when the love between you and Shiloh fades?"

Jake's hands tightened around the edge of the table, forming fists. His voice shook with the effort to remain in control, to keep a lid on all the hot emotions boiling within him. "It won't."

"It *will*. You might not ever see each other again, and eventually the distance will cause your affections to fade. Or maybe she'll find someone else, or you will find someone else. But, eventually, it ends. Love always ends; in death or in heartbreak or in betrayal, but it *ends*. And then what happens, hm?" Sawyer scanned him up and down. "Your motivation for fighting Arcadia ends with it."

The last of Jake's control snapped. He jumped to his feet and slammed his fist down on the table, the sound exploded through the room, shaking like the bomb at the Cleansing that had ignited beneath his feet and ignited his world.

"It's not just about her! I love Shiloh with the very air in my lungs, and yes, I *want* to fight for her. I want to burn this whole froqing world down for her. But I also want to do it for Hope, and Nic, and the Garcia family" —Reese sucked in a breath, but Jake continued— "and Stefani, and Val, and the Haven girls getting locked in closets, and a thousand other names I know of people who've been murdered, or hurt, or been barred from loving the people they love." He dragged a breath through his teeth, grabbling with his control, but his shoulders still trembled. "I am tired of watching innocent people suffer. Of watching innocent people *die*. I am tired of hatred masquerading as peace. I am tired of doing nothing but dream about a better world because I *can* do something about it and you *know* it!"

Silence rained upon the table as they all stared at him. Sawyer's eyes seemed impossibly darker now as they drilled into him. Froq. How could Jake have ever seen a similarity between Sawyer and her niece? Shiloh's eyes held starlight. Sawyer's held only ruin.

Reese leaned close to Sawyer and whispered something to her. Sawyer's scowl only deepened. Slowly, all the people at the table moved their attention from Jake to Sawyer, as though the whole room held its breath, waiting for her to respond.

Sawyer turned to Reese and said only one word; a word that reverberated in Jake's chest.

"No."

Sawyer swept her attention back to Jake. "Whatever pretty words you say, at the end of the day, you are still an Osgood. You will *always* be an Osgood."

If Sawyer had been able to peer deep into Jake's soul, she could not have chosen a better combination of words to shatter him. Words that confirmed his darkest of fears: Jake was his father's son, and that was all he would ever be. Jake tried to breathe around the knife in his chest, but there was no air. No words.

Reese put her forehead in her hand with a sigh. Paul looked furious, and Amelia even reached across the table toward Jake's hand in a distinctly motherly gesture. Jake whipped his hand away.

At the other end of the table, Grim smirked at him.

Jake shoved away from the table and toward the hallway. Behind him, an explosion of noise erupted as more than one voice began to talk at once. Jake didn't stop, flinging himself around the corner so quickly he nearly tripped over Nic, who stood in the shadows, clearly eavesdropping.

The look of pity she gave him felt almost as bad as the words Sawyer had spoken.

"Jake—" Nic began.

"Don't," he snarled. He flung open the door to the room and collapsed on the bed. All this time, he'd wanted nothing more to join ROGUE—but ROGUE had rejected him. The leader of ROGUE formed yet another barrier that would stand between Jake and Shiloh.

Which meant he had to formulate a new plan.

If ROGUE wouldn't trust him, then he would find another way to destroy Arcadia. Even if that meant doing it on his own.

EIGHTEEN

Gauzy clouds and sparkling stars floated above Val's head, projected from Stefani's tablet. The dark bedroom filled with the melody of bird songs and soft waves breaking on shore. Stefani always said she wanted Val to sleep in paradise, never realizing that just being in Stefani's bed—Val's arm wrapped around her, her nose buried in her back—was the only heaven Val could ever want.

Normally, Val slept so easily in Stefani's bed, waking only to sneak back into her own bed before dawn, but tonight rest evaded her. Ever since she'd been pulled from her father's arms when she was five, Val had always felt like the next loss waited just around the corner, threatening to take her legs out from beneath her. Now, it loomed over Val like a monster, stealing the air from her chest.

Stefani mumbled softly in her sleep, nuzzling her face into her pillow. Val slid away and sat up, rubbing her hand across her aching eyes and molten cheeks.

It isn't supposed to happen like this. Not to Shiloh...

Stefani rolled onto her other side, a painted hand reaching out across the sheets to seek Val in her sleep. When she found nothing, her eyes peeked open, a drop of sea visible through Stefani's eyelashes.

"You okay?" Stefani whispered, then cringed. "Sorry. That's a *really* stupid question."

"It's fine," Val mumbled, pulling her knees to her chest and setting her chin against it.

Stefani threw the blankets off her and bounced onto her knees. "Hey, don't do that."

"Do what?"

"Go all turtle hiding in its shell." Stefani flattened her palms on Val's knees, trying to push down her shield. "Talk to me."

Val huffed but lowered her knees. "What's there to froqing talk about?"

"Oh, I don't know. The fact that your sister is in mortal peril, and her only hope is a boy that you not only don't trust but, quite frankly, despise?"

Val ignored her, turning her head to stare at the window across the room, the one she used to sneak in and out. Snowflakes fell gently against the glass, spreading out like icy thumbprints.

"Come on, Valencia," Stefani pleaded, that name—the one Val hated—a lullaby on her lips.

Val looked around the room—at the scattering of clothes and makeup around the room; at the gentle glow of the hologram pictures that displayed Stefani's adventures outside Arcadia's walls with her happy, happy family: : her parents and two older brothers. Val tried to look at anything... other than Stefani.

"Don't do this." Stefani swept her fingers through Val's hair, pressed her forehead against Val's temple so her warm breath tickled Val's cheek. "Please, please, don't shut me out."

"It should have been me," Val muttered before she could stop herself.

Stefani's eyes widened. "What?"

Val ground her teeth together. *Froq it all!* She never wanted to talk about what she really felt, but somehow, Stefani seemed to be able to cast a spell to unloose her tongue. *Froqing witch, this one.*

Stefani began, "Val—"

"It should have been me," Val interrupted with a sigh and dropped her head, hiding her face behind her curtain of hair. "It should have been me. Not Hope. Not Shiloh. *Me.* I'm the one who belongs in a prison camp or tied up in some cage."

Stefani shook her head. "You know that's not true."

No, Val didn't know. It was the song and dance she'd been taught all her life, since the moment she'd stepped into the Haven. Drilled into her with every slap, every beat of Mother's cane, every long moment in the dark of the Repentant Closet. According to this world, everything about Val was *wrong.* Wrong parents. Wrong last name. Wrong language. Wrong skin color. Wrong sexuality. There wasn't a single thing about her that was right.

Val had long ago realized that her story would end with her behind a prison camp fence. She'd accepted it.

"It *is* true," Val said. "I'm bad... wrong."

"Val, look at me." When she didn't, Stefani cradled Val's face between her palms and lifted her head to see the lights and colors that somehow danced in Stefani's grey eyes. "I know all the froqed up things you been told, but it's a lie. It's this world that has everything wrong. You are *perfect.* Please tell me you know that."

Some part of Val wanted to pull away, to retreat back into the darkness she'd cloaked herself in for comfort. But the light that poured out of Stefani's truth held her captive, illuminating all of her. Because when Stefani looked at her like that, Val almost believed she *was* perfect.

"And Jake is going to save Shiloh," Stefani said without a single waver in her voice.

"And what makes you so froqing sure?"

Stefani rested her forehead back against Val's own, so when she spoke, Val felt the words on her lips. "Because... if he loves her half as much as I love you, there isn't a single thing in this universe that could stop him."

🔥

4 HOURS 5 MINUTES REMAINING...

For twenty-eight hours, Shiloh had watched the hours fade on the timer, seeming to move both fast and slow, counting down the hours she had left. It was in the single digits now, and Shiloh could feel her own mortality hovering like a buzzard waiting for a wounded animal to stop twitching.

She had paced and racked her brain for any possible escape, but now she sat in the shadow of the inevitable. If ROGUE was going to give Samuel Osgood what he wanted, they would have done it by now. And Shiloh was glad. She had no doubt that whatever it was would have destroyed ROGUE. And ROGUE had to survive. The rebels were the only chance for a better world, and Shiloh's life seemed a fair trade for hope.

Unable to sleep, Shiloh stretched across the cool stone floor and broke a Haven girl rule. She remembered, letting the recesses of her mind go to places she hadn't allowed it to revisit since setting foot in the Haven. This time the memories of the Haven didn't assault her, didn't throw up barriers. Instead, a feeling comparable to what she felt when she was with Jake swept over her, the comfort and peace that came with knowing she was loved.

She remembered a man who sang sweeter than a bird. She remembered a woman whispering, "Sweet dreams, my warrior princess." The same woman perhaps, hugging her close, and when Shiloh breathed in, she swore she could still smell the crushed pine smell that clung to the woman's hair.

Shiloh remembered being curled up with Hope and Val — laughing kids, teasing girls, close-knit teenagers. Sisters. She remembered sitting in a tunnel between Jake and Val, with Stefani and Nic, happy that she'd found so many people worth dying for.

But mostly, Shiloh thought of Jake. She thought of his laughter, his touch, the feel of his skin against her, the way his love wrapped around her and filled her up.

Close your eyes, his voice murmured in the stillness. *I'm right here.*

As the minutes ticked away, Shiloh clung to this memory, imagining she was still wrapped up in Jake's arms.

Shiloh must have drifted to an unwilling sleep because the sound of the door opening startled her awake. She flung herself into a sitting position as footsteps pounded toward her. Before she could even turn her head, hands clasped her arm, jerking her to her feet.

"Up, girl," snapped a voice she'd now come to recognize. #111. "Time's up."

Shiloh glanced at the clock. "I still have four hours."

#111 tossed a bundle of clothes into Shiloh's chest. The Arcadian dress pants and a Codex compliant sweater fell to her feet, along with her own sneakers. Of course, the Elite had them. Samuel Osgood must have given them to her.

"Get dressed," #111 snarled.

Shiloh glanced at the door to the cell, left ajar, but saw only a solid wall behind it. When she'd watched people bring her food through the window, she'd seen the wall part and then snap shut behind them. No escape. She pulled on the pants with shaking hands, yanked the sweater over her t-shirt, and stepped clumsily into her shoes.

"I have more time—"

"Shut up!"

#111 seized Shiloh's wrists and whirled her around. An electric handcuff hissed and bit into Shiloh's skin. Cloth descended around Shiloh's face, plunging her into darkness. It smelled rancid, like old blood. A black sack pulled over the face of a heretic about to be led to her death. She'd seen enough executions to know how it ended.

#111 shoved her forward. Well, if she was going to die, then she wouldn't do it whimpering. Shiloh lifted her chin and pulled back her shoulders, but she couldn't still the trembling in her fingers.

Doors opened and shut. An elevator chimed. Feet marched on the marble floor. She was in the Unity Center, Shiloh realized. They had been keeping her in the Vault, where—only days before —Silas had escaped. Where they kept the most dangerous criminals in Arcadia.

Another elevator. Yet another door, and cold air stabbed into Shiloh's flesh. Her steps faltered as her sneakers met snow. Outside. Not the execution chamber.

But why?

Another door opened, its hinges letting out a long whine.

"Get in," #111 barked, shoving Shiloh's head down.

A seat rose up to meet Shiloh as she stumbled into the vehicle. The door slammed so hard it rattled and, seconds later, the car careened forward, driving much too fast through congested Chicago streets. Shiloh didn't ask where they were going. She already knew it would be the last place she ever went.

NINETEEN

Before dawn, the members of ROGUE prepared as though going to war. Strapping on guns, checking their packs, and whispering to each other to ensure their plan was set. Jake watched it all from a corner of the bunker, aware that he did not belong. That he'd never belong.

In less than four hours, Jake would see Shiloh for what could be the last time. He gritted his teeth at the thought. No, he refused to think that. He would figure it out, somehow.

Still, who knew how long it would be? And during the chaos, he wouldn't exactly have a chance to speak to her.

He pried himself off the wall and walked to where Paul stood, packing his bag beside East. The two stopped talking as he approached.

"Paul, do you have paper?" Jake asked, shifting his weight from heel to toe. "I'd like to write Shiloh a note if I can."

Paul nodded and dug through his bag, producing a small notepad and a pencil. Jake took them with a soft "Thanks."

Jake stared down at the paper, trying to conjure what to fit within those handful of lines. There was so much he wanted to tell her.

"We leave in five minutes," Scalpel said.

Think, think.

Jake could feel Paul studying him as the man pulled his pack and then his rifle onto his back. Paul cleared his throat. "Look, um... Jake."

Jake forced himself to look up from the lines. Paul towered above him, a mountain of a man, honed thick with muscle, but there was something gentle, soothing about him.

"Forget what Sawyer said to you," Paul said. "I don't know what chance you and Shiloh have, but I believe that you love her. Men don't let their asses get kicked the way yours was when they don't love a girl."

Jake gave him a half smile, but it hurt Jake's bruised face. He let it fall.

"And I don't believe what she said," Paul continued. "Lots of things end. Lives end. Relationships end. But love?" He let out a breath. "Love *endures*. It's the only thing that can."

As he spoke, Paul's gaze drifted across the room. With one eye still swollen shut, Jake had to turn his head to follow Paul's line of vision. Amelia stood, fussing over Nic, adjusting the straps of her pack, speaking a mile a minute. Nic looked like she was considering swan-diving from a very substantial height.

Jake glanced back at Paul. On the man's face was a look Jake knew well. Paul looked at Amelia like Jake looked at Shiloh. Like she was the only thing he could see.

Jake cleared his throat. "Are you and Amelia..."

"No." Paul snapped his eyes away from Amelia like he'd been caught doing something wrong. The single word held an unspoken addendum. No, *but* he loved her. No, he didn't think he *should*, but his love endured anyway.

"In the meantime," Paul said, pointedly changing the subject, "know that we're going to take care of Shiloh. No one is going to let anything happen to her. Not Sawyer, and certainly not me. She's Alec and Elaine's kid. I let them down once. I'll be damned if I do it again."

Amelia beckoned to Paul. Paul offered a swift goodbye and then trotted over, leaving Jake to glare at the blank lines of the notepaper.

"Three minutes," Sawyer called.

Froq, there isn't enough time.

"Get your endsphere moving, Chuckles," Grim said, aiming a playful kick at the boy, who scrambled from the chair he'd been spinning in to quickly fling on his pack.

Everyone seemed to have moved their speed of last minute preparations from fast to chaotic.

East finally rose from where he'd been kneeling nearby. "Jake." He stepped close and lowered his voice. "Not that you think my opinion matters, but I like you, so I'm going to tell you anyway. I agree with everything Paul said, but that wasn't the only thing I think Sawyer was wrong about. You may be an Osgood, yes. That is unchangeable. But you are not the *same* Osgood as your father. I would hate to think that my son or my daughters would be judged by *my* mistakes. I hope they make plenty of their *own* mistakes to be judged for." He laughed softly to himself, then added more solemnly, "People can think whatever they would like, but at the end of the day, *you* get to choose what kind of man you are."

Jake swallowed down a lump in his throat. East couldn't possibly know how much Jake had needed those words, how they settled into his soul like balm on a wound. "Thank you, East."

"My name," he said, "is Yousef Qadir."

The significance of Yousef offering Jake his name didn't go unnoticed. It was trust of the highest honor.

"Thank you, Yousef," Jake corrected. "Take care of yourself out there. Get back safely to your kids."

Yousef nodded. "As Allah wills it. I hope our paths cross again one day."

"One minute!" Sawyer called.

Froq, froq, froq.

As Yousef turned toward the door, Jake looked back to the paper once more. There was no time to think or second guess. He scrawled. Three sentences. He hoped they'd be enough.

"Let's go!" Sawyer gave the final order.

Grim stepped up to Jake, a blindfold in his hands. "Let's go, rich boy."

"Wait." Jake back-peddled away from him, tearing the piece of paper from the notebook. He launched himself toward Nic before Grim could grab him. "Here." He pressed the paper in Nic's hands and folded her fingers around it. "Make sure that Shiloh gets this. Make sure she knows—"

Grim roughly yanked Jake's wrists behind him, coiling the rope. The blindfold came swiftly after, plunging Jake into darkness, a prisoner once more.

"Promise me, Nic," Jake said.

Her soft hand squeezed his arm. "I promise."

§

30 MINUTES REMAINING...

A car, a plane, another car...

Blind, Shiloh had picked up the clues of where the Elite were taking her in the little things. The rare whispers of the Elite, the announcement of the pilot, the length of the flight. They had brought her back to Minnesota and put her into another car, driving who knows where. But why? Surely, if ROGUE hadn't given what the Council wanted, they could just as easily have killed Shiloh in the Vault.

Finally, the car's tires vibrated on a rumble strip and pulled to a stop.

"Are you sure this is the place?" a man—another Elite whose

voice Shiloh had learned to pick up during the long, blindfolded journey—said.

"It matches the coordinates," #111 grumbled.

Bang! Bang! A car door opened and shut, and then—*whoosh*—a gust of bitter wind sailed in from the door nearest Shiloh, as it was flung open. The Minnesotan wind had teeth and nails, biting into the layers of Shiloh's clothes. The Elite hadn't bothered to give her a coat. The temperature of her skin now matched the frigid fear in her chest.

"Out!"

#111 seized her arm and yanked her from the car. Shiloh sank into deep snow. She struggled to remain upright as the Elite jerked her this way and that, as though they had to avoid obstacles in their path. Trees, Shiloh guessed. They were in the woods.

"Where are we going?" Shiloh asked.

#111 had no answer. They marched in silence for perhaps twenty minutes. Twice, Shiloh stumbled and fell into the snow, and twice, #111 hauled her back to her feet with cruel words. Shiloh's body trembled from the cold. Dressed as she was, she'd likely die from exposure before #111 executed her.

At last, #111 jerked to a stop. "Kneel."

"What?"

"Get on your knees!"

Shiloh's shivers turned to violent shakes, and her mind whirled desperately, begging for a way out. But she'd spent days thinking of possible ways to escape, only ever coming to one end.

She was going to die.

She could face it with dignity, or she could run and take a bullet in her back.

"I said, get on your knees!" #111 forced Shiloh down by her shoulder, and she collapsed to her knees. The snow soaked through her trousers, turning her skin to ice.

"Any last words, Haven girl?" #111 asked, a laugh barely refrained in her throat.

Shiloh ground her teeth together to keep them from chattering, but still she shook. This wasn't how she wanted to die, trembling on her knees. Hope had been strong, unyielding. But Shiloh couldn't stop.

Close your eyes. Jake's voice breathed, like he was whispering in her ear. And though she couldn't see, Shiloh did.

I'm right here.

His hand entwined with hers, warm and strong, an anchor to this uncertain world. Shiloh knew she imagined it, but it felt so real she pretended he was there. Right beside her.

"Well?" #111 demanded.

She clutched the memory of Jake's touch close and raised her chin like she was wearing a crown. "You and all of Arcadia can go froq yourself!"

"Very well, Haven girl."

A gun clicked, switching from tranq to kill. Shiloh clutched her shaking fingers behind her back and lifted her chin even higher. The Elite's breath rose and fell, loud and rasping. And Shiloh thought of Jake and Val and love—only love—until she took her last breath.

Until the Elite pulled the trigger.

Boom!

TWENTY

The gunshot recoiled through Shiloh's body, exploding through every muscle, every nerve. But no oblivion came. The gunshot echoed on and on in her head, but the Elite had fired... into the air.

"Next time," #111 snarled, "I won't miss."

With a rough tug, #111 loosened the blindfold from Shiloh's eyes. Shiloh blinked in the sudden burst of sunlight. It glistened off the snow, almost blinding her with its brightness. Trees towered all around her, stretching toward the sun.

"Alright, motherfroqers," #111 shouted, her head tilting as she searched around her, "I know you're out there. Change of plans. I'm not handing her over until I see Jacob Osgood."

"What?" Shiloh gasped. "What about Jake—"

"Shut up!" #111 grasped Shiloh's arm and yanked her to her feet. Something cold and hard ground against Shiloh's temple. The object was familiar, a sensation she'd never forget as long as she lived. A gun to her head.

"You have three seconds," #111 called out to the wood, "before I put a bullet in her head and tell the Councilor something tragic happened. One."

The wood was silent. Even the wind seemed to still.

"Two."

The gun ground deeper, so hard it was painful. Shiloh bit her lip to keep from crying out.

"Thr—"

The shadows between the trees moved. Shiloh's eyes widened as a person stepped into the light. A scarf and hood covered their face, and in their hands, they carried a rifle that they trained squarely on the Elite. And then, further down, another person appeared from between the trees. And another, and another. Half a dozen at least.

Taking in the hoods, the scarves, the guns, Shiloh knew who they were.

ROGUE.

They'd made a trade.

No, no, no.

One more form took shape, in the center of all of them. This time, it was two people: a hulk of a man grasping the arm of someone blindfolded and bound. Despite the ruin of his face, Shiloh would have known the shape of him anywhere. Her body responded to it like a physical pull.

"Jake!" Shiloh gasped.

"Hush!" #111 hissed in her ear,

Snow crunched, and Shiloh turned her head as figures emerged from the darkness behind her. Elite stepped out to match up with the members of ROGUE, guns trained right back.

"Fucking cowards," called one of the members of ROGUE, the voice rough but distinctly feminine. "Should have known Osgood wouldn't follow direction."

"We're going to let them go at the same time, understand?" #111 said. "If you try anything funny, I'll shoot her in the back."

With a swipe of #111's hands, the electric cuffs fell away from Shiloh's aching wrists. The man who held Jake loosened his hands, as well, then his blindfold fell away.

Their eyes met.

Shiloh's knees almost buckled with relief. She never thought she'd see him again, and she wanted to drink in the sight of him. Bruises and swelling stained his face, but he was the most magnificent thing she'd seen. Jake walked toward her, and a hand pushed her roughly forward.

Shiloh didn't know whether to run or tread carefully, but finally she propelled herself through the snow toward Jake. He sprinted forward. They met halfway between ROGUE and the Elite. Jake caught her in his arms and spun them both around, so he now stood between her and the Elite. Shielding her.

Shiloh brushed her fingers across his bruised cheeks, his swollen eye, his puffy lips. "Jake, what's going on? What happened to you?"

"There's no time." Jake's hands slid across her face, fingers sinking into her hair. "Everything is going to be okay. You'll be safe with them, but you have to go. You have to run."

"Jake—"

He silenced her with a kiss. His lips pressed hard against hers, expressing an urgency that made her heart ache. It was a kiss that tasted of pain and passion and a thousand impossible wishes. A kiss that said goodbye. Shiloh clung to the collar of his coat. *No, no! He* can't *be saying goodbye.*

"I love you," he said pulling away, and then he pushed her away from him.

The man who'd held Jake caught her, his hands firm but gentle. Jake walked backward through the snow to stay between Shiloh and the Elite. The man tried to shove her behind him, but she resisted and locked eyes with Jake one last time.

His lips silently formed a single word: "Run."

So this time, when the man pushed her behind him, Shiloh ran. Or at least, she ran as best she could through the thick snow, half-stumbling. A hand caught her arm, and she almost jerked away until the person spoke.

"Shiloh, it's me."

Familiar blue eyes peered out from the shadows of the coat's hood.

"N-Nic?" Shiloh's teeth chattered. She'd barely noticed the cold for a few minutes, but now she found it had sunk its teeth all the way to her bones. "Nic, w-w-what's happening?"

"I'll explain everything later," Nic said. "We have to hurry."

Nic tugged Shiloh along, steadying her through the deep snow. The rest of ROGUE crashed around her. Snow kicked up all around them. There seemed to be more than the original rebels she'd seen come out of the woods. Shiloh glanced over her shoulder but saw no sign of Elite pursuit. No gunshots fired at their heads, but Shiloh knew better than to think they'd just let them all go. By now, they had Jake secured. Nothing stood between them and ROGUE now.

The members of ROGUE knew it too. They formed a circle around Shiloh, shielding her from all sides. Like they were protecting her. Like... like she was important to them. They rushed faster and faster through the snow, and then, just as suddenly, they stopped. One of the members held up a fist in the middle of the small clearing, only two giant pine trees looming near them.

"Quiet," said one rebel, her voice the same who'd cursed Councilor Osgood earlier.

Everyone obeyed, huddling together. The woman, this clear leader, cocked her head and turned a slow circle, searching for what she'd heard. In the stillness, Shiloh's heartbeat sounded like a drum.

🔥

Jake watched Shiloh and the rest of ROGUE disappeared into the shadows of the woods. A second later, the Elite converged on him, their bodies in their dark suits forming a wall around him. A hand grabbed Jake's arm and steered him in a new direction. They fired questions—Was he all right? What had they done? But one voice rose above all others.

"We have him," said one Elite into the communication device in her helmet. The female. The same one who'd put a gun to Shiloh's head. "You are free to engage."

A scream built in Jake's chest, but he bit his tongue to keep it down and forced himself to keep walking, like a good little puppet. He remembered what Sawyer had said, about expecting his father to lay a trap. He hoped that meant they'd prepared for this. He clung to that hope, even as his rage built, burning through his entire body until the world tinted red.

This... this was why you didn't make deals with Osgoods.

◊

The leader's next words were whispered so low, Shiloh nearly didn't catch them, "Are you ready?"

But the others must have heard because they nodded. Beside Shiloh, Nic let out a shuddering breath and placed a hand around the strap of the rifle across her back. The chattering of Shiloh's teeth seemed too loud in the silence. Someone, with the same pair of bright blue eyes, stepped close to Nic. *Amelia*. The hulking man set a hand on Shiloh's shoulder.

"Sphere!" a woman barked, a second before a round, blue object plopped in the center of the group.

"Stunner!" someone else called.

Someone dove for the sphere, while others scattered. Nic grabbed Shiloh and launched them both beneath the branches of the nearest pine. Shiloh landed in the snow with enough force to take her breath away, but she scrambled to her hands and knees and glanced behind her. The Sphere must have been thrown because it was sailing back in the direction it came. It exploded in the air. Lightning bolts of electricity shot from it, hissing and popping like fireworks.

Someone screamed as a bolt struck their leg, and they collapsed to the ground only a few feet from Shiloh.

"Chuckles!" A lanky heretic launched himself from where he'd landed on the ground and grabbed the fallen rebel. He dragged the limp body beneath the tree to where Nic and Shiloh hid.

"Grim, is he all right?" Nic hissed. The scarf had fallen from Chuckles's face. His eyes stared, unblinking, above him.

Froq, Shiloh thought. He was only a boy, no older than Nic.

"Yeah, just stunned," Grim said, swearing beneath his breath.

Shiloh crawled toward the boy, looking for breathing. Gunshots ripped through the air. She ducked low to the ground and threw her hands over her head.

Bang! Bang! Bang!

Outside of the veil of green, shadowy figures moved among the trees like a wolf pack. Their guns already fired as they drew closer. The members of ROGUE jumped to their feet and scattered behind the shelter of trees on the opposite side of the clearing, drawing guns and returning fire. The bullets pinged off the Elite's metal suits.

The Elite were so close. Too close.

"Come on, you fuckers," Grim murmured, watching as the Elite approached.

Shiloh pressed a hand over her mouth so she wouldn't scream.

The Elite were at the tree line now. They stepped into the clearing.

And a wall of flame exploded at their feet.

Shiloh flattened herself to the ground, arms still over her head, as the heat crackled in the air. Neither Nic nor Grim seemed surprised. They'd expected it.

ROGUE had laid a trap for the Elite, Shiloh deduced. Buried explosives in the snow and led the Elite right across them.

The wall of fire subsided. Flames gnawed at the leafless trees and crumbled bodies of the Elite. In the silence that followed, the wind howled, and the fire roared. And then... more footsteps crunched in the snow... and another line of Elite appeared where their comrades had fallen.

The gunfire resumed.

"Help me, Princess," Grim said, seizing Chuckle's arm. "To the other side of the tree."

It wasn't until Grim set his vivid green eyes on Shiloh that she realized he was talking to her. *Princess?* Who was he calling *Princess?*

Now wasn't the time to ask. Shiloh grabbed the boy's other arm and helped haul him to the other side of the tree.

BANG!

A gun fired so close Shiloh's ears rattled, and she twisted to see Nic flat against the ground, her rifle trained forward. An Elite still twenty feet away fell as her bullet sailed through his faceplate in a spray of glass and blood. The weak spot. A direct hit.

Something flickered through Nic's expression, and then she took aim and fired another shot.

"Stay here, Princess," Grim said, before patting the boy's shoulder. "Ali, you'll be okay, man. I'll be right back."

Shiloh's lips parted, but Grim was already tumbling toward the next tree, where he propped his own rifle on the ground and began to fire. Shiloh squinted around the tree, taking in the chaos. Bullets exchanged with bullets. As one Elite fell, two more seemed to take his place. Some bullets released puffs of blue—Stunner bullets—as they struck the tree, while others exploded in a spray of splinters.

"AWOL," called the leader's voice, "do you have another sphere?"

BANG! BANG!

Shiloh never heard the answer over the bullets. Nic fired again, and Shiloh shielded herself against the tree.

Thud!

Shiloh leaned around the tree to see Nic slump forward, the puff of blue still trailing above her.

Shiloh bit back a scream, ensured no Elite were near, and

scrambled to Nic's side. Her fingers found the curve of Nic's neck. Her pulse beat steadily. Shiloh rolled Nic over and dragged her to lay beside Chuckles-Ali-whoever the boy was.

Shiloh peered around the trunk. Two more Elite marched in their direction. *Froq!* Shiloh glanced at Nic's fallen rifle. She didn't know the first thing about that long, gleaming metal. But a small pistol hung at Nic's side. All Shiloh had to do was point and shoot, right? She reached for the firearm but hesitated.

Bang!

Shiloh twisted back as Grim lunged from beneath the other pine toward the approaching Elite. He lifted his gun and fired. *Bang!* It pinged off the metal suit. The two Elite swung toward him, their attention being pulled away from Shiloh's hiding place. Grim pulled the trigger again, but this time nothing happened.

"Froq!"

Shiloh's breath caught as an Elite lifted his gun, but Grim swung his rifle like a bat into the first Elite's hand. The Elite's gun landed in the snow. Disarmed, the Elite lunged, knocking Grim into the snow with him. They scrambled around, fists thrown, snow flying. The second Elite fixed the pistol on them, waiting for a clear shot. As soon as they had one, Grim would be dead.

Shiloh grasped Nic's pistol and stood. She lifted the gun, heavier than she thought such a little thing might be. When she looked back to Grim, the first Elite had forced him to his knees, wrenching his arms back. Grim struggled, swearing and growling like a caged tiger, without success. Grim's scarf had fallen in the struggle, revealing his face to be young. Far too young to die.

Shiloh took aim, but she couldn't steady her arm. She'd surely miss... unless she was so close she couldn't. Cool sweat inked on her neck as the second Elite pressed his gun to the skin between Grim's eyebrows. An execution.

Just like Hope.

Shiloh lunged from the shadows and lifted the gun straight into the Elite's face, seeing her own reflection in the visor, just like all the times she'd stared into Silas's helmet. The trigger was harder to squeeze than she'd imagined, but she anchored both her hands and drew back with two fingers. The gun bucked in her hands, the force driving her back a step. Glass sprayed toward her, tainted with red as it slid past her skin. And the Elite fell. Dead.

She'd... she'd killed him.

Behind her, Grim shoved to his feet, the shock of the other Elite giving Grim the upper hand. They tumbled into another brawl, but this time, Grim landed on top. He pinned the Elite's arms to the snow with his knees and wrenched the helmet off. His fist landed again and again into the man's face, until both of them were bloody, and the man moved no more.

Grim looked up to where Shiloh stood frozen, trembling from more than cold. His mouth parted as he stood. "Well, fuck," he murmured, his gaze sweeping up and down her body. "I wasn't expecting that."

"Everyone down!" the leader called. She burst from her cover behind a tree and pulled back her arm, a red sphere caught in her fist. She held it, her lips moving as she counted: *One, two, three.* And then she launched the weapon. It soared into the midst of the next wave of Elite and plopped into the snow.

Grim launched himself at Shiloh, knocking her to the ground. He stretched his long body as a shield over her as the world ignited, an explosion twice as big as the first. Heat nipped at Shiloh's flesh, crackling and screaming like a dragon breathing flame. The trees shook as the ground trembled.

And then, just as suddenly, everything was quiet.

TWENTY-ONE

There was nothing.

No gunshots.

No footsteps.

Only the sound of Shiloh's racing heart, and Grim's breath as it rose and fell. After a second, Grim lifted his weight off her. He still hovered above her, his hands on either side of her head, his brow knitted as he studied her face with bright green eyes. "You okay, Princess?"

He was so close she felt the words on her cheeks as much as she heard them. And that was far too close.

She shoved his shoulder. "Get off me."

He rolled away and stood in one graceful movement. He offered his hand, but Shiloh rose without it.

"Shiloh!"

The leader turned in a circle until she found Shiloh. Her hood had fallen, revealing her close-cut, dark curls. She let out a breath, her shoulders sagging in relief.

"Are you okay?" she asked, charging across the distance between them. She lifted a hand, her only hand, and set it on Shiloh's shoulder. Something in how she looked at Shiloh seemed intimate—like she wasn't just a stranger. Like this woman cared about her. Deeply.

Around them, fire crackled in the bare tree branches, and curled up the ferns of the pines. Blood had turned the snow red beneath the remnants of what remained of the Elite's bodies. The body that lay closest—killed by a single shot— was the person Shiloh herself had killed. Maybe she should feel something about that—guilt, regret—but she felt... *nothing*.

"Are you okay?" the leader demanded again, standing closer now.

"Yes," Shiloh said. "But Nic was stunned."

A woman who stood nearby, who was surely Amelia, yelped and tore to the tree where Shiloh gestured. The large man followed her.

"And Chuckles got hit with the Stunner sphere," Grim added over his shoulder as he followed behind them.

The leader swung in a circle as the members of ROGUE slowly came out from hiding, looking over each person.

"Scalpel, here!" called a voice.

The leader rushed forward and, unsure why, Shiloh followed close on her heels. They stopped before a tree. Red streaked down the trunk's chipped bark to the base where a body slumped on the ground. A woman kneeled beside the man. Her hood had fallen, revealing rows of tight braids.

"Yousef," the woman breathed softly.

Scalpel kneeled and checked for a pulse on the man's neck. After a moment, she dropped her hand with a sigh. "AWOL, I'm sorry."

Shiloh stared down at Yousef's face—olive skin, full beard without a hint of grey, wide brown eyes that seemed kind, even now. In the middle of the adrenaline, she'd forgotten about the cold and the damp, but now the shiver returned, shaking her whole body. Her sweater, damp and stiff with embedded snow, clung to her skin, but part of the coldness was something that no blanket could touch.

Guilt.

This... this is my fault.

They'd come for her. Knowing the risks, Yousef, this stranger, had joined this quest to save her. And he'd died for it.

The only question was *why?*

&

They set off quickly again—Ali slumped between Grim and Amelia, Nic slung over the shoulder of a man they called Badger. Despite being Shiloh's own height, he carried Nic like she was weightless. Even Yousef was carried between AWOL and the hulking man, who Shiloh learned was Paul. Nic's Paul.

Shiloh clung to the thermal blanket she'd been given, trying to regain feeling in her numb body, to still her shivering. The farther they went, the worse she became. Her feet still moved, but her head felt like yarn unraveling. The more she grasped at her thoughts, the faster they rolled away.

Hypothermia, some distant part of her brain recognized. *This is hypothermia.*

By the time they reached a large box truck, Scalpel had to help Shiloh into the cab before pulling herself in afterward. AWOL swung into the driver's side, Shiloh trapped in between them. The slam of the doors boomed like the echo of an explosion in her head, and then the truck lunged forward, spinning on ice before it found purchase and raced onto the snowy gravel.

A hand snagged on Shiloh's sweater, trying to yank it up. Instinct broke through the fog, and she shoved the hand away with a hiss. "D-don't!" she said through chattering teeth.

"We have to get you out of these wet clothes," Scalpel snapped back.

"I-I-I k-know." Somewhere in the deep recesses of her mind,

Shiloh recognized it was a good sign that she was still shivering. It was when shivering stopped that hypothermia became deadly. "B-but I can d-do it."

Shiloh peeled the damp sweater off with shivering fingers. She tried to pretend this was just another day in the locker room, and these weren't two strangers who had annihilated an army of Elite. Scalpel dug through her pack, tossing Shiloh a dry shirt and pants. Shiloh pulled on the long shirt before changing into the dry pants. Scalpel rolled the wet clothes in the blanket and tossed the bundle to the floorboard.

Scalpel wrapped a fresh, dry blanket around Shiloh's arms. Then she shrugged out of her coat, something that must have been difficult with one arm, but she made it look easy. She threw that around Shiloh's shoulders too, swaddling it around her like a child being tucked in at night, an action so tender it ached like a poked bruise.

"W-why are you d-doing this?" Shiloh asked.

"Because you're exhibiting textbook signs of hypothermia," Scalpel said.

"I know th-that!" Shiloh clashed her teeth together to keep them from knocking around. "Why did you save me?"

The truck whirled around a corner at a speed that made Shiloh tumble toward AWOL. Scalpel caught her arm, steadying her.

"Hold on to your ass," AWOL mumbled, taking the next curve just as quickly.

The trees outside the window flew by like a stampede.

"Are w-we being followed?" Shiloh asked.

Scalpel inspected the large passenger-side mirror that showed nothing but trees and the tire tracks left in the snow.

"There's a lot of different roads in this forest," AWOL said, tightening her hold on the steering wheel. "I hope no one is following us, but I'm not slowin' down to find out."

Shiloh turned her attention back to Scalpel. Though Shiloh still felt she was grasping through a fog, the shivering had stopped enough to put force into her voice. "I asked you a question, and I w-want an answer."

Scalpel kept her eyes fixed on the mirror. "We can talk about this later."

"No, we can t-talk about it *now*. There's a man d-dead because of me."

Scalpel snapped her head towards Shiloh. "Don't you dare blame yourself. *I'm* the leader of ROGUE. His death lies solely with me."

AWOL inhaled sharply. "Sawyer, don't—"

"Brooks, just drive," Scalpel—or was it Sawyer?—snapped. "And stay off the main roads. They'll probably have them all blocked off."

"You're the leader of ROGUE?" Shiloh repeated.

Sawyer nodded.

Shiloh stared, her head tilting, whirling, spinning. This woman, the one who looked at Shiloh, even now, like she was something important. Like she knew Shiloh. Like she cared.

Shiloh clutched her hands into fists around the blanket. "W-who am I to you?"

Dark eyes stared back at her. Pitch black, just like Shiloh's own.

"You're my niece," Sawyer said at last.

Niece, niece, niece.

The word burned in Shiloh's ears, pounded in her head, slammed against her chest.

Niece, niece, niece.

"Your mother, Elaine..." Sawyer paused on the name for a heartbeat too long. "She was my sister."

"You're my—" The word *aunt* got lodged in Shiloh's throat. The claws of memory—Aunt Morgan's fingernails sinking into her arm, of Aunt Isa's palm meeting her cheek—pierced her mind. It took effort to shake herself free.

"*You're* who they wanted," Shiloh said, the pieces snapping together, "in exchange for me."

Sawyer nodded.

"But you traded Jake instead."

"Yes, we kidnapped him."

"In all fairness," Brooks added, "it was *his* idea."

Of course, it was. Shiloh shook her head. "Idiot." She supposed ROGUE had to make it look convincing, and that explained the bruises on Jake's face. But it could have been worse. Jake could have died saving her. And that wasn't acceptable.

A throb pulsed at Shiloh's temple; a few more shivers coursed through her body. What was Shiloh supposed to feel right now? The truck blazed forward even faster, finding a straightaway. Shiloh stared at the rapidly passing trees as though they might fling her the answer. Beside her, Sawyer clung to the handle above the door and occasionally snuck glances at Shiloh.

Her aunt. An actual living relative. Shiloh should have been overjoyed or grateful, or at the very least, angry that she'd had family all this time but had still been stuck in a Haven. But Shiloh felt... nothing. She was looking at a stranger, nothing more.

But there were more questions.

"If you're the leader of ROGUE, who were my parents?" Shiloh asked.

Sawyer swallowed visibly, still staring out in the blur of white and grey, snow and trees.

"Your parents created ROGUE," Brooks said, glancing carefully at Sawyer. "They were the leaders up until, well..." She stopped and ground her hands into the steering wheel.

"Until they died," Shiloh said, making her tone flat. Uncaring. Too many emotions threatened to make her chest explode to add profound grief to the chaos.

Sawyer's gaze pressed into Shiloh heavily. The truck flung over another bump, sending Shiloh into the air. She steadied herself with a palm on the dashboard.

"I need you to know," Sawyer said, her voice insistent, after Shiloh settled back against her chair, "that I thought you died with them. Until Nic came back to ROGUE, I had no idea you were alive. If I had, I would have come for you. I would have torn every single Haven in Arcadia apart if I had to."

"It doesn't matter," Shiloh mumbled. She closed her eyes, letting her head fall back on the seat. Hiding from the emotions that threatened to drown her. "Arcadia lies."

"It *does* matter," Sawyer insisted.

What was Shiloh supposed to say? She didn't know, so she left her head on the seat behind her and slowed her breathing. She must have convinced them she'd fallen asleep because, a few minutes later, a hand tucked the blanket more firmly around her.

"Does she remind you of anyone?" Brooks said, then let out a low whistle. "She's made of spunk... just like Elaine."

After a long moment, Sawyer spoke, her voice a harsh whisper, "She has to be. I can only imagine what she's had to survive."

TWENTY-TWO

"Oh my Council, Jake!"

As soon as Jake walked in the front door of his home, his mom broke from the front stairs where she'd been waiting and flung herself across the room at him. She hugged him tighter than he'd ever remembered, her arms trembling.

"I'm okay, Mom," he said, pulling her tight against his chest. "I promise."

Over his Mom's head, Jake could see Ana peeking out from the hallway leading to the kitchen, one hand clasped to her chest, another to her tear-streaked cheek. Jake offered her a smile, hoping she'd find comfort in it and believe he really was okay. Even though nothing, at all, was okay.

Mom stepped back and studied the angry bruises on his face. "Oh, my boy. What did they do to you?"

"It's not as bad as it looks," Jake said, but when her fingers barely brushed the bruises on his cheek, he winced.

Footsteps came down the hallway, and Dad burst into the foyer. Upon catching sight of Jake, Dad's shoulders sagged, relief bowling him over. Mom stepped aside, and Dad moved so quickly,

Jake didn't have time to protest before Dad engulfed him in a crushing embrace.

Jake's hands curled into fists at his side. He wanted nothing more than to shove Dad away, slam his fist into Dad's nose, call him all the forbidden words screaming in Jake's head. Right now, Shiloh and ROGUE might still be under attack. Or dead—they could already be dead.

Jake's teeth clenched into his jaw ache. *No, she's not dead! She's not!*

When he could take no more, Jake broke away, putting an arms-length distance between him and Dad. No, thinking of this man before him as Dad didn't feel right. This man was Councilor Samuel Osgood before he was anything, anyone, including Jake's father. It was time Jake gave up any illusion otherwise.

Samuel Osgood's eyebrows pinched together as he met Jake's gaze. "I think we should talk."

"What's there to talk about?" Jake snarled before he could stop himself. He sucked in a breath so deep his lungs felt like they might burst.

Be a good puppet.

Samuel closed his eyes; pained, but not surprised. Samuel anticipated anger, and Jake couldn't act too far out of character without suspicion.

Good. I can do anger.

Jake marched forward until only inches separated them, and Samuel flinched back, like Jake might hit him. But Jake kept his fists at his side. "You had my girlfriend kidnapped out of my arms and threatened her life to—"

"Keep your voice down," Samuel growled, glancing back to where Ana had once stood, but now the hallway was empty. The guards had retreated outside the front door, so Jake and his parents were alone.

"And then," Jake continued, lowering his voice only slightly, "those monsters kidnapped me, beat me, and very nearly killed me because your game backfired."

Samuel winced. "Jake—"

"But you ended up getting exactly what you wanted, because now Shiloh is stuck with them, and I will *never* see her again!" Jake didn't have to fake the tremor of those last words, or the way *never* wrapped crushing fingers around his throat. No, *that* was real.

Samuel glanced to Mom as though for aid, but she only crossed her arms over her chest.

"Jake, I'm sorry," he said, voice low. "One day, you'll understand. I didn't have a choice."

"Of course, you did! But as always, you chose yourself."

Jake marched from his father. Samuel followed, but Jake pounded up the stairs before he could stop him.

"All I have ever done," Samuel protested from the bottom, "is try to keep this family safe."

From the top of the steps, Jake turned back. "Look at me." He gestured to his face. "You're clearly doing a fantastic job."

Without giving the Councilor a chance to respond, Jake spun around and stomped down the hallway.

He hoped Samuel hadn't missed the seed he'd planted. The word *monster* to describe ROGUE had been the only act in the show—a little act to convince Samuel that Jake no longer wanted to be a heretic. That was step one in his plan, the one that had settled into his heart when he realized ROGUE wanted nothing to do with him. He had to regain the Council's trust.

Jake ripped his bedroom door open and, once inside, slammed it so hard the wall rattled.

"Jake," a voice said softly.

He jumped, startled. Ana stood a few feet from him. She wore her dark hair pulled away from her face with a white bandana, her eyes warm and dark. Like coffee on a cold morning. He opened his mouth to speak, but she pressed a finger to her lips and beckoned him closer.

"*Shiloh está viva*," she whispered when only a foot separated them.

Shiloh is alive.

"Ana, what—"

She held up her hand again, glancing quickly at the door, and spoke in Spanish. "I overheard the Councilor—I've been listening at his office door because I wanted to know... I was so scared for you." Her voice broke, and she blinked rapidly. Jake's stomach twisted in regret—regret that he'd hurt his mother and Ana during all this, but not guilt. He'd do it again, in a heartbeat.

"But, just before you came," she continued, "I heard him speak to the Elite—they said the mission failed. No bodies. The Councilor specifically asked about Shiloh, but whatever he did, the Elite didn't find her, so she must be alive."

A wash of relief flooded over Jake, and he crushed Ana into his chest. She smelled like sweet spices and homemade bread, a scent that brought memories of her feeding him cookies for dinner.

"*Gracias, Ana,*" he said, his voice thick. "*Gracias.*"

Still, a dark part of Jake's soul refused to believe Shiloh was truly safe until Stefani heard that song on the ROGUE radio, signaling Shiloh had made it to her new home. But Ana had restored his hope. And as long as there was hope, even the faintest flicker, Jake would fight. No matter what he had to do, no matter how long it took, no matter who he had to destroy— even if it was his own father—he would find his way back to Shiloh.

Because, as Paul had said: *love endures.*

&

Though she pretended to, Shiloh didn't sleep in the hours it took to arrive back at their destination. With every passing moment, she expected to be startled by the sound of gunfire or an explosion rocking the truck off its wheels. But they stuck to back roads—

Sawyer navigating Brooks with a large map—took lots of twists and sharp turns, and finally came to a stop. They'd made it.

Shiloh lifted her head, looking out the windshield at the endless slope of white before them. Brooks and Sawyer shoved the door open and prepared to swing out.

"Sawyer, wait." Shiloh shrugged out of Sawyer's coat, but Sawyer shook her head.

"Keep it," she said. "I'll be fine."

Shiloh opened her mouth, but Sawyer had already swung out and landed knee-high in the snow. Shiloh slipped her arms through the coat sleeves, tucked the blanket against her chest, and then followed.

At the end of the truck, the rest of the heretics were jumping out of the bed. The boy who'd been stunned—Ali—was awake now, though a little dazed. Grim hovered near him like a protective bodyguard—or rather, a big brother. It wasn't a resemblance that gave the relationship away; they didn't look much alike, at all. Ali only came to Grim's shoulder, stocky where Grim was lean. Grim's skin was a warm light brown, whereas Ali's was a cool black. Instead, it had been Grim's actions on the battlefield that gave the brothers away.

Though Ali had woken, Nic remained unconscious, now cradled in Paul's arms. Perhaps the contents of the sphere were not as potent as the bullet that had struck her. Still, her chest rose and fell steadily, a comfort.

The last person off the truck was Yousef. Now wrapped in a blanket, Badger and Brooks lifted him out of the truck, the beginning of a funeral recession. A hand slipped from the blanket, pale on one side, but purple and bloated on the other.

Shiloh swiftly looked away, swallowing against the lump that lodged in her throat.

They climbed up the slope in silence. Shiloh fought to keep her balance on the steep incline, dragging her feet through the deep snow. Halfway up, she stumbled. A hand seized her arm before she landed in the snow.

"Easy there, Princess."

Grim released her as quickly as he'd grabbed her, but Shiloh took a step to distance herself anyway, her face twisting into a scowl.

"Why do you keep calling me that?" she asked.

"Call you what?"

Without waiting for an answer, Grim started walking. With his considerable height, she had to scramble to keep up with his pace.

"Princess," Shiloh said.

"Oh." A slow smirk wound up Grim's face, his bright green eyes sparking with a mocking laugh. He wore long dark curls pulled back in a bun at the nape of his neck. "That's your codename, isn't it?"

"I don't have a codename," Shiloh snapped, and he cast an amused glance at her. A look that said *'there, there, you poor naïve thing'*.

Because, *obviously*, she had a codename. She'd probably had one from the day she'd been born to Alec and Elaine Sanders. The creators of ROGUE.

And Shiloh—their daughter. The princess.

Froq!

Repulsion twisted Shiloh's gut. Had she been the type of little girl—sweet and cute and feminine—for whom the name Princess had been befitting? That didn't seem possible. And no matter who she had been, that little girl didn't exist anymore. Shiloh was far from a princess.

"I don't care what my codename name is, Grim," Shiloh said, clenching her teeth. "Don't call me Princess."

He only smirked again. "Whatever you say... *Princess*." He picked up speed, leaving her behind with ease. He called back over his shoulder, "Oh, and the name's Luca."

It took everything within Shiloh not to hurl a snowball at his head.

When Shiloh finally made it over the ridge, a cool sweat had broken out across her back. Before her, Shiloh found an old, broken ski lodge with tarp-covered windows and splintered wood. Shiloh waited at the top as the last of the members of ROGUE emerged from beyond the ridge, carrying the covered body between them.

They all, even Luca who was in the lead, paused and watched as the group lowered Yousef to the snowy ground. Badger shook his head as he stepped away from Yousef, his scowl so deep that his scars took over his face, a zig-zag of flesh. He marched toward the lodge, grumbling as he passed Paul, "Come on. Let's go get shovels."

Still carrying Nic, Paul headed toward the house. Amelia followed, but Shiloh glanced behind her. The dark blanket around Yousef's body contrasted against the snow. Did Shiloh follow or did she stay to help this man who'd lost his life to save her?

Sawyer paused by her side and answered for her. "Let's get you inside."

The ice covering the porch sparkled underneath the afternoon sun like fire. Shiloh crossed it carefully and slid through the crack in the door Paul had left open behind him. The warm glow of a mighty flame greeted her from the stone fireplace centered on the far wall. Before it sat a young man in glasses, an elderly man, and a small huddle of children. The children—five altogether, ranging from toddlers to preteens—let out a cheer as everyone entered.

Badger paused as the young man broke from the crowd and rushed toward him, calling him by his real name.

"Mick!"

Their brief kiss spoke of a deep, passionate love they didn't have to hide. It flared out like a declaration, a flag that professed freedom, joy, and hope.

Shiloh had stepped into an entirely different world.

A better world.

Mick pulled away, whispered something to the man, whose face paled. Mick turned and left the room. Paul and Amelia headed toward a set of stairs to the left. Shiloh began to follow, but a low whistle stopped her.

"Well, I'll be damned," the elderly man said, rising to his feet unsteadily. He hobbled around a couch toward her. "Shiloh Sanders. I can't decide whether she looks more like Alec or Elaine." He squinted, almost upon her now. One eye was cloudy, unseeing, but the other studied her with an intensity Shiloh fought not to shy away from. "But them's the Ardelean eyes, that's for sure." He looked toward the young man in glasses. "What do you think, Charlie?"

"I'll take your word for it, Wallace," Charlie said with a smile that made his eyes crinkle. He wrapped an arm around the old man's shoulders and steered him back toward the fire. "But let's not crowd the girl."

Shiloh let out a breath and turned to catch up with Paul and Amelia. Sawyer followed behind her.

As Paul and Amelia reached the first step, a woman descended the stairs. A scarf twirled around her head, a rosy mauve that brought out the deep, warm tones of her skin. A hijab. The word came with warning bells in Shiloh's head, an instinctive reaction that years of Arcadian training had drilled into her. *Heresy. Rebellion. A faith that represented only hatred.*

But when Shiloh crammed the instinct down and looked with her own eyes, the woman was beautiful. The fearless, open expression of her brand of heresy made her even more so.

"Oh, Amelia, Paul, you're back," she said, coming to a halt, a soft smile on her face. "Is Yousef outside?"

The fist in Shiloh's chest tightened, crumbling her lungs like paper.

Amelia winced, twin expressions of agony and sympathy. Sawyer left Shiloh's elbow to approach slowly. The smile slipped from the woman's lips, meeting the look on Sawyer's face, and she took a step back like she wanted to flee. Around the fireplace, the kids who'd been talking merrily fell silent. Charlie quickly shooed them toward another room on the other side of the lodge. But the eldest girl stared over her shoulder the whole way, her head wrapped in a hijab like her mother.

How many kids had Yousef left behind?

"Sawyer," the woman repeated, clutching a hand over her stomach, "where is Yousef?"

Sawyer shook her head. "Fatima, I'm—"

Shiloh couldn't hear those next words. She bolted around Amelia and Sawyer and took the stairs two at a time after Paul, who carried Nic up the stairs. Shiloh pretended not to hear the shriek from below, the sound of a world shattering.

Paul slipped through one of the doors off the hallway. The room must have been beautiful once, like the hotel Shiloh had stayed in only days ago. But the mantel of the stone fireplace sagged to one side, and the curtains clung to the rods with the last of their worn fibers. Paul laid Nic on a bed made up with sleeping bags. It sagged beneath her weight, springs groaning in protest.

Paul lovingly tucked the blanket around Nic's shoulders, brushed a few strands of blond hair from her face. The look he gave Nic caused a tight squeeze around Shiloh's heart. It was the closest thing she'd ever seen to what a father might look like—a real father. One who loved his child more than anything else, even if that child wasn't really his.

Paul moved to the fireplace and kneeled before it. He made quick work of starting a fire, adding warmth to the chilled room. He stood, brushing soot off his hands, and glanced between the door and Nic, hesitating.

"I can stay with her," Shiloh said, "if you need to leave."

Paul looked at her, really looked, and Shiloh got the impression that he knew her too, in ways that didn't make sense. "I can't thank you enough for all you did for her. She told us about all you did. She wouldn't be here if it wasn't for you."

Shiloh swallowed. "I couldn't let anything happen to her."

"No. You always did look after her."

"What does that mean?"

Paul rubbed his fingers over one side of his beard. "It's a long story. How much do you remember of your past?"

"Not much."

"I'm sure we'll all be happy to fill you in," Paul said. His attention trailed to the window. Past the fogged glass, Shiloh could see down upon the figures that lingered in the yard, gathered around the friend who was to be buried. He sighed, looking suddenly exhausted. Surely, he'd buried many friends. "Later."

Shiloh nodded.

Paul took a step toward the door but paused before her, looking at her with a soft expression, one similar to what he'd given Nic. She tensed, afraid that he might hug her, but he only clasped her shoulder. "I'm so glad you're here." He walked toward the door, stepped into the hallway, but then ducked his head back in. "Oh, and that boy?"

Shiloh's heart drummed in her ears. "Jake?"

"Yeah." He gave her a warm grin. "He sure does love you."

He left with that, leaving Shiloh with so many questions and a hollowness in her chest that echoed with silent screams. Because whatever had happened, she knew with surety that Jake was gone. That more than miles separated them now. Jake. Val. Willa. Zyla.

I'll never see them again. Not now.

Shiloh gingerly sat on the other side of the bed from Nic, leaning against the wall and drawing her legs tight to her chest. From here, she could see outside the window. She watched as dirt began to fly—a grave being dug.

TWENTY-THREE

Nic slept for what must have been hours, and no one disturbed Shiloh in the room. Only once was there a small knock on the door: Amelia, bringing Shiloh a portion of supper. She checked on her daughter, asked Shiloh if she needed anything, and then lingered in the doorway, studying Shiloh. Amelia's mouth parted once, like she might say something. Then, as though Shiloh had a 'Do Not Disturb' sign hanging around her neck, Amelia softly closed the door.

Shiloh paced between the bed and the window. She watched the grave grow bigger until it was dark, and she could see nothing but shadows. And then lights flickered on, swaying like fireflies, and clustered together near the ridge—a funeral by lantern light.

Pressing her forehead against the cool glass, Shiloh watched the cluster of flickering lights.

A sudden cry made Shiloh jump and whirl around. Nic thrust herself into a sitting position, her fingers grasping at her hip, at her empty holster. Her breath came in gasps.

"Nic, it's okay." Shiloh rushed to the bed and crawled in beside her. "You were stunned, but you're safe now."

Nic searched around the room, her panicked breathing slowly normalizing. "I was stunned?"

Shiloh nodded.

She groaned and thrust the heel of her hand to her forehead. "Great. Now my mother will never let me go on another mission."

Shiloh blinked, unsure what to say to that.

Nic groaned again and then let her hand fall. "Did everyone make it back okay?"

Shiloh shook her head, picking at fibers on the sleeping bag to avoid looking up. "A man called Yousef was killed."

"Oh God!" Both of Nic's hands flew to her mouth. "Fatima... the kids... are they okay?"

Shiloh sealed her eyes closed, even as the crack in her chest widened. "I don't know. I've been with you since we got back. Watching out for you."

"And you're hiding," Nic said.

Shiloh's fingers crushed into the sleeping bag. The stiff, heavy fabric crinkled. "I'm not."

Nic folded her arms over her chest and gave her that defiant expression Shiloh knew well. "So then, why aren't you with your aunt?"

From the bed, Shiloh could no longer see the parade of lights through the window. She tried to think of an answer—her aunt was at the funeral, Shiloh didn't feel like intruding, Paul had been worried about Nic—but none of them felt like reasons Nic would believe.

Nic laid a palm over Shiloh's hand that rested beside her in the bed. "I mean, Shi, you have *family*. Isn't that ... isn't that good?"

Shiloh pulled her hand away. "I already have family. Val is my family. And now—And now, I'll never see her again."

And Jake...

Would Shiloh ever see him again?

"You don't know that," Nic said, but even she didn't seem convinced.

Shiloh looked away.

"Jake gave me something for you." Shiloh looked back sharply as Nic pulled something from her pocket. She dropped the square of paper into Shiloh's palm, Shiloh cradled it like a treasure. It had been folded haphazardly, the corners not lining up, a sloped tear through one side. She unfolded it. The words, written in Jake's sprawl, were quick and simple.

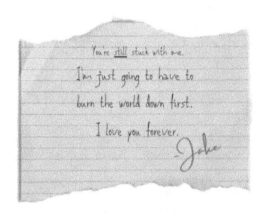

You're *still* stuck with me. I'm just going to have to burn the world down first. I love you forever.

-Jake

A droplet fell onto the page, smearing the lop-sided J. Shiloh let the note drop on the bed and slid her thumbs across her cheeks. The word 'forever' echoed in her ears like Jake had whispered it to her, like he had that night on his roof.

Nic reached for her hand again. "I'm sorry. I thought it might make you happy."

Shiloh brushed away more tears. "It did."

She'd needed that reminder of Jake's love. It ignited something in her blood that she clung to. Hope. Hope that, when pitted against all the evil and desperate odds in this world, their love would prove stronger.

The last refrains of the song came to a halt on the radio, which sat between Stefani and Val on the bed. Val waited, holding her breath. The now familiar syrupy voice began, and Val strangled her fists in her lap.

"Goodnight, Princess."

Stefani let out a squeal and bounced on her knees. "Jake did it! That son of a blight pulled it off."

Finally, he'd done something right. Somewhere, out there, Shiloh was safe, in the hands of ROGUE and, apparently, an aunt. She would be fine, or as fine as anyone could be in Arcadia. The long-lost princess of ROGUE.

Val laughed dryly at the irony.

Stefani stopped her bouncing and cocked her head. "What's so funny?"

"Nothing," Val said, though her lip curled into a sneer. "I bet Shiloh froqing hates her codename."

Stefani's ruby-red lip formed a hard line. "Probably, but Val..." She flicked off the radio and then reached across to grab Val's hand. "Are you okay?"

"Yeah." Val pulled her hand away. "You should call Osgood."

Stefani's bottom lip slipped out, a pout she did when she was worried, but she lifted her phone from her pocket and dialed. Osgood answered on the first ring, his hologram popping from the phone.

"Holy froq on a froqing sandwich, Jake!" Stefani exclaimed. "You look like cow ordure. No, worse, actually. Like the ordure of the bacteria that eat cow ordure."

Osgood cringed and then winced as though the crumpling of his facial features made everything hurt. Val's stomach twisted. Surely, just her dinner settling wrong. Not worry for him. Absolutely not.

"Please tell me you're calling for the reason I think you are," Osgood said, his voice low but urgent.

Stefani nodded, careful not to say too much, and Osgood let

out a breath that sounded like it came from his very soul. His face dropped into his hands for a long moment, his shoulders trembling. When he looked up, his eyes were rimmed with red.

He'd done it. He'd risked everything to save her, and he was... sobbing with relief. It settled in Val's head with the ring of cognitive dissonance—something that couldn't possibly be real but certainly was.

He really loved Shiloh, didn't he?

"I can't really talk now," Osgood murmured. "I'll chat when I get back to school, but um... thanks." His voice crumbled, and he cleared his throat before adding. "For everything."

The hologram disappeared.

"Cut it with the ordure, Val," Stefani snapped, dropping her phone to the bed. "I know you're not fine."

Val stiffened. "Why wouldn't I be fine?"

"Oh, I don't know." Stefani rolled her eyes. "Maybe because your sister got kidnapped and now..." Her voice trailed off.

"Now, I'm never going to see her again," Val said, her tone flat, like she was reading a definition from a dictionary. She stood and stretched her arms overhead, hoping that would ease the tightness in her chest. "It's not like I didn't know this would happen someday."

Everyone always leaves.

"Val—"

"It's getting late." Val snatched her threadbare backpack—which had stopped zipping in seventh grade—from Stefani's chair. "I should go."

Stefani crawled out of bed. "Valencia, wait!" She caught Val's wrist and turned her around.

Froq, froq, froq!

Stefani needed to stop froqing looking at her like that—like she could see past all of Val's excuses. If Val acknowledged the hole being drilled into her chest, she would fall to pieces. And she couldn't... she couldn't face the pain. Not *this* pain. This would surely be the end of her.

Val bared her teeth. "Leave me the froq alone, Stef. I'm *fine!*" Which would have been convincing if her voice hadn't froqing cracked at the end. If the froqing tears hadn't decided to appear in her froqing eyes.

She launched herself toward the door, but it hit—a tsunami of pain that crashed into her and threatened to drown her. She pressed her hands against the door, the force of her sobs bowling her over, making her body quake.

Froq, froq, froq!

"Oh, Val," Stefani sighed as she wrapped her arms around Val from behind.

"Why?" Val gasped between her sobs. "Why does everyone I love leave me?"

Stefani gently turned Val in her arms and held her so tightly it felt like she was the only thing keeping the seams of Val together. "I'm not going to leave you, Valencia. I promise."

"Don't do that," Val said, burying her head into Stefani's chest.

"Don't do what?"

"Don't make promises you know you can't keep."

TWENTY-FOUR

The soft creak pulled Shiloh from the depth of her sleep, the deepest sleep she'd had in days. Shiloh sat up, her throat dry and raw from lack of moisture, and glanced around the room in search of the noise which had woken her. Nic had laid beside Shiloh until she'd fallen into an unwilling sleep. But now the bed beside her was empty. Shiloh glanced at the doorway. A figure peeked in briefly, before disappearing.

"Sawyer," Shiloh croaked. She cleared her throat, licked her dry lips, and tried again. "Sawyer."

Sawyer's face reappeared in the crack of the open door, but she remained in the doorway, waiting. Shiloh wasn't even sure why she'd called out to her. She swallowed again, trying to remedy the desert in her mouth.

"Water," Sawyer said. "You need water."

She disappeared once more, soft footsteps retreating down the hall. Unsure whether to follow, Shiloh twisted the sleeping bag in her hands. A few minutes later, the door creaked again as Sawyer entered, a thermos in hand. She offered it to Shiloh, who took it.

"Thanks." Shiloh unscrewed the cup that served as a lid and poured water into it. The cool water soothed her throat, and she drank it down as Sawyer stood, still as a soldier in a drill line. The leader's eyes flicked around the room as though counting the shadows.

When Shiloh had emptied the cup, Sawyer said, "Drink more. You're likely dehydrated. I doubt the Elite cared for you very well."

Shiloh did as she was told, studying Sawyer over the rim of the cup. Sawyer seemed oddly knowledgeable about medical-related information. What had she said in the truck? *Textbook signs of hypothermia. Codename Scalpel.*

"Are you a doctor?" Shiloh asked.

Sawyer flinched like the question had teeth. "I *was*," she replied flatly. She fell silent, and Shiloh thought she wouldn't say anything more, but after a long moment, Sawyer added, "I was in my third year of surgical residency when the Sundering happened. But I'm not" —She glanced down at where her arm should have been— "I'm not a doctor anymore."

Sawyer looked flat as stone, but Shiloh could only imagine that losing the chance to be a surgeon likely ached like a still bleeding wound.

Clasping the metal cup in both hands, Shiloh changed the subject. "Will you tell me about them? My parents?"

Sawyer blinked then lowered herself onto the end of the bed. She stared out the window, at the dark world outside, like the memories were playing on the glass. "What do you want to know?"

Shiloh lifted one shoulder. "I don't remember anything, really."

Sawyer jerked her head in Shiloh's direction. "Nothing?"

Shiloh took a gulp of water, swallowing down Sawyer's disappointment. She could have explained about surviving in a Haven, about the harsh rules she'd lived by. But she didn't want to. "You said my parents created ROGUE. How did they do that?"

Sawyer shifted, pulling one of her knees onto the bed and tucking her foot beneath her so she could turn toward Shiloh. The position made her look younger, more human than soldier-machine. "After the Sundering, those who went on the run—heretics—were all divided into scattered groups. There was no way to communicate. The only reason we knew each other existed was purely by accidental meetings. Elaine and I..." She hesitated, as though the name of her sister made her lose her train of thought. "We were on our own when we met Alec and his group. Alec—your father—he had a way of making everyone feel like they belonged. I think that's what drew people to him. Alec would never turn away someone in need of help. Not if it was within his power to help them.

"We met a lot of heretic groups those first couple of years and started developing our own little ways to communicate—marks on trees, messages left in code. But it wasn't enough to truly help. Then Elaine figured out how to make the radios work. She was smart... so, so smart." Sawyer paused again, taking Shiloh in. "I hear you take after her."

Shiloh shrugged.

Sawyer's lips twitched, like she was going to smile, but her lips had forgotten how. "You were always smart. Even when you were little."

Shiloh ducked her head, unsure how to respond. "So, my mother made the radios?"

"Yes," Sawyer continued, "and then Alec and Elaine traveled across Arcadia, finding groups of heretics and giving them radios, but also... they wanted to convince people to fight back. When Elaine talked, people wanted to listen, and by the end, she could make them walk through hell. And Alec... well, they'd follow him because they knew he'd walk through hell with them."

"And so ROGUE fought?" Shiloh asked.

"We did. We fought... for years. When you came along, it was a surprise to us all. Elaine never thought she could get pregnant. But from the moment your parents saw you..." The smallest of smiles came over Sawyer's face, her gaze growing unfocused and distant, like she could see Shiloh as a newborn on the bed before her instead of the near-adult she'd grown into. "I never thought anyone could love someone as much as Alec and Elaine loved each other, and then you came along. You were their whole world."

An ache ripped through Shiloh's chest. She could almost feel it —the way they'd loved her—like it had left fingerprints upon her heart. But she knew how the story ended.

"How did they die?" Shiloh asked, her voice steadier than she felt.

Sawyer's eyes fluttered closed. She took a slow breath in and out. Shiloh clutched the cup even harder, wishing she had something more solid to hold.

"We lost," Sawyer began simply. "It's a long story, but a thousand little losses compounded until eventually the Elite got the upper hand. They trapped us in a bunker. We held them off and kept them from entering. We were there for weeks, but eventually, we were running out of food and water. We knew we were done. And so, Alec and Elaine made a deal—authorized by Councilor Osgood." Disgust tainted Sawyer's voice. The same emotion burned down Shiloh's throat. "Osgood agreed that if Alec and Elaine turned themselves over, everyone else would go free."

"And you trusted him?" Shiloh asked, sucking in a breath between her teeth.

Sawyer shook her head. "No. Not entirely. We arranged for Paul, Amelia, and Jason—that was Nic's father—to take you and Nic to safety."

"Why not you?"

"I was too well known. If I hadn't been there when Alec and Elaine surrendered, the Elite would have suspected we held someone back." She took another deep breath and then continued, "There was one exit the Elite hadn't found and weren't guarding, but we would have been noticed if we all tried to leave. In the chaos of the surrender, we thought you'd have a chance." Sawyer's voice crackled at the edges, glass warning that it might shatter. "Sending you away was the hardest thing I had to do. It *destroyed* your parents."

Shiloh closed her eyes against a blazing sting, pinching the bridge of her nose. And in the darkness behind her eyes, old memories resurfaced. She could almost feel it: tears on her cheeks, fingers clutching at her mother's hand, her throat raw as she begged.

"Mommy, Daddy, please, I want to stay! Please let me stay with you."

She could hear sobbing, not just her own. And the final words spoken, *"I love you."*

Shiloh already knew what happened next.

Gunshots.

Screams.

"Samuel Osgood had them executed, didn't he?" Shiloh asked.

Sawyer nodded. "He had *everyone* executed. That bastard Silas Petrovic shot them all one by one in front of Alec and Elaine... and... and me."

Silas. Shiloh inhaled sharply at the name. It landed like a physical blow in her gut. Sawyer fell silent, studying Shiloh carefully.

"Silas... Silas killed my parents?" Shiloh asked. Somehow, Shiloh felt she'd always known this, since Yuletide Eve when she'd heard the conversation between Silas and Councilor Osgood. If her parents were Arcadia's greatest enemies, then Silas would have had great satisfaction. But suspecting it and having it confirmed were two different things.

Sawyer drew a deep breath through her nose, then nodded slowly. She didn't ask questions, telling Shiloh that Nic had already told Sawyer all about what had transpired between Silas and Shiloh. Rage nipped at Shiloh's chest, her gut, her very blood, turning her entire body into fire. Silas was still out there, somewhere, still avoiding the justice of a bullet in his brain. One day, she'd ensure that bullet found him.

One day.

Almost unaware of what she was doing, Shiloh pulled her knees to her chest, a barrier to the rage, the pain—the screams and the sobs welling up inside her. She looked back to Sawyer. "How did you survive?"

Sawyer planted a hand on her hip. "As the Elite came to me, Elaine struggled against the ones holding her and that created a diversion. I was able to get free and run. But I was wearing an exploding cuff on my wrist, and when I got far enough..." She gestured to her empty sleeve, and Shiloh could figure out the rest. "They must have assumed I was dead. I *should* have been dead. By the time I remembered anything, it was days later, and I woke to the news that you were all... all dead. Somehow, you and Nic had gotten separated from Paul and the Howells. You'd told Nic to hide because you were such a smart girl and you always protected her. But the Elite must have found you because you were... you were gone. We never found your body, but the Elite left us a clear message. The Sanders were all dead."

A tear escaped, making a path down Shiloh's cheek. She swatted it away before Sawyer could catch sight of it in the dark. How long had it been since Shiloh last cried for her parents? Probably since she was a little girl, before she'd grown too tired of being locked in the Repentant Closet. But now the grief felt raw like the loss had happened only seconds ago.

Sawyer sat in silence, shifting only the slightest amount, but the whine of the bedsprings gave her away. What should Shiloh say? To this stranger whose pain looked quite like her own?

Before Shiloh could decide how to fill the silence, Sawyer climbed to her feet and headed toward the door. "I want to show you something. I'll be right back."

While she was gone, Shiloh took the opportunity to chase away a few more pesky tears, to breathe slowly in and out until her emotions receded behind the walls she'd built—the place where the grief couldn't touch her. When Sawyer returned, Shiloh stood near the window, watching a few lanterns bob as a guard patrolled around the perimeter of the lodge.

"Here." Sawyer stretched out the object in her hand.

A book.

Shiloh took it gingerly. Sawyer reached into one of the many pockets on her baggy pants and pulled out a small flashlight. In the new light, Shiloh could take in the book. The gray leather cover had worn into a smooth, suede texture as it aged. The yellowed pages waved along the edge and curled at the corners.

"It was your father's," Sawyer explained. "He was always writing in journals. He had many, but this is the only one I have. I think he'd want you to have it."

Shiloh blinked hard. *Froq.* There came the heat of tears again.

"Did he sing?" Shiloh asked, running a finger over a corner of the journal. "My dad, I mean."

Sawyer's lips pulled into a small smile, the first Shiloh had seen. "All the time. He sang you to sleep every night."

Shiloh sniffed, and—unable to help it—wiped a hand over her eyes. Sawyer shifted uncomfortably and then gestured to the journal. "If you open it, I have a picture of Elaine."

I don't want to... I can't....

But Shiloh flipped the cover open anyway. The picture sat on the front page, just over the scrawl of a signature. Alec Nicolas Sanders. Two girls stood side by side. One must have been Sawyer, over thirty years younger, and dressed in long black robes and a silly puffed hat with tassels. Elaine stood beside her. The two sisters looked similar. Same long black curls; same dark, dark eyes. But where Sawyer's smile was subdued, Elaine's dominated her face, shining from within. Where Sawyer's curls were carefully contained in her cap, Elaine's sprang wildly about her head.

Shiloh searched her mother's face, trying to find something familiar. But more importantly, trying to find bits of herself. The eyes were obvious. The blackness of her hair, definitely. But that was where the similarities ended. Elaine was beautiful, the kind of beautiful that didn't quite seem real. Her passion shone through the picture. She felt strange and foreign as a woman in a magazine, and yet Shiloh ached to meet her, to know her. She wanted more than just the memory of the smell of pinecones.

"I'm sorry I don't have pictures of your father," Sawyer said.

Shiloh only nodded and closed the book, offering it back.

Sawyer shook her head. "Like I said, you should keep it."

Maybe Shiloh should have insisted Sawyer take it back, but she didn't want to. She clutched it between her hands. "Thank you."

Sawyer shifted back and forth on her feet, her gaze sweeping through the room, tracing the paths of moonlight that slipped into the window and draped across the floor. "I was wondering..." She stopped.

"Yes?" Shiloh asked.

"May I—" She hesitated, shifting anxiously once more. "May I hug you?"

Shiloh stiffened. Affection from strangers was not something she was comfortable with, but Sawyer was her *aunt*. She had loved Shiloh all her life, even though she'd believed Shiloh dead for most of it.

Shiloh nodded. "Okay."

Sawyer stepped forward hesitantly, wrapping her arm around Shiloh's shoulders loosely. When Shiloh stretched her arms around Sawyer, her embrace tightened until it nearly hurt. But it didn't feel suffocating. It felt *safe*. Shiloh inhaled and breathed Sawyer's love in deep.

A scent filled Shiloh's nose. Like the lullabies her dad used to sing or the sound of her mother's voice, it was distant, quiet, but familiar.

Sawyer smelled just like crushed pinecones.

The thud of the journal as it slipped from Shiloh's hands drew them apart. She hurried around Sawyer to where the book had dropped, scooping it up like Shiloh used to scoop up Willa after she fell. The picture had fluttered out of the book. Sawyer bent to pick it up, while Shiloh reached for another folded paper that had fallen from the pages.

Curious, Shiloh unfolded it. Her heart stilled in her chest.

"I forgot I put that in there," Sawyer said, thrusting out a hand.

Shiloh gazed for one long moment at the picture of Councilor Bennett kissing his guard. Then she folded it up, rose to her feet and returned it to Sawyer. "Jake gave you that." It wasn't a question.

Sawyer tucked it into a pocket of her vest. "Yes."

"Why?" Shiloh asked, though she knew exactly why Jake had done it. He'd wanted to help ROGUE since the moment he knew they'd existed, but she wanted to hear it from Sawyer.

The woman from moments ago—who'd hugged Shiloh so fiercely—had disappeared within a heartbeat. Sawyer was back to being the commander, her back straight, her face blank, her tone emotionless. "He offered to be a spy for ROGUE."

A rush of emotion warred in Shiloh's head. Concern, pride, and hope all vied for position. It was a tremendous risk, but Jake was only himself if he was rebelling. And more—If he spied for ROGUE, he'd remain close to Sawyer. Which meant he'd form a bridge back to Shiloh.

"And what did you say?" Shiloh asked.

Sawyer lifted a shoulder in a shrug. "I said no."

Shiloh flinched. She hadn't expected that. "Why?"

Sawyer watched her for a moment, not answering, like she already knew Shiloh wouldn't like the answer. "Because he's an Osgood."

In the silence that fell between them, the wind outside wailed through a crack in the window, curling around Shiloh's skin with the same chill that now streamed through her veins.

"Did you say that to him?" Shiloh hissed, her voice equally cold.

Sawyer didn't answer. She didn't need to. Those words—those

unforgivable words—would have eviscerated Jake. Jake, who'd dreamed of helping ROGUE since the moment he'd learned they existed, rejected because he couldn't escape the shadow of a man he both loved and despised.

"Jake is *not* his father," Shiloh said, her hiss turning into a snarl. "He is good and kind and just. He would do anything to see Arcadia fall."

Sawyer's eyes narrowed. Just a fraction, just enough to show the anger rising within the commander. *Shut up,* some part of Shiloh ordered. The one that was used to being silent and telling others what they wanted to hear. Shiloh ignored it. No more good girl. Not for Arcadia, and not for ROGUE either.

So, instead, Shiloh lifted her chin and added, "It's a stupid decision, not accepting his help."

"Your opinion is noted," Sawyer said. "But it's my decision to make."

Shiloh opened her mouth, prepared to argue, but Sawyer had already turned. "Good night, Shiloh," she said, a second before she closed the door behind her.

TWENTY-FIVE

"Shiloh, it's time to wake up," Nic said, shaking her gently. Shiloh cracked her eyes open, surprised at how much sunlight poured through the window. Shiloh sat up, but then clutched the sleeping bag to her chest. The fire in the hearth had turned to embers, and a stiff winter chill awaited her outside the warmth of the bed. Nic was already dressed in layers, twin blond braids peeking from her knit cap.

"You need to eat breakfast," Nic went on. "We're leaving in two hours."

"Leaving?" Shiloh repeated. Steeling herself, she slipped out of the bed. She could feel the cold wood through her socks.

"We're going to a different camp," Nic explained. "Sawyer and Brooks don't want to stay here in case the Elite are trying to track us."

Shiloh picked up her shoes, but they were still damp and stiff with snow.

"I think someone is working on something better for your feet," Nic said.

Shiloh nodded and didn't put her wet shoes on. She waited for Nic to head to the door, but Nic didn't move. She shifted her weight from foot to foot, staring somewhere past Shiloh's shoulder.

"Shiloh, uh…"

Shiloh raised an eyebrow, waiting.

"I think I should tell you that…" Nic clenched and unclenched her fists. Her face flushed a blazing red. "Well, when I said goodbye to Jake, when I escaped the school—"

"You kissed him," Shiloh finished for her.

"He told you?" Nic asked, her voice almost squeaking.

"Of course, he told me." Jake had admitted it over the tablet at the hospital within a few days of the kiss. He'd acted ashamed, reassuring Shiloh he felt nothing other than friendship with Nic. If he'd expected Shiloh to be mad, he'd been relieved, because she had only shrugged and said, *"Okay."*

"I'm really sor—"

Shiloh held up a hand and sighed. "This really isn't necessary, Nic."

"It is, though. I'd never do anything to hurt our friendship. I don't know why I did it."

Shiloh did. Nic had seen the side of Jake that few people got to see, the side Shiloh saw: the Jake who was behind the mask and puppet strings. And if Shiloh—with her bruised, cold heart—couldn't help but fall for him, how could Nic resist? Nic, who was passion and warmth and goodness.

But ultimately, how Nic felt didn't matter, because Jake loved *Shiloh*.

Shiloh rested her hands on Nic's shoulder. "Stop. There's nothing to forgive."

Nic blinked rapidly, and Shiloh knew it was more than relief that made Nic's eyes momentarily glaze over. She quickly spun around and led Shiloh down the stairs, back to the lobby. Shiloh pretended she didn't see the way Nic swiped at her cheeks.

Nic's heart had not been the only one Jake had ever broken,

but it was the only one Shiloh felt any regret for. But Nic would survive. She'd survived so much worse.

The lobby buzzed like a hive, people squirming this way and that, gathering supplies and stacking them by the door. Nic weaved expertly through them, toward the fire at the heart of the room. Shiloh started to follow, but a voice called her name.

Shiloh turned.

The woman in the mauve hijab approached Shiloh with a bundle of cloth in her hands. Shiloh's stomach lurched into her throat. Yousef's wife. What had Nic called her?

"I'm Fatima," she said, stopping before Shiloh. Her honey-hued eyes bore red at their edges, but otherwise, she did not look like a woman who'd just lost her husband. She seemed serene, stoic. "I'm sorry we didn't get the chance to meet yesterday."

I'm the one who should be sorry, Shiloh thought, but she couldn't bring her lips to form words.

"Here," Fatima offered the bundle in her hands, and Shiloh took it. "I know you came here with nothing but the clothes on your back. You look to be about my size, but we can adjust anything if needed."

It felt heavier than mere cloth, and as the bundle shifted, Shiloh realized a pair of boots sat within the clothes.

"The boots may be a bit big," Fatima added apologetically. "But Yousef always said that he had small feet. His one imperfection, he'd always joke." Fatima gave a smile at that, and it was both happy and profoundly sad. A glistening of tears formed in her eyes.

"I'm sorry," Shiloh finally managed. "I'm very sorry. I wish he hadn't come."

"I'm *not* sorry. Sawyer didn't force us. Yousef chose to go because that's who he is—who he *was*." A diamond of a tear rolled down her cheek, sparkling in the faint light. Fatima swiped the back of her hand across each cheek and blinked furiously until the dampness in her eyes disappeared. "He would have wanted someone to go if it was one of our children. And if he had not gone, then... well, he would not be my Yousef."

Shiloh swallowed hard against a lump forming in her throat. She didn't know what to say. She remembered watching Jake get shot by Elite #111 and the fear that he was dead. The very seams of her soul had ripped open. If that was anything like what Fatima felt, Shiloh didn't know how the woman was upright, except that she had remarkable strength.

"Let me know if you need the clothes altered," Fatima said, her voice thick. "If you'll excuse me."

Shiloh let out a breath of relief when Fatima walked off. She turned to catch up with Nic, who now sat on a couch near the fireplace, holding a bowl and spooning a thick substance into her mouth. The warmth of the fire soothed the chill on Shiloh's skin.

"Good morning, Shiloh," said the young man with glasses from where he sat on the stone hearth. A little boy sat beside him, looking at a worn picture book upside down. The man picked up a bowl from the floor and ladled a spoonful of oatmeal from the pot that hung above the flames. He offered the bowl to Shiloh. "It's not much, but I try."

Shiloh set down the bundle of clothes in a nearby chair and took the bowl, staring down into the globs of white. "Thanks, uh—"

"Charlie," he said, squinting between the wire-thin glasses as he smiled. He gestured to the boy beside him. "And this is Ezra. Say 'hi', Ezra."

Ezra looked up from the book to Shiloh. Realizing there was a stranger in his midst, he promptly stuck his thumb in his mouth, clambered onto Charlie's lap, and buried his face in his chest.

"He's shy," Charlie said softly, rubbing circles on the boy's back.

"It's okay," Shiloh said. She stared at the back of the boy's dark head. In another life, that boy would have been destined to be a

Haven, but here he was, free of that cruelty. Clearly loved. A small miracle.

Shiloh spooned some oatmeal into her mouth. It was dry, but a touch of sweetness graced her tongue. Cinnamon, maybe.

"Well?" Charlie asked.

"It's not bad," she said. "I've had worse cafeteria food at school."

"Oh, I remember," Charlie said with a laugh.

Shiloh studied him. He was young enough that he certainly could have attended an Arcadian school. So how had he gotten here? Everyone here had to have a different story, something that had brought them to ROGUE. Maybe, like Nic, they'd been born into it, but likely many had run away from Arcadia, choosing a life on the run over a life of chains.

And this was *her* life now.

Shiloh looked around her as she perched on the edge of a chair, the oatmeal slowly warming her stomach. She watched Ali, Luca, and Mick, stacking cans of provision near the door, Fatima giving orders to her children, and Wallace in a chair nearby reading a book to another little girl. This life of frequent moving, of constant danger, of death waiting around the corner... it was not a perfect life, but it was an honest life. There were no masks here. No chains. This life was a life of choices, something Shiloh had never had before.

And even though she missed Jake so much she felt it with every exhale, like a permanent hitch in her side, she was grateful that her life of pretending was done. Now all that was left was for her to decide what to do with this new life before her.

What would you do, Jake had asked on the rooftop only three days ago, *if your life wasn't already decided for you?*

"Nic," Shiloh began, pushing the last ball of oatmeal around the bowl, "who trained you to fight?"

Nic paused, the spoon in her mouth. She dropped it in her bowl and said, "Mostly Paul, though my dad did some too."

Shiloh nodded and stood. She handed her bowl to Charlie with a "thanks" and crossed the room to where Paul stood.

"Paul?"

Both Paul and Brooks turned.

Paul gave her a warm smile, more visible in his eyes than in his beard-covered lips. "What can I do for you?"

"Teach me to fight," Shiloh said. It wasn't a request; she didn't want to give him the opportunity to say no.

A more solemn look replaced Paul's smile, but beside him, Brooks folded her arms over her chest, looking amused.

"I suppose we'll have to," Paul said. "You have to be able to defend yourself."

Shiloh nodded, but it was more than that. She had a promise to keep.

Jake will never forgive you, she'd told Councilor Osgood, *but I'll be the one to make you pay for it.*

"So, you'll teach me?" Shiloh pressed.

Paul nodded. "Of course. Though Brooks here" —He inclined his head toward the woman beside him— "is far more skilled than I am."

Shiloh cocked her head. Beside Paul, Brooks looked like a small child, not even coming up to his chest. Still—looks could be deceiving.

"I was in the Arcadian Armed Forces," Brooks explained, her amused smile flickering out like a light.

Shiloh swallowed as she pictured Brooks in the fatigues the Armed Forces wore. The army was separate from the Elite, who exclusively hunted heretics, and from the Protectors, who patrolled the streets and enforced common laws. The Armed Forces protected Arcadia from any outside force. They were the reason that no compassionate country would dare come after Arcadia for the crimes it had committed against its own people. The Armed Forces were well-trained, heavily armed, and ruthless.

Brooks went on like she felt she had to explain, "I was eleven at the time of the Sundering, and I was... impressionable. My parents drank the medicine the Council offered like it was the draft of immortality. So, when I got put on a Military Track at one of the early Arcadian schools, I was eager to serve my country, but it turns out I didn't have the stomach for what serving my country actually meant." A shadow crossed her face, and she shook her head, her long braids swaying with the movement. "I stayed for far longer than I should have, was trained and made into a soldier. Into a killer, really. But then, long, dark story short, I couldn't anymore. I deserted. Went AWOL.

"I was on my own for a bit, and then Alec and Elaine found me. I thought they'd hate me for what I'd done in my past, but... well, Alec and Elaine weren't exactly the hating type." A tone of admiration crept into Brooks's voice, followed quickly on its heels by a tone of sadness. "They were good people, your parents."

"The best," Paul agreed, beneath his breath.

Better than me, Shiloh thought. She, herself, carried plenty of hate within her. Not for Brooks, who'd questioned and run from the horror she'd been forced into, but for Beck, and Samuel Osgood, and Silas. Hate boiled so hot within her, she thought she'd breathe fire.

Shiloh pushed the thought away and asked Paul, "Who taught you to fight?"

"Your father did," Paul replied. "Before the Sundering, he served in the United States Navy as a specially trained soldier they called a Navy Seal. I was only a boy, several years younger than you now, when Alec found me—about six months after the Sundering. My family, well..." He coughed. "Arcadia didn't need much reason to come after people who looked like me if they didn't fall in line."

Shiloh swallowed. His skin was a rich black—just like Hope. It had only taken one small mistake, the tiniest act of heresy, and they'd sent her to a prison camp. Hope hadn't even been worth the effort of sending her to a Reform home.

Brooks nodded her agreement, showing she knew personally.

She'd been given a track of honor in Arcadia, but only because she and her entire family had fallen so perfectly in line. It had been a tremendous risk for her to run from the army. She had to have known, if she was caught, there would have been no second chances.

Skin darker than white received no mercy in a world that didn't tolerate differences.

"Alec took me in," Paul continued, "and trained me. He made sure everyone in ROGUE was trained, and I've just passed down what he taught me to Nic and to others who've joined ROGUE."

Shiloh looked between Paul and Brooks. "So, you'll train me? Both of you?"

"It'd be my honor," Paul said.

"Of course," Brooks said, one corner of her lip flicking upward. "In fact, I'll give you your first two lessons now." Brooks stepped closer to her. "Are you ready?"

Shiloh nodded, listening closely.

"Lesson #1." Brooks held up a finger. "Never let down your guard."

Shiloh nodded again. That seemed rather obvious.

Brooks flicked up another finger. "And two..."

Shiloh never saw Brooks move. But one moment, Shiloh stood, and the next, her back slammed into the ground with a thud that made the room fall silent. All the air left her lungs. Shiloh dragged a breath through her teeth. Even that hurt.

Somewhere, someone barked with laughter, and somehow, Shiloh knew without looking it was that boy, Luca. She twisted her head to the left, but instead of seeing him, she saw Sawyer. She frowned, as though disappointed. The heat of shame licked at Shiloh's cheeks.

Brooks leaned over Shiloh, filling her vision, an amused smile on her face. Brooks wiggled two fingers. "Lesson #2: Always watch your feet."

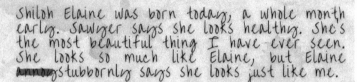

April 7, 2093

Shiloh Elaine was born today, a whole month early. Sawyer says she looks healthy. She's the most beautiful thing I have ever seen. She looks so much like Elaine, but Elaine ~~annoys~~ stubbornly says she looks just like me.

Maybe it's the ~~mix~~ blend of us weaved together in her that makes her so ~~ama~~ extraordinary. Whatever the case, she is perfect. I didn't know something so little, so tiny could take up so much room in my heart, but there's no doubt.

She owns every bit of it.

Shiloh took a breath, fighting against the waves of emotion crashing in her chest, and closed her father's journal. The truck vibrated and swayed as it struck a bump on whatever road Brooks steered it down. Shiloh leaned her back against the crate of provisions strapped to the wall, steadying herself so she wouldn't slide into Nic who sat beside her.

The Sparrows had left the lodge an hour ago, carrying their provisions on a makeshift sled down the slope and loading everything they possessed into the back of the box truck. Brooks and Paul had taken the cab of the truck, but everyone else sat in clusters. A lantern had been fastened to the inside roof, swaying in circles and flaring light around, enough that Shiloh could make out the words of the journal if she squinted. But those who sat in the corners of the trucks became only shadows.

In one corner, Fatima comforted her three children. Their sobs had turned to sniffles now, mourning that they'd left behind the place where they'd buried their father. In another, Becca, Ezra, Charlie and Mick formed another group of shadows—Ezra being lured to sleep on his sister's lap, Charlie and Mick sitting in silence, their hands entwined between them. Ali's laughter floated from where he and his brother sat on a stack of luggage. Wallace and Amelia sat side by side across from Shiloh and Nic. Amelia pretended to listen to Wallace's jabbering but glanced frequently at her daughter.

And then there was Sawyer. She sat on Shiloh's other side. The light swayed back and forth across her face, which remained unreadable as she glanced toward Shiloh every few minutes.

"What do you think?" Sawyer asked, gesturing with her chin at the journal in Shiloh's hands.

The emotions within Shiloh's chest were too numerous to name, and she'd never been good at putting what she felt into words. She was even worse at trusting people with those emotions. Shiloh ran a fingertip along the inside of her arm, feeling the prick of stitches that Amelia had placed after cutting out Shiloh's implanted ID before they left. Apparently, Amelia had learned quite a bit from Sawyer before Sawyer had lost her arm.

Shiloh spoke at last, replying to the question with a question. "Is my birthday April 7th?"

Sawyer nodded.

"Not March 28th?"

"I'm certain of the date. I was there."

Shiloh nodded. She shouldn't be surprised. Arcadia had taken her parents from her, her last name, her past. Why not her birth-date? It'd help hide the fact that they'd let the Sanders' child live, and it wasn't so large of a difference that they'd have to work hard to convince a six-year-old, not when they'd erased her memories. Not that birthdays were even celebrated in the Haven.

No, that didn't surprise Shiloh. What did surprise her was the significance of the date.

"April 7th is Jake's birthday," Shiloh said.

Sawyer fiddled with a zipper on her vest. "Yes, I recall a news story about his birth—the grandson of Councilor Jacob Osgood. You two were born on the same day."

Shiloh tried to imagine it. Reagan Osgood and Elaine Sanders —two women destined to be enemies—laboring to give birth at the same time. Reagan had likely been in some hospital, pampered with the best care, while Elaine had only Sawyer in whatever camp they'd been in—an abandoned building, a tent, a barn? It was as though Shiloh and Jake's fates had been bound together as they both came screaming into the world within hours of each other, even though they were born worlds apart. By all rights, they should have been enemies, but they had become something else entirely.

Something impossible.

Shiloh flicked open the journal to the last page, where she'd carefully taped Jake's note. *Forever.* She could almost hear him whispering that word he'd written, the way he'd whispered it against her ear on the roof, vibrating against her skin, coiling deep in her stomach. Shiloh shook the feeling off, lest she combust in front of everyone.

I have to burn it all down first, the note said.

Me too, Shiloh thought. *I have to burn it down.*

"Sawyer," Shiloh asked, "what do you plan to do with the picture of Councilor Bennett?"

Beside her, Nic shifted. Her head had listed against the crate, balancing on the edge of sleep, but now she drew herself up, listening.

Sawyer drummed her fingers on her thigh, her long legs stretched out in front of her. "I'm not sure yet."

"I think you should do what Paul said," Nic said. "Distribute it. People deserve to know the truth. And, like Jake said, truth is dangerous."

"You were supposed to be sleeping," Sawyer said flatly, barely glancing at Nic. "Which probably means you overheard everything."

Nic squared her jaw, not flinching. "I did."

"I agree people deserve to know," Sawyer said. Around her, Shiloh noticed other conversations were fading, the lantern catching the whites of eyes as they shifted toward their leader. Perhaps they had all heard about the picture, too. "But the reality is, even if we found a way to distribute the picture into the hands of citizens, the United Council will simply report that it's fake. Digitally created."

Wallace tapped his fist lightly against the metal floor of the truck; it made a *tsk, tsk* noise like the cluck of a tongue. "The people in power will always tell their lies, but it doesn't make speaking the truth any less important. Those with willing eyes will see the truth. Everyone else will choose to remain blind, but it's a choice everyone should be allowed to make."

"And what would you suggest?" Sawyer swept her gaze around to include everyone, an invitation into the conversation. "What do you think we should do with them?"

"We could make copies," Nic said quickly. She'd obviously been thinking of this. "And then we could post it around major cities, on major roads and stuff."

Shiloh's heart picked up in her chest at the thought, imagining citizens, walking on their morning commute on a street lined with the image. She was sure it wouldn't take long for Protectors to rip the picture down, but not before people saw. And if they saw, people would speak. Sure, the media could report it was all a lie, but if it happened in multiple cities throughout Arcadia, it would instill doubt.

And doubt was a seed that grew and grew until it eroded the walls it had been planted in.

Sawyer cocked her head back and forth, showing she was considering the idea. "Most major cities have strict curfews. Anyone out at the time would be questioned. It'd be dangerous."

Shiloh's heart hammered even louder now, picking up a steady rhythm until it sounded like a war drum. "It wouldn't be impossible," Shiloh said. A crooked smile curled onto her face. "Not if they can't see you."

Sawyer frowned, but Nic shared Shiloh's grin, understanding.

From the corner, someone scoffed. *Froqing Luca.* "And what? You have some kind of incantation for invisibility?"

"Not an incantation," Shiloh said. "But a little bit of science can be a magic all its own."

TWENTY-SIX

T he door to the end of the box truck scrolled open with the thundering of metal. Shiloh stood on aching legs, cramped from the long journey. It had been uneventful, but the length had been tedious, and Shiloh suspected Brooks had done a lot of maneuvering to ensure they were not being followed or to avoid being spotted. She stretched out her sore legs and arms as others jumped off the end of the truck. When Shiloh got to the end, Luca offered his hand from where he stood on the ground. Shiloh ignored it and jumped down, steadying herself on the bumper as she sank deep into snow.

She searched around her. The truck had been pulled into a thick grove, its headlights still casting light on the trees that surrounded it. Shiloh saw Mick and Charlie steer past a line of trees, each carrying a slumbering child in their arms. Becca had fought sleep, but finally succumbed just like her younger toddler brother.

Shiloh followed them, sliding in Yousef's old boots. She stepped out of the shadows of the trees and into moonlight as the line of trees gave way to an open field. In the silvery light of the nearly full moon, she could make out four small homes that bore cracked windows and fallen gutters. In the snow that surrounded them, she could see heaps of rubble peeking out from the white, where perhaps more homes had once been. Far past the homes, Shiloh thought she could see the glistening ice of a lake.

"I need to go check the houses," Mick said, casting a soft look down at Ezra. Both of Charlie's hands were already filled with Becca.

"I'll take him," Shiloh offered, holding out her arms.

Mick grunted, which Shiloh took as gratitude, and he carefully transitioned the boy into Shiloh's arms. Ezra's head lulled against her shoulder, heavy with the pull of sleep, but the weight of a slumbering child was a familiar one. Shiloh thought of Willa and Zyla, the weight of them, but she quickly shook the memory away.

Mick drew his gun and a flashlight on his side and approached the nearest house.

Luca joined him before he made it to the door. They didn't have to push hard for the door to come open. Through the cracked windows of the homes, Shiloh watched the beam of Luca and Mick's flashlight move through the home, searching each room. A minute or two later, they exited the house and moved on to the next.

"What was this place?" Shiloh asked Charlie.

"Native lands," Charlie replied. Becca whimpered softly near his shoulder, and Charlie stroked her back, making soothing noises, before continuing. "These lands belong to the Ojibwe. But after the Sundering, they were driven out, pulled apart from their families and scattered across the states. Forced them to assimilate, and if they refused... well, we all know what happens if anyone refuses Arcadia. History... history has a way of repeating itself, I suppose."

She took in the man, as best she could in the bright moonlight, the golden tone of his skin, the shine of emotion in his eyes. Charlie's tone suggested he knew that same pain in a visceral way—like this wasn't someone else's story he was telling.

He saw her looking, the unasked question in Shiloh's expression, and nodded. "My mom was Ojibwe. She married a white man, my father. We always lived off these lands, but there was something that changed in my mother after the Sundering. I don't think life here was ever perfect or even easy, but at least it was... something. A connection. I don't know." Charlie sighed as he watched Mick and Luca moving from the second house to the third. "I was only five when it happened, and I don't really remember much. But I remember the way the light dimmed within my mom, the way I could sense that we'd both lost something immensely important. She'd tell me stories about our people, our beliefs, our culture, telling me she didn't want me to forget."

A shadow passed over Charlie's face. The wind blew through his sandy hair; the same wind nipped at Shiloh's skin. She shivered and adjusted the hood of Ezra's coat over his ears, before tucking her nose in the scarf about her neck, the one Fatima had given her.

"I didn't forget," Charlie added after a long moment of silence. "When Arcadia forced me to go to a boarding school a year later, I told everyone—my friends, my roommates, my caregivers all about the stories my mother had told me. And when I went home for Christmas, only my father was there."

Shiloh shivered, this time having nothing to do with the cold. She didn't need to ask what had happened to his mother. "I-I'm sorry."

"Me, too."

Silence fell between them, the voices of the other Sparrows and the crunching of snow drifting from behind them as they unloaded the truck.

"Okay, enough sad stories," Charlie said, shaking his head and forcing bravado back in his tone, "when there're so many more exciting things to talk about."

"Like?"

"Like Jacob Osgood." The way Charlie said Jake's name reminded Shiloh of Demi, her ridiculous, gossip-loving Haven sister. Like a squeal hid beneath his voice. "Does he look as good in person as he does on television?"

Shiloh bit her lip to withhold a surprised laugh. The question might have been annoying from anyone else, but it came as a profound relief. Clearly, not everyone in ROGUE hated Shiloh's boyfriend solely based on his last name. Charlie gave her a wink, like he knew. Like he wanted Shiloh to know she had an ally, a friend.

Shiloh let out a breath of relief. "Jake looks even better."

"I want to hear everything about you two, just don't... uh... tell Mick I asked."

Shiloh smiled. "I won't sa—"

A yell ripped through the night air, coming from the fourth and final house.

Followed by a gunshot.

"Mick!" Charlie yelled, plopping Becca down so quickly Shiloh had to grab her arm to keep the half-conscious girl from falling. Charlie tore through the deep snow, toward the final house, pulling a gun from his belt.

From behind, several others ran out of the trees: Paul, Amelia, Nic, and Brooks. Paul, Amelia, and Brooks paused by Shiloh to appraise the situation, but Nic flung herself past Shiloh and after Charlie.

"Nic, wait!" Amelia called, running after her daughter.

Charlie was still twenty yards from the house, when Luca and Mick stumbled out and they were... *laughing?*

Mick held something up between them. Beady, now-dead eyes caught the glow of the flashlight. A freshly shot racoon, dangling by its tail from Mick's fist.

Charlie slowed to a halt, gasping for breath. His voice drifted back to Shiloh. "Mick, what the fuck?"

"Little bastard scared the shit out of me," Mick replied.

"Not as bad as you scared him, though," Luca said, and all three of them laughed.

Shiloh began to breathe again, relieved Ezra hadn't woken in the confusion. Becca blinked around her, dazed. Paul released the strangled grip he'd had on his gun as Amelia grabbed Nic's arm and dragged her back, lecturing her about mindlessly running into danger.

"Oh good," Brooks said, with a huff of a laugh, "looks like we have breakfast."

◈

As it turned out, Brooks wasn't joking about the racoon. The next morning, Shiloh found it roasting on a spit above the fire pit someone had built in the early morning hours in the center of the four houses. Now-empty crates, large stones, and a couple of logs circled around the flame. Shiloh settled on one log, Nic collapsing beside her with a yawn.

It had been a late night of unloading provisions and preparing the homes to accommodate sleep, gathering wood for the wood-burning stoves in the living rooms of the homes. The homes were small and cramped, and so they divided into two of the homes. Soon, they discussed, they'd divide into all four homes, but with it only being February and the wind chills dropping below zero, it was easier to warm two homes instead of four. Shiloh had slept, barely able to move between Sawyer and Nic, but at least with so many bodies in one place and the stove burning, the chill finally left her bones.

Thick lines dragged beneath Nic's eyes. Besides the late night, Nic had also had guard duty with her mother. Everyone, except Shiloh, took turns guarding, two hours at a time.. But Shiloh knew this wasn't the only thing that led to Nic's exhaustion. Last night, Nic had trembled in her sleep, kicking Shiloh awake once. Shiloh didn't have to ask who haunted Nic's dreams. Likely the same man who sometimes haunted hers.

When everyone had arrived at the fire—everyone except Sawyer, Shiloh noticed—Charlie sliced and divided the raccoon among all of them.

"Don't worry," Nic reassured Shiloh. "It tastes like chicken."

And it *did* taste like chicken—chicken which had sat for two days in a bowl of grease prior to being cooked. But chicken all the same.

As they ate, Brooks gave them all assignments for the day. A life like this meant there was constant work to do, and they all seemed used to Brooks assigning jobs. Mick and Charlie would work on breaking the ice at the lake to get water. Paul would go hunting for game and take Ali and Amir with him. Amir needed more training in hunting, and Ali was apparently a "really great shot." Nic and Luca would work on putting tarps over the cracked windows of the homes. On and on the jobs went, from preparing meals to gathering or cutting wood. Even Wallace, who seemed almost too frail to do much of anything, was charged with looking after the youngest children in one of the homes.

Everyone had their role. Except Shiloh.

They all scattered, one by one, until at last, only Shiloh and Brooks remained.

"What about me?" Shiloh asked. "I can help."

"You're training with me," Brooks replied. "Let's go."

She turned and traipsed toward the nearest house, gracefully stepping in the footprints others had left to ease her way through the snow.

Wiping her greasy fingers on her pants, Shiloh rushed to follow Brooks, who lead her behind the first house. A wooden deck stretched off the back, one rail sagging, a few boards missing. Brooks stepped onto it and gestured for Shiloh to join her.

Shiloh's foot slid as it made contact with the deck, and she seized hold of the railing to keep from falling. The railing shuddered beneath her grasp but kept her on her feet.

"You've got terrible footing," Brooks observed dryly. "Before you learn anything else, that has to be fixed. You lose your footing and end up on the ground, then you're dead. Understand?"

Shiloh nodded. "And I have to learn it on ice?"

"If you can hold a fighter's stance on ice, you can hold it anywhere. Now, chin up, shoulders back, feet apart."

Brooks spent the next several minutes critiquing Shiloh's posture, adjusting her feet, her hips, her spine; all to the exact right angle. The ice complicated the task. Every time Shiloh moved the slightest, her feet wanted to slide. Her angle would change and Brooks would make her start all over again. At some point during this time, Luca and Nic had come with an armful of tarps and worked on sealing up the windows along the back of this house. Shiloh tried to ignore them, but she was aware of them both occasionally glancing her way—watching, judging how much she struggled with this simple task.

Finally, Shiloh thought she had it. Brooks cocked her head from side to side as she studied her. She circled around Shiloh, taking in every angle. Shiloh forced her breathing to be still, afraid even too large an inhale might throw her from the position.

"Not bad," Brooks admitted at last. "Not great, but something we can build on."

Shiloh's lips twitched. She'd take it as a victo—

Brooks's boot locked onto Shiloh's ankle. By the time she registered it, there was no time to move. Brooks jerked Shiloh's leg out from under her. She slammed down hard onto the wood and ice.

A bark of laughter from Luca felt colder than the ice that now dampened the layers she wore. Shiloh gritted her teeth as she stared up at the hazy, grey sky far above.

"And just like that," Brooks said, leaning over her with a look of disappointment on her face, "you'd be dead."

The rest of the training went about as well as it started. Brooks led her through a few rudimentary fighting motions and critiqued every angle of motion, making Shiloh repeat every move until each was 'almost perfect' and then several more times. Through it all, Brooks chose random moments to knock Shiloh's feet out from under her. She did it so swiftly Shiloh only saw it coming once, but when she attempted to jump back, she slipped on the ice and fell anyway.

The look of disappointment deepened on Brooks's face, and Shiloh could almost hear what she was thinking:

I expected more from Alec and Elaine's daughter.

By the time lunch came around, every muscle ached and every patch of skin felt tender and bruised. But after lunch, Paul had returned from a successful hunt, Ali having brought down an elk. And it was now Paul's turn to train her.

He made her do sprints through the deep snow and led her through a series of strength-training exercises, like he was the most brutal gym teacher.

"There's more to being a soldier than just throwing a good punch," he'd said.

She'd never complained, gritting her teeth when both her once-broken leg and clavicle ached. Only when she thought she might collapse with the next step did Paul let her sit and rest near the fire at the heart of camp.

Though snow had settled into Paul's beard, he acted like he didn't feel the cold. Shiloh, however, felt like it had settled into her bones. She hovered her fingertips above the flame as Paul walked her through the components of a handgun and then a rifle.

"Will you teach me to shoot?" Shiloh asked.

"Eventually," Paul said with a little quirk of his mouth. "One step at a time."

At last, he dismissed her with a chuckle. "At ease, soldier."

Shiloh limped toward the house she'd slept in the night before. The door's handle was broken, and it stood slightly ajar. Voices floated out, and she paused when she heard her name.

"And what about Shiloh?" Brooks asked.

"Paul and Amelia will look after her." Sawyer's voice rang out in its usual flat monotone. "She'll be safer here."

"Speaking of Shiloh," Brooks said, and then her voice raised, "I know you're standing there. Come inside."

Shiloh didn't ask how she'd known. They didn't survive in the wilderness by not being hyper-aware. Shiloh slipped in. Sawyer kneeled on the floor before her backpack and a stack of dried provisions. Brooks stood over Sawyer, arms crossed. They watched Shiloh as she stepped toward them.

"You're leaving," Shiloh said. Not a question.

Sawyer nodded. "If we're going to distribute the picture, I need to get other factions to agree to help."

I, not *we*. Not that Shiloh needed the distinction after what she'd overheard. This woman—her aunt—had just met Shiloh, after years of thinking she was dead, and was leaving her behind. Maybe Shiloh should feel something about that, but she didn't. Or maybe she did, but she did what she'd always done before with things she didn't want to feel.

She buried it so deep she could pretend it didn't exist. Perhaps her walls hadn't completely crumbled, after all.

"Do you have everything you need?" Brooks asked, an edge to her voice.

Sawyer glanced at the provisions near her. "This should be enough to get me to the next faction. Thank you."

Brooks gave a tight nod, then swung on her heel. She whipped her knit cap from her pocket and yanked it over her ears before stomping back into the snow.

Sawyer climbed to her feet, looking oddly tired as she turned to Shiloh.

"When do you leave?" Shiloh asked.

"In the morning. At first light. If you make a list of the materials you need for the invisibility jackets, I'll find a way to get them and send them back."

"I'll get them made," Shiloh said.

"Thank you." Sawyer lifted her hand, hesitated, and lowered it onto Shiloh's shoulder. For an awkward moment, they only stood, like Sawyer couldn't decide whether or not to hug her. Shiloh ended it by stepping away. Whatever closeness she'd felt that first night had cooled when Sawyer had spoken sharply about Jake, the mask of the commander returning.

She was a stranger to Shiloh. Nothing more.

Sawyer took a careful breath. "Paul and Amelia will look after you. You'll be safe here... or as safe as anyone can be in ROGUE."

"I'll be fine," Shiloh said. "I'm good at surviving."

TWENTY-SEVEN

"Well, look what the big smelly cat drug in," Stefani said, as she opened the door to her dorm room at Ardency. She leaned a hip against her doorframe and folded her arms over her chest, looking Jake up and down. "You still look like something the cat should have left in the litter box. But that's hardly different than usual."

Jake's lips twisted, a half-wince that turned into a full wince when his bruised cheeks pulled. Five days and a doctor to set his broken nose later, and it still froqing hurt. "Can I come in? To work on the project?"

Stefani lifted one eyebrow, and he tried to signal with his eyes. *Play along.* She glanced toward the bodyguard who stood behind Jake, towering like an engulfing shadow. Stefani barely missed a beat and opened the door wider.

"I swear, Osgood, if you get us stuck with a lousy grade like last time, I'm gonna tell the whole school you like to wear girls' underwear."

Jake chuckled as he entered the room. "They just have so many more color and trim options."

Stefani clutched the doorknob with nails painted her classic don't-froq-with-me red. "Is your friend coming?" She nodded her head to the bodyguard.

The bodyguard said nothing, his lips transforming to one hard line.

"Nah," Jake said.

Stefani slammed the door shut, whirled around, and pressed her back against the door like she was barricading it against an evasion. "What the froq?" she mouthed.

Jake put a finger to his nose. "Mind if I put on some music? Helps me think." Without waiting, he walked to the small white box sitting on her desk. With a few clicks, it boomed to life, filling the room with a pounding rhythm and bursts of light. No words filled the melody. Good. Jake couldn't have stomached the Arcadia-praising themes that usually filled Codex-approved music.

Stefani approached Jake so she could lower her voice beneath the wireless speaker's pounding. "What in sweet biscuit-eating Kentucky is with the suit?"

"Apparently, you get kidnapped one time and your parents decide to have you monitored 24/7." And Jake hadn't been able to argue. Playing fearful of what had happened to him would help his goal. Throwing a fit about being spied on would only raise suspicion.

"So what? They're going to follow you around everywhere?"

"One of them even followed me into the bathroom."

"Newbie." Stefani rolled her eyes. "Do you want a drink? You look like you could use one." Before he could reply, she kneeled beside her bed and pulled out an emerald bottle and two wine glasses from beneath.

Jake glanced around the room. "Where's Val?"

Stefani's feet faltered for a moment as she returned to the desk. "Val is—" She set the glasses down beside each other, grabbed a wine opener from her desk drawer, and screwed it into the cork as she searched for the right word. "Well, she's—" The cork popped up, the noise hidden beneath a loud boom of music.

"She's turtling," Stefani finished at last, pouring the two glasses.

"She's what?"

"Turtling." Stefani mimed a domed shape above her head—a turtle shell, Jake supposed. She held out a wine glass to Jake, and he hesitated before taking it. "You know, when a turtle senses a threat, it hides in its thick shell and refuses to come out."

Jake swirled the crimson liquid, staring into the whirlpool. When was the last time he'd had alcohol? Probably at the beginning of the school year when he'd tried to numb the pain of losing Shiloh behind a fuzzy brain and girls who couldn't compare.

"Val's hiding from you?" Jake asked,

The sip Stefani had been taking of her wine turned into several large gulps. She licked the residual from her lips. "She won't even respond to my messages."

"Why? What happened?"

"Shiloh happened."

The reminder landed like a physical blow. Jake winced. "So, she's hiding from the pain?"

Stefani nodded, glaring at the floor.

Turtling. Now, Jake understood. Hiding from everything behind a shell until you believed nothing could hurt you. When in reality, the pain was already inside the walls. Shiloh sometimes did that, too. It wasn't fun being on the outside looking in.

"She'll come around," Jake encouraged, though he wasn't sure he believed it.

Stefani shrugged. "She generally does. But when Hope was arrested, it only took her two years to speak to Shiloh again."

And like Hope, Val must think she'll never see Shiloh again. Shiloh likely felt the same. The thought of Shiloh dealing with the grief of losing someone else she loved made the hole in Jake's chest burrow even deeper. It was already cavernous—a great, empty space where Shiloh should be, a place that bled and echoed. He missed Shiloh so much it hurt to breathe.

"Hey, you okay?" Stefani said, setting her wine down on her desk.

Jake set his glass down as well, untouched. "Yeah, I'm fan-froqing-tastic."

Stefani laid a hand on his shoulder, giving it a gentle squeeze. "I'm really sorry, Jake," she said, so low he barely heard her over the pounding music. "I'm sorry you lost her."

Jake whipped away from her touch. "I didn't lose her!" he snapped, louder than he meant.

"Okay, okay. Froqing *chill*!" She glanced at the door and then gestured to her music box. Catching the movement, the machine turned the volume up.

"I didn't *lose* her," Jake repeated, less loud. "I'm going to get her back."

Stefani picked up her glass of wine and swirled it toward him extravagantly. "Tell me, sir knight. What is this great plan you have to rescue your fair lady?"

Jake stepped closer until he and Stefani stood only a hand's-width apart. "I'm going to expose all of the United Council's dirty secrets."

Stefani snorted. "Seriously? That's what my mom has been trying to do since before I was born."

"Not rumors, Stefani. Actual evidence."

"My mom hasn't been able to dig up much evidence. They keep all that close."

"Exactly. *I* can get close. They've all known me since I was born." His tone grew insistent, a pleading sewn into it: *Please believe me.* After Sawyer's rejection, he needed someone to believe in him.

It seemed strange to be in this position. Up until a couple of months ago, Stefani was a royal pain in his endsphere. But here he was... needing her. Because, without her, he couldn't pull this off. But more importantly, he *really* needed a friend.

"I've already given evidence to ROGUE," he said.

Stefani's eyes sparked, the gossip's interest perked. She jumped up to sit on the edge of the desk, swaying her feet like a little kid. "Oh? And what is this juicy piece of truth you've been hiding?"

He told her, and she spat her sip of wine back into the glass. "E-excuse me. What?"

She looked like she might drop her glass, so Jake took it from her and set it on the desk.

"So, it's not a rumor then?" she asked.

"No, it's not a rumor."

"Froq," she murmured. She stared at the holograms of pulsating rainbows dancing around the room. The delight at the scandal faded from her face, leaving her brows knitted together.

"What?" Jake asked.

Stefani hesitated, twirling a now-pink strand of hair around two fingers. "I don't care that Councilor Bennett is gay." She sighed softly. "I'm glad *he* gets to be with the man he loves. It just seems so..." She sniffed, turning her head swiftly and blinking carefully. Jake pretended not to see the sheen of tears she clearly didn't want him to see. "So froqing unfair."

"It's really froqing unfair." Jake's stomach twisted in sympathy, but before he could decide the best way to comfort her, Stefani brushed the side of her hand across her cheeks and tipped her head back to let the rest of the wine run down her throat.

She set her face in her usual cat-who-ate-the-canary expression. "What are they going to do with the picture?"

"I don't know yet. They hadn't decided. Expose it... somehow."

"And you're going to get more?"

Jake nodded.

"And give it to them?"

Jake stiffened. "That's where I'm not sure. Sawyer made it quite clear that ROGUE has no desire to work with an Osgood any further."

Jake realized too late that he hadn't used Sawyer's codename, but no confusion crossed Stefani's face, so she must know who he was talking about.

"She said that?" Stefani asked, wrinkling her nose. "That's *rude*."

Jake lifted one shoulder. "It doesn't matter. I'll find a way to expose it... even if I have to do it on my own."

"Hey." Stefani poked his leg with her bare toes. "You're not *alone*."

A bubble of hope ballooned in Jake's chest.

She held up her finger. "I mean, first I want to say, for the record, that I think you've gone utterly insane. But, not gonna lie" —A slow smile took over her face— "I kind of love it." She poured herself another glass. "All right, let's hear it, Jakey-boy. What's the plan?"

Jake lowered himself into the desk chair beside Stefani, and she leaned her ear close to hear him. "First chance I get, we hack into my dad's computer. He must have all sorts of things hidden in that thing."

Stefani scoffed. "And probably about thirty-five layers of security to get through. Not to mention any important files are going to be encrypted. Did you become a computer scientist while you were kidnapped or some—" She stopped, her jaw dropping. "Wait. Did you say *we*?"

"You just said I wasn't alone."

"That could have meant anything, Jake. It could have meant I supported you emotionally—that I'm rooting for you. Like, yay, go, Jake!" She pumped a fist in the air. "But you just *assume* I'm going to help you hack into a Councilor's computer?"

Jake rolled his eyes. "Are you in or *not*?"

"Well, of course, I'm in, prighead." She huffed. "I'm just mad you *assumed*." She hid her impish smile behind her glass. "But that's just your father's home computer. I'm not convinced there will be much on it. What comes next?"

"Next, I apply to be a United Councilor's summer intern. It'll give me access to the Unity Center and the Councilors."

"You think you'll get in?"

"My dad has basically been holding a spot for me since I was born."

"But after all the ordure you just pulled? Surely at least Madison Beck suspects you've gone heretic."

This time, Jake couldn't hide his cringe, because that was what he'd realized, after Sawyer had rejected him. For his plan to work, he'd have to regain the trust of the Councilors. "It means that, from here on out, I have to... behave."

More than that, he'd have to seal on the mask the Council expected him to wear, so they saw exactly what they wanted to see from him. Someone who regretted they'd ever had any association with ROGUE. He'd have to pull off the masquerade performance of a lifetime.

Stefani blinked at him. "Jakey-boy, are you telling me you're going to be a good boy? However will you survive?" Jake flipped her off. She stuck out her tongue. "You think you can convince them?"

"Stef, I've danced to their puppet strings all my life. All I have to do is convince them I still move to them."

"But you won't." Stefani lifted her glass in a cheering salute. "Not anymore."

"No," Jake agreed, raising his own glass to clink against hers. "Never again."

"Hold the presses, ladies and gents," Stefani announced grandly. "Jacob Osgood is a real boy now!"

PART THREE
MASQUERADE

WE ALL WEAR MASKS,
AND THE TIME COMES
WHEN WE CANNOT REMOVE
THEM WITHOUT REMOVING
SOME OF OUR OWN SKIN.

— ANDRE BERTHIAUME

TWENTY-EIGHT

TWO MONTHS LATER...

*D*ing, ding, ding!

The fork clinking against the champagne glass chimed throughout the ballroom. All around the Osgood ballroom, the buzzing of conversations faded, and everyone's attention turned toward the center table, where Samuel Osgood now stood, his champagne glass raised.

Jake adjusted his smile as the spotlight of the room fell upon him. A camera shaped like a golden balloon floated closer to their table, picking up his father's voice and making it resonate through the crowd.

"Thank you, everyone, for joining us to celebrate the eighteenth birthday of our son." Samuel lifted his glass higher. "I know it means so much to myself and my wife to have you here." He gestured to Jake's mother, who beamed a radiant smile up at him. It was the most affection Jake had seen exchanged between the two in the short time he'd been home from school over the weekend.

Polite applause tapped through the room, and Jake lifted a hand in a wave. *Smile pretty. Smile pretty.*

His parents had spared no expense for the party. Black and gold decor draped across the ballroom. Foil balloons bearing the numbers '18' floated everywhere, sparkling in the late afternoon sunlight that poured through the wall of windows. Jake was accustomed to extravagant birthday parties, but this one outdid them all.

Compensating for something...

"Well, it's not every day you turn eighteen," Samuel had explained.

But Jake saw through it. This birthday was a message, a show. Polishing the Osgood family until it once again gleamed in the light. *See, look at us. The Osgoods: strong, powerful, beautiful, happy. Oh, those rumors that one of our relatives betrayed us and was convicted to die before escaping? Total hogwash!*

Already this evening, Jake had watched his mother lie through a brilliant smile when someone asked, "Where's that brother of yours?"

"He was unfortunately unable to join us," she said, her smile never wavering.

Unfortunately, Jake had thought, *he isn't dead.*

Of course, it also meant Jake's aunt and cousins were missing, but Jake tried not to think about that, lest it crush something in his chest.

State Advocates, Councilor Bennett, Councilor Beck, and so many other well-connected individuals filled the tables around the ballroom. Few guests were Jake's own age. Even fewer were people he considered friends. Well, actually, there was exactly *one*. From where Jake sat, he could see Stefani sitting with her mother and father a few tables over. For once, her auburn hair did not contain a colored streak, but she made up for it in her outfit: a long jumpsuit striped with vibrant shades of pinks, yellows, and oranges that combined to make her look like a fiery sunset. The front of it angled down her chest in enough of a scandal that the elderly ladies in attendance had clucked their tongues is disapproval any time they fluttered past Stefani's table.

As Samuel droned on, Stefani caught Jake's eye. She stuck a finger down her throat, faking a gag. Jake bit his cheek to keep from laughing and tucked his head down so the camera didn't capture the amusement flickering over his face.

Thank his lucky stars for Stefani. He wouldn't have survived these last two miserable months without her. She'd kept him in line, reminding him of his ultimate goal, in the moments he missed Shiloh so much he thought he'd go insane from the longing. Without Stefani, he would have run away weeks ago to find Shiloh in order to relieve the pain that resided permanently in his chest.

"Jacob."

Jake fixed a smile back on his face as he lifted his head to look at his father.

Samuel held his glass out to him. "Jake, I have been so honored to be your father. I'm so proud of the man you've become."

Yeah, I sincerely doubt that.

But Jake only said, "Thanks, Dad." Despite his quiet tone, the microphone on the balloon-camera picked his voice up, so everyone heard it anyway.

Play the part.

Jake stood from his chair, lifting his own glass of nonalcoholic wine. "And thank you to every single one of you. Long live Arcadia!"

The entire room lifted their glasses and echoed his cheer. He drained the entire glass, but it didn't wash away the sour taste the words left curdling in his mouth.

The waiting staff wheeled in a cart bearing a massive-tiered cake. Then it was time for Jake to blow out his candles. The waiters served the cake, and then the dancing began—opened, of course, by the Councilors in attendance. Jake's parents seemed stiff as they swung across the dance floor. This was the first time Jake had returned from school since his kidnapping, but he could tell.

Even if Mr. and Mrs. Osgood put on a good show for everyone else, something was amiss. Clearly, his mother hadn't forgiven his father any more than Jake had.

Jake glanced over to Stefani once more. She cocked her head toward the door and mouthed, "Ready?"

Jake shook his head. If he left now, someone would notice his absence. "Soon," he mouthed back.

When his parents returned to the table, Samuel pulled out Mom's chair before sitting down himself. Jake watched as more couples swung onto the dance floor.

"You should dance, Jake," Samuel said, lifting his fork and stabbing at the cake before him. "Katerina Beck is here." He nodded toward the table where Madison Beck and her husband took their seats. Her granddaughter sat across the table from her, next to her bald-headed father. "I'm sure she'd appreciate being asked."

Jake's hand froze, the bite of cake an inch from his lips. He forced himself to shove it into his mouth. Chew it. Swallow it. Buying time. The sweet icing turned to ash on his tongue. Once again, like dozens of times before, Samuel pushed Jake toward Katerina. The only difference now: Jake *knew* it wasn't merely his father's foolish hopes. It was iron-clad reality. Seven years from now—maybe even sooner given Katerina was two years older than him—Jake would receive his marriage decree, and Katerina's name would be on it. He felt it—that same anger he'd felt when he'd learned the truth. His blood turned to a boil, sending liquid fire through his veins.

Breathe, Jake, breathe. Be a good puppet.

"Well?" Samuel asked.

"Enough, Sam," Mom said, so quietly she barely moved her lips. "It's his birthday. He can do what he wants."

"It's fine," Jake said, as he pried himself out of his chair. Then he forced himself to add more enthusiastically, "Dad's right. What kind of host would I be if I ignored a pretty girl in need of a dance partner?"

Jake forced himself to weave through the tables toward the Becks. The conversation came to a lull between the four as his shadow fell over the table.

"Hello, Councilor Beck," Jake said. Greeting her took effort. Every nerve in his body, already rattling with anger, screamed at him to release his rage. He slipped his hands deep into his pocket, so he wouldn't be tempted to flip over the table. He moved on quickly. "Mr. Beck." He nodded to both men sitting at the table—father and son. And then, finally, Jake looked to the other side of the table and forced his smile to widen for her. "Katerina."

Beck's granddaughter swiveled her green eyes up to him and offered a manufactured smile, the perfect amount of teeth showing through her painted-red lips. She'd swept her scarlet hair to the side and tucked a white flower where it gathered. The blue satin of her dress dipped the right amount of low for an esteemed young woman—low enough to promise, but high enough not to tease. Shiloh had been right about Katerina. She was, objectively, beautiful. Anyone who wasn't completely blind could see it. But Katerina wasn't *Shiloh*.

It was like comparing a candle to a wildfire.

"Thank you all so much for coming," Jake said.

Councilor Beck's smile was as synthetic as her granddaughter's, but her lips curled thin. "We wouldn't have missed it."

It took all of Jake's will to not let his smile collapse. Was there any truth to what he'd overheard during his mother and father's conversation at the hotel in Chicago? Had Beck ordered Shiloh's kidnapping? And what about Silas? Had Beck orchestrated his escape? And, if she had, why had she done it? What was her goal?

Dangerous. That was what it was.

Beck was a dangerous woman, an alligator camouflaged as a harmless log along the shore. The rest of the Council feared her.

Jake wasn't sure why, but he was froqing going to find out. One of the secrets that he intended to expose.

"You've grown so much, Jake," Beck said, bringing her glass of wine to her mouth. "I remember when you were born. Your grandfather was so thrilled. Time surely does fly." She sipped her drink.

"Yeah, it does." Jake shifted his gaze to Katerina. "Could I have the privilege of this next dance?"

Katerina glanced toward her grandmother, who gave the smallest of nods.

Permission asked. Permission granted.

"I'd love to," Katerina said, like she might have meant it.

Jake offered his hand, and she took it. He led her onto the dance floor, picking a spot where both his father and Beck could see him. He laid his hand on the slant of her waist, slid his other hand through hers. As he pulled them into the steps of the dance, Jake kept as much distance between them as he dared without making his resistance obvious. Some small amount of rebellion against the destiny forced upon him.

As they swayed, a golden balloon-camera floated closer. Surely, Jake and Katerina would be the subject of some cute e-magazine piece. He could see the headline now: *Prince and Princess of Arcadia. Is this the start of a budding romance?*

Jake breathed in to calm his nerves, but his nose flooded with vanilla and roses. Katerina's scent was much too rich, the opposite of the fresh, natural scent that clung to Shiloh's skin. The thought made him ache, a twist of the knife buried in his heart.

Froq, I miss her. I miss her. I miss...

"So, what happened to her?" Katerina asked, tilting her head back to look up at Jake.

The question yanked his tie tighter, strangling him. "Who?" he asked, the sound almost a pained exhale, even though he knew exactly *who.*

"The girl from the Yuletide Ball."

Jake expected her to add, *You know, the Haven girl*. But she didn't.

"It's, uh... It's complicated."

"Are you two still together?"

Froq... his tie was getting tighter by the second. He wanted to rip it off, rip off the tight-collared shirt, too. Rip off his skin, even, and keep going until he found the knife twisting into his chest so he could make it stop.

"No," Jake said, unable to keep his voice from sounding thick. "No, we're not."

"I'm sorry." Katerina sounded like she meant it. "You seemed like you really liked her."

Jake nodded. He tightened and then loosened his jaw, hoping that the emotions blazing in his chest didn't make it to his face. He lifted his arm and let Katerina spin beneath it, giving him a moment to take a breath.

"It's difficult, isn't it?" she said, when her hand returned to his shoulder.

"What is?"

She pulled herself near to him, angled her mouth toward his ear, dropped her voice low. "When you want something you're not supposed to want."

Jake stiffened.

"Trust me," she said softly, squeezing his shoulder. "I know."

Jake's mouth opened, unsure what to say.

"You should dip me. Your father is watching, and he'll like it."

Jake dipped Katerina down as the song reached its crescendo, her hair flaring toward the ground in a red arch. He brought her up slowly, trying to read her face. But it remained as serene as always. She wasn't unreadable, not like Shiloh. Instead, her face seemed to show exactly what she was. Sophisticated. Well-mannered. The blood of a Councilor. But in all the years of avoiding her like he avoided every expectation, Jake had never dared to ask himself if perhaps she wore a mask like his.

She smiled and stepped back. "Do you think we appeased them, or should we dance again?"

"Hey, Jakey-boy!" a voice popped by his ear, and he jerked in surprise.

Stefani. Thank froq.

Jake stepped back, and Stefani propped an arm on his shoulder, leaning on him heavily. She looked Kat up and down, a bemused expression on her face. "Hey, Kat. Long time, no see. I love your dress, by the way."

"Thank you." Katerina gave her a gracious smile. "Stefani Andreou, right?"

Stefani blew a bubble of gum and popped it as she replied, "*Yep.*" She pulled the gum back into her mouth. "Mind if I steal a dance with this loser? I've been told that I can't just sit in the corner pouting, and it's either him or ol' man Advocate Stewards, and just between you and me"—Stefani leaned closer to Katerina, shielding her lips behind her hand—"he doesn't know where to put his hands."

Katerina blinked at Stefani, her eyebrows knitting together. Stefani had that effect on people. She was a bizarre, unsolvable puzzle.

"Of course," Katerina said after a beat, gathering her grace around her like she gathered her skirt in her hand. "Thanks for the dance, Jake."

"You're welcome," Jake said.

Katerina glided back to her table.

The strange encounter with Katerina lingered like a spiderweb on his skin. Jake shook it away. It was irrelevant if she, too, felt trapped in a stage performance she'd never agreed to. With any luck, it would be Yuletide before he'd have to see her again. And maybe... maybe... he'd have lit the whole froqing world on fire by then.

Jake let out a breath, running a hand through his hair. "Thanks for saving me."

"What?" Stefani said, turning toward him and setting a hand on his shoulder. "You mean, you *weren't* enjoying every moment with your betrothed?"

Jake glared at her. "Don't joke about that."

"I've always been curious. Does she come with a dowry? How many pigs did your dad barter for her? Or did she require a few horses?"

Jake gritted his teeth against the desire to snarl something unkind back.

Easy, Jake, she doesn't know it's not a joke.

"Move your feet, Jakey-boy," Stefani said, kicking at his foot with one of her spiked heels. "It's like dancing with a statue."

Jake took Stefani's hand and forced himself into the steps. He glanced around the room and back toward his parents. His father stood from the table, turned, and sauntered toward the ballroom door. His mother, however, watched Jake and Stefani with a look of curiosity.

Stefani moved her hand from Jake's shoulder to his bicep. She squeezed it and gave a fake squeal of surprise. "Jake, is that a muscle I feel under here?"

"Shut up," Jake hissed.

The last thing he wanted was his mother to get the wrong idea of who Stefani was to him. But Stefani, predictably, did not shut up.

"All that time in fight club has paid off."

"You're a pain in my endsphere, you know that? And it's not fight club."

Though it wasn't *too far* from the truth. Since returning to school, Jake had convinced the school to take him out of his other sports and allow him to take up training with those on a Military track—stating that his father wished it. And what Samuel Osgood wished for happened. The switch meant demanding workouts and training for hand-to-hand combat. Each time Jake sparred with another fellow student—frequently having his endsphere handed to him—he remembered the female Elite who'd pinned him to the ground like he was a weakling. He'd drive himself harder, and then spend hours of free time in the gym, pushing his body as hard as it could go. Because he swore to froq, he'd never feel that powerless again.

Jake snuck another glance at his mother and found her sweet-talking Advocate Stewards. Somehow, she hid her cringe.

Maybe the birthday boy wouldn't be missed now.

"You ready to sneak out of here?" Jake asked, pulling Stefani closer so he could keep his voice low.

Stefani scoffed like it was a stupid question. "I've *been* ready. You're the one who's been slow about it."

"Ten minutes and then meet me outside." He smiled, and for the first time tonight, it felt real. "It's showtime."

TWENTY-NINE

"Steady now," Paul said lowly from beside Shiloh.

They laid side by side on the cool, damp ground, the tall grass rising high above their heads. The rain from last night soaked through Shiloh's pants and tight black jacket. She blocked it all out. The chill. The wet. Paul's watchful eyes. She focused only on the steel of the rifle in her hands and the three deer who grazed only twenty yards upwind from them.

"Still have it in your line of sight?" Paul asked, studying Shiloh's hold on the rifle.

She squinted through the rifle's scope, adjusted her aim slightly until it lined up with the tawny flesh of the doe nearest them. She nodded.

"Good. When you're ready, exhale and take the shot."

Shiloh took a breath. *Breathe in. I won't miss this time. Breathe out.* She pulled the trigger.

No matter how many times she fired the rifle, the power amazed her. It exploded in her hands, kicked back against her shoulder. The boom awoke the quiet field around them, startling birds out of the line of trees behind Shiloh. Two deer raced forward. The one Shiloh had aimed for buckled, then took after its herd, dragging a leg behind it.

"Froq!" Shiloh said.

Paul leaped to his feet and swung his own rifle toward the retreating doe. *Boom!*

The doe crumpled into a heap. As Paul approached it, Shiloh climbed to her feet. She looped the rifle—the one she'd borrowed from Mick—over her shoulder, strangling the leather strap between her hands. She'd been training for *two months*. Two months of days full of shooting and hand-to-hand combat practice. Two months of having her endsphere handed to her—by Brooks and Nic and Luca and Paul and Ali. Two months, and Shiloh *still* couldn't bring down a froqing deer.

Paul glanced from the lifeless deer back to her. "Well... at least you wounded her. That's improvement."

Not good enough.

Compared to Brooks, Paul was the gentler trainer, the encourager, the enforcer of good habits. Brooks was the one who still knocked Shiloh on her endsphere at moments she didn't expect—standing in line for supper, walking to her house. She occasionally dodged Brooks, but most of the time, Shiloh ate dirt.

"Fucking Christ, girl, when are you going to learn the most basic of lessons," Brooks always said, not trying to disguise her disappointment.

Shiloh saw the same disappointment reflected in the eyes of anyone who'd known her mother and father. She could almost hear them thinking: *Are you sure she's really the Sanders' daughter?*

Paul drew his knife from his belt and handed it to Shiloh. "Want to do the honors?"

Shiloh took the knife. This was yet another thing she'd been learning since they'd arrived here. Gone were the books of sciences and math that had once been her hopes of survival. Now, survival meant fighting, hunting, and scavenging, and she'd had much to learn. She could now recognize which plants were safe to eat and which would kill you, how to make fire and shelter, and perhaps most importantly, how to send messages through the ROGUE network.

Charlie had taught her that. He had a mind for the hundreds of codes that ROGUE used—different ones for different days. Different radio stations, too. Shiloh had watched him translate messages like it was plain English and not what had sounded to her as gibberish coming over the radio. Shiloh worked to memorize them all, and that, at least, came a little easier. Brooks had even let her take apart a radio and put it back together to show her what made it different from other radios, that allowed them to transmit and receive unique signals that weren't picked up by Arcadia. Shiloh had, at least, been able to do that. Perhaps, in one way, she was like her mother.

After skinning the deer and packing up the pieces, Shiloh and Paul headed back to camp. They trampled through the tall grass and back through the woods toward camp. They'd been out all day, looking for game, and now the last rays of scarlet sunlight slid toward the horizon. As the sun faded, it took with it the early spring warmth that had felt sweet against Shiloh's skin after such a long winter.

Despite the fading daylight, the camp buzzed like a hive of worker bees, as it always did. Currently, Fatima hung one last load of washing on the lines strung between the homes, with the help of her eldest two children. Others marched around the parameter standing guard. The tale-tell crack of an axe hitting wood as someone prepared more firewood behind one of the houses.

Paul stopped near the great firepit at the center of the homes. A foot-high wall of stone was built around it. The fire within burned high, awaiting dinner to be cooked. As they approached, Charlie rose from the log where he sat, moving the bouncing Ezra off his knee. Ezra wrapped one chubby hand around Charlie's pant leg.

"Did you get something?" Charlie asked, his eyes sparking bright behind his glasses.

Paul let the bag fall at Charlie's feet. "A whole deer."

Charlie clapped his hands. "Fabulous. Did you get it, Shi?"

Shiloh's hand tightened around the rifle strap once more. She shook her head.

Someone snorted behind her. "Did you at least stay on your feet this time, Princess?"

The hair on the back of her neck stood on end as she faced Luca—like an aggravated cat about to face a dog. He towered above her, the faintest of sneers twisting on his lips. In the two months she'd known him, she'd learned that Luca wasn't a guy of many words, but when he spoke, she often wished he hadn't.

"Yes," she snapped. He'd been there to witness the first time she had fired a rifle, and the recoil had sent her straight to the ground.

"She even clipped it," Paul said, with a smile.

"Did you?" Charlie asked. "See? You'll get it next time."

He clapped her on the shoulder affectionately, and Shiloh shied away. He meant it to be congratulatory, but it only felt demeaning. It made her wish Brooks was there to tell Shiloh she couldn't bring down a deer unless it ran straight into her bullet.

Shiloh glanced around her for an escape—some excuse to get away from these three men who tormented her, even if two of them didn't mean to. She let out a breath as she caught sight of Nic coming from behind one of the houses, her arms filled with firewood. Ali trailed behind her, his own arms full, as well. Typical. That boy seemed to have chained himself to Nic's heels—following after her like a lost puppy—but Nic was as oblivious to him as she was to her own shadow.

Nic caught sight of Shiloh and picked up her speed. When she was still a few feet away, she announced, "Sawyer's back."

Shiloh swallowed. "She is? Since when?"

Nic let her arm of wood fall near the fireplace. "About an hour ago." She started to form a pyramid of the wood next to the fire pit, using Ali's own stack without glancing at him. "She wants to see you."

Oh, does she really? Shiloh sucked the words back down her throat, not letting the skepticism reach her lips. "Where is she?"

"In our house with Brooks," Ali replied.

The Sparrows had since divided into all four homes: Amelia, Paul, Shiloh, and Nic in one; Mick, Charlie, and the Singer siblings in another; the Qadirs and Wallace in the third; and finally, Brooks camped with the brothers.

Ali nodded his head toward the smallest brick dwelling.

Without a word, Shiloh handed Paul back the rifle to return to Mick, slipped around the crowd, and headed toward the home.

Shiloh pushed past the tarp that had been hung to replace the door to this home. The few remainders of sunlight poured through the cracked windows, shadowing the living room in a soft grey. Brooks sat with her legs crossed beneath her in an ancient, dusty armchair, and Sawyer and Amelia sat on the sagging, torn couch, bent over at the paper Sawyer held in her hands.

At the sound of Shiloh's footfalls, the three women turned their heads.

"Shiloh." Sawyer's lips twitched in the whisper of a smile, as she rose from the couch. "How are you?"

"Fine." Shiloh hesitated a few feet away, and they stared at each other for a long moment.

Sawyer had stayed true to her promise, ensuring Shiloh had the supplies she needed for the Cloaks. Sometimes the provision came through the ROGUE network, which must be deep and extensive. Someone would drop them in the nearby woods for the Sparrows to find. Twice, though, Sawyer had returned herself. It wasn't only supplies for Cloaks, but also provisions the Sparrows needed— medicine for Wallace, clothes and boots that actually fit Shiloh, ammunition. Both times Sawyer stayed only a day or so, leaving with completed Cloaks to distribute to other factions. Each time she returned, though, this first awkward moment stretched on between them, waiting to see how Sawyer would react. Would Sawyer hug Shiloh this time? Take even a step closer? But she didn't budge, and neither did Shiloh.

"Here." Sawyer held out the paper she'd been holding.

Shiloh approached to get a better look and her breath caught.

The fliers were complete. And they were beautifully reckless. Bright red words of defiance were printed below the picture of Councilor Bennett and his husband: *If your love is accepted, why isn't ours?*

"What do you think?" Sawyer asked, studying her face carefully.

"It's perfect." Shiloh lifted her gaze from the paper. "Do we know when?"

Sawyer glanced at Amelia and Brooks. Even if Brooks was the official leader of the Sparrows, Sawyer and Amelia had known one another since Amelia was younger than Nic was now. In Shiloh's time here, she'd learned Amelia's story. She'd been a part of Alec Sanders' original group—members of the congregation where Alec's father had been a pastor, who Alec had fled with at the time of the Sundering. Now, the trust between the old friends, Sawyer and Amelia, ran deep.

"Soon," Sawyer said, and they nodded their agreement. "But some of that depends on you. Show me what you've been working on."

Shiloh nodded and turned around. She led Sawyer out of the house and into the backyard. A little shed, built from wood with chipping blue paint, leaned at an odd angle. With the amount of rusted gardening tools that had been in this shed previously, Shiloh suspected it had once held a small indoor garden. She pushed open the squeaking door and flicked on the solar lantern sitting on the desk near one of the windows. The light shone off the tools, metal, and glass Sawyer had scrounged up to make the cameras and projectors. A jacket hung from the corner of the desk.

"This one is almost done," Shiloh said. Her chin lifted a little higher as she spoke. No matter her failings in other areas, this was a place where she felt confident. "I should have it finished by tomorrow."

Sawyer nodded, fingering the hem of the jacket. "I brought enough materials for two more. I need all three done in a week."

"A week? That's pushing it—"

Sawyer turned to face her, her hand planting on her hip. Shiloh let the words die on her lips, realizing this wasn't a request. It was an order by the Commander.

Commander. That was how Shiloh thought of the woman. *Aunt* was merely an interesting fact that Shiloh had tucked away in the recesses of her mind.

Shiloh nodded. "I'll get it done."

"Thank you," Sawyer said, her expression softening a little. She took a step forward, and Shiloh thought Sawyer might hug her, but Sawyer only rested a hand on her shoulder for a moment. "I have something for you."

Sawyer swung her crossbody backpack over her neck and set it on the desk to rifle through. She brought out a bundle of cloth, neatly wrapped with twine, and offered it to Shiloh. "Happy eighteenth birthday."

Shiloh took the bundle with hesitation. March had come and gone, like a breeze, with no mention of her birthday. She hadn't even thought about it because no one but Val and Hope had ever celebrated her birthday, which meant the last few birthdays had gone by without notice. But then she realized.

"It's April 7th," Shiloh said. Her *actual* birthday.

Jake's birthday.

Her chest ached at the thought of Jake, a reminder of the gaping hole his absence left—the permanent hitch in her side that prevented her from taking too deep a breath. She dealt with the pain the way she always did; she pushed it down and forced her mind elsewhere.

"It is," Sawyer said. "I know it's hard to keep track of days living like this."

It was true. One day bled into another. The date didn't matter in places like this.

"But you remembered," Shiloh said, staring down at the package in her hands.

Sawyer's lips twitched again, but this time, it didn't seem like a smile, at least not a happy one. "April 7th has been a date I've remembered every single year since you've been born. This one is the first in a long time when it wasn't a sad day."

Shiloh swallowed hard. Moments like this, she could tell how deeply Sawyer cared for her. It was all the other moments that Shiloh couldn't trust.

Shiloh pulled at the twine and unfolded the package. A gleaming handgun sat in the cloth, along with a holster and belt. The gun looked new: double-barreled, with a switch to slide between killing and stunning bullets. Shiloh trailed a finger across the polished black metal. She didn't have a gun or rifle yet. She had been borrowing someone else's for practice all this time. Even eleven-year-old Eris had her own gun here; a small thing that she kept hidden in the rolls of her skirt. Holding her own weapon in her hand sent a thrill through Shiloh's body.

A shiver of warning followed the thrill, though. A gun shouldn't make her feel powerful. It was dangerous, Paul always lectured, never to be used lightly. But maybe that was what Shiloh felt—like she was dangerous. And maybe there wasn't much difference between being dangerous and being powerful.

"Thank you," Shiloh said. She slid on the belt and holster and tucked the gun into it. The gun pulled at her side, a steady weight that she'd have to grow used to.

Sawyer nodded, then cocked her head toward the door to the shed. "Come on. I'm sure Charlie has cooked up something good."

They left the shed behind, Shiloh adjusting to the way the gun swayed with each one of her steps. The rest of the Sparrows crowded around the fire at the center of camp. When Sawyer and Shiloh turned the corner of the house and came into view, they all turned toward her. She was still ten feet away when they yelled in unison:

"HAPPY BIRTHDAY, SHILOH!"

Shiloh jumped, her heart slamming into her ribcage. The thunderous noise had been so loud a flock of birds near the lake had taken flight, squawking their furious disapproval. In the front of the crowd, Ali led the littlest children in a merry jig, singing a birthday song. Nic beamed a smile as she broke away from the crowd and looped an arm around Shiloh's.

"Happy birthday," she said again, pulling Shiloh forward.

Shiloh's heartbeat slowed to normal as Nic led her into the center of the crowd. Fatima gave her a gentle smile; Mick slapped her back so hard she stumbled; Amelia pulled her into a side-hug; Paul playfully tugged at her ponytail. Even Luca gave her a grudging smile. Brooks stood at the edge of the crowd, near where Sawyer had stopped. Brooks's arms crossed, but her lips tilted upward. When Naia, Fatima's youngest, pulled on her hand and demanded she sing, Brooks sang. Loudly and off-tune.

Nearest to the flame, Charlie waited with a pan filled with... *Is that cake?*

It had to be. Somehow, he'd made a chocolatey cake, even slathered with frosting—the thick kind that came in a can. And in the cake were birthday candles. Shiloh didn't count them, but she knew instinctively that there were exactly eighteen candles.

"Happy birthday, Shi," Charlie said, smiling softly.

A rush of emotions flooded Shiloh's chest, so many she couldn't name them.

"Go on, girl!" Wallace said, waving the walking stick he'd recently begun using to steady his weakening gait. "Blow out your candles. Make a wish."

"I—" Shiloh began, but she stopped, words catching in her throat.

She closed her eyes and pinched the bridge of her nose, the way she did when she thought she might cry.

Nic whispered in her ear, "Are you okay?"

Shiloh nodded. Her lips tried to form words, but she didn't know which ones to make.

"What's wrong, sweetheart?" Charlie asked, lowering his voice and taking a step closer so that others couldn't hear.

Shiloh hated this—feeling vulnerable. But when she opened her eyes, Charlie waited, calm and patient. Wallace cocked his head, and Nic slid her arm around Shiloh's shoulders. No one looked at her with judgment.

At last, Shiloh tried: "It's just I... well, I've... never had a birthday cake before."

Charlie's smile turned sad, not with pity but understanding. Nic rested her head on Shiloh's shoulder, pulling her close in a sideways embrace. Shiloh leaned into her in return, perhaps surprising them both.

Wallace gripped his stick tighter, shaking his head. "All the more reason you should enjoy it, girl. You deserved eighteen birthday cakes. Fuck Arcadia for taking that from ya."

The vulgar language on the old man's tongue made Shiloh laugh. The candles on the cake flickered with her breath but didn't go out. Beads of wax trailed down them, forming multi-color puddles in the frosting.

"Thank you," Shiloh said.

"Don't thank us. This is what family does," Nic said.

Family.

Shiloh looked around her, at the faces of the people she'd come to know over the past eight weeks. They looked back at her expectantly, waiting, smiling, but more than that, they looked at her... like she belonged.

Shiloh knew little about family, but she knew that family

didn't mean blood. It meant belonging. Shiloh had belonged with Val and Hope. She had belonged with Jake. And now, Shiloh belonged here—with the Sparrows.

But there were two faces missing in all those who looked at her. *Val and Jake.*

And Shiloh knew what she'd wish for.

"Hurry up," Paul teased from behind her, pulling her ponytail again. "Before the whole cake goes up in flames."

Shiloh smiled back and drew in a deep breath. Exhaling, she made her wish and blew out the candles.

THIRTY

It took a full fifteen minutes for Jake to escape from the ballroom, constantly intercepted by all the people who wanted to wish him happy birthday, or reminisce about *how the years have flown by*, or ask questions to put in a magazine piece featuring the birthday boy. Finally, Jake slipped out onto the veranda.

The sun had now disappeared behind the horizon, and the night air still clung to the memories of winter's frost. The glow from the ballroom shone across his backyard, so bright it hid the stars from sight. Jake pulled his suit jacket around himself tightly and ducked his head as he hurried away from the sounds of music and laughter. He rounded the corner of his house and slammed straight into Stefani.

She yelped, and Jake shushed her.

"You, *shh*," she hissed back, pressing a finger to her lips. "You scared the ordure out of me. And you're late."

Jake rolled his eyes. "Don't be such a drama queen."

Her mouth dropped, as she draped a hand to her chest like he'd driven a knife into it. Jake glanced around them, but they were alone in the shadows, tucked behind the tall hedges that surrounded his house.

"Come on."

Stooping beneath the top of the hedges, Jake darted below a few windows until he reached his target: the window of Dad's office. Jake had to stand on his tiptoes to pry fingers beneath the windowpane and shove it open. During the party, his father had ensured this office was locked tight, so he'd snuck in earlier to unlock the window. A camera also trained on the front of the office, which is monitored at all times by guards. This was the only means of entry into the office, but the bottom windowsill fell at the height of Jake's chin. Far too high for Stefani to make it on her own.

Jake bent and cupped his hands together. "All right. I'll boost you up."

"If you drop me," she whispered, putting her foot in his hands, "I'm going to—"

"I'm not going to drop you," Jake said.

Stefani reached for the window ledge, hoisting her other foot off the ground, still muttering under her breath. She cut off mid-word, her body going tense. "Guard," she hissed.

In the corner of Jake's eye, the light shifted.

Froq!

Jake thrust upward hard, shoving Stefani through the window. She tumbled across the sill and landed inside the office with a thud. Jake dropped onto his belly, shimmying beneath the bushes. Branches and roots clawed at his suit.

The light of the Guardian orb swept across the ground, buzzing as it scanned for anything amiss, its unblinking eye recording everything that it came across. The orbs had been added to the property after Jake's kidnapping.

After the Guardian passed, Jake launched himself upright. He grasped the ledge of the window. He was almost in when Stefani grabbed the back of his suit jacket and hauled him the rest of the way through the window with a suddenness that sent them both back to the floor.

"Peace and harmony," Stefani panted, "did you have to eat all the birthday cake?"

Jake slid the window closed. "Hurry up. We don't have much time before I'm missed."

White wood made up the office. Towering white bookshelves lined the walls of the room. Their shelves displayed a few select books and cases of rare artifacts that the Osgood family had collected through the centuries. An ivory bar displayed bottles of dark liquor, which cast long shadows in the dark. The only splash of color disturbing the white was the oriental rug lying beneath the half-moon desk at the center of the room.

Stefani plopped into the desk chair and tapped on the desk's white surface. It purred to life—the glowing outline of the keyboard forming on the wood; the screen hovering above. She frowned at the word on the screen, spinning a piece of hair on her fingertip.

Password.

"Got any hints for a password?" she asked.

"Maybe a few," Jake replied.

Stefani reached down the front of her jumpsuit and, after some maneuvering, pulled out a black metal box. She slid it open to reveal the tiniest of keyboards. "Cool. Start listing."

Jake rattled off some things—family birthdates, where his father went to college, his parents' wedding anniversary, the name Gwen.

Stefani's fingers froze, stopping her furious typing. "Wait. Who's Gwen?"

Jake swallowed. He'd never told anyone about his sister who'd been stillborn. Except Shiloh. "I'll explain later."

After he listed a few more possibilities, she opened the door in the desk that hid the components of the computer and connected the device to a port. Immediately, dots appeared in the password box on the floating computer screen. *Wrong password,* it said. Then more dots.

Wrong password.

"What's it doing?" Jake whispered, glancing toward the office door.

"Analyzing the information you gave me and working through all possible combinations." Stefani set her elbows on the desk and placed her chin in her hand, watching the screen with a bored expression as if they had all day. Jake shifted his weight back and forth. How long would they have before they were found? His father could walk in at any moment. He shifted again, back and forth.

"Okay, Mr. Fidget." Stefani shot him a glare. "Why don't you make yourself useful?"

"And do what exactly?"

"I don't know... search for secret doors in the bookshelves. Hollow books filled with dark secrets."

"This isn't a spy movie, Stef."

She flicked her fingers in a dismissive gesture. "Just do something... not here."

Jake paced away from the desk toward the bookshelves. Other than sneaking in this afternoon, it had been a while since he'd been in Dad's office. There'd been a time he'd sneak in here during the summer whenever his Dad was gone, mostly to raid the bar. But he hadn't really taken in the details since he was a boy who liked to stare at the things locked behind the glass cases in the bookshelves: an old telegraph machine; an antique compass set on a plaque that read *From the navigation panel of* The Enola Gay; the pen that Jake's grandfather had used to sign the agreement of the Sundering; a framed, aged fabric flag with a striking snake.

The few antique books nestled on the shelf bore leather-bound or worn hardbacked covers. Jake stroked a finger across their spines, just to have something to do with his hands. He glanced over his shoulder at Stefani who alternated between leaning back in the chair and tapping on the keyboard. Each second coiled his chest tighter, feeling like an eternity.

"How's it coming, Stef?"

She didn't even turn to look at him. "Found that secret passageway yet, Jakey-boy?"

Jake glared back at the books. A title in the center caught his eye, and he immediately tied it to a memory of Yuletide Eve, when he'd taken Shiloh into the library of their home. She'd spent an hour amongst the shelves of real, physical books while Jake had been content to watch her. She'd tenderly pulled books from the shelves, turned each page like they were spun gold, filled his ears with facts about this author or that classic book. Finally, she'd chosen one to carry back to his room, where she'd read to him as he held her. He hadn't understood anything she'd said, but he could have listened to her all day.

This book bore the same title as the one she'd picked out. Jake slid the book from its place on the shelf and flipped it open. Somehow, holding it in his hands made him feel closer to Shiloh. He began to read the pages, trying to conjure the way the words had sounded on her lips.

Wait. His hand tightened on the spine. *This... this isn't right.*

> *Principle #123: Marriage relationships*
> *shall be ultimately determined*
> *according to compatibility of partners,*
> *but more importantly, the benefit of the*
> *companionship in the service of the*
> *greater community.*

Jake knew those words. He, like every other child in Arcadia, had been forced to memorize and recite this principle and so many others. They'd repeat it over and over until it echoed in their heads.

This was The Codex. Then why was it covered with a different book sleeve?

Jake folded the sleeve back to look at the front cover beneath. Few physical books existed in Arcadia, but The Codex could be found in every room at Ardency. Jake recognized the red cover instantly. But the title and author were wrong.

Manifesto for a Perfect World

The One World Society

His mind spinning, Jake flipped through the next pages, pausing on the copyright page. He stared at the date until his vision blurred. Then he blinked and read it again. The Codex had been written *after* the Sundering, which had been nearly thirty years ago. But this book... it was dated over *fifty* years ago. Decades before the Sundering.

Jake flipped through the pages faster and faster, his heart racing to keep in time with the flicker of the pages. Surely, it was a coincidence. Maybe, his grandfather and the original Council had borrowed this single principle from a different book. But each page was as familiar as the last, each principle the same number he knew. This was The Codex.

And it wasn't.

What the actual froq.

"Jake," Stefani said, craning around the desk chair to look at him, "I did it."

Jake clutched the book in his hands. It had to mean something, but right now, he didn't have the time to sort it out. Jake slipped the cover back on and slid it back with the rest of the books. Later. He'd have to think about it later. He returned to Stefani's side, staring at the screen. Her hands sped across the surface of the desk.

"Now all I need to do is make a copy of the hard drive onto my device," Stefani explained without slowing, "then erase any trace I was here."

"How long will that take?"

She pursed her lips. "It depends on how up-to-date this computer is. Anywhere between fifteen minutes to two hours. Probably fifteen, though."

"We don't have two hours."

"I said *probably* fifteen."

When she'd set up the file transfer, the computer screen showed it would take twenty minutes. Twenty minutes for which Jake would be forced to sweat and watch the door, hoping that he wasn't being missed and searched for. As they waited, Jake's thoughts couldn't help but wander back to the book on the shelf.

"Have you ever heard of the One World Society?" Jake asked.

Stefani pursed her lips, twirling her hair again. "No. Why do you ask?"

Jake watched the timer on the computer counting down. Ten more minutes. "Just something I heard. Wasn't sure what it was."

The next three minutes crawled by. Footsteps began in the hallway, voices rising and then falling away, disappearing only with the boom of the front door closing behind them. Some of his party guests were leaving. Mom and Samuel were likely furious that Jake wasn't there to wish them well and wondering where he'd gotten himself off to. Jake pulled at his tie, loosening it around his throat.

Five minutes remaining, the computer screen read.

Footsteps came again, but this time they grew louder, not walking away, but closer. A cool sweat broke out on Jake's neck as the sound approached the door. With it came voices, voices he knew well.

"He's pushing his boundaries, Madison," his father said, "like every teenage boy since the dawn of time. It's nothing dangerous."

"Dissent is *always* dangerous," Beck replied, her voice cold and hard. "Dissent is gasoline. If even a little is in the air, a single spark could set the world on fire."

Jake's breath stalled in his chest. Stefani glanced to Jake, her eyes wide.

Samuel's response was too low to be heard, but Beck's voice thundered her command, "Handle your son, Samuel, or I will handle him for you."

Footsteps sounded again, the crack of high heels on wood floors, carrying Beck away. Jake glanced at the computer screen. They still had ninety seconds until the transfer was complete.

The door handle jiggled; metal scraped as a key slid into a lock. The noise screamed in the silence.

"Jake, what do we do?" Stefani hissed.

Froq, froq, froq.

Samuel was going to find them. What possible explanation could Jake give to him about this?

And they still needed thirty seconds.

Jake glanced at Stefani, and the idea hit him. He grabbed Stefani's wrist and pulled her out of the chair. He spun to take her place in the chair and then yanked her back down onto his lap.

"What are you *doing*?" she said in a low squeal.

"Shh," Jake said, pulling her against his chest. "Just go with it."

The door creaked open.

The file transfer dinged as it completed.

Jake jerked Stefani's device from the computer and tucked it into the pocket of his suit, even as Stefani twisted just enough to shut down the computer with a few quick pushes of the button.

The door opened fully, and Samuel stepped into the room. Stefani and Jake both jumped to their feet. Samuel froze in place, looking between the two of them.

Jake forced a sheepish smile, sweeping his hand through his hair to hide how it trembled. "Uh... hi, Dad. Sorry, um, Stefani wanted to see granddad's pen from the Sundering agreement, and I thought I'd show it to her."

Stefani didn't miss a beat. She even managed a flush of embarrassment, though maybe it wasn't faked. "I just love history, you know. And, uh... um, you have a really lovely office."

Samuel looked between the two of them. Jake knew the conclusion Samuel was coming to and knew he'd seen Stefani sitting in Jake's lap. To his credit, Samuel remained perfectly calm. The only thing that gave him away was the faint purple tinge to his ears. What was making him angry? That Jake had been making out with a girl in his office, or the fact that the girl wasn't Katerina?

Or maybe that he feared Jake had heard what Beck had said.

"Stefani Andreou, right?" Dad asked at last.

"Yes, s-sir," Stefani said, with the perfect fake tremble in her voice.

"I think your parents are about to leave."

"R-right, I'll just get going," Stefani said, already rushing toward the door.

"Sorry, Dad," Jake said, faking a chagrined smile. Then he hurried out the door and down the hallway, after Stefani's retreating back.

The hall outside the ballroom was crowded with people now, waiting for their cars to pull up. Jake and Stefani hurried past them and ducked into the first door Jake knew would be devoid of people. Which happened to be the same broom closet Stefani had pulled him in during the Yuletide Eve Ball.

Jake pressed his back against the door. Gasping like she'd run a marathon, Stefani sagged next to him.

"Oh, sweet froqing harmony." Stefani held a hand to her chest, where her heart likely slammed against her ribcage, like Jake's own hammered at his. "That was close."

"Too close. Good thing I think quick on my feet."

"Oh, and about that." Without warning, she punched his arm. Hard. "That's for putting the moves on me, sicko."

"It was an act," Jake said through his teeth, rubbing his arm. "And it worked, didn't it?"

She shrugged. "I suppose."

Jake's breath returned to normal as he pulled the device from his pocket and handed it to Stefani. "So... what do you do with it now?"

Stefani held up the device, staring at it like a puzzle she couldn't wait to solve. "I start searching for buried treasure."

THIRTY-ONE

Work. Froq you, work!

Shiloh pressed the button on the jacket once more to turn the cameras on. Patches of fabric remained visible, while most of the garment disappeared. She gritted her teeth as she flicked the button off. Why wasn't it working? She went over it all once more. The position of the projectors? Check. The connections between the cameras and the projectors? Check. Then the problem must be within an individual projector, a component failing to launch? The only solution was to pull each projector apart and check the small components within it. But that would take hours... hours she didn't have if she was going to meet Sawyer's deadline.

Shiloh sank heavily back in her chair, rubbing fingers over her aching eyes. The sweetness of her birthday cake had long since faded from her tongue. What time was it? How long did she have before morning arrived, and Brooks woke her for drills or practice? It didn't really matter. If she was going to fulfill Sawyer's command, Shiloh couldn't afford the luxury of sleep.

Val's voice rang in her ears. *Pull it together, Starchild. You're embarrassing yourself.*

Shiloh often conjured the voices of those she'd left behind, a way to keep them near. It was harder to imagine what Jake would say if he was here. But perhaps that was because, if he was here, she wouldn't need him to say anything at all. She ached to rush into his arms and tell him to never let go. To kiss him and to ask him to touch her like he'd touched her the night in the hotel. And *more*.

Froq, how she wanted *more*.

Shiloh sighed, rubbed her eyes again, and picked up one of her tools.

"Getting tired there, Sleeping Beauty?"

Shiloh jerked her head to find Luca in the doorway, leaning against the doorframe with his arms crossed as though he might have been there for hours. His dark clothes and complexion seemed to fade into the shadows beyond the light of her lantern, but his green eyes always shone bright.

"What did you call me?" she snapped.

"Sleeping Beauty?" He took a step toward her. "That's a type of princess, isn't it?"

Shiloh tightened her hold on the screwdriver in her hand. "Did Sawyer send you to check on me?"

It was in the early hours of the morning. Maybe they'd grown worried she'd been eaten by bears.

"Nah," Luca said, coming to the opposite side of the desk. "I saw your lantern through the window from my bedroom." He gestured toward the window, and if Shiloh squinted through the yellowed glass, she could see the back of the house and a window she hadn't realized belonged to Luca's and Ali's room.

"Do you spy on me often?" Shiloh asked.

Luca scoffed. "I have better things to do with my time."

He lowered his lanky form onto the stool on the other side of the desk. The stool had been there ever since Nic had carried it in to keep Shiloh company. Sometimes, one of the other Sparrows would occupy the stool. Paul and Amelia liked to tell Shiloh stories of her mom and dad. Charlie liked to hear stories about how

Shiloh had met Jake, sighing at all the right moments and professing to being a romantic at heart. Wallace and Ali had both been banned from the workshop. The repetitive stories and the magic tricks, respectfully, made it impossible to focus.

Luca had never visited her. Other than a few terse conversations and his frequent jabs, they'd never spoken. What could he possibly want?

He picked up a metal circle from the desk, turning it around in his fingers.

She snatched it from his hand. "Can I *help* you with something?"

"Nope." He folded his arms on the desk, like he planned to stay a while. "How many more do you have left?"

"Three." Shiloh pulled one projector back out of the jacket and twisted open the back panel, squinting at the tangle of components within.

"Looks more like you're pulling those apart. Isn't that counterproductive?"

Shiloh tightened her hold on the projector, feeling a violent urge to fling it at Luca's head. But if she swung at him, she knew—just like the handful of times she'd sparred with him—he'd only dodge her easily and then, the next thing she'd know, she'd be on the ground looking up at him.

Instead, she took a breath. "Look, I'm really busy, okay? I have a week to get all of these done, and I really don't have time to be your source of amusement."

"A week, huh?" he repeated.

"Yes."

"Think you can do it?"

"I don't really have a choice."

"Then let me help you."

The offer came out so sincerely that Shiloh blinked at him, sure he'd transformed into someone else. And then she scoffed. "This isn't killing a turkey or hand-to-hand combat, Luca. It would take more time to teach you than to just do it myself."

"Surely there's something I can help with." Luca gestured at the jacket before her. "A trained monkey can punch holes in a jacket."

Shiloh shook her head. Much as she hated to admit it, he had a point. "Fine." She grabbed one of the new jackets and a permanent marker from a desk drawer. With the swiftness that came from having done this a dozen times, she drew a 'X' where the projectors and cameras went. "On one condition," she added when she was nearly done.

Luca arched an eyebrow. "What's that?"

She thrust the jacket at his chest and slid the leather puncher toward him. "No talking."

Luca picked up the puncher as Shiloh returned to inspecting her work on the projectors and camera.

He made it only two minutes before he spoke again. "So how did you and the rich boy meet?"

Shiloh said nothing.

"And by rich boy, I meant—"

"I know who you meant," Shiloh hissed.

Luca snapped the puncher harder than necessary, but his voice returned to his same nonchalant tone. "Easy there. I'm only trying to make conversation, Princess. You're a hard girl to get to know."

Shiloh gripped her screwdriver so hard it hurt. "And you're so transparent?"

She'd learned so many stories of the Sparrows through the past two months. She'd learned how Fatima and Yousef had belonged to two different factions in ROGUE, before one day they met and never parted... until he died two months ago.

She'd learned Mick had run away on his twenty-fifth birthday rather than be forced into a loveless marriage with a woman. He'd been a loner for years, until he stumbled upon the Sparrows. According to Charlie, it had taken a long time for Mick to believe he had a chance for love, but eventually he stuck around long enough to find out.

But Luca—he was a closed book. Shiloh had figured out enough to know that he hadn't been born in ROGUE and had lived in Arcadia most of his life. He never talked about his past. And his brother—chatterbox that Ali was—didn't talk about it, either. They wouldn't even give a last name. Whatever Luca was running from, it had to be bad.

Luca's scowl deepened. He opened his mouth once more, but Shiloh pointed the screwdriver at him. "I said no talking. I need to focus."

His nostrils flared, but he returned to his work. The solar lantern beside the desk flickered, a warning she wouldn't have much more time to work before her light gave out.

"I just don't get it," Luca said.

Really? Five minutes? After months of giving her nothing but jaded one-liners, he'd decided to talk to her now. And *this* was what he chose to talk to her about? He'd never once mentioned Jake to her before, but she'd seen the look on his face whenever Jake's name came up in a conversation with someone else. The way his lip curled and his eyes darkened.

Hatred. Pure, unbridled hatred.

Sawyer wasn't the only one who refused to look past Jake's last name.

"No talking," Shiloh hissed. But he ignored her.

"How'd a girl like you end up with a guy like him?"

Girl like her? The tension in Shiloh's shoulder moved down her spine, every muscle coiling in on itself. She'd heard this before. "Why? Because I'm a Haven girl?"

Luca recoiled. "No, of course not. Because you seem too smart to fall for someone like him."

"You don't know him," Shiloh said coolly, refusing to look up from the projector before her.

"I know him enough." Luca gave one more rough clip of the

puncher, before setting it aside. In the moonlight, his narrowed, green eyes almost glowed. "I may have never stepped foot in Minnesota before I joined ROGUE, but rich boy was certainly well-traveled, if you catch my drift. The tales of the '*Prince of Arcadia*'—or whatever the fuck the e-magazines call him—are legendary. I mean, it's been, what? Two months since you got here? Do you really think he's just waiting around for you?"

Shiloh's fingers froze over the projector, the screwdriver limp in her hand. Many thoughts had tortured her over the long weeks: how she and Jake would find a way back together; what would happen to Jake if, after the photo was released, it was discovered that he'd been the one to take that picture. But she hadn't even considered this.

Shiloh shook her head. "He wouldn't do that."

"Wouldn't he?" Luca asked, his tone full of pity.

Underneath Luca's scrutinizing gaze, Shiloh's stomach pinched in doubt. At the beginning of the school year, after she'd been forced to break things off with him, Jake had been quick to jump back into his old ways. Poor coping habits for his first broken heart. How was he coping now?

Or, in her absence, had he realized she wasn't worth waiting around for?

The pinch in her gut twisted into a wrenching ache. She thought she might be sick, but she tried to keep her face placid and her movements sure as she set the projector down.

Luca must have thought she'd been unaffected because he poked against the bruise he'd created. "I mean, he knows he'll never see you again. Sawyer made it quite clear to him that she'd never allow—" He stopped, sucking in a breath as though he could inhale the words back down his throat.

A frigid cold swept over Shiloh's skin, a cold that had little to do with the breeze cutting through the cracks in the window. When she spoke, she barely recognized her voice. It was dark. Deadly.

"*What* did Sawyer say?"

Luca shook his head. "Nothing. I didn't mean..."

"Yes, you did. *What did she say?*"

He eyed the screwdriver Shiloh clutched in her fist. "Fuck. Sawyer's gonna kill me."

Shiloh pressed her fists on the table and leaned forward. "Did Sawyer tell Jake that she wouldn't allow us to be together?"

In the silence of the night, Luca's swallow was audible. "Yes."

Rage.

There were no thoughts, no words, no other emotions. Just rage. It echoed like a long scream in her head, over and over.

Rage, rage, rage!

Shiloh hadn't escaped Arcadia only to be controlled by someone else.

It took all of Shiloh's will not to storm into the house where Sawyer slept and outwardly roar the rage in her head, but Shiloh would likely wake the entire camp. And what good would it do to scream like a spoiled teenager who'd been told no for the first time? Defiance was much better when conducted in secret, so the ones being defied couldn't prepare.

She forced herself to breathe. *Inhale. Exhale.*

And what if Luca was right? What if, after being told by the leader of ROGUE that Jake had lost Shiloh forever, he'd finally given up? What if he'd decided there was no point burning down the world?

What if he'd accepted that Shiloh wasn't worth the effort it took to love her?

Shiloh sealed her eyes shut against the waves of emotions that collided within her. Luca must have seen it, because he sighed, "Look, Princess, I'm sorry—"

At the word *Princess*, Shiloh's restraint fractured. She pulled back her arm and flung the screwdriver. It soared past Luca's head and bounced against the wall of the shed, rolling along the plywood floor before settling in a crack.

Luca burst to his feet like he was preparing for another attack. He'd been lucky she had chosen to miss his head.

"Get out," she hissed. Her voice was scarcely more than a whisper, but it held a warning, the quiet rattle of a snake about to strike.

The shadows he wore like a veil over his face seemed to grow darker. He sat back down. "No. You need my help."

The rage inside Shiloh froze every part of her, crackling and wailing like a winter storm. Words cried inside her head, fighting to be set free.

I'm not *a princess.*

You're not *sorry.*

And what did I do to make you hate me?

She'd opened her mouth to let all the words spill out, when the solar lantern died, plunging them into darkness, turning Luca into only a shadow. And with the light went Shiloh's desire to fight. It fled from every muscle, leaving nothing but exhaustion.

"I can get another light," Luca offered, his voice strangely gentler than before.

"Don't bother." And Shiloh was already out the door by the time he spoke again.

"Shiloh, wait—"

The use of her actual name almost made her stop. Almost.

Instead, she carried herself out of the shed and into the moonlit night. She'd left her jacket inside the shed, and the April air nipped the skin of her arms, bare in her sleeveless shirt. She slipped through the backyards and into her house. She glanced toward the couch in the room, where she'd thought Sawyer might be sleeping. She wasn't there. Good. Shiloh didn't know what she would do if she had been.

Shiloh padded softly into the bedroom she shared with Amelia and Nic, passing the second room where Paul slept. Despite Shiloh's attempt at silence, both Amelia and Nic peeked open their eyes as she stepped in, but they quickly fell back asleep when no threat presented itself. Shiloh slid onto the lumpy full-sized bed she shared with Nic. Amelia slept on a smaller mattress set directly on the floor.

Shiloh slid her fingers between the mattress and the headboard, pulling out her father's journal. She'd read the journal so many times, she nearly had the words memorized. She could imagine her father saying them. But it wasn't her father's voice she sought tonight.

She flipped to the back cover, where she'd tucked Jake's note. It was too dark to read it, but she traced her fingertips across it, picturing the slope of the writing, letting the words echo within her. Especially the last one.

Forever.

She'd accept nothing else.

Shiloh limped her sore, tired body into her workshop following the workout and sparring session with Brooks. Though it was more brutal than usual, at least Luca hadn't been there. The two remaining jackets had been laid out carefully on her desk. She trailed her finger against one sleeve, the one Luca had been working on, and found the holes for the projectors and cameras all lined up where they were meant to be. Not just on this jacket, but on the second one, as well.

Luca had continued working, long after she'd left. It would have taken him hours to do this. Was this supposed to be some kind of an apology?

Shiloh shook her head and sat down to get to work. It didn't matter. She didn't have any intention of accepting it.

THIRTY-TWO

Nic watched as her mother pulled up the zipper of her newest Cloak, the soft sigh of metal-meeting-metal loud in the silence of their room. As each tooth met, Nic's stomach coiled into another knot. She curled her fingers even tighter to keep from exhibiting the anxiety on her face and leaned against the wall as though she had not a care in the world. As though her heart wasn't pounding in her chest, in a bitterly familiar cry.

Please, please don't go.

Mom pulled the hood up over her tight, high ponytail and then twisted this way and that, testing the movement of the jacket. "I think it fits quite well," she said, looking to Shiloh for confirmation. Shiloh had explained that a good fit was essential. If the projectors didn't lay right, they would cross paths and distort the image.

Shiloh cocked her head, arms tight against her chest as she took in every detail of the Cloak. "It's a little tighter on the stomach than I remember it being when we first tried it on, but I think it'll be okay. Turn it on."

Mom made a face and quickly slipped a hand into the pocket

where Shiloh had hidden the switch. Then—poof—like magic, Nic's mom was gone. How had Ali described it when Mick had tried his own around the campfire earlier at lunch?

Abracadabra! Now you see it. Now you don't.

Despite knowing what the Cloak did, Nic found it unnerving. Perhaps because this was *her mom*, and she didn't like the idea of Mom disappearing.

What if she doesn't come back?

Shiloh had Mom walk around the room. Unlike Nic's had been, this Cloak seemed to move seamlessly. Perhaps making a dozen had helped Shiloh work out some kinks. At last, Shiloh nodded her head, and Mom flipped the switch once more.

Mom's smile curled wide. She stepped toward Shiloh, her arms parting as though she might hug her. Mom must have noticed Shiloh stiffen because she stopped, letting her hands drop to her side.

"Your parents would be so proud of you," she said, her voice low with emotion.

The words raised a lump in Nic's throat, but the composed expression on Shiloh's face never wavered. Shiloh lifted one shoulder in a shrug, before she grabbed the last remaining Cloak where it hung on the bed and handed it to Amelia. "Can you give this to Sawyer for me?"

Mom frowned. "Don't you want to give it to her yourself?"

Shiloh's lips drew into a hard line, a small crack in her mask. "No. I've checked it over and it works fine. She knows how they work, since she took them to the other factions."

Mom hesitated, then took the jacket. "But shouldn't you at least—"

Before Mom could finish, Shiloh slipped out of the room without a backward glance.

Mom sighed softly and set the jacket back down on Nic's bed. "Is something going on between Shiloh and Sawyer? Shiloh's been avoiding her all week."

Nic shrugged. "I don't know. She never tells me anything."

The mask that Shiloh had been forced to wear in Arcadia appeared to still be planted on her. The birthday party had been the first time Nic had seen her emotions slip since that first night. She knew Shiloh was adjusting to an entirely new life, that she missed Jake and Val terribly, that she struggled with her training, but Shiloh never admitted to any of it. Never let any of it show. As strong and unemotional as stone.

Like aunt, like niece.

Mom unzipped her own jacket, the noise drawing Nic's attention back to the present moment. The silence hovered between them, and in it, Nic's pulse felt loud.

What if she doesn't come back?

"You leave tonight?" Nic asked, though she already knew the answer to the question.

Mom nodded. "We'll travel to Minnesota's bunker, and then in three days' time, we post the truth."

Nic bobbed her head in acknowledgment, unsure what to say.

Mom stepped closer, studying the lines of Nic's face. "Are you all right?"

"Fine," Nic said tightly, glancing toward the door. Two steps, and she could be out.

"You don't sound fine." Gentle fingers landed on Nic's chin and drew it upward to meet Mom's eyes. They searched Nic's own, deep enough that she thought for sure Mom might read the words flinging around in her head.

What if I never see her again?

"Nic," Mom sighed, sad and yet so drenched in love that it shattered Nic's resolve, "please just talk—"

"Why does it have to be you?" Nic blurted.

Mom dropped her hand like she'd been struck. Nic ground her teeth together, a wall against any more words that might come up.

"What do you mean?" Mom asked.

"Forget it!" Nic spat, darting toward the door.

Mom seized Nic's arm and hauled her around. "I won't forget it. *Talk* to me."

A storm of emotion rattled in Nic's chest, unsure whether it wanted to settle on the swirl of panic or the crackle of fury.

Don't talk.

Just shut up.

Don't—

But the words came anyway. "Why does it have to be you? Why can't someone else go?"

Mom's lips opened and shut, then opened and shut once more, like Nic was some strange creature she couldn't muster words around. And perhaps she was. The Nic a year ago would never have asked such questions. She'd been excited that The Family was brave enough to fight. But a year had been so long ago. Before cages and madmen and promises to return left unkept.

"Paul could go," Nic said, but when she thought about it, she didn't want him leaving and never coming back either.

Mom shook her head. "You know the Cloaks didn't fit him."

"Then let someone else go!" *Anyone else. Anyone but* my *mom.*

"I can't do that."

"Why not?"

Mom pressed the palms of her hands onto her hips, glaring down at the worn, musty carpet at her feet. "I just can't, Nicolette. Sawyer asked me, and I have to go. You have to fight for what is right. I thought I taught you that."

The words stung worse than any slap. Nic's cheeks burned because she knew. *Of course,* she knew. She was just saturated with fear to the bone, but she couldn't admit *that.* She couldn't admit to her mother—to anyone—that Nic was terrified... all the time. She couldn't admit she was *weak.*

"Then let me go with you," Nic insisted. That was a better idea. If Nic could fight, instead of sitting around doing nothing, maybe she'd feel as though she was doing something that mattered.

Like *she* was something that mattered.

Mom's reply was a growl. "No."

"Why not? I can take Sawyer's place. I can be a lookout. I'm as good a shot as her anyway, and we shouldn't risk her—"

"No!"

"But—"

"Nicolette, *I said no!*"

Mom's voice pierced Nic straight through. Nic laid a hand over her now-aching stomach, as if that single hand could hold back her emotions, could stop her from ripping open.

"But," Nic said, her voice feeling weak on her lips now, "why not?"

Mom's mouth hardened into a line, saying nothing.

"Just tell me why," Nic pleaded. One good reason. That was all she needed. Something other than what whispered in the dark recesses of Nic's mind.

Because you're too weak.

Because you're not strong enough.

Because... because...

Mom shook her head, offering nothing else to fill the void. And so, the words settled in Nic's soul, like flood water rising. Everything she'd done, everything she'd survived, every single pain the Elite had inflicted, and Nic hadn't talked. She'd been brave and loyal and true—and it wasn't *enough.*

She wasn't enough.

"I need to go," Mom said, stepping around Nic toward the door.

"You don't trust me," Nic hissed. She replaced the brittleness in her voice with a crackle. The storm within her had finally settled on a single emotion. Anger. *Good.* It was easier than pain.

Mom spun back around. "What?"

"You don't trust me," Nic said again, louder. "That's why you don't want me to go. You don't trust that I'm strong enough. You think I'm weak... that I'll just fall apart!"

Mom took in a breath and reached for Nic, but she stepped away from Mom's touch. "That's not true."

Nic coiled her hands into fists. "Then tell me why I can't come."

Mom made a few noises, as though she might be trying to speak, but in the end, nothing came out.

"See," Nic said, her nails biting into the palm of her hand, hard enough to draw blood, "you don't trust me."

Nic darted toward the door. In more proof that Nic was right, Mom didn't even try to stop her.

Nic heaved the stone toward the lake, but instead of skipping as she intended, it sank beneath the surface. She picked up another and another, heaving them with all her might, watching them shatter the lake's serenity. The ripples spread and spread, but the movement didn't seem enough to rid everything inside her threatening to explode.

Maybe she should go back. After all, the sun was setting, casting streaks of orange and pink across the water. The sky to the east inked into the purple hue of coming darkness. Mom would leave any moment, and if she never returned, did Nic really want those to be the last words she'd said to her?

No, but Nic couldn't bring herself to move. Her booted feet seemed to sink even deeper into the mud at the lake's bank. She tried to gather all her thoughts, put a name to everything she was feeling in the chaos, but it was all too big a mess, like a tangled web she couldn't unweave.

She weighed another rock in her hand.

"Hey," said a voice from behind her, deep enough that Nic had no hope it was Shiloh—the only person she really wanted to be around at that moment. Shiloh was perhaps the only one who might understand how Nic felt. In the past weeks, when Nic had woken from her nightmares, it was Shiloh who'd looked at her with dark eyes that understood, who took her hand and said nothing, knowing words didn't have the power to soothe away horrors that were actually memories.

"Hey, Ali," Nic said. She spared him only the briefest glance over her shoulder to confirm it really was him. Then she turned back toward the water, tightening her arms to her side, hoping her stiff posture would send the message.

Go away.

He didn't. Instead, he came to stand beside her. Despite the warmth growing in the air, Ali still wore his knitted cap low over his ears.

"Are you okay?" he asked.

Nic nodded.

One eyebrow raised, disappearing beneath his cap. "Are you sure? You seem sad."

Nic gritted her teeth. "I'm not sad."

"Well, you seem—"

"I'm not *sad*!" She should have stopped with that, but the words kept coming. "I'm *angry*. Really, really angry." The pressure rising within her, she heaved the rock in her hand toward the lake.

Plop! It sank straight through.

Ali didn't flinch at her tone. Instead, he carefully selected a stone from beneath his feet, considering a couple before finally choosing a palm-sized flat rock. He picked up a stone at his feet and tossed it back and forth between his hands, his expression thoughtful. "At who?" he asked at last, pulling back his arm and letting the rock sail. The stone bounced, once, twice, three times before sinking.

Nic bit her lip as she looked about the bank for a new stone. Now there was a good question. Who *was* she angry at? Her mom for treating her like a broken toy? Paul, too? Yes and yes, but somehow, her anger seemed bigger than that—so massive it could not be directed at just one person. She was angry at Silas and the Elite and Arcadia and God.

God?

Nic blinked out at the surface of the water. The wind picked up, pushing dark clouds across the sky, seeming to hasten the arrival of nightfall. Faith was supposed to make things better, right? It was supposed to take away the pain. But the pain was there. Constantly.

Nic finally selected another stone, this one flatter than the last. She tried to hook her arm the way she had seen Ali, but hers still landed with too much force and disappeared into the water.

Yes, Nic was mad at God. If God was real, if God loved her, why was the pain still there?

Maybe God isn't real.

The thought was terrifying. She'd never once, not once, doubted. It was too much, this war within her, and she couldn't begin to explain it.

So instead, she murmured, "I don't know."

He cocked his head again, as though he didn't believe her. "Do you wanna talk about it?"

"No," Nic said, a growl quite like her mother's appearing just beneath the one-note word, a melody of warning not to push.

"Okay." He found another stone and turned back to the lake.

They stood in silence as they cast stones. The last embers of the sunset sparked across the surface of the lake like wildfire. It was the quietest Ali had ever been–making him seem, for once, like the fifteen-year-old he actually was and not an errant toddler–but Nic should have known it certainly couldn't last.

He swung to face her, bouncing from foot to foot with his usual nervous energy. "Hey, want to see a magic trick?"

Nic sighed, too tired to keep the irritation out of her voice. "No, Ali, I don't want—"

In a heartbeat, he'd closed the distance between them, his arms parting and then wrapping around her and then... and then... God, he was *hugging* her.

As his arms folded around her shoulders, drawing her forward, Nic stiffened, her fists curling until her nails bit in. But she didn't yank away, though she wasn't sure why. This boy wasn't a stranger, but he wasn't a friend. She wasn't sure she liked him, and he certainly drove her insane. But... in that moment, his kindness washed over her like a cool balm, soothing away the edges of the pain in Nic's chest, if only just a little.

Almost of their own accord, her hands opened like flowers blooming in spring, and she rested them on his back, ever so lightly.

"This is a hug," Ali said, as soft as a sigh, "and it's the greatest magic I know."

Ali stood taller than she realized, her head fitting beneath his chin. The muscles of his back felt firm beneath her hands, and his arms cradled her with an unexpected strength. Being hugged by Ali differed sharply from hugs she'd received from others before, somehow more intimate. Like when Jake had hugged her.

Nic jerked away at the memory of Jake, escaping from Ali's touch. Heat blazed to her cheeks. What was she doing? She shouldn't be hugging Ali. It was wrong... it should have felt wrong...

It *shouldn't* have felt wonderful.

Ali looked at her, mouth parted, as though shocked by her sudden retreat. The need to run bolted into her legs, and it was all Nic could do to keep her feet planted.

"We should, uh..." She shifted uncomfortably. "We should go back before it gets dark."

Ali nodded, letting out a sigh. It was the only sound he made the entire way back to the houses. And by the time they arrived, Mom, Mick, and Sawyer were already gone.

❦

Nic stared at the shadows that played along the ceiling, broken only by the shifting moonlight and the occasional beam of a flashlight as someone on guard duty paced the parameter. Shiloh rested peacefully on the twin mattress on the floor, the one meant for Nic's Mom. She'd grown weary of Nic's restless turning and had moved there a couple of hours earlier.

Anytime Nic closed her eyes, her heart picked up speed. Images taunted her.

Her mother being discovered as she posted the pictures. Getting shot.

Her mother not making it home.

Her mother... gone.

Nic sighed and stood, sweeping her wild hair from her face. Surely, it would be her turn for guard duty with Paul soon. She might as well get up and go to the bathroom first.

The frigid floor stung her toes. She padded toward the door, as quietly as possible. Until her foot caught the trash bucket they kept at the end of the bed. It clattered on the floor, and trash shot out.

Shiloh jerked upright, hands fisted at her side.

"Sorry," Nic whispered. "So sorry."

Shiloh relaxed visibly, mumbled something Nic couldn't make out, and then laid back down. Nic scrambled to pick up the trash that had scattered. She must be more fatigued than she felt. It wasn't like her to be so clumsy.

Most of it was old wrappers from provisions; a tin can from beans Shiloh must have carried in, and—

Nic blinked at the flattened box in her hand. Her breath caught at the words printed on the side. *Pregnancy Test.*

Nic's heart fluttered in her chest. Something long and thin lay within the box. Nic tipped it toward the opening and caught the pregnancy test in her palm. The pink plus sign stared back at her.

Oh, my God.

Oh. My. God.

Nic shoved the pregnancy test back into the pail and rushed to the door, no longer concerned about noise, but at the door, she glanced back. A patch of moonlight gleamed off Shiloh's dark hair, casting shadows over her eyes.

It seemed her emotions weren't the only thing hiding behind her mask.

Shiloh was pregnant.

THIRTY-THREE

V al played with fire again, wishing she could burn the whole froqing forge down. The metal at the other end of her tongs glowed orange, and she pulled it out, bringing it to the anvil. This would be the last of the flowers she was making for Stefani's undying bouquet. Graduation loomed less than two months away, which meant Val could feel their time together drawing to a close.

Just one more loss. Surely, she should be accustomed to grief by now. But if Shiloh's loss hadn't ended Val, surely Stefani's would.

The school never addressed where Shiloh had gone. She'd just left due to an accident and then never returned. There were rumors, and Val hated that those rumors only existed because Shiloh had been Jacob Osgood's girlfriend. If it had just been a Haven girl going missing, no one would have cared.

Val gritted her teeth and slammed the hammer down once more. Sparks flew.

Her tablet beeped. She ignored it, but it came again. And again. And again. Val pulled off her gloves and pulled her tablet out of her bag. Stefani had sent a string of texts.

SOS.
COME TO MY ROOM
QUICKLY.

Val threw a cover over the bouquet of flowers and ran. Minutes later, she pounded the door to Stefani's dorm, breathless. Stefani swung open the door, and Val charged into the room.

"What's the matter?" Val demanded, rushing toward her. "What's wrong?"

Stefani kicked the door closed, grabbed Val's face between her hands and kissed her. Val almost pulled away in surprise, but Stefani's tongue traced Val's bottom lip and froq whatever she'd really come here for. Val opened her mouth and twirled her tongue with Stefani's. Her fingers curled around Stefani's hips, yanking her close, grinding her own hips forward. Stefani moaned, a sound that was drowned out by the thumping music that poured through Stefani's room, but still vibrated all the way to Val's core. That sound. That froqing sound.

Val's entire being sparked to life, electricity flaring through her body, making her come alive in the way she only did with Stefani.

After several long moments, Stefani pulled away, "What's the matter is it had been twelve hours since I kissed you, and I couldn't stand it anymore."

Val huffed in a breath, trying to steady her panting breath. "You just texted me SOS because you wanted to kiss me?"

Stefani pulled a lush, purply lip between her teeth. "It did seem like an emergency at the time."

Val shot her a glare then swiftly returned to kissing her. Lightening. Sweet, static, hot—a brewing storm rumbled through Val's body as she walked Stefani back toward the door and pressed her against it. Val's hands drifted past the fabric of Stefani's shirt, up that froqing perfect curve of Stefani's waist, her soft skin gliding beneath Val's palm.

"And where exactly did you want me to kiss you?" Val asked,

between the kisses and nips she scattered across Stefani's jawline and down her neck.

"Anywhere," Stefani said, her voice turning into a whimper. "Everywhere."

A laugh, low and dark, found its way up Val's throat as her fingers made quick work of Stefani's shirt buttons. Everywhere else Stefani was the certain one, the confident one, but here...Val took the lead. It hadn't been like that at first. Stefani had to teach her a few things. But now, when Stefani's body was a melody Val could sing from memory, it wasn't hard. Something primal within Val wanted to possess Stefani, to claim every inch of her body in whatever way Stefani would allow, for however long they were given.

Val caressed her mouth, her tongue, then her teeth across Stefani's collarbone. "Here?"

"Yes," Stefani hissed, tangling her fingers into Val's hair, pulling with the exact pressure that made Val lose her froqing mind.

Val laid a string of kisses down Stefani's sternum and her ribcage. Swirled a tongue around her navel. "Here?" Val asked again.

"Lower," Stefani pleaded. "Please."

And *froq!* How could Val ever froqing refuse her? What could Val do, but fall to her knees before Stefani and worship her?

Every sigh. Every taste. Every brush of skin against skin. Every cry Val drew from Stefani's lips, and every curse Stefani forced from Val's own—it all threatened to ruin Val and save her all at once. It frightened Val how good this felt, how desperately Val wanted Stefani even after all this time. Stefani was the sweetest of defiance. The most perfect of heavens.

Val would have sacrificed every froqing little thing she had for a lifetime of these moments with Stefani. But Val knew—even as she lost herself in Stefani's light, her goodness, her passion, her love— that this unbearably beautiful joy was never destined to be Val's. So, Val clung to this moment, stole each second like a thief in the night, storing it away in her soul—a treasure she would cherish until she inhaled her last breath.

After, when Val and Stefani both lay panting on the floor, clothes hanging from doorknobs and desks, Stefani admitted the truth behind her summons. She leaned close to Val's ear so she could hear over the music Stefani had turned on for privacy.

"Actually," Stefani said, "there was a different reason I messaged you. But you looked so 'I'll-slay-whatever-dragon-distresses-lady' that I had to kiss you. And well, do all the other things, too."

Val made a mental note to look that way more often. She sat up, pulling her sweater over her bare chest and shimmying into her pants. "Okay, what is it?"

Perhaps Stefani had finally found something of interest in the files from Councilor Osgood's computer. Val glanced toward Stefani's desk, where Stefani had spent the better part of the week since she and Jake had returned from 'celebrating Jake's birthday' over the weekend. And by that, they meant committing heresy. So far, they'd found a lot of nothing—finances, new policies for the schooling system, a few soon-to-be-renewed treaties with other countries.

But maybe now...

Stefani climbed to her feet, grabbed a robe from where it hung on the doorknob of her bathroom and shrugged into it. The way the white satin draped over her honeyed skin—barely hiding the swells of her chest—was very distracting. Stefani fell to her knees beside the bed. She swept aside the bed skirt and had to shimmy halfway underneath. She was going for the loose floorboards and the compartment underneath where she hid things she didn't want found. When she wiggled back out and sat up, she held a thick, large yellow envelope in her hand.

She beckoned Val close, and Val lowered herself next to Stefani. "What's that?"

"This," Stefani said, colors dancing in her eyes as she opened the envelope, "is the stuff of revolutions."

Stefani whisked out a paper from within and handed it to Val. Stefani had told Val about the picture Jake had handed over to ROGUE, but seeing it personally made her body stiffen. The sound of crumpling paper was a warning, and she forced herself to loosen her grip.

"Three nights from now, these will be posted all over five cities across Arcadia," Stefani whispered, so quietly that, if her lips hadn't been so close to Val's ear, she might not have heard.

Val shivered, a thrill soaring down her spine. "But why do *you* have these?"

Stefani stroked her fingers across the envelope. "Arcadia is going to do their best to pretend this never happened. With the next generation all secluded at schools, the students might never know."

"Just how they want it," Val muttered. Those who controlled the narrative controlled the way people thought, and no one was more controlled than kids at school.

"So, I suggested to my parents that they get these into the schools," Stefani continued. "Mom had a few connections with some teachers in some other states, but not at Ardency. All Ardency has is me."

"Your parents are letting you do this?" Val frowned. The Andreous gave Stefani a longer leash than most. Her father had taught Stefani what he knew about hacking; they kept her informed, but Val thought they meant to prepare her for later. When she was older and could join in their fight, like her two older brothers. But mostly, Stefani was uninvolved. Rescuing Nic and helping arrange Jake's kidnapping had been the exception.

"Of course not," Stefani scoffed. "They'd think this was reckless and stupid. But—"

"But you're going to do it anyway," Val finished.

Stefani nodded, without a hint of shame. "I stole the flyers, and three nights from now, I'm going to put them up across campus."

Val should have felt scared. This was reckless and dangerous. But Val could only imagine the students finding the posters. What would they feel? Fury, disgust, disbelief, and maybe... hope.

Stefani set the envelope down and grasped Val's hand, threading her fingers through hers. "Do you want to help me?"

Val's heart thumped. "Is Jake helping, too?"

Stefani cocked an eyebrow. "I think that's the first time I've heard you call him Jake instead of Osgood."

Val shrugged and grumbled something non-committal under her breath. She wasn't saying she wanted to be best friends with the guy, but well... he'd saved Shiloh. And now that Shiloh was gone, Val might have expected him to go back to his old ways—picking through the girls who were now throwing themselves at him since his girlfriend was out of the picture. But Jake was clearly miserable without Shiloh. He could either be found in the gym, plotting heresy with Stefani, or—annoyingly so—checking in with Val to *'make sure she was okay'*. Telling Val she *'could always talk to him'* about her feelings. Gross. She normally just glared at him until he skulked off.

Still, calling him Osgood—which always made Val think of Jake's father—didn't feel right anymore.

"I'm not going to ask him," Stefani finally replied. "Jake can't risk it. ROGUE needs him. They don't realize it, but they do. He's the closest they'll ever get to the Council."

Val nodded.

"And you, Val. I know I shouldn't risk you. But I know you." Stefani lifted Val's hand and laid a kiss on it. "You're not really alive unless you're fighting."

Val grinned and leaned forward to brush a kiss against Stefani's lips. "Let's do it. Let's commit heresy."

🔥

A cool sweat plastered Jake's skin on his shirt as he returned to his dorm. He tossed his gym bag onto his bed. Earlier, during hand-to-hand combat practice, the instructor had said Jake showed immense improvement in the small time since he'd joined the classes. That compliment had fueled Jake for the two hours he'd remained in the gym, slamming into the punching bag, running drill after drill, and putting his body through the demanding strength-training exercises. Whenever his body threatened to give up, he pushed it harder. He wouldn't stop until his body never failed him, until he never felt weak again.

Jake collapsed onto his bed, his muscles sagging in relief to lay down and rest. Perhaps he should call Stefani to get an update on the files... There had to be something there. She just hadn't found it yet. Maybe he should take a second look at everything she'd shown him. Maybe he'd missed something, too.

He reached into the pocket of his sweatpants for his phone. Then a knock at the door interrupted him.

Jake sighed. The only people who ever came to his room anymore were girls using some excuse to get near him. There had been no end to the girls who threw themselves at him now that his "Haven girlfriend" had disappeared with little explanation. But they were so... tiresome.

If he ignored whoever was at the door long enough, his body-guard—always stationed in the hallway—would eventually send her away.

But the knock came again, more insistent.

With a groan, he rolled himself off the bed and closed the distance to the door in two strides. "Whatever it is," Jake said, as he opened the door, "I'm not inter—"

His word died in his throat; his heart plummeted into his stomach.

Councilor Samuel Osgood stood in the doorway.

THIRTY-FOUR

"**D**ad?" Jake's voice was almost a wheeze as his chest tightened. "What are you doing here?"

His father drew in a deep breath, steadying himself. "I want to take you somewhere. Grab what you'll need for one night away."

Jake's hand tightened on the doorknob. "Dad, it's 9 pm. I have classes in the morning."

"It's been handled."

Of course, it had been. One word from Councilor Osgood and all would bend to his will. He was the Councilor most heavily involved in the school system, and Principal Clark would have licked his shoes clean if she was asked.

When Jake hesitated, still clinging to the doorknob, Samuel spoke again, "Do you want to grab your bag, or should I grab it for you?"

A choice that wasn't a choice. Samuel wasn't taking no for an answer. Two guards hovered behind Samuel, one Jake's own and then the head guard. Rakes glared at him with an intensity that said, should Jake refuse, he'd be more than willing to throw Jake over his shoulder like a disobedient toddler.

"Sure, just... uh, five minutes, okay?" Jake shut the door.

What the actual froq is happening?

His heart pounding, Jake plied his sweaty clothes from his body and slipped into a clean Arcadian uniform. He'd have preferred to shower, but his father didn't look like he'd have the patience for it. Instead, Jake tossed a spare uniform and his phone into his gym bag and shrugged into his jacket.

Samuel was pacing the hallway when Jake opened the door again. Samuel spun toward him. "Ready?"

Froq no.

Jake held up his right wrist, where two bands coiled. One his phone-connected watch and the other his tracker. "What about—"

"It's been deactivated. Are you ready?"

Jake nodded, and Samuel led him out of the dorm, the guards trailing behind them. Two cars waited in the road before the Legacy dorms: the guards' hulking SUV and a sleek, black foreign-made car that had sat dormant in Jake's garage for years. Samuel had driven here independently. His father *never* drove.

"Get in," Samuel said, jerking open the driver's side door and swinging in.

Jake glanced around him as though he might find an escape. A shadow descended the steps of the female Legacy dorm. He recognized the dark hair, the permanent scowl on her face. Val stopped at the bottom step and squinted toward the cars. Her mouth fell open.

Samuel hit the car horn, the explosion of noise causing Jake to jump. He flung open the door and slid into the passenger seat. The slamming of the door sounded like the bang of a gavel. Before Jake could toss his bag into the back and fasten his seatbelt, Samuel gunned the ignition.

The car flew down the road leading out of the campus and past the houses where the professors resided. Clouds hung low in the night sky, cloaking most of the moonlight. The headlights illuminated the fields and woods as they charged past them.

Still, his father said nothing. He worked his jaw and flexed his hands around the steering wheel.

Jake's watch vibrated, and he glanced down to see the hologram message on his wrist.

Stefani: Holy froq, are you okay???!!!

Jake pulled his jacket sleeve over the watch, hiding the glow of the message. The watch vibrated again—another message—but he ignored it.

When the car pulled onto the highway that led to Minneapolis, Samuel's voice finally shattered the silence. "I really need you not to lie to me."

"Oh-kay," Jake said slowly, trying to keep his voice calm.

"What did you take from my office?"

Froq, froq, froq.

It took all of Jake's will to keep his face straight, to not let the panic show in his voice. "Your office? What are you talking about? I didn't take anything from your office."

Samuel jerked the wheel, taking a bend in the highway too sharply. Jake caught the ledge of the door to keep from sliding. "I said don't lie to me. I'm sure the Andreou's daughter was a convenient excuse to get in there, but I'm not buying it. You had another reason you wanted to be in my office. You wanted in there so badly you went through the window. Do you think I wouldn't look through the camera footage and realized you never used the door? I need to know what you took."

"But I didn't—"

"Dammit, Jacob!" Samuel slammed his fist onto the console between them, and Jake flinched again. Jake had seen his father furious, but this was a new level. This went beyond anger. His voice was etched with *panic*. "I'm trying to protect you... to keep you safe, and you keep making that more and more difficult for me."

Jake locked his teeth together and growled through them, "I didn't take anything from your office."

Samuel yanked the wheel. The tires thumped as they hit the rumble strip. Samuel slammed both feet on the brake. Tires squealed before it jerked to a stop, launching Jake against his seatbelt hard enough to wind him. He gasped, trying to catch his breath. He glanced into the rearview mirror to see the guards' SUV pull over, but he knew better than to think they'd come in between Jake and his father.

Samuel threw the car into park and spun in his seat to face Jake. "Look at me."

Jake met his eyes.

"Do *not* lie to me. Tell me the truth."

"I *am* telling the truth."

Samuel glared at Jake, and Jake forced himself to stay firm. To grit his teeth and not buckle under his gaze.

After several long moments, Samuel swore again. "Fine."

He pulled back onto the road, his knuckles white from his tight grasp on the steering wheel.

"Where are we going?"

Samuel didn't answer, not then, and not for several long moments of excruciating silence. The buzzing of Jake's watch screamed in the quiet, and Samuel glanced out of the corner of his eye at Jake's wrist.

Jake tilted his hand so his father couldn't see Stefani's messages.

Jake?
JAKE??!
Oh froq, you're being murdered aren't you?

He quickly typed back on the hologram keyboard.

No.
At least, I don't think so.
Stop texting.

His phone buzzed one more time—Stefani sending a single emoji making a crude gesture. Jake tapped the thin metal band of the watch, turning it off in case she tried to message again.

Outside the window, fields stretched out. The headlights splashed off the fresh green buds of grass that slowly replaced the sprigs of brown. Spring had arrived, and on its heels would be summer, which meant Jake had little time to convince the Council he deserved a place in the internship. Clearly, with the way his father was acting, the last few months of Jake behaving himself hadn't even put a dent in their doubt.

His father's next words confirmed this.

"You're making a mistake," Samuel said, his voice level now, but after the long silence, it still seemed to echo through the car, "if you think throwing your lot in with ROGUE is going to benefit you. They are every bit as bad as you seem to think the Council is."

Jake worked his jaw. He knew he should say something, deny it. But denying Samuel's accusations wasn't going well.

"They killed your grandfather," Samuel said flatly.

Jake shook his head. He remembered when his grandfather had died. He'd been young, but not that young. He remembered watching the coverage on the news. He remembered the day: the news coverage on the television, Mom's tears, and Samuel sitting mute—staring at the phone in his hand like it had fangs. Jake remembered it so well because his entire life had changed after that day. That day he stopped being the grandchild of a Councilor and became the *son* of a Councilor.

"Grandpa died in a car accident," Jake said.

Samuel gave him one long look before turning back to the road. The look said enough. Of course, that story wasn't true. Arcadia lied.

"He was assassinated," Samuel explained. "By ROGUE. Their leaders fired into a crowd he was giving a speech at."

Jake drew in a breath. ROGUE's leaders at the time would have been Alec and Elaine Sanders, Shiloh's parents.

"Jake," Samuel continued, emotion clogging his voice, "there were children there. Children died. Do you think they cared?"

Jake's fingers coiled around the door handle. He wanted to laugh at his father, to snarl at him. Because Councilor Samuel Osgood was the *last* person who could take a moral high-ground when it came to the deaths of children. And there was a difference between casualties and intentional orders.

But Jake forced his hand to loosen. He adjusted his metaphorical mask, pressed it deeper into his skin.

Dance, puppet.

"I know they're not the good guys," Jake said. "They beat me up, remember?"

"For fuck's sake, Jake, how stupid do you think I am? Do you think for one second I don't know you handed yourself over to them to protect Shiloh? I don't know how you contacted ROGUE —and please, don't tell me because I'd never be able to explain how I knew the information without damning you with it—but I know you did it."

Froq. Jake let his head fall back on the headrest. He was royally froqed. Outside, the fields they passed were a blur. If Jake jumped from the car, how dead would he be? *A little* dead or *a lot* dead?

But there was no escaping it. Instead, Jake asked, "If you thought that, then why did you make the trade?"

"Because Sawyer Ardelean *would* have killed you. She had you in her possession. She wouldn't have hesitated to kill you if Shiloh had come to harm. Surely, you know that."

Jake swallowed. He hadn't thought about that at the time, unwilling to believe that his father *wouldn't* make the trade, unable to care about anything other than saving Shiloh. But he, like

Shiloh, had been hours away from death. Sawyer would have put a bullet in his skull and then—what had her threat been?

Tear him into so many pieces, there won't be been enough left to bury.

"I know," Jake said.

"Working with them will only end up with you dead," Samuel said.

"I'm *not* working with them."

Samuel snorted.

"I'm *not*," Jake insisted. "If they hate Osgoods so much, do you think they'd work with me?"

Samuel cocked his head; he was considering it. Jake forged on.

"Dad, I haven't had anything to do with ROGUE since the kidnapping. I swear it to you."

Samuel sighed, his shoulders sagging. "I just don't know whether to believe you anymore."

Jake rested his head against the coolness of the window as silence fell between them again. It lingered and lingered, like a virus you couldn't quite get rid of. The minutes on the dashboard clock slowly shifted upward.

"Where are we going?" Jake finally asked again.

"Somewhere I can show you how dangerous heresy really is."

THIRTY-FIVE

Shiloh's punch met flesh for the third time that day. Nic barely flinched. She barely even moved. Shiloh took a step back, panting from the parrying. Still, Shiloh knew better than to think she was improving. Nic's head seemed to be in the clouds. All three punches that had gotten through Nic's defenses had landed because Nic wasn't trying—at least, not really. Nic barely swatted away Shiloh's blows, and she hadn't thrown a single one back.

"What's going on with you?" Shiloh hissed, low enough that her voice wouldn't reach where Paul stood watching them, leaning on the railing of the back porch of their home.

Ali and Luca were also near, lounging in the grass a few feet away. Shiloh suspected that this time, Luca only showed his face because his brother wanted to watch Nic fight—well, Ali seemed to want to watch Nic do anything. Luca and Shiloh, though, hadn't even exchanged pleasantries—or verbal jabs—since the night of her birthday.

Nic shook her head. "Nothing's going on."

"Let's go again," Paul called. "Nic, keep your hands up."

This time, Nic knocked away Shiloh's punches, spun away

from Shiloh's attempts to hook a foot behind her leg, but never swung back. Heat pooled into Shiloh's face, stronger than exertion alone. Was this how pathetic Shiloh was now—that Nic had stopped even trying to beat her? Soon, Shiloh threw a jab that slid right under Nic's arm, into her ribs.

This time, Nic let out an 'oof,' wind sailing from her.

Shiloh gritted her teeth. "Why aren't you fighting back?"

A tinge of pink flushed Nic's face, but not from heat. The early morning sun had caused a sheen of sweat on Shiloh's arms, bare in her tight black tank top, but Nic hadn't exerted herself enough to have even a drop of sweat.

Nic bit her lip. "I, uh—"

Shiloh took a step closer because she really didn't want people hearing the next part. "Are you taking it easy on me because I'm terrible at this?"

"What?" Nic's eyes widened. "No, I... I just..."

"You just what?" Shiloh hissed.

"I—" Nic shifted uneasily, side to side. Her gaze dropped to Shiloh's stomach and jerked back up to her eyes. "I don't want to hurt you."

Shiloh scoffed. "That's never bothered you in the past."

"That was... um... *before*."

"Before *what*?" Shiloh's voice rose a little on the last word. She resisted the urge to shake Nic by her shoulders.

"Girls," Paul said, coming down the porch stairs. He crossed his arms over his chest. "What's going on?"

"Nothing," Nic said, but her nervous tone made it clear it was *something*.

Paul stepped a little closer.

Great. Now he'd definitely get to hear this. Even Luca and Ali had stopped their jabbering and were sitting up straight, watching.

Fan-froqing-tastic.

"Before *what*?" Shiloh demanded again.

Nic's eyes shifted to Paul. "Maybe we should talk about it later."

Shiloh shook her head. "Tell me *now*."

Paul looked between Nic and Shiloh, a question pressed into his furrowed brow. Nic tucked her head toward her chest and took a deep breath.

On the exhale, she said, "Before I found out about the baby."

"Baby?" Shiloh sputtered. "*What* baby?"

"*The* baby," Nic repeated, as though that explained anything.

Shiloh glanced at Paul, like he might have an answer. He murmured a curse as his eyes dipped down to Shiloh's stomach.

Baby.

It clicked. A new, profound rush of heat flooded Shiloh's face. "What... how..." She stopped her bumbling and sucked in a breath. Still, she felt far from calm. Embarrassment clawed for first place in her chest, competing with confusion and, yes, even a little bit of anger. "Are you froqing kidding me? You think I'm pregnant?"

Nic gnawed on her lip before nodding. "I saw the pregnancy test in the trash in our room."

"Holy—" Ali muttered, but he trailed off, his mouth gaping like a fish.

"Shit," Luca finished for him. "Sawyer is going to skin Osgood alive." A corner of his lip ascended at the thought, but then he sobered. The flicker of concern that crossed his face made Shiloh want to squirm out of her skin.

"If you found a pregnancy test, then it isn't mine," Shiloh insisted.

Nic took a step closer and laid a hand on Shiloh's shoulder. "You don't have to pretend anymore. We can figure—"

Shiloh shrugged off her hand. "Nic, if someone is pregnant, it isn't me. It is *literally* impossible."

"I know you have the birth control but—"

"You can trust us, Shiloh," Paul pushed in, using his kindest voice, though something in the set of his jaw made it seem like he wanted to skin someone alive, as well.

Peace and harmony. Shiloh pinched the bridge of her nose, shutting her eyes. A throb started behind her eyes. She couldn't believe she had to say this. "I can't be pregnant. Because Jake and I haven't had sex."

Nic's nose wrinkled in confusion. "But... what... I thought—"

"Seriously?" Luca barked. "Why not?"

Shiloh shot him a glare. "None of your froqing business!"

Luca smirked, and Shiloh was seconds away from finding something else to chuck at his head. But Nic's small voice pulled her attention back.

"But I saw the pregnancy test. It was positive."

The answer should have been obvious. Shiloh glanced between Nic and Paul, waiting for them to grasp what she suspected. When their expression didn't change, she said, "If the pregnancy test isn't mine, and it isn't yours, Nic, then..."

Paul must have realized it first because his face turned ashen. The heel of his hand rose to his temple. The look that crossed his face belonged to a man caught in complete surprise, but more than that—a man whose life had utterly changed in a single moment.

Nic took longer to realize, with confusion written into her brows. Finally, her mouth dropped open, and she jerked her head toward Paul. Emotions flickered across her face like a wheel spinning around: surprise, confusion, concern, frustration. Then finally the wheel stopped, landing on anger.

"Is my mom pregnant?" Nic snapped.

No one answered her.

"Paul, *is my mom pregnant*?"

❦

"Jake, it's time to wake up."

Jake grunted, surprised at the burst of light that welcomed him as his eyes opened. Last night, Samuel had driven them straight home, saying little else besides goodnight and telling Jake to be prepared to leave first thing in the morning. Which meant Jake hadn't slept, but stared out his window at the night, like the stars that reflected off the Mississippi at the edge of his backyard might offer some kind of answer to his problem.

How do I pull off this masquerade? How do I make them believe me?

Jake's mother had been conveniently away from home, doing some fundraiser for her charity, and Ana had already been sleeping, so neither of them could take his mind off it all.

It had still been dark when his father drove them to the Minneapolis airport and ushered him onto their private jet.

There, in a plush chair leaned all the way back, Jake had finally fallen into a reluctant sleep.

"What time is it?" Jake asked, rubbing the sleep from his eyes so he could make out Samuel crouching beside him. Someone must have covered Jake with a blanket after he fell asleep because one was draped over him.

"Almost 10 am." Samuel stood. "We landed a few hours ago, but I wanted you to be well-rested when we went. It gave the guards time to clear the area."

"What area?" Jake glanced toward the window, but the one closet to him was closed, and he couldn't get the right angle to make out much through the others. "Where are we?"

"Washington," his father said. He straightened his jacket. He'd put on a non-Codex corduroy that he only wore when outside Arcadia.

Jake frowned. "Marovia?"

"No, Washington D.C." Samuel started toward the front of the plane. "Or what remains of it."

Jake scrambled to his feet, almost tripping as the blanket got tangled around his legs. He grabbed his jacket from where he'd tossed it on an airplane seat and half-sprinted after his father, catching him at the still-sealed airplane door.

"Why are we here?" Jake asked. "I don't understand."

Samuel took something from the guard seated closest to the door and pressed it into Jake's hand. A gas mask. "You'll need this."

Samuel took another and fixed it over his nose and mouth, fastening it behind his head. Jake hesitated a long moment before putting on his mask, too. Rakes stood from his chair and started to pull on his, which had been hanging around his neck.

Samuel held up a hand to stop him. "That won't be necessary. You won't be going with us."

Rakes protested, "But, sir—"

"You've already searched the parameter. I'll be fine. There's no one out there."

Rakes's eyes looked like they might bulge from his head. "But... sir..."

"This isn't up for debate. You and your men will stay here."

Finally, he nodded. "Yes, sir."

A flight attendant handed Jake and his father suits that zipped over their clothes. Jake put on the hood, pulling it tight around his chin, and then slipped into gloves and clear protective eyewear given to him next. With the gas mask in position, only his eyes were left visible.

The guards moved away from the airplane's door, and when it opened, Jake expected a roaring wind, a brutal heat. The kind of thing that he'd seen in movies of astronauts exploring other planets. But as the stairs descended from the plane to broken asphalt, only stillness met his ears. The sort of stillness that belonged in a graveyard.

Jake followed Samuel down the steps and onto the asphalt that must have been a city street once. The pilot had shown great skill, landing them on this patch, because everywhere else would have been impossible. A seemingly endless rubble stretched out in jumbled grey and tan hills. Jagged metal rose like broken bone from the ruin. Skeletons of buildings towered toward the blue skies that seemed to be too dazzling for the dark scene before him.

Jake had seen the ruin before in pictures... but they could not convey how this felt—standing at the heart of such destruction and seeing nothing but ruin. How many lives had ended here in only a matter of moments? How many people never even had the chance to scream when the bomb came? Those who survived the initial blast didn't survive the chemical bomb that followed, so deadly even the air remained unsafe decades later.

Jake glanced to his father, who stood at his side, taking in the scene.

"Is this where you murder me?" asked Jake, trying to keep his tone light.

"No, son." Samuel shook his head. "This is where I try to save your life."

Thirty-Six

"Paul, is my mom pregnant?" Nic repeated for the third and—she swore to God—final time.

Paul's mouth opened and shut until finally, he croaked out, "I don't know. If she is, she didn't tell me." He ran a shaky hand over his beard. "It could be possible that it was someone else who took the pregnancy test. Fatima or... or Brooks..."

But the doubt in his voice made it clear he didn't think that was the case. Because maybe he was putting together other clues, the way Nic was now. Shiloh had said that Mom's Cloak was tighter around her stomach than it had been originally. Her mother had refused cake the night of Shiloh's party. Once, while on guard duty, she'd stopped to puke behind a tree and blamed it on undercooked deer meat.

"*Could* she be pregnant?" Nic asked. Because she couldn't bring herself to ask it outright.

Is my mom having sex?

Is she having sex with Paul?

Paul's throat bobbed up and down. "Yes."

"I-is the baby yours?"

Paul's gaze swept across Shiloh, Luca, and Ali, who all stood in silence. Without a word, Paul swung around and marched away.

It was a better *yes* then if he'd said the word.

Nic couldn't breathe.

My mom's pregnant... with Paul's *baby.*

Nic's mind screamed the thought over and over, trying to make sense of it. She felt like the world was crumbling around her, fracturing and reforming around this new reality where Nic was going to be a sister.

A sister!

Nic shook off the feelings. She charged after Paul, up the porch and into the back door of the home. She found him pacing in the living room, his head in his hands, the floorboards squawking a protest beneath him.

"Are you and my mom together?" Nic demanded. How could Nic have missed it? How much had her mother really been hiding?

Paul shook his head. "No." The single word was a groan. "While you were gone... things... happened." He stopped pacing and sagged onto the moth-eaten sofa. "But she ended it. When you came back, she ended it."

There was so much behind that word *she*. *She* and not *we*. Nic thought about it, the touches she'd seen exchanged between them, the clasped hands, the standing close. It was always her mother who pulled away first.

Nic studied him, still with his face buried in his hands. All her life, Paul had seemed unshakable: a gentle, unmovable mountain of a man. But now he seemed... broken. Heartbroken.

Nic softened her tone. "Do you love her?"

He let his hands drop from his face. His sigh sounded like it came from the depths of him, the places he must have kept hidden for a long, long time. "Nic, I've been in love with your mother since we were kids. But your father was my best friend, and I would have never gotten in their way."

Nic tried to imagine it, walking back the years. Watching the girl you loved fall for your best friend, get married, have a child; helping to raise that child; seeing your best friend shot down, but then continuing to keep a distance because how does one cross that line?

She thought briefly of Jake, of what she had felt and what she could have felt if situations were different. How, simultaneously, she'd never stopped hoping that Shiloh and Jake would get the happily-ever-after they deserved. Maybe, she understood a little. How you can be both heartbroken and happy all at once.

And maybe it wasn't one-sided. Maybe, if Nic thought about it, something had been slowly—so slowly—changing between Paul and her mom since her father died. Their deep friendship had grown closer: lingering touches, shared glances, longer walks while on guard together. It had been there: a spark. Just a tiny little spark. She just hadn't noticed; maybe her mom hadn't really either. But it had been there all the same.

It would have been easy then, with Nic gone, with the rest of their family dead, for Amelia and Paul to lean into one another. For the boundaries that had once been there to fall away against the tide of grief and loneliness. For that spark to turn into a fire.

"Why did she end it?" Nic asked because suddenly that seemed the only unbelievable thing.

Paul shook his head. "That's a question you have to ask her."

"But she isn't here, and she doesn't tell me anything. Surely, she gave you some kind of reason."

Paul ran a hand over his face once more. Nic crossed the room and sat beside him.

"She gave me a lot of reasons, Nic. None of them I really believe. At first, it was because she wanted to be sure what she was feeling didn't have to do with grief. And then it was because she was afraid of what you'd think. That us being together might harm you somehow."

Nic shook her head, her fingers curling around the edge of the cushion. "I'm not made of glass."

Paul gave a hollow laugh. "Oh, I know. Believe me, I know. You are made of sharpened steel and concrete. But you also went through something horrible. Something that would have broken anyone—even the strongest of us."

Nic ground her teeth together. "I'm not *broken*."

Paul set a hand on her shoulder and rubbed it down her back, the way he used to when she was little and she couldn't fall asleep. "We're *all* a little broken. Every single one of us. And that doesn't mean we're not strong. The strength lies in doing the work to put ourselves back together."

Nic jerked away from his touch. "They didn't *break* me!" She refused—*absolutely refused*—to admit that. If she admitted that, then Silas would win.

"Okay, Nic." Paul sighed, "okay."

"For the record," Nic said, pointedly changing the subject, "I'd be okay with it. You and my mom."

Behind Paul's beard, a corner of his lips tipped upward. "Yeah?"

"Yeah." Nic slipped her hand into his and gave it a squeeze. "If people love each other, they should be together."

He gave her a small smile, one that didn't banish the sadness in his eyes. But it was a start.

A long silence settled between them as they watched the sunlight slipping through the cracked window, forming stripes along the floorboards.

"What are you going to do?" Nic asked at last. "About the baby?"

Paul hesitated. When he spoke, each word was careful. "I don't know. I know what *I* want to do, but ultimately, that choice belongs to your mother."

Nic swallowed. It hadn't occurred to her that maybe her mother wouldn't want a baby. That she hadn't told anybody about the pregnancy because it was something that she meant to make disappear. Ending a pregnancy had long been illegal even before the Sundering, but Sawyer would certainly have resources to make it happen. Living the life they did in ROGUE, pregnancy and birth were dangerous. Having a baby could be even more deadly.

It was a choice Nic was glad she didn't have to make.

"But, whatever happens," Paul added, slipping an arm around her shoulders and pulling her into him, "between your mother and me, with this baby, I want you to know that nothing changes between you and me."

Nic's throat clogged with a sudden welling of emotion. Nic leaned her head into Paul's side, feeling safe in his arms.

"I love you, soldier," he breathed into her hair, "and I couldn't love you more if you'd been born to me."

🔥

Samuel led Jake through the rubble in silence, not indicating where they were going. Jake sucked in air, each breath making a wheeze and gasp as it traveled through the mask. Not even birds disturbed the desolate landscapes, as they, too, knew not to come here.

"You know the story of what happened here?" Samuel said, his voice hollowed and echoing through the mask.

"Yes," Jake said, "of course."

"Tell me."

Jake glanced at him sideways. *What was this? History class?* "The Sons of David dropped massive bombs on the city, and then followed it with a chemical bomb which made the air toxic."

"And who were The Sons of David?"

"They were an ultra-religious cult."

"Otherwise known as..." Samuel whirled his hand to signal Jake to complete the answer. Jake had to unclench his jaw to do so.

"*Heretics.* Otherwise known as heretics."

But that was the problem. Anyone could be considered a heretic through the right viewpoint.

"Mmm," Samuel said, bobbing his head. "This way."

He turned off the cracked asphalt street they'd been traversing and led Jake up a hill of rubble with an ease that surprised Jake. Samuel offered Jake his hand, and he grabbed it, letting his father help him to the top. From this perspective, a little higher up, even more of the devastation was visible. In the distance, the framework of a domed roof could be seen, what must have been the famous White House. Close to it, a peaked spear lay broken on its side, the remnants of the Washington Monument.

"Do you know how many people were in this city when the bombs dropped?"

"You saw my history grades. What do you think?"

Samuel raised his eyebrows as though to say '*Fair point.*' "Just over 700,000."

The number was unimaginable, too massive for anybody to fully comprehend.

"Do you know what the building beneath our feet used to be?" Samuel asked.

Jake looked down at it, but the rubble looked identical to everything else. He shook his head.

"It was an elementary school." A shadow crossed Samuel's eyes. Jake couldn't read him. Sadness, perhaps. "Did you know I went to college for teaching?"

Jake shook his head.

"Before the Sundering, I was in college at Howard. It's where I met your mother. I was doing an undergrad in early childhood education. I came to this school often as part of the program. By all rights, I should have been here when the bomb fell. But I'd just proposed to Reagan, and your grandfather insisted we come for a spontaneous engagement party. The morning after, the bombs fell. It was 10 am on a Tuesday. One of the bombs hit the school directly. We don't know how many died, since so few bodies were ever found."

Each word cut into Jake's skin, and he did his best not to imagine it. Laughing children, young and innocent. All their pure light snuffed out in the blink of an eye. But the images slammed through his head anyway.

"The Sons of David did it because they hated us," Samuel said, his fists coiling at his side, his voice trembling. "Because that was what religion teaches people. To hate. That's why it cannot exist."

Jake understood where his father was going with this. Looking around him, Jake couldn't deny it. Religion could be dangerous. Harmful. Toxic. Maybe not for everyone—not for people like Nic, whose faith had driven her to fight and to love and to accept. But religion had turned this place into a barren wasteland.

Still, the same could be said for any unyielding belief. Any belief that was unwilling to admit when it was wrong, that built lines of barbed wire between *us* and *them*. When differences were demonized, pain and suffering and blood were the only results.

Arcadia was no different.

"And what about love, Dad?" Jake asked. This... this was perhaps not the best play, but he couldn't stop himself. "Why forbid people from marrying whoever they love? Why was that ever necessary?"

Samuel folded his arms over his chest. "It was yet another area people could never agree upon. And where there is disagreement, there can never be peace." Samuel paused. "But maybe... maybe the Council went too far."

Jake looked toward him sharply. He hadn't expected that.

"A world without religion would be an infinitely better world," Samuel said. "But the Council's solution wasn't perfect by any means. But can you blame them? Look around you. Your grandfather and Beck—they made decisions because they were scared. Decisions made out of fear are never good decisions."

"If you feel that way, then why don't you change it?"

"Because I am not—" Samuel stopped, looked down at his feet, started again. "I am not a good man, Jake. I understand that I am the villain in your story and in many stories. I am too selfish to risk the cost of dissent. I risked it once—*only* once—when I told your grandfather I didn't want to follow in his footsteps, that I didn't want that life for my family. The consequence of that action..." Moisture appeared in his eyes, and he blinked it away. "There's not a single moment that goes by that I'm not aware that you should have a thirteen-year-old sister now... had I had a little less courage."

No, he couldn't mean...

An invisible hand wrapped around Jake's throat. *Gwen.* The sister who had been born stillborn. A cruel act of nature—except that maybe it hadn't been natural. Jake had been so young; maybe he didn't remember what had happened right at all. If what Samuel was suggesting was true, it had been an act of cruelty to remind him of the consequences of not being obedient. By Jake's grandfather? No, that didn't seem right. By Beck, likely. It would have been so easy; some poison ingested or injected. Not enough to kill Jake's mom, but enough to harm the vulnerable life within her.

And looking at his father, stooped at the shoulders, his pale cheeks peeking above the mask: Jake knew the lesson had been effective.

It took a long moment for Jake to work past the emotions strangling him. His words were thick with them when he spoke, garbled behind the mask. "Does Mom know?"

Samuel winced at the question. "I find your mother generally knows everything. I never told her my suspicions, but whatever they did, she got so sick... We're lucky I didn't lose her, too."

Jake fought to breathe around the hitch in his chest. "Why are you telling me all of this?"

"Because, like I said, I am not a good man. But *you*, Jake?" Samuel took a step toward him. "*You* are—you are your mother's son. You have a compassion for others, and a thirst for justice that I

do not possess. And you will... you will be a better man than me."
Samuel raised a gloved hand and rested it on Jake's shoulder. "But
joining forces with ROGUE?" The hand on Jake's shoulder tightened, not hard, but like Samuel was resisting the urge to shake
some sense into him. "That is a stupid decision. You are so incredibly short-sighted. You don't see the opportunity before you. Beck,
Smith... they won't live forever, and Bennett and Jameson are
puppets. *You* could create change—*real change*—from the
Council seat. If you were patient, if you were willing to take risks
and make sacrifices, you could create a better world."

Jake looked away from his father, past the rubble, as far as he
could see, until the blue sky met the horizon. It was the first time
Jake had ever let himself picture it. Becoming a Councilor. Sitting
on his father's throne.

He'd spent so long hating the idea of becoming like his father
that he'd never even imagined. The power—the responsibility of
the Council—had turned his father into a monster. But...

But what if Jake used that power for good?

It wouldn't come without a cost. The things he'd have to sacrifice... the kind of man he'd have to become in the meantime... How
much necessary evil would he let himself commit in the name of
the greater good? How much innocent blood would be on his
hands by the end?

In the end, would Jake become a monster too?

As though sensing Jake's doubt, his father pushed one more
button. "Do you not understand the type of power that comes
with being a Councilor? You could have whatever you wanted."

Jake tightened his jaw, still focused on the horizon.

"You could have Shiloh."

Her name on Samuel's lips caused rage to erupt in Jake's chest.
He jerked his head toward his father, seething. "You're a froqing
liar."

"Am I?" Samuel asked.

Jake spun away, nearly losing his footing on loose stones. He descended the rubble pile as swiftly as he could, away from his father and his manipulation and back toward the plane.

Stone scattered as Samuel hurried after him. "Jake, wait a second."

On more level ground, Jake whirled around to face him. "*Don't*," he snapped. "Do not stand there and pretend that my marriage isn't already decided. That you haven't already determined I'll marry Katerina Beck."

Samuel took a long, steady breath. Jake expected a lie, but it seemed his father had decided to be honest with him. "I didn't do it to curse you, Jake. If you love nothing, the Council has no power over you."

"That's what you want for me? A life without love? A life of misery?" Jake spun around again, but he'd only made it a few more feet before Samuel's next words caused him to freeze in place.

"I'll resign."

Jake's heart leaped into his throat. He turned around, expecting to see mockery in his father's face. But Samuel's face was serious as stone.

"Before either you or Katerina are made to marry," Samuel said, carefully approaching Jake. "Then you'll be the Councilor and you can choose for yourself."

Jake didn't like it: the way the idea tasted sweet on his tongue.

"They'd *never* let me be with Shiloh," Jake said.

"They might," Samuel said. "If they thought it meant you'd obey."

"You mean, so long as I agree to be their puppet?"

"So long as you *pretend* to be. We both know you're good at breaking the strings and carrying on the tune, anyway."

Jake gritted his teeth. No, no, he shouldn't even be considering this. It was the last thing he'd ever wanted. And yet...

And *yet*...

A choice stood before him. Not a choice between dissent or obedience, but between which path of rebellion he'd take—the way of fire and gasoline or the way of an ember in ashes. Both could surely burn down a house, but which would be right?

And which would bring him Shiloh?

His father took one last step. Both of his hands settled on Jake's shoulder. His eyes, identical to Jake's own, bored into Jake. And in those eyes, Jake could see there wasn't just a calculating Councilor here. There was a desperate father who, despite how it seemed, loved his son.

"Son, I am begging you," he said. "Choose the path I'm offering. If you continue down your current path, I will not be able to save you. Beck will not let me rescue you again. If she catches you rebelling, there will not be a place on this earth where I can hide you and she will not be able to find you. She will execute you, and she will make me watch, and *it will be the death of me*."

Jake didn't know what to say. What could he say, except: "Okay, Dad."

Samuel's shoulders sagged with relief. He yanked Jake toward him in a death grip of a hug. "Promise me."

Jake wrapped his arms around his father, so he couldn't see his hands turn into fists. "Cross my heart and hope to die."

THIRTY-SEVEN

"**I** think this is mighty fine work," Stefani said, stepping back from the tree and setting her palms on her hips.

The circle of trees Val and Stefani stood in—where, surely, there would be at least one gathering of partygoers this weekend—now bore a decoration of heresy. On every other trunk, a nail speared a flyer to the tree until, everywhere around Val, a drop of silver moonlight fell on the truth.

The same flyers were now all over the campus—slid under the front doors of dorms, taped to the windows of the Commons, tucked into the loose bricks of the aged buildings. Val and Stefani were limited to where they could avoid the cameras of the ancient security system, but Val was satisfied that enough people would see the picture before the security and teachers tore all of them down.

"It's a masterpiece," Val agreed, smiling behind the dark scarf that hid her face. In the spring night, the scarf and hood she wore drew up a sheen of sweat, plastering the material to her skin.

Stefani turned toward Val. Val could see the smile in her eyes, sparkling bright even in the dimness. Stefani bumped her hip against Val's playfully. "Come on, heretic. Let's get out of here."

Clasping each other's hands, they headed back through the

woods, avoiding the trodden path. They didn't dare make a sound the closer they got to campus, even to whisper to one another. The first pink tinges of sunrise hadn't made it through the dense trees yet, but dawn would soon be upon them. It was an extra risk, remaining out for so long. The campus might soon be waking up, the fresh patrol of security guards taking the place of the fatigued night shift.

When they reached the edge of the wood, Val pulled her hand reluctantly from Stefani's. They approached the view of the cameras. From here, they would have to time their movements exactly—running between the cameras in the seconds between when each snapped their stills—until they made it back to their separate dorms.

Val glanced from behind the last tree, taking in the long stretch of lawn and beach between the Quadrangle and Lake Harmony.

"Ready?" Stefani asked.

Val nodded.

As one, Stefani and Val raced toward the large tree halfway between the wood and the Quadrangle. Heart hammering in time with her feet, Val flung herself against the tree. Stefani pressed herself beside her only seconds before the flash lit up the darkness, capturing the picture.

Without time to hesitate, they ran, aiming for the wall of the Quadrangle beneath the camera. Stefani reached the wall first and glanced back over her shoulder at Val, still a few feet away. Stefani's eyes flung wide; her mouth formed Val's name in a silent scream.

Froq!

Val propelled herself faster. Her hands slapped the brick on the side of the building, just as a voice boomed, "Hey, you two!"

A beam of light sliced through the shadows and landed upon Val and Stefani. A hulking form stood behind the blinding glow: a security guard, clutching his flashlight.

"Run!" Stefani screamed, but they were both already fleeing.

Feet pounded against the soil, back toward the woods they'd just left.

"Stop!" the security guard bellowed as he took after them.

Val barely heard his command from beneath the slam of her feet against the ground, the furious cry of her heart, and the scream of her thoughts:

Don't get caught. Don't get caught.

If she did, it would all be over. Her only future would be barbed wire and the impossible labor of a prison camp. And Val could make peace with that—she'd always known it was her fate. But *not* Stefani... Stefani couldn't get caught, and Val... Val wasn't ready to lose her.

Run faster...

A force of weight slammed into the back of Val's leg, and she was falling... falling... falling... unable to right herself. She slammed to the ground and gasped as all the air left her lungs. She kicked out wildly, but the guard held fast and avoided her flaring legs. His knee dug into her back as he wrenched her arms behind her. Electronic handcuffs bit into her wrist.

It's over. It's all over.

Val craned her neck to look up, at Stefani's soaring feet, now only yards away from the woods. She'd make it. She would make it! But Stefani tossed a glance behind her, as though sensing Val was no longer running beside her. When she saw Val pinned to the ground, her steps faltered... and then stopped.

"Run!" Val screamed. "Froqing run!"

A moment's hesitation was all it took. A figure jumped from the darkness—another guard, who swiftly took Stefani to the ground.

"No!" A tirade of rage shot through Val's body as the electric handcuffs bit into the flesh of Stefani's delicate wrists. "*Hijo de putas!*"

"Shut up!" Val's guard growled. He yanked her to her feet.

But Val couldn't stop. She screamed more Spanish curses and

wrestled to be free of the guard's touch, even though he only grabbed her tighter and tighter. Until it hurt.

"Why did you stop?" Val snarled to Stefani, as the guards fell side-by-side and steered the two girls toward the front entrance of the Quadrangle.

Stefani only glanced her way, a beam from one of the guard's flashlights illuminating her face. In her eyes—turned stormy grey in her fear—was the answer, one Val already knew.

Because Stefani loved Val.

You see... love destroys us all in the end.

THIRTY-EIGHT

"**S**it!"

The guards shoved Val and Stefani hard toward the chairs lining the hallway outside the Principal's office. Val's knees slammed against the edge of the chair. She wobbled and, with her hands behind her back, she couldn't correct her balance. Her bottom slammed onto the floor. Stefani stumbled, too, but somehow managed to remain upright.

"Don't you think the handcuffs are a bit..." Stefani paused and then gave the sweetest of smiles to the two guards. "A bit much?"

The two guards might as well have been ogres, all jowls and violent eyes and dumb expressions.

"I said," growled the taller of the two, "sit down."

"Froqing ordure," Val said, following with another string of Spanish curses. With her hands tied behind her back, she couldn't get off the floor. "Do you have to be this stupid to be a security guard or will they train you?"

"Watch it, missy," snapped the shorter of the two. He made up for his height with his considerable gut. He took a step toward Val.

"Do you realize who I am?" Stefani said, jumping between Val and the guard. She tossed her head, her hair flying. "My mother is

State Advocate Andreou, and she is going to be so angry when she finds out you put her daughter in handcuffs like she committed murder or something."

The guards shifted and glanced at one another.

"What do you think we're going to do?" Stefani asked. "Beat you up?"

I might. Val bit her tongue. She finally managed to climb to her feet.

The guards hesitated for one second more, but finally the tall, lanky one stepped forward and pulled the electric key from his belt. Stefani turned around so he could release her, facing Val.

She mouthed two words, each syllable slow and exaggerated.

Distract them.

Stefani's hands now free, she stepped to the side. The guard reached for Val next, and Val spun around. Her heart pounded in her ears. Distract them? Out of the corner of her eye, Val saw Stefani fiddle with something beneath the sleeve of her dark jacket.

Val didn't know what was happening, but she trusted Stefani had a plan.

With a swipe of the guard's hand, the electric cuffs fell away, and Val released her temper like a rubber band. *Snap!* She threw an elbow back and low. A deep groan told Val she'd struck where she'd aimed, the guard buckling to his knees.

"Hey!" bellowed the stocky fellow. He launched himself at Val. She tucked herself like a bull about to charge and drove her shoulder into his broad gut.

"Back up," the lanky man hollered into the communicator attached to his collar. "We need back up."

Five minutes later, Val wore *two* electric handcuffs, one around each wrist with the other side clipped to her chair's arms. Four security guards stood against the opposite wall from her, panting.

"Come here, you motherfroqer," Val snarled, glaring particularly at the lanky guard. "I'll hit you in the other testicle. You can have a matching set of squashed balls, you overgrown nutsack!"

"Val," Stefani said softly, resting a still-free hand on Val's knee. "Stop."

Val glanced at her, and Stefani gave her a smile, one that seemed to say that she'd done it. What she'd done, Val didn't know. She didn't know what would save them from the prison camp that awaited them, but if anyone could do it, it was Stefani.

Val chewed on the inside of her cheek. The four guards watched her, like gazelles inspecting a prowling lion from a hopefully safe distance. She resisted the urge to lunge at them and see if it made them scream. Froqing motherfroqers, where did they get these useless endspheres?

The time seemed to pass like it was crawling backward. Val rested her head on the wall behind her, staring toward the ceiling. A splash of gray dawn light spread through the window at the end of the hallway and made shadows play above her. What were the guards waiting for? For the principal? Or was it beyond that now? Would the Elite come to haul her and Stefani away?

Val's chest tightened like a fist had clamped around her heart. *Not Stefani. Whatever happened, not Stefani.*

Finally, a door at the end of the hall tore open. Heels slapped against the hardwood. Principal Clark charged toward them like a billowing storm.

"Get them in my office," she thundered, barely glancing toward the girls as she passed. She threw open the double doors.

Stefani slowly rose but didn't take a step toward the office. She twirled a strand of hair around her finger, glancing between Val and the door at the end of the hall.

The guards looked at each other like they were silently drawing invisible straws. Finally, the stout fellow decided to be brave. He released Val from the chair, only to quickly snap her wrists together behind her back.

"Let's go," he said. "Both of you."

Val didn't resist as he grabbed her arm and pulled her after Stefani into the room. Her hands clasped tightly behind her back, Clark paced back and forth behind her desk, her heels popping like gunshots. The guard pushed Val into one chair, and before he could even look to Stefani, she took the seat next to Val.

"You can leave now," Clark said to the guard.

"But this one—" He stabbed a finger toward Val. She bared her teeth like she might snap at it, and he jerked his hand back. "She—"

"Leave!" Clark demanded.

The guard left, slamming the door closed behind him. Its boom echoed in the thick silence that followed,

Clark spun toward Val and Stefani. The principal reached into the pocket of her uniform, drew something out, unfolded it, and tossed it onto her desk.

Val didn't have to look to know what it was.

"Do you girls care to explain what this is?"

To her credit, Stefani pulled off the *I've-never-seen-that-before* look brilliantly. "That's, uh…" She cocked her head at it. "What even *is* that?"

"Let's not waste our time playing stupid," Clark snapped. "You know exactly what this is."

"I—" Stefani began, but Clark's hand cut through the air, silencing her.

"Valencia Haven"—Clark's lip curled at the last name—"I wish I could say I'm surprised by you, but given your record, I can't even pretend. You couldn't escape the heresy of your parents, could you?"

Val's face burned. She jerked at her handcuffs, imagining what it would feel like if her fingers wrapped around Clark's throat.

"But you, Stefani?" Clark's eyes flicked to her, "I would never have imagined—"

"Hey!" a voice in the hallway cut off Clark's words. "You can't go in there."

"It's quite urgent that I speak with Principal Clark," replied a calm, feminine voice that sounded vaguely familiar, but Val couldn't place it. "Step away, please."

"Ma'am—"

"Listen. You seem like a nice fellow, and I'd really hate for you not to have a job come tomorrow, so please step aside."

Beside Val, Stefani let out a breath of relief. Val frowned at her.

"For the Council's sake," muttered Clark. She marched to the door and yanked it open. "What in Arcadia is—oh, Advocate Andreou!"

This time, Val exhaled. Of course! Stefani's mother was here. When Val had distracted the guards, Stefani must have used her watch to contact her. During the struggle, the guards never would have seen her typing a frantic message, begging for help.

Reese Andreou had made impeccable time; she must have sped the entire way. Now, Reese pushed past Clark into her office. How was it possible for someone to look so unassuming yet powerful at the same time? Reese wore a wrinkled Arcadian uniform and tennis shoes, her Arcadian-length brown hair finger-combed. Perhaps it was the tilt of her chin, the square of her shoulders, or the surety of her steps as she neared Val and Stefani that gave off an air of authority.

Reese stopped, glancing between her daughter and Val. Reese's face flashed hard and then smoothed again when she turned toward Clark.

"Why is the girl in handcuffs?" She calmly folded her hands together in front of her. Her sweet tone held a serrated edge. "Are you arresting students now? Principal, surely you know that is beyond your authority."

Clark shut the door and approached Reese wearily. "It seems Ms. Haven attacked two of our guards. Her hands are bound for our safety."

"Oh, dear!" Reese said, looking genuinely concerned. "If a

teenage girl took down two of your guards, what does that say about the security of your school, Principal?"

Clark cleared her throat. "Well, Valencia Haven has been known to be quite... temperamental."

Reese shook her head. "I kindly request you release her."

"But—"

"*Kindly*," Reese repeated, "but if I have to ask again, it will *not* be kind."

Clark hesitated, her knuckles cracking as they curled into fists.

Reese drew a phone from her pocket. "Councilor Osgood will not like being woken up this early, but he'll surely want to know how his schools are being run. And we are such good friends."

Clark didn't wait another beat before ducking into the hallway. She returned seconds later with the key. She swiped it over Val's wrists, freeing her. Val rubbed the tender skin and rolled her joints, but she never looked away from Reese Andreou. Val was used to seeing Reese's persona on television: the sweet, devoted, bow-down-to-the-Council personality. But Reese was far more like her daughter than Val realized–beneath the cotton candy exterior, was not cardboard, but a spike.

"Now"—Reese rested a hand on Stefani's shoulder—"do you mind telling me what all this fuss is about?"

"Your daughter and her"—Again, Clark wrinkled up her nose as she looked to Val—"friend... were caught outside of bed. Somehow, they removed their trackers."

"That's it?" Reese frowned. "They broke curfew? Forgive me, I must be missing something."

Clark nodded. "You are." She tapped a finger on the flyer of Councilor Bennett sitting on her desk. "We found these around campus."

Reese took a step closer. Not a flicker of panic crossed her face, even though Val's heart shuddered in her chest as it dawned on her. If Stefani was accused of heresy, what would that mean for her family? What would that mean for ROGUE?

The fist in Val's chest tightened. It hurt to breathe.

"What is that?" Reese asked, spreading fingers over her chest, her nose wrinkling.

"That," Clark said, stabbing her finger against it, "is some faked photo meant to humiliate our beloved Councilor."

Of course, she would say it was fake.

"That's horrible!" Reese said. "Who'd do such a thing? Surely, you should be looking for the culprit instead of wasting time with my daughter—for what? Breaking curfew with a friend? Unless—" She drew in a sharp breath, clutching the collar of her shirt. "Peace and harmony, Principal Clark. Don't tell me you think my daughter is responsible for *this*."

"They were the only ones out tonight."

A deadly stillness swept over Reese. She glanced at Stefani, almost imperceptibly. Stefani took the cue.

"I didn't do that, Mom," she cried. "I'd *never* do it!"

Reese twirled her hand in the air. "Well, there, see. There's been a mistake."

Clark's cheeks burned hot. She almost vibrated with fury. "We have *not* made a mistake."

"Help me understand what makes you so certain. Did you capture them on camera?"

Clark sucked in a breath. "No... your daughter must know how to avoid them because we didn't catch them on camera until they were being pursued by the guards."

"These cameras must be dinosaurs," Reese said. "If these girls could avoid being seen, surely someone else could, too. And you should be out there looking for them."

"But—"

"Principal Clark." Reese took a step toward her. Though Reese stood a full head shorter than Clark in her heels, Clark grew tense, as though being approached by a predator. "Surely, you are not accusing my daughter of this. This goes beyond heresy. This is sedition. *Treason*."

Clark swallowed. "I know."

"And if you're accusing her," Reese said, taking one last step towards the principal, until only a foot separated them, "you're accusing *me*."

Stefani shifted in her chair, gnawing on her bottom lip. Val stopped breathing completely now.

"No, no," Clark said, shaking her head quickly. "Of course, I'd never see it that way—"

"But the Council will." Reese's voice dropped to a deadly whisper. "Principal Clark, are you accusing me of treason?"

Clark's gaze flicked from Reese to Stefani to Val. "I—"

"Stefani." Reese walked back to the two chairs where Val and Stefani sat. "Please tell Principal Clark the real reason you snuck out of bed tonight."

Stefani shook her head in confusion. "I—"

Reese's eyes jerked once, twice, to Val. Stefani followed the signal, looking to Val. A message was being sent from mother to daughter, that Val couldn't read, let alone Clark, whose view was blocked by Reese's back.

"What were *both* of you doing out there?" Reese asked.

A flash of horror crossed Stefani's face. She shook her head, her lips forming the word '*No*'.

"Stefani," Reese repeated firmly, "tell Principal Clark exactly what you were doing. No matter how bad it is. If you tell the truth, things will be easier."

A flash of tears leaped in Stefani's eyes. She looked down at her lap, her fingers strangling her knees as though she needed to grip something. "We, um... well..."

"Go on," Reese said, her hand landing on Stefani's shoulder. Squeezing it.

"We wanted to be alone together," Stefani said, glancing at Val from the corner of her eye. A tear slipped down her cheek, a soundless apology. "You know, to *be together*."

No.

The fist in Val's chest crushed her stony heart. It shattered, turning to dust that rained to Val's feet.

No, no, no, no.

Stefani couldn't tell Clark that. She couldn't voice Val's darkest of secrets. She couldn't be putting a nail in Val's coffin.

No, no, no, no.

Reese turned to Val, a note of sadness flickering through her eyes. And Val understood. Better for them to think Val and Stefani were doing this type of heresy than for them to be doing something that could get all three of them executed.

Stefani and Reese could survive this accusation.

Val would not.

But then, Val had always been doomed from the start.

Val swallowed hard, closed her eyes, and forced herself to breathe. How did Shiloh teach her once? In through the nose? Out through the mouth?

"Oh," Clark spoke at last. One syllable, but so packed with disgust it made Val feel ill. "I see."

"Well," Reese said, one vague word that Clark could interpret how she wished.

"Principal Clark, perhaps you and I should discuss how best to handle this on our own."

"Perhaps we should."

With only a look from Reese, Val and Stefani climbed to their feet. Stefani looked like a withered flower, wilted at the edges, its color fading. Val forced her feet to move, out into the hallway where two of the guards still waited. They watched Val wearily, but now even their fear couldn't bring her joy.

She slumped into the chair in the hallway. Stefani collapsed beside her. Her fingers brushed Val's hand, but Val pulled away.

Twenty minutes of silence later, Reese stepped into the hallway and shut the office door behind her. "Could you leave us please?" she asked the guards.

This time they looked relieved to be sent away.

Reese stood between the two girls. Her shoulders slumped and suddenly, she looked very, *very* tired.

"Mom, I'm s—" Stefani started, but Reese held up a hand.

"Not now. Not here."

Stefani swallowed and nodded.

"What did they decide?" Val asked, unsure how she got the words past the swelling in her throat.

Reese crouched down, so she was below their eye level. She dropped her voice. "You're lucky that neither of you are ending up in a prison camp, though you, Stefani, will likely be serving detention until you graduate."

"And Val?" Stefani whimpered.

Reese dropped her head, her hair falling forward to cast her face in shadows. "I'm really sorry, Val," she breathed, an apology that came from the depths of her. "I tried. I really did try, but—"

But she could only do so much without looking like she sympathized with lesbians. Her daughter was one thing, but her daughter's *lover*... Reese would look like a heretic herself, which she couldn't afford. *ROGUE* couldn't afford it.

But if Val wasn't going to a prison camp, then...

Val felt the truth settle deep into her gut like she'd guzzled poison willingly. "They're sending me to a Reform Home, aren't they?"

"No, they can't!" Stefani cried. She grasped Val's arm, like she could physically keep her there if she just held on. "Mom, please, there has to be something that we can do."

"If there was, I would have done it." Reese rose to her full height. "Principal Clark wanted you sent to a prison camp, and I barely persuaded her to back down from it."

Val nodded. She should have been feeling fear or rage or... *something*. But instead, she felt only resignation. She had been watching this train hurtle toward her all her life. Feared it. Hated it. Now that it had finally collided with her, there was nothing left to feel.

"No, no, no!" Stefani tightened her grip on Val's arm until her nails sank in. She still looked at her mom. "You know what Reform Homes do to people like us. They'll torture her. They'll break her."

"No, they *won't*," Val growled.

Arcadia had taken enough from her; they wouldn't take *this*. Not this deep, unchangeable part of her. Not how she felt about Stefani. The Reform Home could do whatever they wanted, their anti-gay conversion therapy or whatever they wanted to call their torture. But this truth would remain. Val Haven liked girls. And she loved Stefani Andreou.

"They won't break me," Val said again.

Stefani, at last, turned toward her. She pulled both of Val's hands between hers. "They *will* break you, or they'll send you to a prison camp."

Val met her gaze steadily. Unwaveringly. "They *won't* break me."

Stefani's lips parted, and Val wanted so badly to taste those lips just one last time.

Reese looked at the watch on her wrist. "The Protectors will be here any time to take you to the Reform Home. I suggest—" Her voice broke, and she cleared her throat before continuing, "I'm so sorry, girls, but I suggest you say goodbye."

She turned her back and walked to the far side of the hall, giving them space, perhaps being a lookout.

Stefani clung to Val's hands. Her breath came in gasps that threatened to turn to sobs. "Valencia, listen to me. Please, listen. You have to pretend, okay? Pretend that you're changing. Let them see what they want to see."

Val sighed and shook her head. "I'm so tired, Stef. I'm so tired of pretending to be something I'm not. I was never very good at it."

"Val." Stefani quaked as though she might shatter at any

moment. She brought Val's hands to her mouth, leaving kisses on her fingers, kisses that were damp with tears. "Val, please..."

Val couldn't bear to see Stefani hurting. Val hated it, and yet, she felt honored that someone like Stefani Andreou had somehow placed Val so deep in her heart that goodbye was this hard.

"Stef." Val pulled her hands back so she could lift them to Stefani's cheeks. She could hear footsteps on the stairway now, pounding hard. "Listen to me. *I love you.* I will love you until I breathe my last breath, and no one will take that from me. Loving you has been my salvation, my light, in a horribly dark, froqed-up world."

"D-don't say that," Stefani said, in between sobs. "Don't say that like you're saying goodbye."

Footsteps. Closer now.

"Stefani, shut your gorgeous mouth," Val said, "so I can tell you thank you. Thank you for loving me. Thank you for making me believe I was worth loving."

"Val," Stefani gasped, "you're... you're worth *everything*."

As the door flew open, Val pressed her lips hard against Stefani's, knowing this one last kiss had to be enough to last her a lifetime.

But Val also knew, as the Protectors put her in cuffs and slid a black sack over her head, as Reese clung to her daughter as Stefani screamed, as Val was led into a waiting car and something sharp pierced into her forearm—some medicine to make her calmer, more pliable—the kiss hadn't been enough.

Forever wouldn't have been enough.

THIRTY-NINE

"**H**ey, Osgood, is it true?"

Jake dropped his hands from the punching bag, sweat dripping down his spine as he turned toward the voice that had called his name. Generally, this early in the morning, still an hour before breakfast, Jake had the gym to himself. But today, a group of boys had been loitering in the corner, exercising their mouths but not much else. Now, one—a boy named... froq, Jake couldn't remember—approached him. His friends lingered back in their corner, casting glances their way.

"Is what true?" Jake said, resuming his fighter's stance. *One, two.* He aimed the combination into the bag, timing it with his breath.

"About Councilor Bennett."

Jake's blood turned cold. His hands fell to his side, and he spun toward the boy. "*What* did you say?"

The boy took a step back, swallowed. "Um, I... we just saw the flyers. In the lockers."

"What flyers?" Jake snapped.

"Here!" The boy thrust a paper toward Jake, his hand shaking.

Jake took off his gloves and tossed them on the floor before snatching the flyer from him. Jake tried to hide his reaction as he looked at it. The picture Jake had taken.

This must have been what ROGUE decided to do with it—how they distributed it. A flyer, for people to see. It wasn't a bad idea, but surely ROGUE never would have chosen to target Ardency, a lone school. They would have chosen major cities, political targets, and strategic—

Which meant...

Jake's heart sounded like a siren in his ears.

No, no! Froq, Stefani! Please tell me you weren't this stupid.

And Val? Was Val involved, too?

Jake had to find them. Without a word, Jake tossed the flyer back at the boy and spun toward the exit.

"But, um," the boy's voice stopped him, "is it true?"

Jake couldn't confirm it. He was good-boy Jake now. Future-Councilor Jacob Osgood now. But he couldn't bring himself to deny it, either.

So, he simply raised an eyebrow. "What do you think?" he asked and then stormed out of the gym.

Because, in the end, it only mattered what each person chose to believe. And Jake hoped the boy believed the truth, even if it was a bitter pill to swallow.

Jake wrenched his phone out of his sweatpants pocket as he stepped into the cool morning air. He frantically dialed her number, strangling the phone as he pressed it to his ear. It rang, and rang, and rang...

Froq, Stef, pick up.

"You've got Stef," cheeped Stefani's voice. "Haha, just kidding. Leave a message and I'll get back to you. Maybe. If I feel like it. Or if you say pretty, pretty please with ice cream and sprinkles on top. That generally works, but you better not be lying about the ice cream."

Jake ended the call, but before he could dial again, his tracker beeped just before an announcement boomed over the school speakers.

"Attention all students, please immediately proceed to the Diligence Stadium for an emergency, mandatory meeting." The message repeated itself three times. Jake's tracker beeped again, telling him he wasn't in the location he should be and had five minutes to get there.

Froq.

His stomach twisted in knots as he turned toward the stadium. What would he see when he got there? His friends wearing black cloths over their heads, being hauled off to a prison camp? Could he just sit there and watch it happen? It could quite possibly be the end of him.

Jake climbed into the bleachers, up to the highest row. As the bleachers filled with the crowd of students, he searched in vain for Stefani and Val.

The speakers popped and then crackled over the noise of the crowd as the Arcadian anthem began. Jake rose to his feet, putting a hand to his chest. Below his fingers, his heart pounded out an unsteady rhythm.

Please be okay. Please be okay.

A lone figure approached the 50-yard-line on the field. It wasn't a pair of Elite marching a hooded figure, but Jake's heart rate didn't slow as Principal Clark took her position. She touched her ear, adjusting the small amplifier that had been fitted there. When the last crescendo of the anthem faded, her voice rose.

"Citizens of Arcadia, this morning a monstrous act of heresy has marred our great campus. As some of you must know, posters displaying our beloved Councilor in a most vile act was passed around."

She paused, as though waiting for murmuring to die down. But no one uttered a word. They knew better. Everyone sat in stiff silence as she scanned the crowd. One false move—one flinch—was all it would take for them to be accused.

"This—I assure you—was a terrible prank, a doctored image meant to sully the good name of our leader. It. Is. Not. *Real*," she continued, enunciating each word carefully. "This heresy shocks and appalls me to my very core. A good citizen does not usurp their leader. A good citizen shows diligence. Faithfulness! *Loyalty!*"

She turned a full circle, like she could somehow meet eyes with each and every one of the hundreds of students. Several ducked their heads, others nodded along with every word, and some stared back stonily—wearing whatever mask ensured their survival.

"If any of you know who is responsible for this," Clark said, "it is of great importance that you come forward with what you know."

Then they didn't know... And if they didn't know, then Stefani and Val were safe.

Jake let out a breath. They were safe.

"Anyone who hides heresy is a heretic. If any of you still have one of these posters, you should come forward now so they can be properly destroyed. If you give them to me now, you will not be punished, but anyone found with one of these pictures after the close of this assembly will be regarded as a disloyal citizen."

She didn't have to follow with any threats of consequences. Everyone knew what disloyalty meant. Jake's hands curled around the edge of the bleacher, the metal biting into his hands as he watched students stand, one after another, and make the walk down the stairs and onto the field. They kept their heads tucked with shame riding on their stooped shoulders as they handed Clark the paper. She thanked each of them for their loyalty before instructing them to rip it up. Again and again, until what remained in their hands was confetti, remnants that were cast aside and crushed under the heels of the next approaching student.

The theater continued until the field was strewn with little bits of truth, buried once more beneath the lies. There was more playing—and singing—of the anthem, more lecturing on the attributes of a good citizen, and forced parroting of the rules from the Codex, the whole crowd reciting it like a sea of robots. When Principal Clark was finally satisfied that the puppet strings had been tightened, she dismissed the students.

Jake pried his fingers from their grip on the edge of the bleacher. An angry red line formed across his palm, anger that leached into his fingers. He buried his hands into his pockets to hide their tremor as he took the steps two at a time, pushing past the slow-moving crowd. As he reached the bottom, remnants of paper crunched beneath his feet, caught and blown by the wind— ashes of a revolution he'd failed to start.

A doctored image.

A lie.

There had been no mention that anywhere else in Arcadia had received these pictures, but surely they had. But the same lies would happen there. Media would say it was fake. Arcadia would bury the truth behind more lies. But what had he expected?

His fists tightened in his pockets as he joined the crowd leaving. Then he saw her.

Stefani!

He hesitated for a second, noting that the person ahead of him, while resembling Stefani, didn't seem like her. She was hunched over, tucked into herself, with her feet dragging through the grass. But her hair was the right shade of auburn, streaked with a hint of blue.

Jake lunged forward, weaving past the students between them. "Stef, wait!"

She stopped, and Jake sprinted the last step toward her. A sigh of relief formed on his lips as he stepped in front of her.

But then he caught sight of her face and the sigh froze. Everything froze. His heart, his breath, the very blood in his veins.

Devastation. That was the only word for her expression.

"Stef, what's wrong?" He didn't care to voice the next question that entered his mind. *Where's Val?*

She opened her mouth, but no words formed—only a slight

sound, as if a hand was wrapped around her throat. She glanced at all the people, and Jake understood without asking. He gently grasped her elbow and steered her away, across the campus toward his dorm, ignoring the beep of his tracker as it warned he wasn't headed toward his expected location.

Beside him, she moved unsteadily, as if at any moment her legs might buckle. They made it to his dorm, stumbled up the stairs, and entered his room. Jake gave a command to start the music, and it thrummed out of his speakers with a pulse that made the soccer trophies on his wall tremble on the shelves. But it wasn't loud enough.

Stefani's wail could not be drowned out—a scream that came from the deepest places of desolation. She collapsed, and Jake lunged forward to catch her before she crumbled to the floor.

"Hey, hey, hey!" he said soothingly as he lowered them both to the floor. "Stef, what's wrong?"

Her only answer was more sobs. Jake was helpless, unsure what to do, only certain that his friend was breaking. So, Jake held her tightly, as though maybe he could hold her together. Each scream, every whimper Stefani made, sliced into his soul until finally her sounds became words.

"She's gone. Oh, my god, Jake, she's gone."

❦

The silence might have been worse than the tears. It lingered and lingered. Long after Stefani had explained, and they had both faked ill to get out of scheduled activities, Stefani laid curled in Jake's bed, knees tucked to her chest and blanket pulled to her chin. The tears seeped down her cheeks, sticking her damp hair to her face. Jake watched her from where he slumped in his desk chair, feeling like utter, useless ordure.

Do you understand the power of being a Councilor?

His father's words from a few days ago hadn't ceased to haunt him, nor had the promise he'd made without being sure why. If Jake had any type of power, he'd ensure that every single Reform Home be burned to the ground. He'd see to it that Val and Stefani never had to be parted.

If Councilor Bennett could practice heresy, Jake would be froqing sure everyone else could, too.

At last, Jake could bear the silence no more.

"There has to be something we can do." Jake shoved a hand into his hair and tugged at the roots. "It's a Reform Home, not a prison camp. There's a chance. They could release her; she could come back."

Stefani wiped a hand across her nose and cheeks, only smearing the dampness onto her palm and his blankets. "You didn't see her, Jake. She won't let them break her... won't even pretend... and if she doesn't—" Stefani stopped, unable to say it.

"I know." Jake sighed.

She clutched the blanket tighter. Now only her eyes peeked out.

This is killing me.

Stefani was vibrant and spunky and obnoxious—to the point he wanted to strangle her at least once daily. But seeing her like this was like watching the earth fade from vivid color to black and white. Or maybe it was because he knew this pain—of being separated, of fearing for the one you love—all too well.

"But what about your mom—" Jake started.

"Jake, stop," she moaned. "My mom can't do anything. I almost got her and my entire family ex—" She gulped. "Executed. Short of going to the home and breaking Val out, there's nothing we can do." A fresh torrent of sobs rose. "There's n-nothing... we can... d-do." She yanked the blanket over her head.

Jake sprang to his feet. "Then we break her out."

Stefani didn't respond.

He marched to his bed. "Stef, did you hear me?" He grabbed

the blanket and yanked it away from her head. "We should go get her."

With a growl, Stefani seized one of his pillows and chucked it at his head. It missed his right ear and slammed into the desk behind him, knocking a holographic frame off with a crash. "You pompous, pinheaded prighead! Do you have ordure for brains?" she snarled, but at least, she was sitting upright.

"I'm not giving up on her," Jake snapped back. "She's Shiloh's sister."

And there it rested, another reason why the loss was one he simply couldn't handle.

Stefani rubbed her palms into her eyes and took a long, trembling breath. "I know, Jake. I know. But think it through. The Reform Home is surrounded by Protectors. We'll get caught. And I can't put my family at risk. Val wouldn't want that. And you would ruin everything we've been working on."

Froq. Froq. She was right. But Jake had to think of something. There was only one possible chance, a dim hope deep in his heart.

"Then we get a message to ROGUE," Jake said, "and ask them to help."

Stefani clutched her knees to her chest. "Do you think they will?"

Honestly, Jake wasn't sure. Practicality told him ROGUE wouldn't risk everything for one girl—at least one who didn't have a personal connection to the leader. But Val was Shiloh's sister, and that was the point. At the very least, Shiloh—and, to a lesser extent, Nic—deserved to know what had happened to Val. Even if it would break Shiloh's heart.

"I know a couple of them who would," Jake said. "Rule #4, right? Haven girls always look after each other."

FORTY

"Froq," swore Shiloh as Nic's fist connected with her ribs with enough force to knock the wind from her lungs.

"Move your feet," Brooks said from where she leaned her shoulder against a nearby tree, but the command was half-hearted, almost bored.

I am moving my feet, Shiloh wanted to growl, but she was too busy stumbling back, trying to avoid Nic as she attempted to hook a foot behind Shiloh's knee. No matter how fast Shiloh was, Nic was *always* faster, anticipating her movements. Today was worse than usual.

Two days ago, Nic had treated Shiloh like she was made of glass, thinking she was pregnant. Now, she seemed to be making up for it. Ever since she'd found out about her mother's secret, her mood had turned sour and bitter. It remained that way, even after receiving the message this morning that the mission with the fliers had gone safely. The fliers had been deposited in all five cities, and thanks to the Cloaks, there were zero casualties.

Nic's punches and kicks came in a flurry, and Shiloh barely remained upright.

"Any day now, Sanders," Brooks drawled. "You gotta fight back sometime."

Shiloh swung. Nic stepped aside as if Shiloh's punches came in slow motion, seized her wrist, and before Shiloh was sure what was happening, she was on her stomach, Nic twisting the wrist behind her. Nic released her swiftly, and Shiloh scrambled upward... in enough time to see the pained look on Brooks's face.

Shiloh brushed off the dirt from her tank top and skin-tight leggings, grateful that Luca wasn't lingering around. He and Ali had gone hunting with Paul, and his absence was a reprieve.

Brooks shook her head with a sigh, her braids sliding back and forth. "I think that's enough for today."

They'd barely been at it for thirty minutes. Brooks normally kept Shiloh busy for hours, sparring or exercising or running miles through the dense woods and rocky terrain of the lake. The dismissal could only mean one thing.

She was giving up on Shiloh, on any hope she'd ever improve.

Nic must have sensed it, too, because she snapped out of whatever dazed, sour cloud she'd been lost in. "We can go again," she insisted. "Shiloh did better that time."

Shiloh shot her a glare. It was a lie, and all three of them knew it.

Brooks peeled herself off the tree. "I don't see what the point would be."

"I *am* trying," Shiloh said.

"I'll tell that to the next Elite you find yourself up against. That you're *trying*." Brooks rolled her eyes and turned to march back toward her home next door. She muttered her next words under her breath, like she didn't mean for Shiloh to hear.

"...Such a disappointment..."

There it was. The truth that Shiloh had known all along. Her teeth ground together, and she told herself not to respond, not to give in to the fire that was building within her. But as Brooks took another step, the words broke from her lips.

"I am *not* my parents!"

Brooks froze, her spine snapping into a rigid line. She twisted around slowly, and thunder rumbled in her gaze.

Calm, controlled, obedient, some instinctual part of Shiloh murmured, cowering in the face of an angry authority figure. But this wasn't the Haven, and Shiloh wasn't a child anymore, terrified of being locked in a closet.

So, she lifted her chin. *Show them what you're made of.*

"Nic," Brooks said, without breaking eye contact with Shiloh, "leave."

Nic glanced at Shiloh. "But—"

"Leave," Shiloh said. Whatever words she and Brooks were about to exchange, they could do it without an audience.

Nic growled in frustration at the dismissal, but marched away, disappearing around the corner of the house. Brooks strode across the distance between them. Despite being shorter than Shiloh, fierceness marked every movement like a tiger moving in for the kill. Shiloh's heart fluttered in warning, but she dug her heels in, forcing herself not to retreat.

"Damn right, you're not your parents," Brooks snarled when she stood toe-to-toe with Shiloh. "But that's not why I'm disappointed in you."

Shiloh blinked, surprised.

"You're supposed to be the girl who bested Silas Petrovic. The commander of the Elite. ROGUE's number one enemy. The scariest, most manipulative, most evil bastard I've ever met. This scrawny, pale little thing, and yet somehow *you* managed to beat him at his own scheme." Brooks looked her up and down, a lip curling like she didn't like what she saw. "But now here you are, and you can't last three minutes sparring."

Shiloh's tongue felt tangled in her mouth. She hadn't realized that Brooks knew so much about Shiloh's past. Nic had probably told Sawyer everything, and Sawyer and Brooks were close. Shiloh shook the surprise away and fumbled with the words that left her mouth. "All of you have been training for years—"

"You don't *have* years!"

"I'm... I'm doing my best—"

"No, you're not!" Brooks threw up her hands. "You're trying to fight like your parents would fight, or like Nic, or like Luca. But you're not doing *your* best."

"What does that even mean?"

Brooks's fingers perched on her temples, like it should have been obvious, like this effort was giving her a headache. "Look, take Nic." She gestured to the direction Nic had gone. "She's *fast*. Quick and agile. Luca is tall and strong and has enough unresolved anger that he'd take on a bear if it looked at him funny. And Ali—" She hesitated. "He's flighty and distracted in sparring, sure, but he's scrappy and fights like a badger when his people are threatened. And he can shoot a deer between the eyes from two hundred yards. But you're none of those things."

"Thanks," Shiloh muttered.

"Don't get your panties all twisted," Brooks said. "My point is that you'll never be faster than Nic, or stronger than Luca, or as scrappy as Ali. So, stop trying."

"If I'm not those things, then what am I?"

"You tell me." Brooks cocked her head. "How did a scrawny teenage girl defeat the commander of the Elite?"

Shiloh gritted her teeth. "I don't know what that has to do with sparring. The only time I fought him physically, I only won because I knew he underestimated me." For a second, she could almost feel it—the gun digging into her temple, the explosion in her chest as the same gun swung toward Jake. "He didn't expect me to fight back."

"And *how* did you know that?" Brooks asked. "How did you figure out his weakness?"

The answer came to her in the memory of Silas' words, Beck's words. *You're a smart girl...*

"I'm smart," Shiloh said.

Brooks lips tugged up on one side, a spasm of a smile. She tapped her own temple. Shiloh had gotten it right. "You're *smart*."

"But what does that have to do with fighting?" Shiloh asked.

"You tell me," Brooks replied, and attacked.

The movement came so quickly that Shiloh barely saw it: the shift in weight, the hitch back of a shoulder, the other hand lifting to shield Brooks's face. She had only enough time to fling herself backward, Brooks's fist grazing her ear, but not landing true. The next blow launched just as swiftly, and Shiloh flung up her hands to block it. Shiloh had sparred with Paul a few times when he'd showed her the basics, slow and easy. But Shiloh had never sparred with Brooks, and Brooks wasn't holding back. Within seconds, Shiloh was on her back, her ankle aching from the kick that had taken her feet out from under her.

Brooks towered above her, flexing her fingers in and out of fists. "Again."

Shiloh jumped up, only to be thrown back down within a minute.

"Again!" Brooks barked.

And Shiloh went again... and again... and again...

"Figure it out," Brooks said, during yet another round, her breath effortless despite the flurry of her movement. "What's my weakness? When am I letting down my guard?"

Shiloh tried to watch, to study the movements as they came, but Brooks was too quick... too flawless. She didn't hesitate between moves, or flinch when Shiloh tried to throw one back. She moved both feet with grace and balance. She never stopped until she'd flung Shiloh to the ground and then stood like an unmovable statue, knowing Shiloh had been defeated.

Knowing, once she hit the ground, Shiloh would stop fighting.

She expects me to stop.

This time, Shiloh saw it, Brooks's quick move that sent Shiloh off balance. Shiloh let herself fall, right beneath Brooks's feet. Brooks's hands dropped; her shoulders sagged. And Shiloh launched out a leg, swiping Brooks's legs from beneath her. A look of surprise crossed Brooks's face as she stumbled, trying to keep her balance, and then she fell onto her knees. Shiloh lunged, but it took only moments for Brooks to pin her back to the ground. A forearm pressed to Shiloh's throat, and a knee crushed her ribs, but Brooks smiled.

"Better," Brooks said, climbing to her feet. And for the first time, she offered Shiloh her hand.

Shiloh took it and let Brooks pull her to her feet, every movement aching. Shiloh sucked in a breath, her lungs moving in heaves. When she smiled, it tugged at where her bottom lip had split open.

"You'll never be the strongest warrior or the fastest," Brooks said. "But maybe, one day, you'll learn to be the smartest."

"Brooks!"

Brooks dropped Shiloh's hand, and Shiloh turned to see Charlie as he made his way across the long prairie grass on the side of the house.

"Message," he said, lifting the radio he held in his hand.

"You can go now," Brooks said, barely glancing at Shiloh as she strode toward Charlie.

Relieved, Shiloh followed after, heading back to the main street where the old, abandoned houses were lined. Dirt, grass, and sweat covered every inch of her clothes and bare skin. Maybe she'd find Nic and they could go drench themselves in the lake. At this time of year, the water still felt like ice, but the steadily growing stiffness in Shiloh's muscles told her that might not be a bad thing.

"Who's it from?" Brooks whispered to Charlie as Shiloh walked past them.

"From someone called the Lion Cub."

Every muscle in Shiloh froze; every neuron ceased to fire. Her feet planted, refusing to take her any farther.

Jake.

Shiloh looked back over her shoulder to where the two stood. Charlie clearly didn't know the codename, and Brooks's face showed no recognition, but her eyes flicked toward Shiloh. She knew.

"And what did he say?" Brooks asked.

"It was odd," Charlie said, his brows knitting together behind his wire-thin glasses. "Maybe I translated it wrong, but something about a girl being taken to a Reform Home."

A punch sharper than any punch Brooks had thrown slammed into Shiloh's stomach.

No, no, no, it can't be.

"What girl?" Shiloh demanded, charging toward Brooks and Charlie.

Charlie jerked his head toward her in surprise but didn't speak instantly. Which was too long for the panic building within Shiloh to wait.

"*What girl*, Charlie?"

Charlie glanced to Brooks, but Brooks looked at Shiloh steadily. "What girl?" Brooks repeated calmly.

Charlie squinted over his glasses at the pad of paper in his hand, making sure he had it right. "Someone called the Starchild's sister."

Starchild's sister.

Two words that snatched the air from the world.

No, no, no....

Charlie continued talking—"But I don't know a Starchild, and Wallace didn't know either, and he knows"—but his voice echoed like it came from the end of the dark tunnel forming at her vision.

"Charlie, shut up," Brooks snapped, her voice echoing, too.

Somewhere, past Shiloh's spinning vision, Charlie adjusted his glasses with a frown. Brooks stepped toward Shiloh, a firm, but kind hand settling on her shoulder. Anchoring her.

"Shiloh, who's Starchild?"

"I am," Shiloh said, nearly choking on the words as her throat closed up. Her voice shook, just like her knees.

"But," Charlie said, "you don't have a sister."

In the dark, all Shiloh could see was Val. Cruel hands on her body. A black bag over her head. Her face behind the twisted wire of a prison camp fence.

"Val," Shiloh murmured, and with that name, reality crushed her. Her knees buckled, and she slumped against the house, splintered wood jabbing her back.

Air. There was no air.

Hands caught her, keeping her upright, and voices came from far away.

"Breathe, sweet girl," said Charlie.

Brooks echoed it, her arms and words wrapping around Shiloh as they both slid to the dirt. "Breathe, Shi, just breathe."

FORTY-ONE

"Maybe... maybe she'll be okay," Nic murmured much later that night. She paced back and forth in Nic and Shiloh's room. Shiloh sat on their bed with her back against the wall, staring up at the ceiling.

"No, she won't be," Shiloh murmured, her voice flat. She'd been ravaged by every possible emotion in the last hours—grief, rage, frustration, guilt, and annoyance. Annoyance, as Charlie, and then Fatima and then, finally, Paul, when he returned from hunting, attempted to console her. And Shiloh didn't want comfort. She didn't want hugs or reassuring words or reminders that she should eat. As soon as the shock faded, she wanted to rage, to tear Arcadia apart, to find that Reform Home and burn it to the ground for daring to lay a finger on Shiloh's sister.

Even Luca hadn't said an aggravating thing all night. When she'd left the campfire, he'd even jogged after her. "I'm sorry," he'd said when she paused, looking like he'd rather be anywhere else, like he was so uncomfortable he wanted to crawl out of his skin. "That really fucking sucks."

Shiloh hadn't said anything back and hadn't spoken to anyone but Nic since. Nic, who was perhaps the only one who understood. Nic, who loved Val, too.

Still pacing, Nic curled her hands into fists so tight they'd surely leave fingernail cuts. "But maybe—"

"She's in a *Reform Home*," Shiloh cut her off. "You don't know what they do to people there."

Nic froze, her eyes growing distant as she stared into the shadows in the corner of the room. "I can imagine."

Shiloh swallowed because, of course, Nic could.

"She won't make it out of there, Nic. She won't let them break her... and they'll send her to a prison camp."

Nic's arms wrapped around her chest, shivering although it was the first warm night they'd had since spring set in. She didn't argue. She moved to Shiloh's side, sitting shoulder to shoulder against the wall. "We have to do something," she insisted, steel creeping into her voice.

"I intend to," Shiloh said. Moonlight skittered across the dusty floor. "I'll ask Sawyer to help. She's due back tomorrow."

"Do you really think she'll help us?"

A thin line formed between Nic's eyebrows, and Shiloh could read the doubt there. Would the commander really risk all of ROGUE to rescue one girl from a Reform Home? Probably not. But Shiloh didn't mean to ask the commander—she meant to ask her *aunt*. Maybe, her aunt, the one who'd risked everything for Shiloh, was somewhere behind the commander who was all Shiloh had known for the last two months. Maybe, just maybe.

"She has to," Shiloh said. "She just has to."

❦

Sawyer, Amelia, and Mick returned to camp as the sun climbed high in the sky the next day, bringing with it a sticky heat uncharacteristic of April. Sweat plastered Shiloh's shirt to her back as she watched the truck rumble to a halt, a cloud of dust rising behind it as it broke from the tree line. The dirt and sweat had formed layers on Shiloh's skin as she tried to kill the hours of waiting without going insane: running the shoreline of the lake, doing pushups and lunges until her muscles shook, and sparring with Luca and Nic... having her endsphere handed to her despite trying to fight "smarter."

Shiloh wasn't the only one who stood waiting on the truck. Nic sat beside her on the porch step, and Paul leaned against the railing. They had their own reasons to be waiting, a whole different kind of showdown when they'd see Amelia again. And yes, the whole pregnancy conversation was one that needed to be had, but Shiloh couldn't care less at the moment.

Not when, right now, Val could be getting tortured. Every second that went by was a second more past when Shiloh should have saved her.

The truck's doors opened with a groan, and Sawyer slid out of the passenger side. Shiloh hurried off the step, and Nic jumped to follow her. But they and Paul must not have been the only ones waiting.

Brooks somehow appeared instantly at Sawyer's side. "How'd it go?"

"About as well as could be expected," Sawyer said, stepping aside so Amelia could climb down. "I'm sure a lot of citizens saw the flier, but the Councilors already spread through the media that the pictures were doctored."

Brooks made a sound of disgust. "Surely people aren't that stupid."

"They've been conditioned to be stupid," Sawyer responded, her gaze shifting from Brooks to Shiloh and Nic.

Amelia launched herself across the distance that separated her from her daughter, flinging her arms around Nic. "See? I told you I'd be fine."

Nic drew out of the hug quickly, her eyes darting down to

Amelia's stomach. If Amelia noticed, her face didn't show it. Paul appeared beside her, having followed Nic and Shiloh.

"Paul," Amelia greeted him warmly, tossing an arm around his neck in a friendly hug. Paul swept his arms around her and pulled her close. The affection in the embrace—the way he bent his head to breathe her in—made it obvious how desperately he loved her.

"We need to talk," Paul said when Amelia was first to pull away.

Amelia raised her eyebrows. "That sounds serious. What about?"

"I think you know what," Paul said.

Amelia frowned. "No, I—"

"About the pregnancy test," Nic snapped.

Amelia turned white as a ghost, looking frantically between Paul and Nic.

On the other side of the truck, Charlie, who'd been embracing Mick, uttered a squawk of surprise. "Oh, dear sweet harmony," he murmured.

Mick swung Ezra into his arms and yanked on his husband's shoulder to haul him away. "Let's go... anywhere else."

Brooks raised both eyebrows, but Sawyer didn't look surprised at all.

Shiloh sighed and dug her toe into the dirt beneath her shoe. Did they have to do this now?

"The—the what?" Amelia gasped.

"Amelia," Paul said, meeting her eyes, his tone firm, "are you pregnant?"

Amelia glanced at Sawyer, who held up her palm as though to say, *Leave me out of this.*

Amelia twirled her wedding ring she still wore on her finger, looking anywhere but to Paul and her daughter. Finally, she sighed. "Yes."

Nic sucked in a breath sharply. Paul stared at Amelia's stomach.

Amelia glanced around her once more. "Paul, can we talk about this somewhere else? Privately?"

"Yes, I think we should," Paul said, and maybe Nic knew they should, too, because she didn't protest like Shiloh expected. Instead, she watched them slip side-by-side into the woods.

Nic looked toward Sawyer. Finally, the mission at hand. Shiloh stopped just out of arm's-reach from Sawyer. Sawyer's lips parted to offer a greeting, but Shiloh spoke first, "I need your help."

Sawyer blinked, the only sign of surprise. "With what?"

Brooks crossed her arms over her chest, glancing away, and Shiloh tried not to read too much into it.

"Did you hear the message from Jake?" Shiloh asked.

Sawyer nodded. "It was careless and stupid."

Shiloh stiffened. "He sent the message for *me*."

"As I said, careless and stupid."

Shiloh's fingers curled into fists, Luca's words returning to her mind like a bomb. Sawyer, who wanted to keep her and Jake apart. *Don't think about that,* Shiloh told herself. *Right now, she's the only one who can help me save Val.*

Shiloh took a deep breath and said it on the exhale, "My sister is in a Reform Home."

Shiloh studied Sawyer's reaction carefully—or, really, her lack of one. No line between her forehead, no crease of her mouth, nothing cracked the cool stone exterior of her face. Sawyer glanced at Brooks, who gave a nod of confirmation.

"Someone from the Haven?" Sawyer clarified.

Shiloh nodded. She didn't bother trying to explain that it was so much more than that. Unless you'd been in a Haven, it wasn't something you could understand.

"I'm sorry." Sawyer allowed a small flickering of sympathy to pass through her face and rested her hand on Shiloh's shoulder. Shiloh ignored the instinct to pull back. "What do you need my help with?"

"We have to go get her," Shiloh said. "We can't—*I* can't—leave her there."

Sawyer's hand recoiled, her already dark gaze growing even more shadowed. "No."

The answer came so swiftly, so firmly it landed like a slap on Shiloh's cheek, leaving her face stinging.

"It's too great a risk," Sawyer explained, in a cool, matter-of-fact manner. "The closest Reform Home is in the heart of Minneapolis. It's guarded by Protectors."

"We have the Cloaks," Shiloh said.

"I can't risk my people to save one girl."

The heat from Shiloh's cheek had spread down her throat, into her chest. Blazing so hot it hurt. "You did it for me."

"And a man is dead because of it," Sawyer hissed.

The echo of Fatima's scream when she learned of her husband's death ran like talons across Shiloh's mind, down her spine. Following it were flashes of Yousef's young children crying or throwing tantrums about the smallest things, too young to understand why they really felt sad and angry. The grief that clung to a widow no matter how many brave faces she wore.

My fault, my fault, my fault.

"You said—" Shiloh began, but she sounded winded, breathless. She paused—*Breathe in, breathe out*—and started again, ensuring her voice was flat. Emotionless. "You said he went willingly."

"He went because I asked him," Sawyer said. "And I won't ask them to make a choice like that again."

Shiloh looked to Brooks, pleading silently for help. Brooks only crossed her arms over her chest and looked away, carefully concealing whatever she felt. Nic's face burned red, her fists clenched so hard they shook, but she kept her promise to let Shiloh lead.

Shiloh tried once more. "But if we just ask—"

Sawyer growled through her teeth, one word at a time. "I. Said. No."

And the commander had spoken.

Shiloh knew the conversation was pointless now. Perhaps, she recognized that frozen part of Sawyer because it mirrored something within herself. Sawyer was immovable.

Fighting would be useless, but Nic erupted from behind Shiloh. "But we have to! They are *torturing* her." Nic choked on the word again. "*Torturing* her. And when they get bored, when they realize they can't break her, they'll send her to a prison camp."

Tears gleamed in Nic's eyes, and Shiloh's stomach churned. For what Nic had been through. For what Val was going through now. Sympathy fractured Sawyer's stony exterior, and she looked over Nic's shoulder like she couldn't bear the sight.

"Nic," Sawyer said, her voice softening, "I'm sorry for what happened to you—"

"I'm *fine*!" Nic snapped, swatting angrily at a tear that dared to leave her eye. "This isn't about me. This is about *her*. She's my friend. I never would have survived without her."

"I *am* sorry," Sawyer said again. "Sometimes, when you're a leader, you have to make decisions you don't like."

"That's funny," Shiloh said, her voice cold. "Jake told me that his father says the exact same thing."

Even Sawyer's seemingly impenetrable mask couldn't hide how deep those words cut. She winced visibly, jerking back, her mouth falling open like she'd been struck. Good. Shiloh had meant it to hurt. Without waiting for a response, Shiloh swung around to walk away.

Sawyer's hand seized Shiloh's upper arm and whipped her around, lips twisting into a snarl. "Do *not* compare me to *him*!"

Her fingers ground deep into Shiloh's bare skin, and it wasn't just Sawyer's hand. It was Mother's. It was Aunt Isa's and Morgan's. It was Silas's. Shiloh locked her mask on tighter so Sawyer couldn't see the way panic had welled up inside her.

Instead, Shiloh bared her teeth and hissed, "Whatever you say, *commander*."

Sawyer's hand spasmed. Shiloh had hit another nerve. "Don't call me that. I am a leader only. I don't issue commands."

"Could have fooled me."

Shiloh yanked away from Sawyer's hold. She expected Sawyer to grab on tighter, to fight with her. She almost craved that battle. But Sawyer released her.

"We follow out of love," Brooks protested. "Love, not fear. There's a big difference."

"Is there?" Shiloh looked between them. "Because love can be used as a weapon, too."

Sawyer planted her hand on her hip, inhaling and exhaling roughly, like she was attempting to remain in control.

Shiloh took a step forward and lifted her chin. "But you won't control me."

"I've never tri—"

"Oh really?" Shiloh interrupted. "Then you didn't tell Jake that you would never allow us to see each other again."

Sawyer inhaled sharply through her teeth. Brooks swore, and from the corner of her eye, Shiloh saw Nic visibly wince. So, Nic had overheard that conversation, too. It stung, just a little, that Nic hadn't warned her.

"Who told you that?" Sawyer asked, glancing to Nic.

"Luca," Shiloh said. Sawyer could take it out on him. "So, it's true then? You said that?"

Sawyer's chin moved a fraction of an inch. A nod of confirmation.

"Then please tell me how *your* chains are any different from Arcadia's." Shiloh spun on her heel once more, storming away.

Gravel crunched behind as Sawyer followed. "I'm only trying to protect you. To keep you *safe*."

Shiloh paused and turned halfway around. From here, she could see the rest of the Sparrows. They were all watching. Sawyer and her voices had to have been loud enough that they'd heard everything. Charlie pretended to be stirring a pot but peered over his glasses. Wallace clutched his walking stick. Fatima turned from hanging up the washing, twisting a shirt in her hands. Luca and Ali paused near the edge of the woods where they'd been walking on guard duty, Luca scowling and Ali looking worried. Even the kids had all stopped their chores and their playing to look to them with wide eyes.

Froq. This conversation had digressed far past where Shiloh had wanted it to go. The focus had completely fallen off Val. But then, maybe these were words Shiloh should have said to Sawyer a long time ago.

"A cage might be a safe place to live," Shiloh said at last, her voice calm, "but it is *still* a cage. I let myself live in one my entire life because I used to think it was better to be safe than to be free. But I was wrong. And now that I've escaped that cage, I'll be damned if I live in one again."

Shiloh turned away again, and this time, she refused to stop. Her name on Sawyer's lips sounded like shattering glass, falling fractured to the floor.

"Sawyer," Brooks protested when Sawyer took a step to follow, her voice soft but firm. "She's angry. Give her time to calm down."

The footsteps stopped, and Shiloh didn't glance back. As she slammed through the door to the house, Nic's voice rang out.

"Her name is Val, by the way. Shiloh's sister. My friend. Her name is *Val*. Not that you even cared."

When Nic stomped into their room, Shiloh was already sitting on her mattress, leaning against the wall. Nic flopped down beside her in bed. "What do we do now?"

Shiloh pulled her legs up to her chest and lowered her voice. "Rule #4, Nic. I'm going to go get her."

Maybe that had been Jake's intention. Maybe he'd known Sawyer would never risk everything to save Val, but Shiloh would tear the world apart for her.

"Then I'm coming with you," Nic said, without hesitation. "And don't you dare try to argue. I know I wasn't there for long, but I'm a Haven girl, too, and I'm not letting you tell me no."

"I wasn't going to."

Nic let out a breath of relief. "Good. Then what's the plan?"

Shiloh didn't have a plan. Yet. But she was a smart girl, and she always thought of something.

Shiloh rose from the bed and walked to the window, arms crossed over her chest. Outside, Brooks was climbing into the truck, likely to move it from where Mick had parked it, back into the spot they normally kept it, partially hidden in the woods.

"Nic, do you know how to drive?" Shiloh asked.

Nic stepped beside her, glancing outside to watch the dust rise beneath the truck's wheels. She swallowed audibly. "Sort of. Paul showed me a few things... just in case."

"Good. Then we leave tonight."

FORTY-TWO

The plan came together quicker than Nic expected.

While everyone was at dinner, Nic snuck into Brooks's home, where the Sparrows stored most of the supplies in the kitchen, filling a backpack with canned provisions and bottled water. Meanwhile, Nic knew Shiloh was requesting Sawyer return the Cloaks—and by that, she knew Shiloh was asking Charlie to ask Sawyer, who agreed. Shiloh had reasoned she needed to look them over to ensure the Cloaks were in proper working order. When Charlie returned them, Shiloh carefully folded all three into a backpack. Nic had snuck her mother's map out of her backpack, tucking it into her own. Before she'd fallen asleep for the night, Nic also checked on the truck, ensuring that the keys were still sitting in the ignition, where they always left them.

By the time Nic and Shiloh had laid down for the night, Nic's heart pounded in anticipation. She should have been terrified; what they were doing was reckless. But it felt... *good* to finally be doing something. To fight against Arcadia instead of just sitting and twiddling her thumbs.

The door creaked softly, booted feet padding into the room.

Nic creaked an eye open, but then wished she hadn't. Her mother, whom Nic hadn't seen since she'd walked into the woods with Paul a few hours before, creeped across the floor, her feet light on the old floorboards. Nic hoped that the long time Mom and Paul had talked meant they were resolving things between them—they certainly had a lot to talk about. Some part of Nic wanted to know exactly what that conversation contained, but the other part didn't want to know. Not right now. Not with their plan looming over her head. If Nic so much as talked to her mother, she might see their plan written on her face.

Nic closed her eyes, but it was too late.

"Nic," Mom said softly, "are you awake?"

Nic mumbled a sleepy grunt—her mom wouldn't buy that she wasn't awake, but perhaps she could pull off half-asleep. Beside Nic, Shiloh's breaths came evenly, but Nic doubted she was asleep, either.

"I think we should talk," Mom said, crouching beside the bed.

"About the baby?" Nic asked.

"About lots of things."

Nic's heart twisted in her chest, but she made herself say the words. "Mom, I'm really tired. Can we talk in the morning?"

Nic kept her eyes closed and turned her head into her pillow, but Mom's soft intake of breath spoke of surprise and... was that sadness?

"Oh," Mom murmured, "okay. Maybe we'll both be a little more clear-headed in the morning."

"Mmm." Nic forced her breaths to slow—*in and out, in and out*—until she heard the soft exhale of Mom's mattress as she laid down. Her stomach toiled with guilt because she knew when morning would come, neither Nic nor Shiloh would be there.

🔥

Amelia's deep breaths of sleep were their signal to leave. Shiloh and Nic folded their sleeping bags under one arm and stole toward the door, careful not to step on the boards they knew creaked. Shiloh held her breath as they slipped out of the bedroom and toward the front door. Nic pushed the door back toward its frame, careful so that the hinges didn't squeak.

The moon shone bright against a blanket of stars. In the center of camp, the fire had dulled to embers, and no one sat around it. Lucky. Whoever stood guard tonight likely trailed on the perimeter, nowhere to be seen. Nic grabbed the two packs from where they'd stashed them beneath the overgrown hedges, handing one to Shiloh. Inside, Shiloh had carefully packed the Cloaks, their supplies, and their guns.

"Ready?" Shiloh mouthed to Nic.

Nic nodded, steel in her eyes.

Shiloh's heartbeat turned unsteady as she stepped off the porch and headed toward the place where Brooks had moved the truck amongst the trees, closer to the road leading away from the lake. Shiloh moved swiftly but carefully, glancing around her for any sign of the guards. She wasn't sure who it was tonight, but she certainly didn't want to find out.

They made it into the cover of the tree line. The thick foliage of the trees blocked out the moonlight, leaving only a hulking shadow to reveal the outline of the truck. Shiloh paused to allow her vision to adjust to the lack of light, but Nic moved without hesitation, her booted feet moving soundlessly over the leaves and twigs, until she reached the driver's side door. The door whined as it swung open, a sound like a gunshot in the silence. It propelled Shiloh forward, rushing to the passenger side seat. Her door cried out as well, and she threw herself into the truck.

The keys dangled from the ignition, where they are always left in case of emergency. No one person could have the keys, Paul had explained, because one person could be killed. They'd never imagined that someone in the Sparrows might steal the truck.

It made it almost too easy.

Nic's hands landed on the keys. Shiloh reached to close her door—

Just then a hand seized Shiloh's arm and yanked her from the truck before she could even take a breath to cry out. Instinct driving her, she whipped back and swung with her other arm. Her captor snared her other wrist like snatching a fly from the air and pulled her close, taut against the immovable wall that was his chest.

"Why am I not surprised I found you doing something incredibly stupid?"

Luca. Shiloh's teeth gritted together. Of all the people on guard tonight, why did it have to be him?

Nic sprinted out of the truck and back around the front of the car but froze a few steps away. "We were just going for a walk," she said, but her feet slid apart. A fighter's stance.

Luca jerked his head toward Nic. "You," he growled, "are a terrible liar. Your voice rises a full octave."

Nic glared. "It does *not*."

"It's okay," Ali said as he stepped out of the shadows. "It's cute."

Froq, it's both of them.

Shiloh jerked her wrists back, but Luca held her like a set of handcuffs. "Let go of me," she said through her teeth.

"Why?" Luca asked. "So you can go and get yourself killed trying to get your sister out of the Reform Home? Your aunt would never forgive me."

"Sawyer never needs to know you saw me trying to leave." She kicked his leg, hard enough he hissed and released her, but not before swinging them both around so that he now stood between her and the open truck door.

"*I'll* know," he said. "And oddly enough, I don't want to see you dead, either."

"How touching. You don't have to pretend to care."

Something strange flickered over Luca's gaze, the corners of his lips drawing down.

"We're not going to get ourselves killed," Nic said, her hands becoming fists at her side.

"Oh, really?" Luca crossed his arms over his chest and glanced between both of them. "Let's hear this great rescue plan, princess."

She glanced around. *Think, Shiloh. Think.* There had to be a way to get past him. She just had to keep them talking long enough to distract him.

"Well?" Luca said when she didn't speak, gesturing impatiently. "How do you even plan to make it to the Reform Home?"

"Obviously, we were stealing the truck," Shiloh said.

"And do either of you know how to drive?"

"Yes," Nic said.

Luca rolled his eyes. "A *full* octave."

Nic crossed her arms over her chest and amended, "Well, sort of. I've driven a boat."

"That is not the same thing. You'll end up in a ditch within two miles, that's what'll happen."

"You know how to drive, Luca," Ali said.

Luca and Shiloh snapped their heads toward Ali, who now leaned against the truck, his arms folded over his chest, a contemplative expression on his face.

"Your point?" Luca demanded.

"We should go with them."

Shiloh's heart stuttered in her chest. Surely, she'd heard him wrong... or he was joking. But Ali stood there, a batch of moonlight sprinkling silver across his face, looking more serious than Shiloh had ever seen the boy. Nic stared at him, mouth agape, and even Luca looked horrified.

"Are you crazy?" Luca asked.

"Probably." Ali shrugged. "But I still think we should go."

"You want to help us?" Nic said, her voice barely more than breath.

Ali glanced at Nic, and the warmth that crossed his eyes told stories of his true motives.

"Y-yeah," Ali stammered, adjusting the brim of his beanie with nervous fingers.

Luca strangled the strap of his rifle, which was slung over his chest between both his hands, like he wished he was strangling something else. "Sawyer would skin us both alive. Brooks will have our balls made into Yuletide decorations."

"So?" A bit of steel crept into Ali's tone. From him, it sounded fearsome. Like finding out a kitten had a roar. "You would go if it was me. You, of all people, know how bad a Reform Home is."

Shiloh sucked in a breath. Luca's hands froze on the strap of the rifle, every muscle in his body tensing. The look he gave his brother could have melted iron.

Think, Shiloh.

They were wasting far too much time. The change of guard would arrive soon and come looking for Luca... and besides, her plan would work better *with* Luca and Ali. Nic had packed enough supplies for three people for a week. They wouldn't go as far with two extra mouths, but they'd go long enough they should be able to get to Minneapolis and back—if nothing went severely wrong.

"Come with us," Shiloh said to Luca, softening her voice. Letting down her mask just enough for him to see the pleading in her eyes.

Luca's head turned between Shiloh and Ali and back again, something not unlike panic creasing his forehead. "This is a *really* bad idea."

"Come with us," Shiloh repeated, "or get out of my way. Because you won't stop me."

"I could," Luca said.

Nic took a step forward, nothing but grim determination in her voice. "No, you won't." Her fists shook at her side, her gaze darkened. Shiloh had seen this Nic before when she faced Harper in the locker room at school. Nic the Warrior was a sight to behold.

Luca studied Nic for a moment. "Maybe I couldn't stop you," he told her before looking back at Shiloh. "But I could throw *you* over my shoulder."

Shiloh knew that. Nic could probably have held her own, long enough to take off in the truck, but Luca could stop Shiloh easily. But with what she lacked in physical training, she made up for in stubbornness.

"Maybe," Shiloh admitted, "but I'll just keep trying over and over and over again. What will all of you do? Tie me up?"

"Don't tempt me," he said through his teeth.

Perhaps... perhaps she needed to try a softer approach.

Shiloh stepped closer. She took off her mask completely, just for a moment. Just long enough for him to see her desperation, her fear, her love for Val, whatever he needed to see. "Luca, *please*. I don't beg often, but I'm *begging* you. Help me save my sister."

Luca's breath trembled on his lips as his gaze traced the lines on Shiloh's face, over her moon-highlighted cheekbones, into the depths of her eyes. His darkened, every speck of green lost to the night, a look so intense that Shiloh nearly stumbled back. She forced herself to remain nearly chest-to-chest, hoping beyond hope.

"Fuck," he groaned finally. "I'm *sooo* going to regret this."

Nic uttered a breath of delight, and Ali pumped a fist into the air at his victory.

"I have to get a few things," Luca said.

Before Shiloh could protest, he marched away, ordering over his shoulder, "Ali, you stay with them. If they try to leave, shoot them."

He faded into the shadows, back toward the homes. Shiloh glanced at the truck door, only a few steps away.

"Don't even think it," Ali said, though his tone was back to its normally bubbly nature, hard to take seriously.

Nic scoffed. "You wouldn't actually shoot us."

"No." Ali gave another casual shrug. "I'd shoot the truck tire, though."

Nic glared.

"Are you as good a shot as people say?" Shiloh asked. She'd never actually seen him shoot.

Ali grinned, showing all his teeth. "Better."

With that, they waited, though the minutes that bled by seemed to slow to a trickle. Shiloh watched each shadow, each shift of the leaves, and listened to the hoots of different animals. *Finally,* she heard the crunch of leaves and braced herself to dive for the truck if necessary—but it was only Luca returning. A pack now hung on his back beside the rifle.

"Get in the truck before I change my mind," he said.

Shiloh didn't hesitate. She leaped into the passenger side, as Luca pulled himself behind the wheel. Nic and Ali scurried into the back. Luca carefully placed the rifle on the floor in between them, out of sight but still within reach. Shiloh held her breath as Luca's hand landed on the ignition, the truck grumbled to life as he shifted the gears. The truck bumped its way toward the broken asphalt outside the tree line. She stared out the window, expecting someone to come from around the tree to stop them. She didn't let out her breath until the trees that marked the edge of camp were distant in the rearview mirror.

Grabbing tight to the door to steady herself as they rocked across the broken road, Shiloh studied Luca and the hard line of his jaw. She had no idea what changed his mind. Even after months, she barely knew him.

"Luca, about what Ali said—"

"You should go to sleep, princess," he interrupted, his fingers tightening on the steering wheel. "We've got a long day ahead of us, and we're going to need your brain well-rested if we're going to pull this off."

It would be impossible to sleep in the truck with each bump

rattling through her body, and they both knew it. *Silence it is then.* She should have been grateful for the reprieve, but the air felt still between them—filled with the fear that came from clinging to a crumbling mask. As if Luca was terrified that she—or anyone— might see who he really was.

Shiloh knew that fear all too well.

FORTY-THREE

Their progress was slow.

After finding the Arcadia-maintained highway, Luca dragged a folded paper from his pack and thrust it toward Shiloh. It unfolded to nearly her entire arm span. Sketched roadways crisscrossed the page with red X's slashed across some of them. Checkpoints, Shiloh learned. Nic had mentioned something about getting a map from her mother, and Shiloh assumed a copy of this was what Nic meant. Shiloh had the duty of navigating Luca down the different roadways in order to avoid them. They diverted miles out of the way down winding gravel roads, even cutting through a field once, making what should have been a few hours' trip take all night.

When the sky lightened to a navy gray, Luca turned off the road and squeezed between the trees to park within the woods, out of sight. "We need sleep," he said, rubbing eyes brimmed in red.

They opened the back to join Nic and Ali who slumped on opposite sides of the truck. Nic gave Shiloh a look that was half-pleading, half-relief.

"If he shows me one more magic trick," she whispered against

Shiloh's ear so neither of the brothers could hear, "I'm going to push him out of the truck."

Shiloh hid the twitch of her lips as Nic rationed out some of the food and water between the four of them. Ali jabbered while they ate, and Nic looked at him like she might not just push him from the truck—she'd run him over, too.

Having gotten some sleep while riding in the back, Nic volunteered to take the first watch. Shiloh spread out her sleeping bag, but before she lay down, she pulled her gun from her pack and set it beside her head. Ali and Luca both used Nic's sleeping bag, unzipped fully to form a blanket, to separate them from the cold bed of the truck.

Shiloh's mind spun in dizzy circles, thinking of what lay ahead. She wasn't sure she could sleep, but eventually, the ache in her eyes drew them shut.

When she woke again, a back laid against her own, and light flooded the truck. She sat up carefully so she wouldn't disturb Nic. Luca sat at the end of the box truck, his feet over the tail, his back toward her. She made her way over and sat next to him.

"I can take over guard if you want," she said.

Luca didn't turn to look at her, still peering out at the trees. "Good morning, Rapunzel."

"Let me guess. That's another princess?"

Finally, he looked toward her. His eyes didn't seem as dark as they were last night, now gleaming with amusement. "Don't you know anything about fairytales?"

"I know enough to know I'm not a princess. Princesses are helpless and in constant need of rescuing from dragons and mortal peril and—I don't know—mud puddles."

"I do recall rescuing you a few times," Luca said.

"And I recall saving your endsphere when we first met. *Princess.*"

Luca threw back his head and laughed, and if Shiloh didn't need him to drive the rest of the way to Minneapolis, she would have strangled him. But perhaps she should be angry at herself. She knew he liked getting under her skin, and she let him do it anyway.

"Fair enough," he said. "And would you knock it off with the endsphere and the froq already? You're not in Arcadia. You aren't bound by the Codex anymore. You don't have to censor yourself. You can swear like a normal person."

Shiloh chewed on the inside of her cheek. The words she used were so ingrained, she hadn't considered it. But begrudgingly, she had to admit Luca had a point.

Luca leaned sideways, closer to her, his shoulder brushing hers. "And do you want to know why I really call you 'Princess'?"

Shiloh gave him what she hoped was a disinterested expression. He went on anyway.

"You're the one in love with a prince. The Princess of ROGUE and The Prince of Arcadia. Sounds like a fairytale if I ever heard one."

Shiloh tightened her jaw. She was not discussing Jake with him again. "You're an idiot," she hissed instead. "And I'm not a princess of anything."

"Fine." He leaned away from her "If you're *not* a princess, then what role do you play in this fairytale?"

"There's *no* fairytale, Luca," Shiloh said, her voice turning to an angry hiss.

And somehow, she'd already lost. Luca was laughing again, like seeing her angry was his greatest joy in life.

A rustle in the trees sucked Luca's laugh from his throat. His hand flew to the rifle at his side. Shiloh cursed herself for leaving her gun by her sleeping bag, even as her gaze swept through the towering trees and tangled brush for the source of the noise. A squirrel darted out of its hiding place beneath a fallen log. Leaves rustled as it scampered to the next tree.

Luca let out a breath, the teasing in his demeanor extinguished. He twisted, leaning his back against the truck wall, crooking one long leg toward his chest. "Okay, let's hear this plan of yours. How are we rescuing the damsel in distress?"

"Val," Shiloh said. "Her name is Val. And if she heard you calling her a damsel in distress, she'd skin you alive."

"I like her already." Luca twirled his wrist in a '*go on*' gesture. "The plan?"

"We can use the Cloaks."

"And?"

"And..." Shiloh hesitated. "I haven't gotten any further than that. I'll figure it out."

"Let's hope so," Luca muttered. He glanced toward his brother who slept a few feet away, one arm flung over his eyes. Luca swore beneath his breath and ran a weary hand over the back of his neck. "All this because someone had to go and catch feelings. Girls are nothing but trouble."

"I'll try not to take that personally," Shiloh said.

He smirked. "Oh, you should *definitely* take that personally."

Shiloh bit her lip to hold back a sharp retort. Outside the truck, the sunlight sneaked through the canopy of leaves to create a kaleidoscope pattern amongst the budding grass. "Is that why you changed your mind and agreed to help? For Ali?"

"Yes," he said, and then he sighed, his head falling back against the metal of the truck. "And no."

Shiloh waited, remembering Ali's words. *You, of all people, should know how bad a Reform Home is.*

The silence lingered on and on and on. Shiloh watched another squirrel skitter around a tree and began to give up hope he'd ever explain his cryptic answer.

"Our last name was Haven."

Shiloh's breath froze on her lips. She jerked her head toward him, expecting to see some humor in his gaze, but there was only grim sincerity.

"Before ROGUE," Luca went on, "Ali and I—our last name was Haven."

Shiloh stared at him. She hadn't known any Haven boys before. The closest Haven for boys had been in a different district from Ardency, so they'd never been at her school. Yet she knew enough that no matter how far apart the Haven, they shared the same wickedness. The horror of it could be glimpsed if she dared look deep enough into Luca's eyes. She felt a connection, an understanding, snap into place between the two of them—like enemy soldiers who'd survived the same bloody war.

Shiloh swallowed, her mouth suddenly dry, not sure how to respond to the truth he'd entrusted her with. "Oh," was all she could manage.

"Oh," he echoed as though it said it all.

"Then is Ali really—" She bit her lip because it didn't matter whether or not an ounce of blood was shared between them, Ali really was his brother, just like Val was her sister. "I mean..."

"I know what you mean. I know the bonds between Havens can run deep, but yes, he's my blood brother," Luca confirmed. "We had the same mom, different dads. I don't remember much about her, to be honest. It was fourteen years ago. I was six at the time, and Ali was barely one when we went to the Haven together. We are all each other has ever had."

A thousand questions bounced in Shiloh's head. What it had been like for them there... If his Haven had a Repentant Closet, too... If Ali had really meant the words he'd said about the Reform Home, and if so, why Luca had ended up there...

"For fuck's sake," Luca said, rolling his eyes toward the roof of the van, "stop looking at me like you're trying to solve a puzzle and just ask."

"Are you gay?"

"What?" Luca barked a laugh. "Where the fuck did that come from?"

"I heard what Ali said. About you going to a Reform Home."

The laughter died in his throat, vanishing from the air as though it had never been there. His hands tightened on his rifle.

"Not everyone ends up in a Reform Home because they're gay, Princess."

"Then why were you there?"

Something flashed in his eyes, something bright and sharp, like the white-hot pain of being shot. He glared down at the rifle beside him. After a long moment, he shrugged. "I told the truth."

The word pricked at Shiloh's skin. *Truth is dangerous.*

"About what?" Shiloh asked.

He shrugged again. "It doesn't matter. Something I should have kept my mouth shut about. But I wasn't at the Reform Home for long, and after I got out, I couldn't stay in that... place any longer. So, I took Ali, and we ran."

"How did you escape?" Shiloh murmured, thinking about sensors on windows at her Haven, the Protectors who patrolled the area.

He turned to look at her. Curls fell into his face, casting him into shadow. "That, Princess, is a story for another time."

Shiloh nodded, chewing on the inside of her cheek. She understood, all too well, that the Haven was something best left not thought about. Perhaps that was why he hated her—because her presence was a reminder, rough sandpaper rubbing at the edges of painful memories.

"You should go to sleep," she said.

He didn't argue but stood. He swept a low mocking bow. "As you wish, Princess."

Shiloh's fingers curled, the familiar irritation returning. Whatever sad story rested behind his cool exterior, he was still... he was still...

"You're a froqing—"

Luca quirked an eyebrow

She caught herself, fumbled with the words, and then spat them out. "You're a fucking asshole."

"That's more like it," Luca smirked, proud, as he laid down

next to his brother. "And what a relief. For a second there, we were getting along way too well."

⚜

"That's it... that's your plan?" Luca asked, staring at Shiloh like she'd grown a second head. Or maybe three separate heads. "Your whole plan?"

Shiloh nodded. "I understand it's a bit... rudimentary..."

"Rudimentary?" Luca huffed, crossing his arms over his chest. "You're supposed to be some star of intelligence, and that is the only plan you have? I could have come up with that."

In the back of the truck, Ali and Nic sat a few feet away, gnawing on protein bars and sharing a bottle of water. Nic glared at the back of Luca's head, while Ali wore a goofy little smile, so different from his brother's smirk.

"If you can think of any other options," Shiloh snapped, "I'd love to hear it."

Luca groaned. "Girls are—"

"If you finish that sentence again," Shiloh said, "I swear I'll hurt you."

His smirk widened, flashing a bit of teeth, as he swept his gaze back to her. "Don't threaten me with a good time, Princess."

Ali snorted, trying too late to hide the noise behind a sip of the water. Nic timed the elbow she thrust into his side well, and he let out a gasp and a fine spray of water.

Shiloh felt like she was missing a punchline, but she ignored it. "If you're chickening out, I can find a way to get Nic and myself the rest of the way to Minneapolis."

"Fine, Princess, fine." Luca's nostrils flared. He stepped closer, until Shiloh had to crane her neck up to meet his gaze. "But mark my words: you're gonna be the death of me."

FORTY-FOUR

Someone knocked on the door to the Reform Home, but when the Corrector—a razor-thin, balding man—opened the door, he found no one on the doorstep.

A few feet away, Shiloh pressed herself lower to the ground, beneath the bushes that surrounded the front porch of the Reform Home. The movement should be unnecessary. If the Cloak was doing its job, no one could see her.

From the outside, the Reform Home looked almost romantic, with its slanted porch and stone facade that made it look like it might have been a bed and breakfast once. Pretty wrapping paper on a literal hell. Shiloh and her comrades had watched the Reform Home for several hours, timing the rounds of the Protectors who drove by. Every fifty-five minutes. They'd been gone for only five minutes when Luca, Nic, and Shiloh had put on the Cloaks and left Ali with the truck a few blocks over.

And then Luca had enacted Shiloh's plan: to just waltz right up and knock.

The Corrector took one more step onto the porch. Beside Shiloh, Nic let out a soft breath, the only sign that she was there, hidden behind the Cloak's projections. The exhale was almost a signal because Luca sprang from where he must have been, invisible on the porch. He slapped a hand over the Corrector's mouth, becoming momentarily visible as the Corrector's body blocked the cameras and projectors. The Corrector cried out, the sound muffled behind Luca's hand as he hauled the man down the steps.

Shiloh sprang up, stepped close, and put a tranq bullet into the Corrector's chest with her gun—the only one new enough to be able to tranq. The Corrector collapsed in Luca's hold.

Luca dragged the man's limp body into the bushes and dropped him. Now that he was this close, Shiloh could see the object that hung on the Corrector's belt. An electric prod—the same kind the Elite carried. The memory of the prod's sting still echoed in the nerves throughout her body like a silent scream.

Did the monsters who ran this place use the prod to perform their corrections? It was after midnight, and the Corrector still wore it on his belt. Did he like to use it in the middle of the night, so the tortured kids couldn't even sleep without fear? Had he used that on Val?

Shiloh's fingers twitched on the trigger of her gun, some part of her wanting to put a bullet between his eyes. She gritted her teeth against the desire. The noise of a real bullet would give them away.

"Let's go," Luca whispered, from somewhere on Shiloh's left. She heard his footsteps climb the porch and saw the front door sway as he charged in. She rushed after him, trusting that Nic was right behind her.

Once inside, Shiloh tried to get her bearings. A staircase rose straight up before her, a wall to her left, and a room set with a circle of chairs on her right, with a hallway branching off it.

"Upstairs," Shiloh whispered.

"Hello?" Floorboards creaked to her right. A light flashed on in the dining room. Another man—another Corrector, surely—

rubbed at sleepy eyes and the sudden light. "Wells, who was at the door?"

He blinked right at them, and Shiloh held her breath. "What the—" he murmured, walking past them. Shiloh leaped back a step, out of the way, and her allies must have done the same because someone collided with a coat rack set by the door. It clattered to the ground.

The Corrector spun, eyes wide. He looked around himself, seeing nothing. "W-who's th—"

A gunshot exploded. Blood sprayed through the air, speckling Shiloh's face. Some must have coated their projectors too, because Shiloh could see splotches of Luca and Nic now. A hip, an elbow, Luca's gun, trained forward.

"Luca!" Nic growled. "What did you do?"

"Get the girl," Luca snapped, "and let's get out of here!"

The house was waking up. Cries came from upstairs after the sound of the shot, and Shiloh heard footsteps pounding. Shiloh lunged for the stairs, taking them two at a time.

🔥

Val's eyes flung open at the explosion of sound. She hadn't been sleeping, but she had learned quickly that if any of the three Correctors caught her with her eyes open at night, she'd be rewarded with another "reprogramming" session.

What was that? Val's heart slammed against her chest like it was trying to escape. *A gunshot?*

"What's happening?" whispered one of the girls in the room. She was younger than Val, and her voice squeaked.

A few more of the girls murmured answers, and Val shushed them as she heard distant yelling. It sounded like it was coming from down the stairs. She couldn't make out much, but she heard the words 'get' and 'girl'. And then... feet on the stairs.

Val sat up. Her entire body hurt. The electricity of the prod had made her body stiffen and jerk until every one of her muscles remembered the tension even now.

The voices drew closer. "There's a lock."

"Stand back," replied a second voice.

Boom!

The girls in the room screamed, all but Val. The gunshot was so much closer now and paired with the sound of splintering wood. Cries of alarm came from the boys' room. Whoever this was, they'd shot the padlock off the door.

Val forced herself to her knees next. She couldn't run, not with the tether on her ankle, its anchor latched onto the metal footboard of her cot. They had set the eletrical bound so tight that Val couldn't even get off the bed, let alone make it to the door. But she could fight. She could die on her feet.

Planting her feet on the mattress, Val stood.

The girls murmured, asking what they should do. Someone was crying. Someone was saying "I don't want to die."

We're already dying. Arcadia is killing us all.

But Val didn't want to die like this either, in this froqing ordure-hole of a place. She didn't want to die with the memories of the days she'd spent here, of what the correctors' sessions included. The burning agony of the prod was a relief compared to other methods the Correctors employed, particularly the largest one of them—Corrector #3. They didn't have names, only numbers. The way he'd touched her, the way he'd forced her to touch him.

Do you feel that? This is what you're supposed to like.

In the moment, Val had jerked away and cursed at him in Spanish—the language of her parents, the language of her heritage, the language Arcadia had tried to take away from her. Her entire being had shrieked, *I will not break!* She'd fought until the pain of the prod pressed against her skin had turned her curses into a scream.

But now...

Now...

Val's stomach heaved; the desire to cry built up in her chest. She didn't want to remember the touch of Corrector #3. She wanted to remember the few good things in her life. She wanted to remember her parents' loving arms—the few, shadowy memories that the Haven hadn't stolen from her. She wanted to remember Shiloh and Hope, who always loved her for exactly who she was. And most importantly, Val wanted to remember the way Stefani had touched her—like she was unwrapping a Yuletide present she'd waited for all her life. She wanted to remember the urgency of Stefani's lips on her collarbones, her hips, the most intimate parts of her.

If her body was tattooed with anything, Val wanted it to be love. She wanted it to be *Stef*.

Val raised her fists to her chin, moved her feet apart. A fighter's pose. If whoever was about to come through that door meant to take her, then she'd die fighting, with Stefani's name as her last thought.

Another gunshot, and the door swung open. And Val saw... no one. No, that wasn't right, she saw a patch of... something... floating in the air.

Froq, she was froqing hallucinating now. *Fan-froqing-tastic.*

But then, in a blink, someone was there when they hadn't been before—or they had been and Val hadn't been able to see them. A single nightlight shown a dim glow in the hallway, illuminating the intruder from behind. A pair of eyes peeked between swaths of fabric. But the stranger pulled down the scarf covering their mouth, and Val realized it wasn't a stranger at all.

"Shiloh!" the name came out as a sob. Oh, froq, maybe Val was hallucinating, because Shiloh couldn't be standing there, looking like some motherfroqing ninja who'd come to rescue her.

But Shiloh's lips twitched, the way they often did instead of smiling. "Val, let's go. I'm getting you out of here."

Another sound left Val's lips, a shaky sob of relief, but then reality set in. "I can't. I'm tethered!"

Shiloh glanced at Val's ankle, the blinking red light and metal circle. Behind her, a shadow moved.

"Shiloh, look out!" Val yelled, but it was too late.

Corrector #3 lunged from the darkness and slammed into Val's sister.

🔥

The force collided with Shiloh like a speeding train, slamming her into the ground. In the dim light, Shiloh could just make out the hulking form of a bulldozer of a man, another Corrector. His heavy weight landed on top of her, his hands fighting for her wrists to pin her.

For fuck's sake, Shiloh, Brooks's voice berated. *When are you going to learn to watch your feet?*

Shiloh thrust an elbow into his throat, and he choked out a gasp, clutching his throat. Shiloh rolled free and leaped to her feet once more.

"Shiloh!" Nic called.

The man was already on his feet again, only a few feet away, looking like a bull about to charge.

"Don't worry about me," Shiloh called, not taking her eyes off the Corrector. "Get Val out of the tether."

The man roared and flung himself at Shiloh. She danced out of the way, reaching for the gun at her hip, her hand landing on an empty holster. Froq. It had been in her hand when she'd fallen. She searched the floor, but in the dim, she couldn't see it. She didn't have long to look because he lunged again. She narrowly dodged him.

You're going to have to fight back sooner or later.

Brooks's voice hummed in her head, thrumming with her racing pulse.

Fight smart.

Shiloh could go invisible again, but then the Corrector might go for Val and Nic. Shiloh could see them in the corner of her vision, Nic pulling at Val's ankle. They needed time. She could scream for Luca, but she heard sirens outside, rapidly approaching, and she knew it'd only be a matter of time before Luca had a host of Protectors to ward off.

She was on her own.

Fight smart.

The Corrector lunged again, and Shiloh flung herself out of his way, closer to the staircase. He was nearly twice her size. Even if he didn't have formal combat training, he might overpower her hand to hand from sheer mass alone. But...

She glanced behind her at the long staircase, descending into the darkness of the first floor.

"Come here, you blight," the Corrector growled.

Shiloh positioned herself before the stairs. "Come and get me."

He lunged just as she dropped to the ground and rolled away. When he stood at the edge of the stairs, his arms grasping the air where she'd been, she kicked out a leg and swept his ankles out from beneath him. The Corrector bellowed a cry as he hit the stairs and then kept rolling. One more thud, and then silence.

A gunshot sounded to Shiloh's right. She spun toward Val's room. Nic—who'd let herself be visible—trained her gun at the bed where the anchor of the tether had been fastened. It now lay in a million pieces. The tether loosened from Val's ankle and fell away.

Crashing came from downstairs, Luca swearing, and two gunshots.

"Hurry the fuck up, Princess!" he yelled.

"Who the froq is that?" Val asked.

"No time to explain," Shiloh replied. "Let's go!"

She located her gun on the floor and snatched it. Nic and Val ran from the room. The children cried behind them, and Nic froze, glancing back.

"What about them?" Nic asked.

"We can't save them," Shiloh said. "Let's go."

Shiloh grabbed Val's hand and tugged her down the stairs. She glanced behind her once to see Nic frozen to the floor, still staring at the children. Nic was a better person than Shiloh would ever be. Because, though she was sorry for these kids, though she'd burn every Reform Home down if she could, all Shiloh wanted was her sister, and she'd sacrifice all of them to have her. Over and over.

"Freebird, we have to go!" Shiloh called, and this time Nic moved, pounding down the stairs after them.

The Corrector laid crumbled at the bottom of the steps, his neck hanging at a crooked angle, his eyes wide and unseeing. Val stopped on the bottom stair and glared down at him, a look of pure hatred crossing her face. Three other bodies lay on the floor: the other Corrector and two Protectors. Shiloh's feet slipped in the blood coating the floor, nearly losing her balance, until a hand wrapped around her arm.

She whirled, lifting her gun halfway, but it was only Luca, now visible, his face splattered with blood. "We have to go. There will be more where these two came from."

Shiloh could hear distant sirens. She yanked on Val's arm, but Val didn't budge, still seething down at the Corrector. Her face contorted with rage and... and something else Shiloh couldn't bear to name. Val brought her leg back and kicked the dead man in the side, once, twice, three times, his limp body caving to it. She screamed with each blow, the sound long and torturous.

Shiloh's heart cracked with the sound. What had this man done to her? But now... now wasn't the time.

"Val, come on," Shiloh said, dragging her toward the door. Val fought Shiloh, crazed in her pain, sending a kick into the man's face.

Nic grabbed Val's shoulders, turned her around, locked eyes with her. "I know," she said. "I know, Val, but we have to go."

Somehow, this got through to Val, and she stopped resisting. Val allowed Nic to haul her forward. They ran for the door, feet sliding in the muck. They left bloody footprints on the white porch. When they hit the yard, all four of them broke into a sprint. None of them bothered to turn their Cloaks back on. They were too splattered with blood to have been a perfect camouflage, and besides, Val didn't have a Cloak.

Sirens wailed in the distance. Shiloh searched around the city street for the blue and red lights, but she couldn't see any. The four rounded a bend in the street, and at the end was the box truck. It roared to life, headlights flaring on. Shiloh could barely make out Ali's form behind the steering wheel. The truck started to roll toward them, faster and faster down the street. The tires screeched as Ali slammed on the brake in front of them.

"Everyone in the back," Luca ordered, as he rushed to the driver's side door.

Ali slid over and Luca threw himself in, as Shiloh led the way to the back. Nic helped Shiloh throw the rolling door open, and they lunged in first. Turning back, they both reached for Val's hand, just as the truck wheeled forward. Running to keep up, Val grabbed their wrists. Shiloh and Nic yanked her up with a force that sent all three of them to the bed of the truck.

The wheels of the truck squealed as they turned a corner. Shiloh braced herself against the metal to keep from sliding as the truck nearly tilted on two wheels. On her hands and knees, Shiloh turned, but the string of the back door dangled above her head, just out of reach. Below the truck bed, asphalt sped by. Farther down the road, a glimpse of blue and red flew toward them. Shiloh climbed to her feet carefully, swaying, and grasped the rope. The truck jumped over a bump, and she flung forward. For a heartbeat, her body hovered over the spinning tarmac. Then a hand seized her jacket and yanked her back.

She slammed into the truck bed, her breath leaving her lungs. Nic shoved the door the rest of the way down and collapsed beside Shiloh and Val.

Shiloh laid still, listening. The only sound between the three girls was their panting, Shiloh's own pounding heartbeat, and the faint sounds of sirens. Sirens that grew quieter and quieter. The truck flung around corners, bounced over potholes, and flew at the highest speed it could manage. Until finally Shiloh couldn't hear the sirens anymore.

Shiloh sat up, her head spinning as the adrenaline faded. In the complete darkness of the truck bed, she could see nothing, but she could feel Val and Nic pressed against either side of her.

"You okay?" Nic asked from her left.

"Yes," Shiloh murmured, "Val?"

All that came was a soft exhale. A sob.

Shiloh sought Val's hand in the dark, taking it into her own. Clothes shuffled as Nic moved, and then light flicked on as she found the lantern hanging from the ceiling. Val's dark eyes glistened in the orange light, wide as they met Shiloh's. Shiloh looked her over; she wore a stiff t-shirt and pajama shorts, baring her warm, brown skin. The damage the Reform Home had done in the short time she'd been there decorated her skin in shades of black.

Shiloh didn't want to think about the damage she couldn't see. That kind of injury was far more difficult to heal.

The fire beneath Shiloh's skin climbed. And she was glad—glad that those Correctors were dead.

"You..." Val sucked in a breath through her teeth, trying to grasp control, but the tears only poured faster.

"You're safe now, Val," Nic said softly, resting a hand on Val's back.

"I thought..." Val stammered, "I thought I'd never see you again."

Shiloh swallowed, unable to admit that she'd feared the same thing.

Shiloh didn't know which of them moved first, but in a blink, Val was in her arms. Val clung to her, sobbing hard into her shoulder. Shiloh tightened her hold, some part of her afraid that, if she let her go, she'd lose Val all over again.

"Thank you," Val gasped. She reached out and yanked Nic gruffly into their hug. "Thank you both... for... for coming for me."

"You're my family, Val," Shiloh said. "I'll always come for you."

FORTY-FIVE

The truck didn't stop until they were well out of the city, until the first drops of light could be seen leaking through the crack of the rolling door. When she felt it slow, Shiloh was leaning against the side of the truck, her eyes aching from fatigue. Val's head rested in Shiloh's lap, her breath finally coming in a steady rhythm. She'd looked like she hadn't slept in the three days she'd been at the home.

The brakes squealed as it finally came to a rest. Two doors opened and slammed shut, and then metal clashed as Luca flung the door open. He leaped into the bed with a force that shook it. Ali clambered in after him, less gracefully.

"Are you okay?" Luca demanded, his gaze fixed on Shiloh.

Shiloh held a finger to her lips and gestured down to Val. "Don't wake her," Shiloh whispered.

"Too late," Val grumbled, sitting up, "I'm awake."

"Are. You. Okay?" Luca asked, enunciating each word through his teeth.

"We're fine," Nic answered for Shiloh, pushing up from her other side.

"Are you sure?" Ali asked. His jaw dropped as Nic stepped into the sunlight. He reached a hand forward like he might touch her blood-splattered face, but Nic jerked away in surprise.

"You're covered in blood," Ali said, voice crumbling at the edges.

"It's not mine." Nic shot Luca a glare. "I thought we weren't going to kill anyone."

"I'm not the one who tripped over a coat rack, genius!" he snapped.

"Hey, don't—" Ali said, at the same time Nic pushed around him to march toward Luca, her hands coiled at her sides. "Shiloh could have tranqed him."

"But she hesitated," Luca said, gesturing towards Shiloh. His words landed like a knife in her chest. "And so, I saved our asses. What do you care about a dead Corrector, anyway?"

"I care because we shouldn't be killing people unless we have no other choice."

"People?" Luca spat. "They're perverts who get their rocks off by torturing children. They deserve far worse than a bullet in their skull."

Nic opened her mouth like she might argue, and then she stopped. She looked at Val, who stiffened beside Shiloh.

Nic crossed her arms over her chest. "Fine, whatever."

A heavy silence fell over them all. The weight of what they'd done clung like humidity in the air, sticky and hot against Shiloh's skin. They'd run away from the Sparrows and broken into a Reform Home. Shiloh had killed someone... again. And Luca had killed three... as though it was nothing. But was she any different from him? There wasn't an ounce of sadness or guilt in her chest for the lives it had cost to save Val. Whatever shade of monster Luca could be, Shiloh bled that color, too.

"So," Val said, breaking the tension. She looked at Shiloh and nodded to Luca. "Who's this endsphere?"

Luca shot her a glare.

"That's Luca," Shiloh replied.

Val leaned close, whispered, "Do we like him?"

Shiloh hesitated. Two days ago, she wouldn't have had to hesitate. It would be a resounding *no*. No, she did not like Luca, which meant Val would not like him in solidarity. Val liked nothing more than to bond over mutually shared hatred. But two days ago, Luca hadn't risked his life, and his brother's life, to drive halfway across a state and raid a Reform Home.

From across the truck, Luca watched Shiloh steadily, as though he'd heard Val's question. As though he very much wanted the answer.

"No," Shiloh said at last, dropping her voice even lower so Luca couldn't hear, "but I don't hate him either. He's just... Luca."

"I'm Ali, by the way," he said, giving a cheery wave. "It's nice to meet you."

Val grunted and lifted a hand in an unenthusiastic wave.

"We like him," Shiloh reassured her softly.

Val's wave turned *slightly* more friendly.

"I need sleep," Luca said. "Just for an hour or so. Then we'll keep going."

"We're not going to wait until dark?" Nic asked.

Luca shook his head. "I don't want to risk someone finding us. Or worse, following us back."

"Do you think we're being followed?" Shiloh asked sharply.

He rubbed a hand against the back of his neck. It was an odd gesture from him, a lack of confidence that he never exuded. "I don't think so. I just feel like the Protectors gave up too easily. This thing" —He stomped his foot on the floor of the truck— "is a dinosaur. They could have caught us easily. I thought Ali would have to shoot out their tires."

"Maybe a Haven girl isn't worth that much to them," Val grumbled.

"Maybe," Luca mumbled, but he didn't seem convinced.

"I kept a lookout," Ali added, bouncing his weight from foot to foot. "I didn't see anyone following us."

Shiloh glanced past Luca to the outside of the truck. Trees, beginning to bud in spring, filled her vision. For a moment, the only sound between the five of them was the wind blowing through the branches and Ali's ever-shifting feet.

"Sleep," Nic said at last. "All of you. I'll take the first watch."

"I can—" Ali started to offer, but Nic cut him off.

"I'm fine. I'm not tired."

She sat at the end of the tailgate, dropping her feet over, her shoulders stiff with the weight of her own demons. Perhaps Shiloh should talk to Nic, but she knew a thing or two about demons. Sometimes, it was best to leave them be.

A few minutes later, Val laid down beside Shiloh on the end of the truck, on top of an unrolled sleeping bag. The two brothers, the endsphere and the goofball, laid on Shiloh's other side, Luca's lean back turned away from them. Val shifted onto her back, staring up at the ceiling, chaos scrambling in her chest.

Hope. Sadness. Relief. Grief. She felt it all at once, unsure what emotion to settle on.

Shiloh was staring at her. Val could feel the weight of her gaze. She tried to adjust her mask, the same impenetrable, nothing-can-hurt-me one that she and Shiloh had learned to wear in their time at the Haven. But Shiloh had always been able to see past it.

"Are you okay?" she asked, voice low enough that Nic wouldn't be able to hear it where she sat at the end of the truck.

Now, Nic—Nic *wasn't* okay. One look at her, and Val knew that what had happened to her all those months ago before she'd come to the Haven had caught up with her. The vibrant, fierce girl looked hollowed out and worn like she'd exhausted herself holding onto the cracks in her soul.

Will I look like that, too?

Did they break me?

The hands. Froq, she could still feel the hands.

"Val?" Shiloh's voice creaked with concern.

Val let out a breath. *Think of something, anything else.*

"I'm going to be living with ROGUE now, aren't I?" Val asked.

"Yes," Shiloh replied.

And there it was, the grief. On the roof of the truck, splattered with rays of sunlight, Val could almost see the slant of Stefani's lips as she smiled. Val's eyes burned, and she blinked hard.

"Do you think I'll ever see her again?" Val asked.

"Yes," Shiloh said without hesitation. Perhaps because, if she admitted Val might never see Stefani again, then Shiloh would have to confess that she might never see Jake again. And if Shiloh loved Jake, like Val loved Stefani, then that possibility was torture.

"You can ask me about him," Val said, turning onto her side to face Shiloh. She did want to ask her. Several times since Val had been rescued, Shiloh's lips had formed his name, but she'd only pressed her mouth shut and said nothing. Probably worried Val was too fragile right now. Froq that. "I know you want to."

Shiloh swallowed visibly. "How is he? How's Jake?"

Val rolled her eyes, a habit when she heard his name. "He's miserable."

"Miserable?"

"Without you. He's miserable without you."

Shiloh closed her eyes and pinched the bridge of her nose, the way she did when she held back emotions. Behind Shiloh, Luca stirred, shifting.

Eavesdropping, probably, the froqer.

"So, there's..." Shiloh paused. "He hasn't been seeing anyone else?"

Rage sparked in Val at the thought. She would have pulled Jake's balls out through his throat, but he'd never given her the opportunity. "No, Shi. I would know. He's either at the gym or with Stefani trying to dig up some truth on the United Council so he can destroy them."

Shiloh let out a breath, a look of profound relief crossing her face.

"Did you think he'd cheat on you?" Val asked.

Shiloh shook her head. "Not really. Just... someone said something. And it made me... it made me wonder why he'd bother waiting around for me."

Luca shifted once again. Definitely eavesdropping. Val could guess who that *someone* was. Whatever Shiloh said, Luca was definitely going on Val's hate list.

Because no one—no froqing person—should ever make Shiloh feel like she was unworthy of love. Val knew that feeling all too well. They've been raised and conditioned to feel lesser, broken, wrong. Bad. A Haven girl didn't deserve love.

But Shiloh did.

"I was wrong about Jake," Val admitted, a groan beneath her words. She'd regret saying this, but Shiloh needed to hear it.

"Wrong about what?" Shiloh asked.

"I didn't think he loved you," Val admitted, staring past Shiloh's shoulder so she didn't have to meet her eyes. "But then he came back after you'd been kidnapped, all bruised and miserable, and I realized I'd been wrong. He'd do anything for you. Jake *loves* you, Shiloh. I'm sure of it. He hasn't even looked at anyone else. I think you're... I think you're all he sees."

Shiloh pinched the bridge of her nose again, taking in slow breaths.

When Shiloh opened her eyes again, she met Val's gaze and promised, "We're going to get them back, Val. Stefani and Jake. I swear to you, I won't stop until we get them back."

🔥

Blood.

So much blood.

Nic could still smell it, could almost taste it in her mouth. She thought of four broken bodies, lying in a sea of red. Why did she care? Why did she *still* care? Those men had tortured children—like Silas and the Elite had tortured her.

A lump lodged in Nic's throat, and for a moment, it choked her, refusing to let her draw a breath. Her heart slammed against her chest, a scream built up in her lungs, and for a moment, she was *there*. All she could see was white, broken only by her own blood.

Maybe some part of her was still there. Maybe, she'd never quite made it out of the cage.

"Hey, Nic," said a voice behind her, jolting her back to reality.

Val flopped down beside her, swinging her legs off the end. "Are you okay?"

Nic studied Val. She looked somehow both unemotional and haunted all at once. "I should be asking you the same thing."

"I'm fine," Val said quickly, shifting her gaze out to the surrounding wood. Her gaze followed a bird that flitted from branch to branch.

Nic took a breath. "You don't have to lie to me, Val. I can't imagine what you've been through."

"No worse than what *you've* been through," Val said, without looking toward her.

Nic's mouth dropped open. "Th-this isn't about me. What happened to me was a while ago. I'm fine."

She glared at Nic. "Are you?"

"Yes."

Val looked away, back toward the trees. "Then so am I."

"Val, they probably did things to you that would break most people."

"I'm not broken," she said, shaking her head. "If you weren't hurt by what happened to you, then why should I be hurt by what happened to me?"

"I—" Nic started, but she didn't know what else to say.

"Can we just sit here for a bit?" Val asked with a sigh. "And not talk?"

Nic nodded. She turned back to look outside the truck, watching a patch of sunlight shift through the leaves across the forest floor. And she wondered if she was so willing to admit that Val had been hurt by all this and think no less of her, why Nic couldn't do the same for herself?

Because I'm supposed to be strong, invincible, the best. I'm not supposed to struggle.

They're not supposed to win.

But for the first time, Nic wondered if being broken meant the villains had won... or if broken simply meant you'd survived what should have destroyed you.

"I missed you," Nic said at last, reaching over to take Val's hand.

Val squeezed it in return. "Yeah, kid, I missed you too."

FORTY-SIX

"Does the name Levi Shaw mean anything to you?"

Jake pressed the phone closer to his ear, even though his bodyguard sat in the front seat and he in the back with the divider in the middle of the car sealed tight. The guard couldn't possibly hear. Still, Stefani could have called at a better time than when he was trapped in a car weaving through the Chicago streets. At least it meant she was upright. Probably. It'd be the first time in the seventy-two hours since Val had been taken that Stefani had gotten out of bed, where she'd been burrowed under the covers.

"No," Jake said, shaking his head, though he hadn't turned on the hologram.

"What about the name Henry *Lyoo*?"

"No. Should it?"

There was a pop on the other end of the line like Stefani was chewing gum and just blew a bubble. "Just something I saw on your dad's computer. It's odd because it was the most heavily encrypted piece of data we got, but it doesn't seem like much. Just a bunch of names, all of which were crossed off except those two names."

A thought occurred to Jake. He sat up straighter. "Wait, do you mean Henry *Liu*?"

"Um... Henry L-i-u," she spelled.

"That's it. It's Chinese. It's pronounced *Le-o.*"

"Okay. Then who is he?"

"General Henry Liu. I've met him at a few events." Jake pictured the middle-aged man who wore his Arcadian army uniform like a second skin, emblazoned with badges that spoke of power and honor. He didn't need the ornaments. The set of his shoulders and hardness of his eyes said enough. "He's one of the highest ranked generals in the Arcadian armies."

"Huh. Hold on. I'm going to look up something."

A long silence passed, filled only with the typing of keys on a keyboard. The car took a corner sharply. Jake clasped the side of the door to keep from being yanked by the seatbelt. The car slowed back down, entering another long line of honking traffic. He hated the Chicago traffic, but his father's guards would never let him take the public transportation system that zoomed through the skies.

"So," Stefani said, "Levi Shaw is apparently a Canadian reporter."

Jake frowned. What was the connection between a Canadian reporter and an Arcadian general? What sort of list was this?

"I can't get any other information on him," Stefani continued, "because all the foreign media is, of course, blocked. I'll try from the office next time I get a chance to be alone."

"Okay," Jake said. A heavy silence fell. "And, uh, I'm glad you're, well... upright."

She smacked hard on her gum, an edge entering her voice. "I have something important later today that I have to be functioning for, so I've been working on this as a distracter. You know, trying really hard not to think about my girlfriend being in a literal hell-hole. So, thanks for the reminder, prighead. Would you also like to bring up my painful regressed memories of when my brother tied a cape to my pet gerbil and dropped it off the balcony because he thought the cape could make it fly? It could *not*, by the way."

Jake winced. "Sorry."

"And good luck on your interviews," Stefani said, skillfully changing the subject. "You nervous?"

Jake gazed out at the cars, so jammed packed within the city streets that they appeared to be crawling past. He should be nervous about all the interviews, but he knew what to expect.

Maxwell Smith couldn't care less about who would be fetching him coffee over the summer. He would barely say two words and let his assistant pick the intern, so all Jake had to do was sweet talk her. From what he'd gathered from talking to her at his birthday party, she was new, young, and glossy-eyed. It wouldn't be difficult. Serenity Jameson would turn into a gabfest as soon as Jake complimented her hair. And he was sure Councilor Bennett had far more important things weighing on his mind; his interview wouldn't be rigorous. And since direct relatives couldn't serve as interns, Jake wouldn't interview with his father.

There was only one that presented a challenge.

"Maybe," Jake said. "Beck hates me."

And if he couldn't win her over, he was sure she'd veto him being chosen by any of the other Councilors. Her words to Samuel at Jake's party still swirled in his head.

Handle your son or I'll handle him for you.

This wasn't going to be easy.

"Just tell her you'll propose to *Katerina* tomorrow," Stefani said, something close to seething in her mouth when she said Katerina's name. "It'll make her happy."

"Stef," Jake warned, "don't."

"Wait, Katerina will probably be there interviewing. What will this be? Her third summer in a row? You could just walk into her interview and drop down on one knee and—"

"For froq's sake, Stef!" Jake snapped. "Cut it the froq out!"

"Froqing ordure, I was only joking!"

Jake drew in a breath, forcing himself to lower his voice. "It's not a joke to me."

"I know your father pushes you toward her pretty hard, but—"

"Our marriage contract has already been made, Stef. Beck will make us get married."

Whatever his father had said, Shiloh was the one thing a Councilor seat would never guarantee him. Besides, he couldn't condemn Shiloh to that life—one of an endless masquerade. She'd worn those chains all her life. He loved her too much to allow her to make all the sacrifices that came with being the wife of a Councilor. If Jake couldn't burn the world down soon enough for them to be together, then he'd burn it down for her to be free.

Stefani had been silent a long time, but she cleared her throat. "So, you too are actually, like..."

"Betrothed," Jake finished for her, using her word. "Yeah, basically."

"How'd you find out about this?"

"Beck told Shiloh."

Stefani let out a low whistle. "Excuse my pre-Sundering language, but that's a bitch move. Blight doesn't even cover it."

Jake couldn't help himself. He threw his head back and laughed. "I sure hope no one has bugged my phone. Beck will have you executed in the morning."

"Worth it," Stefani said. "Can you put 'Died as she lived: calling out useless bitches' on my tombstone?"

"It's a promise."

Jake laughed, and even Stefani giggled, but it sounded hollow and quickly died in her mouth. "Hey, Jake, listen. Maybe you need to try a different approach with Beck. Lying to her just insults her intelligence."

"And what should I do? Admit to heresy and hope she doesn't execute me on the spot?"

"We can have matching tombstones, Jakey-boy!"

Jake groaned. "I'm hanging up now."

"But Jakey-wakey, just think about it. We could even share a coffin and save our families the—"

Jake ended the call.

🔥

"Councilor Beck will see you now," said a slender, middle-aged man who wore the Arcadian standard glasses that Jake had only ever seen in the man's hair and not on his nose.

Jake climbed to his feet and took a breath the way he'd seen Shiloh do, slowly in through his nose and out through his mouth. His other interviews had gone about as well as Jake had figured: he'd charmed the socks off Smith's secretary, gabbed with Serenity, and answered the two questions Bennett had mumbled and then not listened to. The man looked grey as a sheet, and despite the cover-up Jake knew the Council had pulled off, there had to have been repercussions.

Jake almost felt sorry for him... until he thought about Val, sitting in a Reform Home. This man was content to take away the rights of others, as long as the same rules didn't apply to him.

Jake thanked the secretary, who opened the ornately carved door that led into Beck's office. Beck sat at her desk, eyes trained on him already. She twirled a small object in her hand; a domino, Jake realized as he drew closer.

"Hello, Jacob." She gestured to one of the stiff leather chairs before her desk. "Please have a seat."

Jake did, glancing quickly around the office. Each of the Councilors' offices within the Unity Center had a bit of their personality in it: Smith's souvenirs from his frequent travel; Jameson's robin-egg-blue walls; and Bennett's pictures of his children, but predictably enough, none of his wife. Beck's was a blank slate. The ivory-wood-toned desks and bookshelves looked like they'd been purchased directly from a magazine. There were no knickknacks or pictures aside from the one black and white abstract painting. It gave away nothing—like Beck didn't want anybody to know her.

The only thing different was the line of dominos set in front of her, lined up one after another, like an army going to battle.

"I can't thank you enough for this opportunity, Councilor Beck," Jake said.

"Let's not waste time with small talk, shall we?" Beck rose from her chair and paced to her small bar, a stool that held only one decanter of amber liquid and two glasses. She poured both glasses. "We both know you're only being considered for a spot because of who your father is."

Jake worked his jaw, trying to decide how to respond. He decided nothing was the best course of action.

"He's had a spot in mind for you since you were born... or if he didn't... your grandfather certainly did." She turned around to face him, sipping a glass. "It'd be unfair for me to go against their wishes. But—"

She let the 'but' hang between them, bearing the force of a hammer on an anvil, landing on Jake's chest.

"But," he said, "you don't trust me."

She tipped the glass toward him. "Ah, you see, therein lies the issue." She took another sip and then returned to her desk. "I don't want to mistrust you, Jacob. I want to be assured of the future of the Osgood line."

"But I haven't made it easy," Jake said. His mouth went dry as the words left his tongue. Truth, Stefani had recommended. He'd either earn Beck's trust with it or earn a death sentence.

Beck sat down in her chair. "You certainly have not." She stared hard at Jake across the desk, calmly sipping her bourbon. She let the silence linger.

And linger...

It's my move, Jake realized. If only Jake knew which game Beck was playing. Maybe it was chess and the best thing to do was go on the defensive. Fall back and protect the king. Or maybe this was poker, and he had to throw down his cards and hope she hadn't stacked the deck against him.

"You know I did it, don't you?" Jake said, fingers curling around the chair. "You know I helped the heretic escape."

His heartbeat screamed in his ears like an alarm bell. He sure hoped Stefani was right. Or maybe Jake could preorder his tombstone. If he allowed Stefani to do it, it'd be engraved: *Jakey-boy, died as he lived: froqing stupid.*

Beck didn't blink, didn't betray even a shred of emotion. "I am not as easily fooled as some people might think."

Jake shook his head. "Of course not."

She sipped the last of the bourbon and leaned forward to set the drink on the desk, putting it down as gently as possible, as to not disturb her dominos. "The question is, Jake, why are you confessing it to me now? Don't you know that truth is dangerous?"

Oh, don't I?

A bead of sweat trailed down Jake's spine; he felt hot beneath the suit jacket that he wore over the Arcadia uniform. But that was what she wanted—to see him sweat. He forced his body to relax, slumping back into the chair.

He shrugged. "If you were going to send me to a prison camp, you would have done it by now. We both know that if you really want something, you have ways of making it happen. Which means, I'm still useful to you."

"I'm not a wasteful person." Beck picked up a domino from the case at the side of the desk. "Every person is a piece in the grand scheme of things." She set down the domino in her hand, crooked between two others. "But even if one thing goes astray..." She tapped the first domino. The line fell rapidly, one after the other, until it struck the crooked piece, which set the chain reaction astray. In the end, only the final piece remained upright. Defiant.

She flicked the insubordinate piece, and it tumbled off the

desk, clattering to the floor. "But sometimes waste is unavoidable, as unfortunate as it is."

Jake stared at the fallen piece. Froq. If ever there'd been a threat...

"It was a mistake," Jake growled. A lie. "Helping her... that... that heretic."

Beck arched an eyebrow, the only sign she was paying attention.

He gritted his teeth because that was what Beck needed to see. She needed to see a reflection of herself. Rage, hatred, vengeance. These were the things that fueled Beck, and he had plenty of that. Directed not at Nic, but at the woman in front of him. He let the hatred ooze through his mask, letting Beck interrupt it as she saw fit.

"I helped her because all I saw was a helpless kid," Jake went on. "And then less than a month later, she sat by and watched as her people kidnapped and beat me. She would have put a bullet in my head if they'd asked her to. They are... *monsters.*"

Beck picked up her glass and twirled it in her hand. "If that's true, then tell me how you contacted ROGUE to help her escape?"

Careful. He could take the risk of exposing himself, but he could not expose Stefani and her family. He thought quickly, missing only two beats in time before he said, "I never had contact with ROGUE. That heretic wouldn't tell me how. She must not have trusted me fully. Shiloh provided a distraction, while I stole a snowmobile and got the heretic off campus. She was on her own after that."

"And who helped Shiloh?" Beck asked. "There were three sets of footprints in the snow that day."

Silas. Only Silas could have told her though. Her lapdog, indeed.

Jake shook his head. "I don't know. She wouldn't tell me. If I knew, I would tell you."

"Would you? Would you really?"

Beck stared at him, unblinking, and he had no idea if she believed the half-truth.

"Yes," Jake said, adding just the right amount of spite to his voice. "I hate ROGUE. I want nothing to do with them."

Beck shook her head and began straightening her dominoes. "And what do you want, Jake?"

"I want—"

A flash of Shiloh passed before him. He shook the image away.

"Power," Jake lied. "Power enough that no one can hurt me like that again. Power enough that I'll never feel weak again. Power enough to make the people who've hurt me suffer."

Okay, Jake thought, looking at Beck, *maybe that last one isn't quite a lie.*

Beck carefully adjusted each domino, the line steadily growing across her desk. "Do you mean to tell me that you've gone from a lovesick boy risking everything for a Haven girl to a boy who suddenly sees all that he's been given in a matter of weeks? It's a tall tale. Hard to believe."

"Truth doesn't have to be believed to be true."

Beck pursed her lips and laid out three more dominos before looking up. "I think that'll be all." Her eyes dropped back to the pieces before her, an intricate plan only she could see.

Jake's shoulders sagged. He was being dismissed, and he'd failed. Everything—his ability to get close to the Council, to grab evidence, to find a way to release it to the world—rested on him getting this internship—and he hadn't done it.

Feeling ill, he stumbled to his feet and slumped to the door, but he paused with a hand nearly touching the handle. Like he was afraid if he touched it, it'd sear his skin. It'd mean defeat.

Jake spun back around. "What can I do that would make you trust me again?"

Beck looked up from her dominoes, and a small smile turned her lips upward. "What would you *be willing* to do?"

A chill slipped down Jake's spine at the sight of her genuine smile. It was like watching a hyena laugh.

"Anything," he swore.

"I hope you mean that, Jacob," Beck said, putting down one last domino. "I really hope you mean that."

She tapped the starting domino, and they fell one by one, curving around and back down the desk until every single one of them bowed, exactly as Beck had intended.

"Jacob, can you stay in the city for a couple more days? We'll be in touch."

Jake nodded, not trusting his voice to speak. Why did he feel like he'd just walked into a trap?

Beck stood and held out her hand for him to shake. He took it, and it was like he was...

Like he was shaking on a deal to sell his soul.

FORTY-SEVEN

I t was almost too easy.

An uneasy feeling weaved itself through every nerve in Shiloh's body, pulling taut as the truck finally came to a rest with a grunt of the brakes. Nic seemed to feel it, too. She paused before the door, both hands pressed against it. She took a long, deep breath before she yanked the door open. Shiloh almost wished she'd left it closed.

Sure, they'd survived this far. But Sawyer, Brooks, Amelia, Paul, Mick, Charlie, maybe even Wallace and the kids—they were going to want to strangle her. Luca, who'd brought a radio along, had sent a message to the Sparrows earlier that day, telling them they were safe and on their way home.

Home?

Had Shiloh ever thought of something as a home before?

Just Jake. Only Jake.

Outside, it was dark, but Shiloh's eyes were adjusted from the hours of dimness in the truck. She heard the rustling of feet flying through leaves and brush. Nic jumped off the end of the truck, disappearing to where Shiloh could no longer see her.

"Oh, Nic!" Paul's voice boomed. "Oh, thank Christ!"

Shiloh hesitantly took a step to the edge, glancing at Val who hesitated behind her. "Don't worry. Whatever they do, I don't think they'll kill me."

Val gave her a look that seemed to say, '*But there's a lot you can live through.*'

Shiloh inhaled deeply. She'd made this choice, knowing that if she made it back alive, there would be severe consequences to pay. But Val was alive, and she was here. Shiloh would pay any price for that.

Val lingered behind as Shiloh made it to the end of the truck bed. In the splashes of moonlight, she made out the faces: Amelia and Paul, both clinging tightly to Nic, profound relief sketched on their faces. Ali and Luca hesitantly rounded from the cab of the truck, just as Brooks broke from the trees. Even as small as she was, she looked like a hurricane charging toward the coast.

"I am going to skin you both alive," she grumbled, charging toward the brothers. Luca and Ali both froze like deer caught in headlights. "I'm going to turn your hides into bearskin rugs. I'm going to hang up your balls like Yuletide decorations."

The brothers exchanged a look like they might run, but it was too late. Brooks flung an arm around each of their necks, yanking them down to accommodate her lesser height. She called them a series of pre-Sundering words, released them momentarily to threaten their lives again, and then returned to hugging and insulting them.

One last person emerged from the woods. Sawyer froze, and even in the darkness, Shiloh and her eyes locked. Sawyer's face remained in shadows, hiding whatever emotion crossed her face. She had to be furious.

"Who's that?" Val said, stopping beside Shiloh.

"That's my..." Shiloh struggled to form words, "well, that's my... my aunt."

Val flinched at the word.

"Just... wait here," Shiloh said. She jumped down from the truck and landed on bended knees. She took a step toward Sawyer, but someone caught her arm and yanked her into an embrace. Strong, unyielding, but somehow still gentle, arms wrapped around her.

Paul.

"Thank Christ you're okay, girl," Paul murmured. He put her at arm's length, looking her up and down. Shiloh was glad they'd all taken time to wash the blood from their faces, or he might have completely lost it. "You are okay, right?"

Shiloh nodded.

"Good." He hugged her again, for good measure. "Brooks and I are going to make you run so many drills for this," he grumbled good-naturedly.

Shiloh didn't doubt it.

She slipped out of his arms, and this time, he let her go. Sawyer still waited at the edge of the woods, away from the others, her eyes unblinking as Shiloh moved closer. Shiloh paused a few feet away, waiting for Sawyer to begin yelling.

But she didn't. Like a sling-shot, Sawyer shot forward, throwing her arm around Shiloh and pulling her against her chest with an embrace so hard it nearly hurt.

"I'm sorry," she breathed into Shiloh's ear. "I'm so, so sorry." She whispered the word over and over, a chorus of apologies.

Shiloh fought for breath, her arms stiff at her side. Sorry? Shiloh had run away, and *Sawyer* was *sorry*?

A soft snap from behind Shiloh caused Sawyer to draw away. Val being Val, hadn't listened when Shiloh had told her to wait. She stood behind her with arms crossed over her chest in what gave the impression of annoyance, but Shiloh recognized as insecurity in how her fingers brushed up and down her arm.

"Val, this is Sawyer," Shiloh introduced. "Sawyer, this is—"

"Your sister," Sawyer completed for her.

Shiloh blinked in surprise as Sawyer stepped around Val and offered her hand. Val eyed it like Sawyer's palm might have fangs but took it anyway.

Sawyer cocked her head toward the trees that hid the Sparrows' camp from view. Brooks, the brothers, Paul, Nic and her mother were already headed in that direction. "We should get back. There are a lot of people eager to meet you."

Val nodded and took a few steps in the direction everyone else headed. She looked back at Shiloh, arching an eyebrow into a silent question.

"You go with Nic," Shiloh said to Val, pinning Sawyer with a stare she hoped Sawyer would read as *stay*. "I'll catch up in a minute."

Val hesitated, glancing between Shiloh and the commander for a moment before she turned and stomped away. The voices and footsteps grew more distant as they slid past the trees toward the houses.

Shiloh turned back to face Sawyer, who stood silent. Waiting.

"You said you were sorry," Shiloh asked. "Why are *you* sorry?"

Sawyer gulped down a breath and sagged against the bumper of the truck. She looked... exhausted. And that was something remarkable. Sawyer was allowing Shiloh to see behind the stony mask of the commander. She studied the lines in Sawyer's face, the furrows around her eyes, the creases across her forehead. They seemed more numerous than they had the last time Shiloh had seen her, as though Shiloh's absence had etched more into place.

"Where do I even begin?" Sawyer asked.

The question seemed rhetorical, and yet, the silence stretched on. The wind hissed through the trees, teasing goosebumps on Shiloh's bare arms, making the hair that had escaped her ponytail tickle her face.

"I thought you'd be angry with me," Shiloh said.

A light sparked in Sawyer's dark eyes, so bright it was visible even in the moonlight. "Oh, I *am* angry, Shiloh. Believe me. Some part of me wants to yell at you until the sun comes up, and then a little more, for good measure. But"—She took a breath—"I am angrier at myself."

"I don't understand."

Sawyer stood from the bumper and took a step forward. It seemed almost... hesitant, like Shiloh was a bird that might startle away. "Because I should have listened to you. I should have heard you out about Val, instead of simply shutting you down. I have... I've been the leader of ROGUE for a long time, and after I lost Elaine and Alec and you, the leader of ROGUE was *all* that I was. I forgot how to be anything else. I forgot how to be a friend, or a person, or..." Sawyer swept her arm toward Shiloh. "Or an aunt. I especially forgot what it meant to be a sister. If it'd been Elaine in Val's place, nothing... *nothing* would have stopped me from going to get her."

Shiloh sealed her eyes closed, unsure what to feel—frustration, validation, sympathy? It all blurred together, stirring up a cyclone in her chest.

"And I should have gone with you," Sawyer went on. "Not as the leader of ROGUE. I should have gone because you needed me, and because I love you." Sawyer's voice dropped, barely louder than the gentle breeze. "And I've done a terrible job of showing that."

Shiloh dropped her gaze, digging her boot into soft dirt. If she looked at Sawyer now, Shiloh thought her heart might crack open and bleed a wound she didn't want to admit existed. She'd always thought of her heart as a cold, broken thing. That she was content without love. But love was the thing she craved most, the thing she needed to survive. Jake's, and Val's, and Nic's and the love of those she'd grown to know as friends. As family. And yes, somewhere along the way, she'd craved Sawyer's love, felt incomplete without it.

"When I woke up and you were gone..." Sawyer groaned, like

words were not enough to express the agony. "I felt like the world had been pulled out from under my feet, and I was the only one to blame. I hated myself. I would have given anything, *done anything*, to have you back."

A branch cracked beneath Sawyer's feet as she took a step closer, close enough to hug Shiloh now if she wanted. She didn't, though. "So, I'm sorry, and I'm also sorry that I made a lot of choices for you without consulting you. In my head, you were still that six-year-old girl I'd lost. But you're an adult. And you get a say in your life. Always. Understand?"

Shiloh let out a breath, exhaling the tornado in her chest, and focused on only one emotion. She lifted her chin and forced herself to meet Sawyer's eyes, "And what about Jake?"

Sawyer let out one long exhale. "I'm not going to lie to you, Shiloh. I think he's going to break your heart." Shiloh opened her mouth to argue, but Sawyer held up her hand and finished quickly, "*But* no one should get to dictate who we choose to love."

Something in Shiloh's chest warmed at those words, the spark for Jake that not even all this time and distance could dim. Love was fire, and she burned for him.

"I love him, Sawyer," Shiloh said. "I'll *always* choose him."

Sawyer planted her hand on her hip and nodded, sighing one more time. "Okay, okay, but if he hurts you, I'm going to kill him."

Shiloh's mouth twitched. "He won't, but I think Val would fight *you* on first dibs. I'm pretty sure she's already threatened to castrate him numerous times."

Sawyer's mouth parted in a laugh. The noise almost startled Shiloh. "Did she? I think I'm going to like her." She shook her head. "Scratch that. *You* love her, so *I'll* love her. She's family."

Shiloh's mouth opened, but no words came out. She didn't know what words she could say to summarize all she felt. Gratitude that the commander had let down her mask. Hope that she would get to keep the aunt behind the mask—because *her*, Shiloh might like. *Her*, Shiloh might just love.

No words. Shiloh was useless with them, so instead she let her mask drop, too, and lifted her arms to pull her aunt into another embrace.

FORTY-EIGHT

Charlie let out a cheer as the group exited the woods and stepped into view of the fire. Nic raised her hand in greeting from where she remained tucked into her mom's side. Val dragged along behind everyone. And Paul—Paul stayed close and distant all at once. He walked beside Nic so that she created a barrier between him and Amelia. Nic studied him—the slump of his shoulders, the drag of his steps, the way his smile had slipped from his face when she wasn't watching .

He looked sad.

Nic stopped so quickly Val nearly collided with her back. As Brooks and the two brothers continued toward the fire, Nic turned toward her mom.

"What did you decide about the baby?"

Out of the corner of her eye, Nic saw Val mouth, "*Baby*?"

Mom looked over Nic's head to Paul, who cast his eyes upward, toward the stars that twinkled above their heads.

When neither one of them spoke, Nic asked more pointedly, "Is there going to be a baby?"

"Yes," Mom said, "there is."

Nic's heart leaped in her chest. Fear? Excitement? Both?

It was definitely both.

"So, are you and Paul together now?" Nic asked.

Mom's eyes widened, shimmering in the moonlight. Paul flinched, like Nic's words physically hurt. And Nic's heart sank down deep into her gut.

No.

Mom said, "Paul and I had a long talk before you left—"

No. No. No.

"—and we decided we were better as friends."

"You mean *you* decided," Nic accused.

Nic glanced at Paul, who cast his eyes toward the starry sky, his jaw locking. All the confirmation she needed.

"Why?" Nic demanded.

"I think you and your mother should talk," Paul said. Before Nic could protest, Paul cast a look over his shoulder at Val, whose neck might have been getting whiplash from how she jerked her head between all of them. "Come on, Val. I can introduce you to everyone."

Val muttered under her breath in displeasure as she sulked after Paul, sending Nic a look that clearly read *Why hast thou forsaken me?* Nic felt bad about it, but she needed to talk to her mom. Now.

Mom watched Paul go, his shoulders slumped low, then cocked her head toward the direction of the lake. "Walk with me."

She led the way, and Nic stomped after her. A steady scream built up in her chest. This was all so *stupid, stupid, stupid*. Why weren't they together? They should be together. Paul and Amelia. In this stupid world where so little made sense anymore, *they* made sense.

Nic and her mother walked in painful silence for the first several minutes, passing Mick, who must have been on patrol. He scowled at Nic. "Give her an earful for me," he told Mom.

"Thanks, Mick." Mom tossed him a mocking two-fingered salute. "But I got it."

He grumbled angry Spanish under his breath as he stomped on. Nic couldn't help but think that he and Val would get along brilliantly.

The tall grass near the lake shore teased Nic's fingertips, disappearing into the crunch of stone beneath her feet. Fractured moonlight danced in the ripples of the water. Mom came to a halt, her boots inches from the lake's edge. She stared out at the water and took a deep inhale.

"Have I told you how much I always liked the water?" Mom asked.

Nic nodded, though she wasn't sure. Her mom *must* have, at some point. Except Mom so rarely talked about herself, about what she liked, about what she wanted. Every conversation seemed focused either on the needs of the group, the mission of ROGUE, or on Nic. Always, suffocatingly, on Nic.

"It always made me feel close to God," Mom said, "when I stand on the shore of something so beautiful."

Nic exhaled roughly. This... wasn't what they were supposed to be talking about. But Mom's words stirred up something within Nic. She thought of standing in almost this same spot, skipping stones when Mom had left. She hadn't felt close to anything or anyone. Well, Ali's hug—heat crept up Nic's neck at the memory —that had been something, but it hadn't quite patched the cavernous ache within Nic's chest, the emptiness that threatened to tear her apart.

"Maybe one day I'll take you to the ocean," Mom went on. "It's breathtaking... and terrifying. It makes you feel so small... and yet, so vastly important."

Nic wasn't sure why she said it. But the words built up inside of her, hammering against her lips, burning on her tongue, until she spat them up.

"Mom, what would you say if I told you I'm not sure I believe in God anymore?"

Mom started, and Nic stared out at the lake. She didn't want to see whatever expression crossed Mom's face. The moments of silence stretched out, yanking open the cracks in Nic's chest. Finally, Mom's fingers touched the hair on Nic's shoulder, a sweet caress.

"Nic, my love, I'd say that's okay."

Nic jerked her head toward Mom, eyes burning. Surely, she'd heard her wrong. Mom swept Nic's hair back away from her face. "Sweetheart, whether or not you believe in God is your own decision. And if you want to talk about it, we can talk about it. But it would never change how I feel about you. Nothing—not a single damn thing—could make me love you less."

"You don't think I'm weak?" Nic asked, hating the croak in her voice. "For doubting my faith?"

A humorless laugh crossed her lips. Like it was ridiculous. "Nic, I could never, not in a million years, think you're weak. You are the strongest person I know. And I am so *very* proud that you are my daughter."

Nic curled her hands into fists, trying to regain control of her emotions. The nails stung as they dug in. She unfurled her hands and inspected her palms. Little scabbed crescent moons had formed on both her hands, the evidence of how tightly she had tried to hold on all this time. She'd been hammering boards to hold up a cracking foundation, while every day they splintered wider. She was damaging herself, cutting herself apart, to try to keep herself together.

"I don't understand," Nic said, taking a step back. "You treat me like I'm a broken toy. You and Paul just keep me locked away, keeping secrets from me. You don't ever give me the chance to fight."

Something Shiloh had said echoed in Nic's chest, where it had planted itself.

A cage may keep you safe, but it is still a cage.

A sob broke from Nic's lips, coming from somewhere deep. "Mom, I feel like I'm *still* in that cage."

The tears came now, a flood of them, and Nic feared that now that they'd started, they'd never stop. She turned her back, not wanting her mother to see. Her feet ached to run, far and fast, but Mom's arms wrapped around her waist, pulling Nic against her chest. Clinging to her.

"Nic, it has never been you, okay? I'm the one who's been afraid."

Nic sucked in a shaking breath, trying to regain control, but the sobs hiccupped past her lips.

Mom turned Nic around gently. Her own tears glistened in the moonlight. "Baby, when I lost you, when you were gone, I felt like I died. I thought losing Jason... losing your dad... was the worst pain I could ever feel, until losing you. I wanted to lay down and never get back up again, and if it hadn't been for Paul, I might have. I got a miracle when you came back to me. If I'm holding on too tightly, it's because I am not strong enough to survive the pain of losing you again. But maybe I have held on so tightly that my arms have become chains, and it isn't fair. I'm so sorry. But it was *never* because I didn't think you were strong enough. You are braver and stronger than I am. I"—She let out a shuddering breath —"am a coward."

Nic forced herself to inhale through her nose. She scrubbed the heels of her hands into her eyes. The tears didn't stop, but they slowed. "Is that why you think you and Paul are better off as friends?"

Mom blinked rapidly. "What?"

"Because you're afraid?" Nic sniffed, changing the subject. Focusing on this was easier than focusing on all the emotions she'd let spill out of her chest. She knew it was only a small reprieve, but she'd take it. "Are you afraid you might lose him like you lost dad?"

"I... I don't..."

"Do you love him?" Nic asked.

Mom threw up a hand like it was a silly question. "Of *course*, I love him."

"That's not what I mean. Are you *in love* with him?"

A look not unlike panic crossed her eyes. "I—I don't—"

Nic took one of Mom's hands between both of her own. "Be brave, Mom."

Mom swallowed and then swallowed again. She twirled her wedding ring around her fingers. Then at last, she closed her eyes and breathed out truth, "Yes, I'm in love with him."

"Then you should be together. And not as just friends."

"Your father—" Mom protested, but Nic shook her head.

"Dad would want you to be happy."

Mom shook her head, but she lifted a hand to hide her small smile. "When did you get so smart?"

Nic smiled in return, contrasting the tears drying on her face. "I got it from my mama."

"I'm not so sure about that." Mom reached forward, sweeping her fingers to wipe Nic's face, but more tears replaced the ones she'd banished. "Are you okay, sweetheart?"

The automatic words—*I'm fine*—sprang to Nic's lips, but she sucked it down. What if she was honest? Truly honest? Maybe it would be as Paul had said. Maybe she'd be able to do the work to put herself back together.

She let out a trembling breath. "No, Mom, I'm not okay. I haven't been okay for a really long time."

Mom pulled Nic into her arms, and the strength of the embrace seemed to hold Nic together. She'd spent so long clinging to all the fractures within herself, maybe it was time to let someone else hold the pieces.

"Does that change your mind?" Nic said, through the sobs. "Do you think saying that makes me weak?"

"No, soldier. I think admitting you're not okay is the strongest thing you've ever done."

🔥

Val couldn't stop staring at Mick and Charlie's hands. She'd been sitting here, holding a bowl of venison stew, for thirty minutes now, and she couldn't stop staring at their hands. Paul had led her to the fire and introduced her to Charlie—who'd given her the bowl of stew—and some old dude named Wallace, who tried to tell her his entire life story within minutes of meeting. Val had to bite her lip to keep from telling him she didn't give an ordure. Apparently, there were more people in the group, a woman named Fatima and a handful of kids, but they were all already asleep. Which had been fine with Val.

She was quite peopled out.

But then a guy called Mick had stomped back over to the fire and gave Ali and the gilipollas an earful about skipping out on guard duty and leaving them defenseless, which Luca had explained had only been for a matter of minutes. Mick had still let Luca and Ali have it—cursing them up one way and down another in both Spanish and English.

And then—when Ali's eyes were wide enough, they looked like they might pop out and Luca scowled so deeply it looked like he might get stuck like that—Mick had sat down... and taken Charlie's hand. Without shame, without worry, without fear.

"What's on your mind there, dear?" Charlie asked Val, adjusting his glasses with the hand not holding Mick's.

"Are you two..." Val paused, unsure how to put it.

"Married?" Charlie finished for her, an enthusiastic smile breaking over his face.

Married. The word echoed in Val's head, like a beautiful dream she'd woken up from, to find herself in a nightmare.

Val shook her head. "Gay marriages aren't legal."

Mick growled low beneath his breath, scowling so deeply his scars looked cavernous. "I don't remember asking for the government's opinion."

"Just because idiots don't recognize something," Charlie said, "doesn't mean it isn't real."

Val nodded, still transfixed by the way Charlie's thumb caressed over Mick's knuckles. And no one came running. No one else who sat around the fire—not Paul, who slumped sullenly on a log, or Wallace, who looked like he might be falling asleep sitting up, or Brooks, who'd followed through with her threat to send the brothers immediately to guard duty—even seemed to notice. Like it was normal. Like it was expected.

Like it was *right*.

If they were right, then maybe... maybe, Val was—

"What's her name?" Charlie asked softly.

Val's fingers clutched her bowl to prevent herself from dropping it. She took a breath, fighting for air as the name lodged in her throat. "Stefani," she said at last.

"Beautiful name," Charlie said. "Does she feel the same?"

Val glanced around the circle. It was strange, being asked questions about Stefani. Val had never been able to talk about her. But no one so much as wrinkled a nose as they listened. Paul nodded his head when her gaze landed on him, and Brooks offered a smile.

Something—not wholly unpleasant—clenched around Val's chest. Not like a fist, but like an embrace.

She'd spent her whole life feeling as though every part of her was wrong, unacceptable, broken. But here, maybe who Val was, wasn't inherently wrong. Maybe, Val was just right.

"Yes, she loves me," Val answered at last. "I don't know how I got that lucky, but she does."

"Stefani?"

Val twisted to look over her shoulder. Shiloh's aunt—the leader of ROGUE—approached their circle. Shiloh walked by her side, looking more relaxed than when Val had left. As Sawyer approached, everyone else seemed to sit up straighter, as though snapping to attention and waiting for the next order. Even Wallace jerked upright, and he'd been snoring.

But Sawyer gave Val a twitch of the lips, a sort of smile that was so profoundly a Shiloh expression, it was a bit unnerving. They really were related.

"That doesn't happen to be Stefani Andreou, does it?" Sawyer asked.

Val nodded.

Shiloh plopped down beside Val, sitting close enough that their shoulders brushed. Val would never admit it, but she was grateful for the closeness.

"I can get a message to her," Sawyer said, "to let her know you're safe. I'm sure she's worried about you."

"But you'll need a codename, girl," said Wallace, tapping his walking stick on the ground. "Whatcha think? Make it a good one."

Val squirmed, looking into her stew as though it might have the answer. All she saw were some bruised carrots and thickened gravy. She looked to Shiloh. "Yours is Princess, right?"

Shiloh's nose wrinkled, and Val almost laughed. She knew Shiloh would hate it.

"Actually," Brooks said. "It's Starchild. Right, Shiloh?"

A smile curled over Shiloh's lips. She nodded. "Yeah."

Here Shiloh was, still bearing the nickname Val gave her. The one that reflected the Haven she'd come from. How she'd been put into such a dark world, and she still shone so bright. Maybe, Val's should be something like that. For so long, the Haven... no, all of Arcadia... had made her feel like every part of her was wrong. Too brown, too gay, too *bad*.

Maybe, she should own it.

"Bad Child," Val said, with a smirk. "They'll know it's me."

FORTY-NINE

The squeal on the other end of the line pierced Jake's eardrum. He yanked the phone away from his ear, but still, the screech blared louder than the hover crafts that zipped above Jake's head where he stood on the rooftop garden of his father's Chicago condo.

"JakeJakeJakeJakeJakeJakeJake!" Stefani yelled from the phone.

Still holding the phone away from his ear, he snapped, "For froq sake, *what*?"

"They did it!" She let out a strangled sound. She was crying again, but this time, the tears weren't sad. They were happy. Relieved. "She's safe, Jake. She's safe."

Jake's fingers tightened around the phone as he pulled it back to his ear. He paced a few steps, unable to sit still. The rooftop garden hadn't changed in the months since he'd been here with Shiloh. The same planters, the same pathway, that same gazebo right in the middle.

"How do you know?" Jake asked.

"My mom called me. ROGUE played the song. You know, the one about home? And the name was Bad Child. And I thought that must be her. If Shiloh is Starchild, then of course, she'd be Bad Child. My mom said that there was a report of a Reform Home in Minneapolis being attacked. Two Correctors and two Protectors of the Peace were killed."

"Holy ordure," Jake whispered. His feet still led him through the garden, back to the gazebo.

"She did it!" Stefani let out another sob. "Shiloh really saved her."

Jake swallowed. "Of course, she did."

That was his Shiloh. The one with the power to burn the world down if someone she loved was in danger. He stepped into the gazebo, his eyes drawn to *that* lounge chair. He could almost feel her here—the demand of her lips, the give of her soft skin, the arch of her body, the grip of her legs around his hips.

Don't stop.

His skin grew hot and sticky from want. He ached for her.

Froq, I miss her.

On the other end of the line, Stefani fell strangely silent, making little soft gulps. Jake could no longer tell if the sounds were happy or sad.

"You will see her again," he said. To Stefani. To himself.

Stefani scoffed. "Of *course*, I'll see her again, you dingbat! I never thought I wouldn't."

"Oh."

She let out one more indignant sniff. "How did the interview go?"

Jake turned his eyes from the lounge chair and forced himself to breathe. "It went..." He brushed aside a curtain on the gazebo and stared out at the Chicago skyline, toward where the Unity Center beamed its blue, red, and white lights. "It went well, I think."

"Why do you sound like that's not a good thing?"

Jake sighed, massaging two fingers into his temple. Then he

realized that was a gesture too like his father, and he dropped his hand. "I don't know. I just can't shake this feeling that—"

The imprint of Beck's handshake lingered like a shiver gliding down his spine.

"That, what?" Stefani asked, her voice eerily soft.

"That everything had just played right into her hands."

&

For once, the silence between Sawyer and Shiloh didn't prick Shiloh's skin uncomfortably. Instead, it soothed across her like a gentle breeze. They walked a wide perimeter around the camp toward the lake and woods that surrounded the north side. The four homes stood silent in the distance, everyone already fast asleep.

Brooks had been intent on having Ali and Luca serve double guard time as punishment, but Shiloh had volunteered to take Luca's place. He'd looked at her as though she'd sprouted horns and buckteeth, but the exhaustion hung off him visibly. It was the least she could do after he'd risked so much. He needed sleep, and with the events of the day, Shiloh's skin buzzed with an inability to sit still.

But as soon as Shiloh had volunteered, Sawyer had volunteered too.

"Fine," Brooks had said, scowling. "But double shifts start tomorrow for you two." She'd given the brothers both a stern look, but then hugged them once more before shooing them to bed.

Shiloh practiced her steps as she moved across the grass, trying to move as silently as Paul had taught her. Beside her, Sawyer barely made the blades of grass bend, her steps were so light. All the while, Shiloh's eyes swept around her, as though she might memorize the shadows of the trees, the sparkle of each drop of moonlight. At least, the moon shone bright tonight. They hadn't even turned on the flashlight that Sawyer wore on her belt next to her gun.

"Did you know your mom hated camping when we were young?" Sawyer said, breaking the silence at last.

"What?" Shiloh scoffed. She tried to picture it. A girl who hated to camp growing up to be a leader of the nomadic ROGUE.

"She used to beg our dad not to take us when it was his weekend." Sawyer tested a log in their path with her foot. Once a massive tree, its insides had hollowed, but it didn't budge beneath her foot. She gracefully stepped onto it and hopped onto the other side. Shiloh scrambled over it after her. "He was an avid hunter, and he wanted so badly for one of us to follow in his footsteps. Tomboys though we were, we never quite got the taste of it. Ironic how—"

Sawyer drew up short suddenly, her mouth freezing on the next word, searching around her. Shiloh stiffened.

Sawyer had heard something.

Sawyer's hand fell on her gun, unbuckling the strap that held it in its holster. Shiloh did the same, grasping the hilt tightly. She searched for what Sawyer saw. But there was darkness and trees and a glint of moonlight on—

Whoosh!

Sawyer slammed into Shiloh's side, knocking them both to the ground. Air burst from Shiloh's lungs, but she didn't have time to gasp. Because Shiloh recognized that soft sound: a tranquilizing bullet flying past her head.

"Move," Sawyer hissed through her teeth.

Shiloh clawed her way across the ground, scrambling past long grass and leaves. One, two, more soft gunshots, slamming into the earth where Shiloh had just been. The bullets hissed, letting up a puff of smoke. Whoever shot from the shadows, they wanted Sawyer and Shiloh alive.

Beside Shiloh, her aunt yanked her gun from her belt and returned fire in the direction of the shots. Shiloh didn't dare turn to look. Heart screaming in her ears, she reached the log and flung herself over. Sawyer landed beside her, pressed close to the ground, as—thud, thud—two more tranquilizing bullets slammed into the other side of the log.

"Shiloh, grab the radio off my belt," Sawyer said. "Warn AWOL we are under attack. The Elite are here."

Even as Shiloh's fingers snatched at the radio, her breath came in bursts. Sawyer turned, peeked over the log, and fired. Glass shattered. Someone screamed. Shiloh brought the radio to her lips, stilled her shaking fingers.

The Elite.

The Elite were here, within hours of Shiloh bringing Val back.

The Elite were here, and Shiloh had brought them.

Part Four
Fire and Gasoline

The most powerful
weapon on earth is
the human soul on fire.

— Ferdinand Foch

FIFTY

"Elite!"

One word. It was only one word. Yet, as some called it from outside, Nic jerked awake with a silent scream on her lips. She clawed out from beneath her sleeping bag, leaped from her bed, and landed on the ground in a fighter's stance. Her mom appeared instantly at her side and clamped a hand on her elbow. In the bed, Val shot upright, eyes wide in the dark.

"Everyone awake!" the same voice bellowed. Brooks's voice. "The Elite are here."

"Go!" Mom barked.

Nic ripped her gun belt from where it hung on the bedpost and snapped it over her hips. Mom tossed Nic her pack, and then slung her own over her shoulders. The thundering of floorboards sounded a moment before Paul burst into the room, his rifle in his hand.

"Let's go!" Paul said.

Nic shimmied into her pack. Val had gotten to her feet and was stumbling into her shoes. Nic and Mom pulled on their own boots. Nic grabbed Val's wrist, and then all four of them ran—out of the room and out of the house that had been their home for weeks without so much as a glance behind them.

Outside, the other Sparrows were bursting from their homes to converge in the center of camp. Charlie clutched a wailing Ezra, trying to quiet his cries, even as the man pushed Becca forward. Mick followed close behind. He held his rifle at the ready, as he walked half-backwards, protecting their backs. Luca and Ali had raced across camp to the farthest house to help Fatima, her kids, and Wallace. Now, they were running back. Luca clutched Naia to him, as Fatima dragged her two eldest by their hands. Ali had an arm slung around Wallace, steadying the old man as he waddled as quickly as his increasingly-frail body would allow.

Nic turned a full circle, but she couldn't see anyone else.

"Where are the Elite?" Paul demanded, glancing to Brooks.

In the distance, Nic could hear it. *Pop, pop, pop,* from the woods around the lake. *Behind* the camp. And if the Elite were there, they could be anywhere.

"I don't know," Brooks said. "Sawyer ran into them on guard. Shiloh sent a message."

"Where's Shiloh?" Val demanded, ripping free of Nic's hold.

A look of fear played in the white of Brooks's eyes, but she shook her head, casting it away. "Get to the truck!" she ordered.

Val bared her teeth. "Not without Shiloh."

But what choice did they have? They had to get Fatima, Wallace, and the kids out of here. They were defenseless. And Shiloh wasn't. She'd trained; she was stronger than she gave herself credit for. And Sawyer was with her.

"They're there!" Ali called as he pulled Wallace to the huddled group. He stabbed a finger behind him. "A lot of them."

Nic squinted in the direction. She saw nothing—but then shadows moved. Nic didn't know how Ali knew, but if he was as good a shot as people said, Nic trusted his sight, even in the dark.

"Go!" Brooks yelled again, but she herself moved in the opposite direction. Toward where the shadows were taking shape, an army of Elite forming two hundred yards away. Mick ran with her.

"Nic!" Charlie called.

Nic sprang forward without question, and Charlie thrust Ezra into her arms. "Take him. Take Becca, too. I have to help hold them off."

"No!" Becca screamed. "Don't go. Please, Charlie, please!" She clutched at Charlie's shirt.

Charlie made a strangled noise before grabbing Becca's wrists, trying to push her away. Still, she fought, clawing, clinging, like a wild animal.

"I can't lose you like I lost Daddy and Mommy. Please, please, *please!*"

Nic's chest cracked open.

"Luca!" Charlie cried. "Help me!"

Luca swept Becca up into his arm not holding Naia and flung her over his shoulder. She screamed, pounding her fists onto his back. Ignoring her, Luca broke into a sprint in the direction of the truck. Fatima followed with Eris and Amir, and Ali pulled Wallace after them. Ali glanced over his shoulder, eyes wide as they met Nic's. She took a step toward him but froze when Paul moved—in the opposite direction, toward those who would stay behind.

No, no, no, not Paul.

A gunshot whistled in the air. Brooks and Mick—and now Charlie—used the farthest house as shelter, peeking around the corner and firing. The Elite must be close enough to exchange fire, but Nic still couldn't see them, with the darkness and the houses blocking her view.

"Paul!" Mom cried, grabbing his arm and pulling him around.

"I have to help hold them off." Paul lifted his hand to Mom's face, tracing his thumb across one cheekbone. "Go! Get our kids out of here." His gaze flicked to Nic, and then down to Mom's belly.

Mom blinked rapidly, a spark of tears appearing and disappearing in her eyes. Standing on her toes, she pressed her lips to his in an urgent kiss. "I love you," she said roughly. "Get your ass back to us."

Paul blinked in surprise, then a smile flashed across his face. "Yes, ma'am." He sobered quickly and added, "I love you too." He glanced at Nic. "I love you both."

Nic's eyes ached as Paul jogged away to join the others before she could even say the words back.

Amelia spun to face Nic and Val. "Let's go, girls."

"But what about Shiloh?" Val growled.

"Sawyer won't let anything happen to her," Nic promised. "We have to go!" Ezra squirmed in her arms, still wailing in her ear. Nic clutched him tighter with one hand and used the other to nudge Val forward. "Go!"

🔥

Shiloh yanked her gun from her belt. She hoped that Brooks had received the message, hoped that the camp had woken and gotten out of there. But Shiloh could hear nothing over the sound of Sawyer's gunfire—real bullets, not tranqs. Each pull of Sawyer's trigger lit up the night and made Shiloh's ears ring with the explosion. Sawyer took shelter behind the log as a few tranqs sailed over both their heads and then she popped up again.

Click, click, click.

The sound of an empty clip.

"Fuck!" Sawyer turned around and slid down the log. "Shiloh, cover me."

She said it so simply, like she had no doubt that Shiloh could. Shiloh took a breath, clutching her gun, trying to remember everything that Brooks and Paul had ever taught her. She sprang up, propping her forearms on the top of the log. She caught a glint of moonlight off a shield. She fired.

And missed.

The Elite dove down. So, Shiloh fired again and again. One Elite lifted their gun. Shiloh dropped behind the log as a bullet pierced the air where her head had just been. Sawyer still fumbled with the clip, trying to prop it on her leg, cursing lowly.

"Help," she hissed through her teeth.

Shiloh grabbed Sawyer's gun, slammed the clip home, and handed it back.

Sawyer nodded a thanks. A shot rang over their heads, the bullet embedding itself into a tree beyond them with a hiss. Tranq bullets still. As Sawyer returned fire with the Elite, Shiloh's pulse thrummed. The Elite must know who they were aiming at, and they wanted Sawyer alive. If they captured her, they would torture her for information, and when she gave them nothing, Arcadia would publicly execute her. Her loss would devastate ROGUE, like the loss of Shiloh's parents had. But all that faded behind the fact that Shiloh couldn't bear to lose Sawyer. Sawyer was her family.

And no one came for Shiloh's family.

Shiloh burst upright. Her eyes trained on an Elite, only twenty feet away now. Their face plate was such a small target, but Shiloh narrowed her vision until nothing else existed. She exhaled and squeezed the trigger. Her gun bucked, the bullet flew, and glass shattered.

The Elite fell.

Sawyer dropped behind the log again and yanked Shiloh down with her. In the strange stillness that followed, Sawyer and Shiloh's own breaths sounded loud. They waited, but no more bullets flew. Sawyer lifted her head just enough to glance over the log, and Shiloh peeked too. A handful of Elite lay—dark, dead shadows on the ground. Nothing, no one, moved.

Distant gunshots rang from the direction of the camp. Surely the Elite had split up, trying to lay a trap that Shiloh and Sawyer had stumbled upon. Shiloh's stomach twisted as she thought of them all—Val and Nic, Luca and Ali, everyone now in danger because of her.

Let them be okay. Please.

Despite the relative stillness, when Sawyer stood, she was cautious. She gestured with her gun for Shiloh to stay down. The leader waited, watching for movement in the space of one breath, two breaths, three breaths. She made herself such an easy target, surely, an Elite would have taken the opportunity to fire.

"Let's go," she whispered at last.

Shiloh stood carefully. She glanced over her shoulder, toward where she could hear gunshots, but Sawyer shook her head. "Not that way. Go forward. If you see any more Elite, I want you to run. Find the others. Leave me behind."

Not a chance.

Shiloh didn't protest aloud, but there was no way she would leave Sawyer. She was getting them both out of this alive.

Shiloh and Sawyer moved forward with quiet, hesitant steps, continuing on their route that would eventually arch back toward camp. The wind stirred the branches of the tree. Every shadow bending before the moonlight stretched into sinister steps. Shiloh's chest ached as her thoughts turned to her friends. Where was Val? Nic? Luca? The rest of the Sparrows? Had any been able to escape or were they all—

The shot came from nowhere.

Sawyer's body jerked and then crumpled at Shiloh's feet. Shiloh's hand shot up by instinct, her gun trained on the Elite who'd hidden in the bushes. She pulled the trigger again and again and again, one after another, until the volley of bullets crashed through the Elite's face shield.

Shiloh gasped. She searched the darkness, the trees, the brush. Nothing. But she'd thought that before. She collapsed to her knees beside her aunt. Shiloh's hands shook as they reached for Sawyer's neck. *Please... please...* The pulse hammered strong and steady beneath Shiloh's fingers.

But there was no time for relief.

Think, Shiloh, think.

Shiloh had to get Sawyer back to safety, but there was no way Shiloh could carry her all the way back to camp. But maybe, maybe....

Maybe Shiloh could hide her.

Sliding her hands beneath Sawyer's armpits, Shiloh pulled her aunt back toward the hollowed log. She'd done this once, with Jake, all those months ago when she'd pulled his bleeding, weak body down a hallway. She was stronger now, her body not broken, but a cold sweat poured down her back in the time it took to drag Sawyer back. Sawyer never stirred. Shiloh angled her unconscious body so Shiloh could shove her inside the log. In the dark, no one would be able to see Sawyer here unless they looked straight in. Just in case, Shiloh grabbed handfuls of leaves and grass and tossed them over the opening of the log, over Sawyer's body, until even Shiloh couldn't see her. The wood of the log should also keep Sawyer hidden if the Elite released an Eye.

The sound of crunching leaves beneath feet made Shiloh stiffen and lay her hand on the gun she'd returned to her belt. Her instinct was to run, to get away, but no... Shiloh glanced back at the lump of leaves that covered her aunt. She had to *lead* the Elite away.

Shiloh leaped to her feet and raced a few steps—toward the sound—until she could see them through the trees. Three Elite. From where they stood, they might not have seen her, might have kept walking toward the log. But Shiloh drew her gun. Her bullet pinged off an Elite's armor, sparking in the dark.

"Hey, assholes!" she barked. Then she ran.

A stampede of footsteps sounded against the forest floor as they chased her. Bullets flew as she spun around the tree trunks, whistling past her head, hissing blue smoke as they struck bark. Still tranq bullets.

"Faster!" Shiloh yelled aloud to herself.

And just like that, Shiloh was bait again.

❦

Val hated herself for it, but she did what Nic said and ran. Gritting her teeth, Val bolted in the direction the others had fled.

You better be fine, Shiloh. You better be froqing fine, or I will murder you myself.

Nic and her mother were close behind. Past the tree line, the truck rumbled with the driver's side door open. Luca and Ali stood in the bed of the truck, helping the kids, Wallace, and a woman Val hadn't met, over the bumper.

"I don't understand," Luca was saying, as he pulled Wallace in, "I wasn't followed. I'm sure I wasn't followed!"

Something pricked at Val's mind like the answer to a test question she couldn't quite remember. Nic pushed the toddler she'd been holding into Luca's arm, who set him next to the other four kids. When he turned back around, his gaze searched every person who remained outside the truck. He inhaled sharply

"Where's Shiloh?" Luca demanded. "Did she and Sawyer not make it back?"

Nic vaulted into the truck, but Val hesitated, her hands resting on the bumper.

"She'll be fine," Amelia said. "I'll drive. Luca, take shotgun."

Luca jumped out of the truck, landing beside Val. "I have to go get Shiloh," he said.

"What?" Val said as the same word echoed on Ali's and Amelia's lips.

"Luca, we have to go!" Ali yelled, leaning out of the truck to look down at his brother.

Luca looked up to meet his brother's eyes. "I can't leave her!"

The distant gunshots were louder and more frequent now, two enemy armies battling to the death. How long would the four people Val saw be able to hold off the Elite?

"What are you talking about?" Ali barked. "We have to go."

Luca backed away from the truck, swinging his rifle off his back. "Ali, take Nic and the others and *get out of here.*"

Ali's eyes widened. "Oh," he said like he understood now.

And Val did, too. His motivation for chasing after Shiloh, even though it could be the death of him. *Oh, for motherfroqing sake!*

Amelia reached out a hand to Luca, like she might try to stop him, but he glared at her. She dropped her hand. "Be careful!" She turned and sprinted to the cab.

Luca took a step backward.

"*Seriously,* dude?!" Ali snapped, shaking his head. "I thought you said girls are nothing but trouble."

"They are," Luca said. Then he turned and ran back into the woods.

Val knew she should go with him to find Shiloh, but she had no skills. Luca would have to protect her, instead of saving Shiloh. But the idea of leaving Shiloh behind made Val feel ill.

Nic broke her thoughts, offering Val her hand. "Come on."

Val planted her palms on the bed of the truck, trying to decide. She caught sight of her forearm, the little prick on her skin the Protectors had left.

It struck her like a knife. No, like a needle. A needle piercing deep into her flesh.

What if it hadn't been just medicine the Protectors injected into her arm?

Oh froq.

Val had been the cheese in a mouse trap. And Shiloh had taken the bait. *Snap!*

"Come on, girl!" Wallace barked.

Amelia revved the engine.

"I have a tracker," Val choked. She released the truck and stumbled back two steps.

"What?" Nic asked, still stretching out her hand.

"You have to go!" Val said. "Go without me. I have a tracker."

A grim line formed on Nic's lips. "Then we'll take it out."

How long would that take? How long would the Elite follow them before Nic would manage to dig the tracker out of Val's skin and destroy it?

Five children blinked at Val from where they huddled at the back of the truck. If they were caught, how many of these children would the Elite kill? And how many would end up at the Haven, sometimes wishing they were dead?

The truck started to roll forward.

"Val!" Nic yelled.

Ignoring her hand, Val climbed onto the bumper to grab the string dangling from the rolling door, and jumped back down, yanking it down with her. Nic called out and lunged, but too late. The door slammed down with the sound of crashing metal. It rattled as Nic tried to open it again, but Val threw its latch into place. The truck picked up speed, leaving Val behind.

"Val!" Nic screamed, from behind the metal, thumps sounding from her hands pounding against the steel.

"Goodbye, friend," Val whispered, and then she turned and ran back toward camp.

FIFTY-ONE

"**V**al!"

Nic slammed her fists against the door. The rattle of metal boomed through the truck, but she couldn't hear it past the screaming in her own head. She couldn't hear Ezra's wail, or Becca's sniffles, or even someone saying her name. The speeding truck swayed beneath Nic's feet as it bumped over uneven grounds—away from her friends.

"Froq!" Nic screamed when the door refused to budge.

She'd lost them. Shiloh and Val. Her friends who'd saved her, and she had left them behind, whether she'd wanted to or not.

"Froq!" She kicked the door. Again, and again, and again.

Gentle but firm hands rested on her shoulders, pulling her around. "Nic, stop!"

Ali stooped so he could meet Nic's eyes. Since when was he taller than her? Had he always been, and she hadn't noticed?

"It's okay," he said, his thumbs caressing over the slope of her shoulders.

Nic sagged against the door. "No, it's not."

Ali glanced at the metal door, and he winced. Was he thinking about Luca? "You're right. It's not." He slid his hands down her arms and took her hands in his. The panic in her chest gave way to something else, something not altogether different from a sense of danger, her heart thudding.

"But you did the right thing," Ali continued. "We need you here."

Nic looked behind him, at the frightened children, at Fatima whose lips moved frantically like she was praying. At Wallace, who looked white as a ghost. Ali was right. She needed to get it together.

Pop, pop, pop!

Bullets pelted the side of the truck. The children all screamed. Fatima clutched her three kids close. Wallace bent his body over a sobbing Becca. Ali hauled Nic to the ground before diving for Ezra, covering him with his body. Nic threw her arms over her head. Brakes squealed, the truck tilted and then spun.

Mom!

The truck jolted to a halt. Everything went still. Then the gunshots resumed in a pattern of fire, pause, fire—the pattern of two parties exchanging shots. They were under attack, and Mom was fighting on her own, and Nic was trapped in this stupid truck.

No!

Nic jumped to her feet, drawing her gun from her hip, and aimed at the latch. "Cover your heads!" She glanced behind her once to ensure that everyone had, and then she fired.

The latch exploded.

She flung the door up. The end of the truck faced a line of trees, and the gunshots echoed to her right. She leaped to the ground and peeked around the corner of the truck. Four Elite stood in the bed of an armored truck, firing toward the front of the vehicle. The Elite's truck had been parked to block the road. A trap.

Nic crept to the left side of the truck. On this side, Mom

crouched behind the hood of the truck. She stood and fired over the cab but had to dive back down to cover when four guns fired at her head in unison. A bullet slammed into the hood. Smoke coiled into the air.

Nic returned to the other side of the truck and took careful aim. Her first shot pinged off one Elite's shoulder. The next burst through his visor.

One down, three to go.

One Elite spun away from Mom and took aim at Nic. Nic flattened herself against the bumper. Metal croaked as the bullet struck the side of the truck. Gasoline fountained from the truck's side, and the acrid smell stung Nic's nose as it formed a river on the broken asphalt.

A gunshot exploded—originating from somewhere above Nic's head. Another cry rang out, and another Elite fell. Nic threw her head back, but she couldn't quite see. Ali now lay on the roof of the box truck, pressed so low she could only see the tip of his beanie and the end of a rifle. He took careful aim, fired twice, and the third and fourth Elite crumbled.

In the residual silence, Nic's heart slammed so hard against her sternum that her chest ached. She crept from behind the truck, her eyes darting this way and that. She glanced toward the front of the truck, but Mom no longer stood there. The hood still sparked with the pool of gasoline spreading wider.

"Nic, look out!" Ali bellowed, climbing down from the roof of the truck.

Nic spun around. From where she stood, she hadn't seen the cab of the Elite's truck, or the driver's door swing open. But now the driver faced her with a gun raised. Nic thrust her gun up, but it was too late. The Elite was already pulling the trigger.

The gunshot shook Nic's entire body. She waited for the impact, the burst of pain, of nothingness. But instead, the Elite's visor exploded, and he crumbled.

Nic looked behind her, expecting to find her mother or Ali, but it was Fatima who stood there. Her pistol was raised, her dark strand of hair streaming free of her hijab. The fierceness in her normally peaceful eyes sent a shiver down Nic's spine.

Ali's feet slapped the concrete as he jumped down and rushed to Nic, his hand wrapping around Nic's arm. "Are you okay?" he said, his voice faint beneath the ringing in her ears.

Nic started to nod, but the smell of fire and gasoline tinged her nose.

"Get everyone out of the truck!" Mom snapped, sprinting around the side of the truck.

Ali grabbed Ezra and shoved him into Amelia's arms. Nic helped Becca and then Naia down, while Ali and Fatima assisted Wallace. Soon, everyone was on the ground, shoving little bodies into the woods and up the slope that led away from the road. Behind them, the world hissed as fire exploded and the truck erupted in flame. Heat blazed against Nic's skin, and the night bled a hot red light. Nic glanced back. Through the trees, she could see the truck crackle, see the fire spread through the river of gasoline until it reached the tires of the Elite's truck. Soon, flames consumed that vehicle, too.

The group paused and turned back for a moment. Nic looked around her. Fire played in the children's wide eyes. Fatima clutched her children to her, looking ready to devour anyone who dared come near. Wallace leaned exhausted on his walking stick, one hand on Becca's shoulder. Ali held Ezra to him. And Nic's mom stood, one hand clutching a gun, the other spread over her lower belly. She looked fine, just fine.

Nic let out a small breath.

They'd all survived.

For now.

Shiloh's feet pounded against the forest floor. She ran as hard as she could through the thick brush. The weeks of training, of running through these same woods, made her faster than the Elite. She twirled around the trees, leaped over fallen logs, avoiding the thickest brambles. The Elite crashed through the brush just behind her. Bullets whistled from behind Shiloh, and bark splintered as they embedded into wood.

Faster, faster.

Finally, the trees fell away. Shiloh slid into tall grass, down a slope, and sunk into soft mud that swiftly turned into the uneven rock of the shoreline. The lake stretched out before her, sparkling indigo and silver as it reflected the night sky. Shiloh had two options. She could run along the shore, but that would put hers in a vulnerable angle to take a bullet. Or she could dive into the water.

She inspected the rippling lake surface, the distant shore, and then she splashed into the water. It bit at her skin like ice. No more bullets flew. She had to get under the water before the Elite started to fire again; they wouldn't be able to hit her if she was underwater. She was up to her waist, about to dive, when she heard...

"Shiloh!"

That voice.

That fucking voice.

After all this time, it still had the power to chill Shiloh to her core. She told herself to dive, but her head had a will of its own. It swiveled around, and the sight made her feet plant in the mud.

Because the fourth Elite who had joined the three on the shore wasn't alone.

Luca.

One of the Elite's held a gun to Luca's temple, their other hand fisted in Luca's curls, yanking back his head. Still, Luca held his chin defiantly, his shoulders square, despite the way his hands were bound behind his back.

"I think this belongs to you," said the new Elite, his voice stabbing into Shiloh's skin. "I found him wandering the woods, looking for you."

"Fuck you," growled Luca.

The fourth Elite spun his gun around in his hand and slammed the handle down on Luca's temple. The force drove Luca to his knees in the rock. A crack opened along his scalp, a drop of blood trailing from his temple down to his eyes.

"Now," the fourth Elite said, turning his attention back to Shiloh, "be a good girl. Drop your gun and get out of the water."

Good girl. Two words she hated so much. Shiloh's fingers tightened on her gun.

"I'll count down from ten," said the fourth Elite. "Ten, nine, eight—"

"Don't do it, Shiloh!" Luca snapped.

"Shut *up*!" the Elite yelled.

One nod of the fourth Elite's head and another Elite stepped forward, pulling a prod from their belt. And it wasn't fair that he still had that power over another Elite. But that thought faded as the lesser-ranked Elite jammed the prod into Luca's ribs. Luca tried not to scream; Shiloh could see it in the way his face contorted, his muscles twitched, his mouth opened but no sound came out. She knew the pain Luca felt all too well, the electric searing, the way every nerve cried for relief.

When Luca couldn't fight anymore, his scream rattled Shiloh's bones, an exquisite physical pain.

"Stop it!" Shiloh snarled.

They didn't.

Luca's scream went on and on...

The fourth Elite focused his gaze on Shiloh. Waiting.

Luca buckled to the ground, curling into a ball. Shiloh pressed her eyes closed, unable to bear the sight, but she could still hear his screams. One by one, her fingers uncoiled from her gun, until it splashed into the water at her side.

Another nod. The Elite pulled the prod away. Luca lay, gasping on the ground, crumpled at the Elite's feet.

The fourth Elite pushed a button at his neck, letting his visor fall. Framed within the black helmet of the Elite, Silas smiled.

"Good girl."

Fifty-Two

T he gunshots didn't stop until the pink light of dawn broke over the horizon. Val listened to the silence from the spot where she'd hidden herself beneath one of the porches. If it was the Elite who'd survived the night, they would find her soon enough, the tracker leading them straight to her. But soon, Val started to hear voices and names she recognized:

Brooks. Paul.

Val wiggled out from underneath the porch, mud coating her entire front of the pajamas from the Reform Home.

One, two, three, four. She spotted the Sparrows two houses down, and counted, letting out a breath. All four of the people who'd stayed behind—except Luca. And Sawyer. And... where the froq was Shiloh?

Val rushed toward them. Brooks spun and lifted her gun out of instinct, but then lowered it.

"Val, what are you still doing here?" Paul demanded, marching toward her. "You were supposed to be in the truck with the others. Did they get out?"

Val nodded, but then said the rest in a rush, words tripping over each other, "It's my fault. It's my froqing fault. I think they put a tracker in my arm. I think they knew Shiloh would come for me and bring me back here. It's my fault. It's my—"

"Shhh," Paul said, clasping both hands on Val's shoulders and stooping so he could look in her eyes. "Slow down. What about a tracker?"

Val thrust out her arm, pointing to the pinprick in her skin. Despite his size, Paul's hands were gentle. Still, when he slid his thumb over the pinprick to feel for what was beneath her skin, his touch echoed with the memory of the Corrector's hands. A silent scream built up in Val's head. She closed her eyes and breathed as Shiloh had taught her. *Breathe in. Breathe out.*

"It's deep," Paul said, an edge on his throat. "I'm not sure I can get it. We need Amelia."

"Or Sawyer," Brooks said.

When Val opened her eyes, Brooks lifted a radio to her lips. "Scalpel, can you hear me?" She released the button, but only static answered. Brooks's hands tightened on the radio, shaking as she pressed the button again. "Scalpel—"

"Here!"

Val jerked her head toward the sound. Sawyer emerged from the direction of the lake, sprinting toward them. She lifted a hand over her head as she yelled once more, "Here!"

"Thank God," Paul muttered.

Charlie let out a brief laugh, and Mick's lips twisted into what might have been a smile, but it looked more like a grimace. Brooks's shoulders slumped. She rested the fist that still held the radio against her forehead, looking like she might cry for only a second. She pulled herself together like snapping a box closed.

But Val felt sick, like a spike had splintered her chest. Had none of them noticed what she saw—or rather, what she didn't see? *Sawyer will take care of her,* Nic had said. But Shiloh wasn't with Sawyer.

Val pulled away from Paul and stormed toward the commander of ROGUE. "Where's Shiloh?"

Sawyer froze, a deer caught in a hunter's scope. "She's not—" She looked around quickly. "She's not with you?"

"We thought she was with *you*," Paul protested.

Sawyer shook her head. "I was hit by a tranq. I woke up in some damn log Shiloh must have hidden me in and—"

Charlie sucked in a breath. "So, she's out there *alone*?"

"No," Val said. "Luca went after her."

"*Luca*?" Brooks repeated, wavering on her feet like the news had bowled her over.

Mick groaned, muttering in Spanish beneath his breath. Val caught every other word, enough to know what he thought about Luca being stupid enough to chase after a girl.

"You need to go look for her!" Val demanded. "Or someone needs to get this tracker out of my arm so I can."

All the color drained from Sawyer's face. "It's been hours. If Shiloh could, she would have made her way back by now."

Which meant...

Val's stomach lurched, and she nearly bowed over with nausea.

Which meant Shiloh was either captured, or... or...

"No!" Val snapped, shaking the thought away. "We have to go find her! We have to—"

"We can't stay here," Mick interrupted. "The next wave of Elite will be on us soon, and we barely survived the last."

"Mick," Charlie said, his throat strangled.

"I'm sorry, Char. I want them back, too, but we are sitting ducks if we stay here."

Val fisted her hands. "We can't just leave her!"

"One hour," Paul said, glancing at all of them. "We look for one hour. Long enough for Sawyer to get the tracker out of Val's arm. Just to be sure. I won't just leave them. I can't."

They all looked to Sawyer, who hadn't budged from where she stood. "Please," was all she said. And it wasn't the command of their leader. It was the plea of a *friend*. Of an aunt—or maybe of a mother—whose child was lost.

Brooks nodded. "Mick and Charlie, you go west. Paul and I will go east. If anything goes wrong, you get your asses back here."

Val watched them go. Without a word, Sawyer turned, entered one of the homes, and returned a few minutes later with a kit.

"I've only got one hand," she said, "so you'll have to help me."

Which was froqing *not* what Val wanted to hear moments before a scalpel sliced into her arm. Paul had been right. The tracker was deep, embedded in the muscle. Val cursed in Spanish and English through gritted teeth, blotting at the blood as Sawyer fished with a pair of pliers. Sawyer pulled it out—a small device that looked like it might be a capsule of medication. Sawyer threw it to the ground and smashed it beneath the heel of her boot. Using teeth and Val's other hand to hold tools and strings, Sawyer stitched her back up. By the time she finished, Val trembled with pain, but it was nothing compared to the way her soul shuddered when all four returned when the hour of searching was over, hanging their heads in defeat.

Shiloh was gone.

&

When Shiloh opened her eyes, all she saw was white. She kept her face turned toward the floor, her brain whirling from the aftereffects of the tranquilizing bullet Silas had finally struck her with. But even in that state, she recognized quickly where she'd been brought.

The endless white, the four legs of a single metal chair.

They'd brought her back to the cage.

How long had she been unconscious? A long time if this was the Vault, in the capital. And what about—

Luca!

His screams still echoed in her bones because the Elite hadn't stopped torturing him when Shiloh had dropped the gun. Of course, they hadn't.

Shiloh started to push herself up to look for him, but then a voice rattled and made her freeze, slumping back to the floor.

"I did as you asked, Councilor," Silas snarled, his voice dripping with venom.

"I asked for Sawyer Ardelean *and* her niece. I see only half of that request here." This voice. Feminine and fierce, like a storm brewing in her throat.

Beck.

Shiloh tilted her head subtly so she could peek through the hair cascading over her face, hoping they wouldn't see the movement. She caught the shapes of two figures standing behind the window that looked into the cage, certainly the same window where Elite #111 had stood, mocking Shiloh.

"Sawyer wasn't there," Silas protested.

"Shiloh told you that, did she?"

"Yes."

"And you believed her?"

Silas didn't respond, but Shiloh must have finally convinced him. After she'd dropped the gun, the Elite had dragged her and Luca to an armored truck, likely to help hide the screams—Luca's screams. The Elite had only aimed a few slaps and jabs of the prod in Shiloh's direction. Luca had taken the full brunt of Silas's and the Elite's rage. The prod. Their fists. Their feet. Perhaps because Silas had learned that Shiloh could handle physical pain. The emotional pain from harming someone she cared about yielded greater results. And she did care about Luca. Perhaps she hadn't realized it until she'd felt every blow Luca had received like it was her own.

But still, Shiloh hadn't budged. She'd said the same line over and over again, begging Silas to believe her.

"I don't know where Sawyer is. She had already left when I got back, and no one told me where she was going."

And maybe Silas finally had believed her because he'd whipped out his gun and shot Shiloh. She'd thought she'd be dead, but here she was. Alive.

For now.

Beck made a humming sound beneath her breath. "Perhaps I'll find a better means of convincing her."

A long pause.

"You can return," Beck said. "Your services are no long required."

"You can't keep me hidden forever, Beck," Silas said through his teeth. "I want to see my family."

"I can keep you hidden for as long as I want. Need I remind you that you would be dead if it weren't that I'd still found use for you."

"I'm not a trained dog you can keep in your doghouse forever and then call out when there's a rat that needs catching."

"Oh, but that is where you're wrong." The cold of the floor leeched through Shiloh's clothing, but it was the tone of Beck's voice that made her shiver. "Your youngest daughter is a pretty little thing, isn't she?"

The silence between them seemed to snap like a howling, brutal wind. Beck didn't need to make a threat. Reminding Silas that even *he* had things he'd hate to lose was all it took to get him to stop tugging at his leash.

Love was a weapon, and Beck wielded it expertly.

Beck said the words one by one. "Run. Along. Doggy."

Silence...

And then footsteps. The grinding of walls as they opened and shut. Shiloh glanced through her hair once more, seeing only one dark frame in the window, before the window returned to a solid wall.

She pushed herself to her hands and knees. The world spun and tilted, and she closed her eyes until it stilled. Shiloh glanced to her right, and her heart stuttered in her chest.

Luca lay crumpled on his side, his back toward her. Her heart restarted in an erratic rhythm as she watched for the rise and fall of his back. But he wasn't moving. She dragged herself toward him, her chest already aching.

"Luca." She laid a hand on his shoulder, shaking gently. "Luca!"

He groaned.

Shiloh let out a breath, almost sobbing in relief.

She helped turn him onto his back, even as he moaned with every movement. The skin of his face had drained of all color, leaving behind a shade of ash. Dried blood curled from the edge of his lip, his left nostril, and the cut on his forehead. His ripped clothes revealed flesh painted in extravagant shades of purple and black, imprinted in the shapes of prod marks, knuckles, and boot prints. His face was swollen, his closed eyes puffy.

"I'm sorry," Shiloh said, her voice catching on the sob that formed in her throat. She had to be strong now. "I'm so sorry. I couldn't—" *Stop them. Tell them the truth about Sawyer. Save you.* She couldn't finish, but he seemed to understand.

"I know," he said, his words muffled through his split lips. "I know."

"Where do you hurt?"

"Everywhere."

Shiloh didn't know what to do, but she couldn't let him lay there broken on the cold floor. She carefully sat on the floor and guided his head onto her lap. She dropped her voice to a whisper, keeping her head bent so her hair covered the movement of her lips from the cameras.

"Do you know if the others got away?"

"Some got away in the truck." He whispered a few codenames.

Shiloh let out another small breath with each one, a fraction of her chest unclenching, especially as he mentioned Bad Child and Freebird.

Shiloh remembered what Silas had said about Luca looking for her. "Why weren't you with Chuckles? Why did you come for me?"

Luca finally cracked an eye open, one tiny sliver of green flashing up at her. He stared at her for a very long time before replying, "I told you, Princess. You're gonna be the death of me."

When one of Beck's bodyguards showed up at the Osgood's condo door and told Jake his presence had been requested by Beck, Jake knew it *wasn't* a request. His mind raced as he was ushered into a car that drove him to the back entrance of the Unity Center. The bodyguard led him down a hallway to a familiar elevator and commanded it to take them down, down, down.

Jake swallowed. They were going to the Vault.

Jake stepped into the long hallway that led to the sealed metal doors. It swung open before he reached it, and there was Beck, waiting with her arms crossed, her foot tapping impatiently.

"Jacob," was her only greeting.

She nodded to her bodyguard who stepped back into the hallway before the door closed again. Jake's own bodyguard would have been furious—they'd only agreed to stay behind at the condo because they thought Beck's would remain with him. Whatever the case, he and Beck were now alone, except for the two Elite sitting at the desk before the monitors.

Jake began, "Councilor Beck, how nice—"

Beck held up a hand. "Let's skip the simpering."

He hid his hands in his pant pockets so Beck couldn't see them coiling into fists. He made his tone casual. "What can I do for you, Councilor?"

"Did you mean what you said? About doing anything to gain my trust?"

Careful, careful, the unsteady beat of Jake's heart warned.

But he nodded, anyway. "Yes."

She smiled, and it was the smile of a hunter who'd watched a hapless rabbit step right into a snare. She tilted her chin toward the monitors above the Elite's desk, the cameras that looked into the cage. Jake followed the gesture there, taking in the image. Two people in one cage, one a lanky male whose head rested on the lap of a girl. A girl he would have known anywhere.

Jake's heart lurched to a stop.

Shiloh.

No!

Jake kept his face blank, his mask firmly in place. But inside, he screamed.

No! No! No!

It had been months since he'd seen Shiloh, but even through the tiny monitor screen, he could see that the months had brought change. Her tangled, dark hair hung longer than the Codex allowed; her lean body toned with muscle; the once-pale skin revealed by her tank top, now kissed by the sun. His eyes drank her in like a man dying of thirst would guzzle water, even as panic threatened to overtake him.

It clicked together like a puzzle in Jake's head. The way Beck had asked him to stay, at the same time that Shiloh was rescuing her sister. A trap had been set, and Jake had lead Shiloh—and himself—straight into it.

Beck was watching Jake. The sharpness of her gaze drilled into his shoulder, and he knew his next reaction would seal his fate. And Shiloh's.

Dance, puppet.

He took a breath and turned to meet Beck's eyes. "What do you want me to do?"

Her smile didn't waver. "Shiloh has information that we need. I need you to convince her to give it to us."

And of course, of course, Beck would think to use Jake to get it. What had Jake's father said? If you love something, it has power over you. And Shiloh loved Jake. He would be her greatest weakness. It'd also be the ultimate test of Jake's loyalty, to see if he'd willingly betray Shiloh to barter for Beck's trust.

"What information?" Jake asked.

"She knows what we need. All you have to do is convince her to give it to me."

It'd be easier to convince Shiloh to leap from a thirty-story building than convince her to give into Beck.

"And what does she get if I convince her?" Jake asked. "I need to understand the situation if I'm going to convince her."

Beck cocked her head. "I suppose if she proves she can be loyal, she can live."

"In a prison camp?"

Beck shrugged. "I suppose that depends on you, and how well you can convince her to be loyal."

"And what happens if I can't convince her?"

"To her or to you?"

"Both."

Beck cocked her head in the other direction, sweeping her gaze up and down Jake. "I don't need you to successfully convince *her* to prove your loyalty. I need you to convince me. And as for Shiloh"—Her eyes darkened into the green of a forest at night. In contrast, the bright red she wore had never looked so much like blood—"I don't think you really need an answer to that."

Rage bellowed in Jake's ears, but he forced his face not to flicker. He glued his mask into place so it wouldn't budge. Shiloh's life rested solely in his hands, and...

I don't know how to save her.

"You have one hour." Beck swung around and marched toward the doors, speaking over her shoulder. "I have business to attend to. When I return, I hope you will have persuaded her to give you the answers I want. Use whatever means necessary. Oh, and Jake," she said, turning around and gesturing toward the monitors. "I will be watching."

Jake nodded, hoping she couldn't see the way his jaw tightened as he gritted his teeth.

Before the metal doors sealed shut behind Beck, she cast him one more glance over her shoulder. "Convince me."

When she was gone, two Elite remained, sitting at the desk of monitors, as still as statues. Jake looked back to the screens. Shiloh's head was bent over the man whose head she cradled in her lap. It took Jake a second to place the stranger. Grim. The boy who'd taken such pleasure at beating Jake. His stomach clenched as Shiloh's fingers caressed a line across Grim's forehead. Jake could feel that same touch, the way her finger had traced his own forehead, the way he could feel the echo of her touch in every nerve of his body. He'd never thought, not once, that in their months apart, Shiloh might have grown to have feelings for someone else.

It took two swallows for Jake to push down the lump that choked him. Did it matter at all if Shiloh had fallen for someone else? If she broke Jake's heart, would it change what he was going to do in this moment?

No. Because Jake still loved her. Irrecusably. Undeniably. Recklessly.

And yet... here he stood. Jake had only ever wanted to burn down the world for her. To do that, he had to restore the trust of the Council—and that had led him here. He could see no way out —no way out of this trap he'd led them both into. To save Shiloh, he'd have to convince her to betray ROGUE, the one thing she'd never do. To convince Beck, he'd have to betray Shiloh.

He'd said he'd do anything to take down Arcadia—not just for Shiloh. But for Hope. For Nic. For Stefani and Val. For a thousand innocent lives whose blood had been spilled by his grandfather and father, and now stained his own hands. But he couldn't sacrifice this. He couldn't sacrifice Shiloh.

Could he?

His temples thumped. A thousand voices pounded through Jake's head, blending with the memory of Shiloh. Her taste, her laughter, her touch, the silky softness of her skin, the sigh of his name on her lips as she moved against his hand.

Sawyer's voice: *At the end of the day, you are still an Osgood. You will always be an Osgood.*

Samuel's: *Don't you understand the power of being a Councilor?*

Beck's: *Convince me.*

Jake's own: *I'll burn the world down for you.*

Decide, decide, decide.

One way or another, there was a match in Jake's hand, and his only choice was to strike it.

Even if he himself went up in the flames.

FIFTY-THREE

From where Nic leaned against the boulder, she watched as her mother brought the crackling radio toward her mouth and sent the message once more. The dawn light that broke through the trees sparkled off Mom's hair as her lips moved. This would be the third time Mom tried to reach the rest of the Sparrows. The two times before had gone unanswered—because those meant to receive the message were too preoccupied, or because they were dead. Neither option reduced the knot that had formed in Nic's stomach.

They're not dead! They're not.

Becca shifted to where her head laid on Nic's lap. Her little arms wrapped around her brother, who sucked on his thumb as he slept. Across from her, against another rock, Fatima slept, her children gathered in her arms. Wallace curled on the ground, sighing softly in his sleep. Ali, however, was as wide awake as Nic. He rolled a penny over his knuckles, his face so sullen that it seemed like it belonged to someone else. Not Ali. Not the obnoxiously bright boy.

Every now and then, he glanced Nic's way, and she forced herself to give him a small smile, like she was telling him it'd be all right. That Luca and Brooks and the rest of the Sparrows would be alright.

But of course, she didn't know that.

Nic's group had pushed on all night, deeper and deeper into the woods, in no particular direction except straight and away. Still, the going had been slow, with the children and Wallace hobbling. Then Wallace had twisted his ankle when it got caught in between two rocks. It slowed them down even more; Ali had to lend Wallace his shoulder, even with the walking stick.

There'd been no sign of more Elite.

Lucky. They'd been lucky.

If the Elite caught them again, the group couldn't outrun them on foot. Still, Mom and Fatima made the decision to stop. Everyone was tired—the children barely able to remain upright. Ezra had been screaming, and Naia whimpered with every step. Even Wallace's face had been drawn with pain, though he never complained. They'd had no choice but to take shelter within an outcropping of rocks, at the very least hidden from view. Still, Nic hadn't been able to sleep. Her eyes burned, and her arms ached from carrying Ezra, but she feared if she closed her eyes, they would not reopen.

Or worse, they'd reopen and she'd be back in a cage.

Static hissed. Mom sighed.

And then...

A message came through, the words jumbled. Mom gasped and began to write furiously on the paper in her hands, translating rapidly.

"It's Paul," Mom said, with a soft sob of relief.

Nic echoed it, fingers rising to her lips. Ali looked at Nic, frowning because he hadn't heard Mom's words.

"Paul's okay!" Nic whispered—or had tried to. It came out loud enough that Becca groaned in her sleep.

"And Val," Mom added, "and Sawyer, Brooks, Mick, and Charlie."

The tightness in Nic's spine unraveled with each name, but two names stuck in her heart. She hesitated to ask, so Ali demanded it first: "What about Luca?"

"And what about Shiloh?" Nic added.

Mom blinked at them, then brought the radio back to her mouth to send a message back.

&

Val watched as Paul ran a hand over his face, looking like he might cry as Amelia's voice came back from the radio. They'd been marching for hours through the woods in the direction they'd hoped the rest of the Sparrows had gone when they'd finally caught a message. The message that came back from Amelia was gibberish again. *Froq*, Val thought from where she leaned against a tree. She should have listened more when Stefani explained the codes. Charlie, however, wrote furiously. He stopped almost as soon as Amelia finished, looking up.

"She wants to know if Luca and Shiloh are with us," he said, his eyes welling behind his glasses.

There it went. Their last hope that somehow Luca and Shiloh had been found by their other comrades.

Brooks swore and slammed her foot against a fallen log, the bark splintering. Mick clutched Charlie's shoulder. Sawyer remained where she was, frozen against the tree, her face stony, not revealing what lay beneath. Val drowned in grief—hers and everyone else's—and she wanted to scream, to cry, to yell that this wasn't fair.

This is my fault.

Why did she have to froq everything up?

Cringing, Paul cleared his throat and sent a message back over the line, this time, not bothering to use a code, "He's not with us. Neither is Starchild." He paused then added, "We're coming for you."

Amelia had given their group's location in the first message. Sawyer had said it was a couple miles from here. They likely hadn't made it far with the children, so their group should be able to catch up to them quickly if they ran. Sawyer had glanced at Val then, and she could almost hear the *If she doesn't slow us down...*

The radio crackled. Amelia's voice began, but then cut off as screams rang through the radio's speakers.

There hadn't been a single warning.

Nic hadn't heard the mechanical buzz as the Eye rolled through the forest. It just appeared over their heads. It froze, then belted out its alarm. The children all woke screaming. Mom dropped the radio, yanked her gun from her hip, and fired a single shot. The alarm silenced. But it was already too late.

Fatima shushed her children, and Becca clamped a hand over Ezra's screaming mouth, but the silence that fell was deceiving. With her heart pounding in her ears, Nic listened for the rustle of trees. And there it was—the sound of rapidly approaching feet on the forest floor.

Nic pulled Ezra into her aching arms and grabbed Becca's hand, preparing to run. She spared one peek above the rock. The Elite pounded up the slope toward them, weaving around the trees, only two hundred yards away. Close. Too close. Perhaps others knew it too because she saw Fatima and Mom exchange a look Nic didn't like.

Mom pulled her rifle from around her back and set it on the top of the boulder, pressing herself close. She fired a shot. Return fire whizzed over their heads.

Pulling her gun from her side, Fatima turned toward her oldest daughter. "Take your sister and brother and run!" She pushed them around the rock and up the slope as Ali helped Wallace to his feet and started to wobble in the same direction.

Eris reached back to clutch her mother's hand. "But you're coming?"

Nic didn't hear Fatima's response because her own mother interrupted.

"Nic, listen to me," Mom said, even as she fired another shot in the Elite's direction. Ezra sobbed into Nic's shoulder, making it difficult to hear. "I need you to take the kids and run."

"What about you?"

Fatima came to Mom's side. She fired over the boulder with her handgun and then ducked back down. The three Qadir children yanked each other up the hill, Ali helping along the limping Wallace. But the Elite were focused on the two women firing at them.

"If we don't hold them off," Mom said, "no one will make it."

Fire scolded Nic's tongue. She opened her mouth to protest. "Mom—"

Mom turned, her wide blue eyes meeting Nic's. "I'm not asking you to go because I think you're not strong. You're the only one I trust to do this. You have to protect them."

Some part of Nic wanted to stubbornly argue, but she knew— she knew they were right. Ezra still cried into her neck and Becca grabbed her hand so tightly it hurt. Sometimes, the best fighting was staying alive.

"I love you, Mom," Nic said and then raced after Ali's retreating back. She didn't say goodbye because she refused to believe this was the last she'd see her mom.

◈

"Fuck!" Paul roared. "Fuck!"

He made a motion like he might throw the radio in his hand, but he clung to it at the last moment. Everyone turned to Sawyer. Val studied her as she straightened from the tree, as she looked from one person to another, like she was calculating the risk.

In the distance, a gunshot rang out, a mere pop. And then another. And another.

Sawyer said one word. "Run."

And Val ran with them as they turned and sprinted deeper into the woods—in the direction of the gunshots.

FIFTY-FOUR

Despite her leggings, Shiloh's skin froze against the cold floor, but she didn't move. She counted Luca's breaths as he slept. Occasionally, they seemed to hitch and pause, and she feared that he would die right there in her lap. But then his breathing would resume with a soft groan. There was no way to know what damage lay beneath his bruises. Broken ribs? Punctured lungs? Internal bleeding? She didn't know, but if she didn't find a way to escape soon, Luca would die. Either from his injuries or when Beck would decide he was no longer useful.

Shiloh looked over the solid white walls. When she'd been here before, she'd spent almost two days in this same cage, unable to find a way to escape.

Think, Shiloh, thi—

There was a thud as the walls opened, drawing Shiloh's muscles tight. Someone was coming. She carefully laid Luca's head back on the floor, causing him to wake and murmur her name. She ignored him, rising to her feet, and faced the area where she knew the door would appear. Her heart's rhythm picked up, her feet sliding into a fighter's stance, and then—

The door opened.

And Shiloh's heart stopped completely.

"Jake." The name whispered from her lips before she'd realized she'd spoken.

Jake stood, leaning against the doorway, looking so beautiful Shiloh wanted to cry. His hands carried a tray laden with dishes, and his face curled into a crooked smile. His deep brown eyes looked at her like she was all he could see. He was oxygen, and she hadn't breathed in a long, long time.

"Hey, Shi," he said.

A sob broke from her lips, and she took a step, prepared to run to him. But a hand snagged around her ankle.

Shiloh dropped her gaze to Luca, who looked up at her with the slit of a single eye. "Careful," he warned, his voice strained. "If he's here, it's because they sent him."

A chill went down her spine as reality returned. They still stood in the cage with the Elites' cameras directed at them. Luca was right. If Jake was here, it was because Beck wanted him here. What game was she playing?

And what role did Jake play?

Shiloh studied Jake, who had made no attempt to move from the door. The differences in him were subtle, and yet, they stood out like little warning bells. The white Codex-compliant shirt that normally had two top buttons undone was tight around his throat. The sleeves he'd always worn rolled up to his elbows now strangled his wrists. His hair, once loose and wild, was styled into the neat and close cut of a perfect Arcadian male citizen.

A prickle of warning joined the want that thrummed in Shiloh's nerves.

Careful.

Jake stepped into the cage and lifted the tray. The cell door slid shut behind him. "They let me bring you food."

They let me...

Shiloh pulled her ankle out of Luca's grasp and approached Jake slowly. It felt wrong, treating him like a danger. Jake wouldn't hurt her. He *wouldn't*. She just needed to figure out what Beck was up to.

Still, she remained cautious as Jake held out the tray. A plate bore a grilled cheese sandwich cut in a triangle, and a bowl of tomato broth—the offer so perfectly Jake that, for a moment, Shiloh almost dropped her guard. Almost knocked the tray aside to leap into Jake's arms. But she heard Luca stirring behind her. He'd risen to his hands and knees, but he swayed. Shiloh snatched the metal cup of water off the tray and returned to Luca's side. She helped him sit up and lean against the wall, then forced the cup into his hands.

"Drink," she said. Her mouth was parched, but Luca needed the water more.

He didn't bring the cup to his lips. "Princess," he breathed softly, a warning, "don't—"

"Drink," she insisted.

And the whole time, Jake watched them, his gaze heavy on Shiloh's back.

She stood and turned around to face Jake. He lowered himself to the ground, setting the tray on the floor in front of him. She took Luca half of the sandwich, before sitting down as well. The tray separated Jake and Shiloh like a line in the sand. Like they were the enemies they were born to be. It all felt wrong, the distance between them—the way they were moving around each other like two lone wolves sharing a meal, unsure when the other might break a truce and attack.

"How are you?" His gaze swept up and down her body. "Did they hurt you?"

"I'm fine." Shiloh picked up the other half of the grilled cheese and bit in. The sandwich tasted like glue in her mouth.

Jake gave her a tight smile. "Shiloh, we both know that when you say you're fine, it's generally not true."

Shiloh swallowed. "Why are you here, Jake?" she said, done with the pleasantries. "Beck sent you, didn't she?"

Something flickered behind his eyes, but she couldn't place it. His mask was firmly in place—a pleasant but unfeeling expression on his face. He'd never worn a mask around her before. He'd always been an open book, letting his emotions play across his face like words on a page. But now... now she couldn't read him.

"You should eat the soup." Jake gestured to the tray. "You need your strength."

Shiloh glanced down to where a plastic spoon lay beside the bowl. She picked it up. Ran a finger over the smooth edge of the spoon. "Just answer the question."

Jake's jaw worked back and forth for a moment, and then finally, "I'm here to save your life."

Considering he hadn't run in here, guns blazing, there was only one way to survive.

Surrender.

"What does Beck want?" Shiloh asked.

She dipped her spoon into the bowl. If he wanted to play this casual, she could join in that game. Jake's gaze followed the movement of the spoon to her lips. She licked the spoon clean, and his eyes darkened.

He cleared his throat, shifting on the floor. "Information."

"On?"

"She didn't tell me. She said you'd know."

Sawyer. Beck wanted Sawyer, and she believed Shiloh had some way to find her, to lead her into a trap.

"And she thought you'd be able to convince me?" Shiloh said.

Jake shrugged.

Of course, Beck had chosen Jake. If love was Beck's favorite weapon, then Jake was certainly the weapon of choice to deploy against Shiloh. Because Shiloh loved him. She'd told Beck that herself.

But the fact that Jake would be that weapon willingly—

Was he willing? If Beck had summoned him and demanded he walk into this cage, he wouldn't have exactly had the option to tell her no. He could be just as stuck in this sick game as she was.

"So now you're their puppet?" Shiloh asked, watching his reaction carefully.

But Jake didn't react. He didn't deny it, didn't cringe at the word he despised, didn't subtly shake his head to clue her in. He blinked and then began slowly. Like he was saying something he knew she wouldn't like. "Shiloh, I've had a long time to think about what I want and how to get it."

"And what *do* you want?" Shiloh asked.

A line formed between Jake's eyebrows, and her fingertips ached to reach across and soothe the skin. Then she wanted to caress down his cheek, over his lips, against his chest. Did he still feel the way she remembered or had that changed, too?

"Do you really have to ask?" Jake replied.

Yes, because Jake was the compass that she'd directed her life with for so long, and now she felt lost, shaken, like nothing else was certain. "Tell me."

"*You*, Shi." For the first time, emotion entered his voice. His eyes showed a spark of flame. "I want a life with you."

Luca made a low sound of disgust. She shot him a glare over her shoulder before turning back.

"They will never let us be together," Shiloh said, shaking her head. "You know that."

"They might." He paused. "If I was Councilor."

Councilor. Councilor. Councilor.

The word ricocheted around the room, slamming into Shiloh's heart. For a long moment, she couldn't breathe. She could only stare at him, begging him to laugh, to take back the words. But he only met her eyes steadily.

Somewhere in the distance, Luca made another sound. But she couldn't hear him over the gunshot of Jake's words, over her own attempt to rake air into her lungs.

"You've—you've never wanted that," Shiloh finally managed.

He leaned forward. "But don't you see? It's the *only* way. There's incredible power in being a Councilor. Protection. I can be whatever I want. I can *have* whatever I want."

A small smile played across his lips. Those lips, the ones that could make fire flare through her entire body. But now all she felt was cold, from the tips of her fingers to the end of her toes, ice settling into her chest.

"You fucking son of a bitch," Luca growled. He gasped, like the force of his own words caused him pain.

Jake barely glanced Luca's way, focused only on Shiloh.

The handle of the spoon ground into Shiloh's palm. She made her fingers loosen. She forced venom into her words. "At what cost? How many innocent people will you let die while you remain comfortable? How many will you command to be killed because Beck pulled your puppet strings?"

Some emotion flashed behind his face, like the man Shiloh once knew was fighting to rise to the surface. It disappeared in an instant. "I told you, Shi. I'd burn down the world for you."

No, no, no! That wasn't supposed to be what he meant. They were supposed to destroy Arcadia together; not watch innocent people die and do nothing.

"Shiloh," Jake went on, "if you don't tell Beck what she wants, she *will* execute you. Just tell her, and she'll let you go."

Shiloh scoffed. "That's what she said?" Shiloh shoved another bite of the grilled cheese into her mouth, not because she was hungry, but because she needed something to do with her hands.

"Not in so many words," Jake replied, "but I'll make sure you get out of here. I promise."

Shiloh swallowed down another bite, then cocked her head toward Luca behind her. "And what about him?"

Jake turned his head to look. Shiloh slipped the plastic spoon down the side of her pants, along her thigh.

Jake looked back, that line back between his eyebrows. "I don't think I can bargain for two heretic lives."

The word *heretic* dripped with disdain. Shiloh's frozen heart began to splinter. She heard the cracking in her ears, a whine of a cry she didn't dare release. She tossed the sandwich onto the tray.

"Jake, what happened to you?"

Jake shook his head. "I don't know what you mean."

"This isn't who you are."

"Of course, it is. I'm"—He spread his palm over his chest— "the one who loves you. Who would do *anything* to be with you. Pay any price. This is *exactly* who I am."

It's an act, she told herself, even as the fissures in her chest widened. *Please let it be an act.*

He glanced at his wrist, his watch, and his hand curled into a fist. Irritation crept into his voice. "Come on. I'm running out of time here. She's not very patient. Tell Beck what she wants, and we can be together."

Shiloh let herself imagine it, just for one second. Jake, a Councilor, and she, a Councilor's wife. Both of them safe while the world suffered. For so long, the chance to be with Jake had been what Shiloh fought for, but there were more reasons to fight. If she gave up Sawyer, her aunt would be tortured and killed. And then every single member of ROGUE would be hunted down, too.

It couldn't be just Jake anymore. Maybe, it never had been. *Hope and Nic and Val and Sawyer and Mom and Dad and Paul and Amelia and Brooks and Charlie and... and...*

So many names, and so many more she didn't know, but those people were also worth giving everything for.

Rule #1: Fight for the ones you love.

No matter the cost.

Even if the cost was her life. Even if it was her very heart and soul.

"Shiloh," Jake pressed, waiting for an answer. And there was only one answer.

"No," Shiloh said.

The cracks within her heart had reached the edges of her heart —threatening to shatter.

Jake's face paled. "Shi, please," he begged, his voice edged with panic. "I can't watch you die." He reached across the tray and grasped her hand in his.

Shiloh stared at his hand: the familiar curve of knuckles, the veins beneath his skin. That hand—the hand that had held hers in her hardest moments. The hand that, even now, summoned goosebumps to her body and made her yearn for more. The hand that had touched her in ways that had made her ignite. She wished she was back there, body to body, chest to chest. She wanted to rewind the clock to that moment, grab it with both hands, and never let go. But she was here. In the middle of this terrible game. And somehow Jake was standing on the other side of the board.

But there would only ever be one answer.

"No."

His hand tightened on hers. "You once said I was the only thing you wanted, remember?"

Oh, she remembered. How she remembered.

She closed her eyes, a million memories playing in the darkness. His hands, his lips, his goodness, his love, his fire. An impossible dream.

A dream that ended now.

"Not like this," she said, yanking her hand away from his. "Not like *this*."

A single tear crept down her cheek. Only one. She would only give Beck this one tear. When she opened her eyes, Jake's mouth hung open, and at last, Shiloh could read him. Devastation looked wretched on him.

"Shiloh," he croaked, reaching out like he might wipe away the tear.

She jerked away from him and launched herself off the floor so that she towered over him. She pressed one fist to her thigh so that the spoon remained where it was. "Get out!" she roared.

"Shiloh—" he protested.

"Get out!" She kicked the tray, sending the bowl clattering. Tomato soup stained the white floor like spilled blood. "Crawl back to Beck and lick her boots."

Jake scrambled to his feet, hurrying to pick up the scraps of the lunch. He clutched the tray so hard his knuckles turned white. He backed toward the door, laying one hand on the wall. It responded to his touch, swinging open. She thought about charging him, running out, and maybe he wouldn't stop her, but the Elite outside the room would.

He stepped out of the cage, still facing her, and before the door shut, she saw him mouth three words slowly. So slowly there was no doubt what they were.

I love you.

Shiloh bit her tongue to keep from screaming. She stood, her fingers trembling at her side, with a fissured heart bleeding in her chest.

"Shiloh," Luca murmured. There was pity in his voice, and she didn't want it.

"Shut up," she growled.

"Shi—"

She spun around to face him and glared. "Shut up! I'm trying to think."

Luca shook his head but said nothing.

By saying no, Shiloh had just signed her own death warrant. And Luca's, too. It could be hours—no, minutes—before Beck gave the order to put a bullet into each of their heads. Or maybe she would keep Shiloh and Luca here as they'd done to Nic, torture them day after day after day, hoping the day would come when they broke.

Shiloh closed her fingers around the spoon at her side. With the right snap, it would come to a point and become a rudimentary weapon. And then it could be driven through tender skin with enough force. In the right spot—like the tenderness of an exposed neck—it could be lethal. But it would be useless against the Elite's armor. Still, there were... other options.

Beck couldn't use Shiloh... if *she* wasn't alive.

As long as Beck had Shiloh within her grasp, Sawyer was in danger. *ROGUE* was in danger. A plan formed quickly in Shiloh's mind. A stupid plan. A reckless plan. She looked at Luca, feeling like maybe she should apologize for what was to come.

But... there was only one foreseeable way out of the cage. Beck would *never* use her again.

🔥

Froq, froq, FROQ!

As the cell door slammed shut, Jake silently cursed, calling himself every name he could think of. He'd seen it—the way he'd shattered Shiloh's heart. Her eyes had gone dim, like a candle being snuffed out. And he hated himself... hated this game he'd been forced to play. He'd known it would be pointless to try to sway Shiloh. She would never surrender the information that Beck wanted. Some fraction of him had been selfish enough to hope that she would, so she'd live, but her courage, her bravery, made him love her all the more.

And yet, how the froq was he supposed to save her?

His heart pounded, and his breath came in pants. He slapped his hand down on the next wall and it slid away. The Elite had loaded his handprint into the system so that he'd be able to make a quick escape—out of the Vault and through the series of gates—should something go wrong. As he entered the next chamber, Jake looked down at the tray, the spilled remnants she'd barely touched. The plastic spoon wasn't there. Good. It meant Shiloh had taken it, just like Jake hoped she would.

When the Elite had allowed Jake to go to the Unity Center's

cafeteria for food, they'd specifically told Jake not to put any silverware on it. So, Jake had tucked two spoons into his shirt sleeve. He'd waited until he'd entered the multiple gate system that led to the Vault—where the cameras would be trained on his back—to slide one of the spoons onto the tray. Jake had feared the Elite would intervene when they saw Shiloh holding the spoon on the cameras in the cage, but perhaps they were under strict orders not to intervene. But they'd definitely check the tray for the spoon when Jake brought it out.

Before going through the next gate, Jake twisted away from where he knew the camera would be and maneuvered the second spoon out of his sleeve and onto the tray.

There.

Now, they wouldn't suspect Shiloh had kept hers, and she would at least have something she could use for a weapon. Jake had no idea what she'd do with it, but she was smart. She could think of something. In the meantime, maybe Jake could convince Beck to give him another chance, buy Shiloh more time. Maybe he could send a message to ROGUE through Stefani to figure out a rescue plan.

His legs unsteady, he walked through the next wall, and the next. Before he went through to the Elite's lobby, he forced his frantic breathing to slow. To set his shoulders into a casual line, to put his mask firmly back on.

Jake stepped out to where the Elite sat, waiting for him to emerge. He let out a growl of frustration. "Well, that didn't go well."

"What is she doing?" one of the Elite said, still staring at the screens.

Jake spun toward the monitors, to the multiple views of Shiloh. She held the plastic spoon in her hand. In rapid movements, she snapped the spoon at an angle, leaving behind a handle that came to a sharp point.

Froq. Jake's heart leaped to his throat. What *was* she doing? Why was she showing them she had it?

It unfolded in slow motion, in a handful of fractured moments. The two Elite jumped to their feet. Shiloh rotated the spoon in her hand, turning the sharp point toward herself. Jake's mouth parted into a scream.

And Shiloh plunged the weapon into her own neck.

FIFTY-FIVE

Jake flung himself around and slammed both hands against the wall. The wall opened... but much too slowly. The Elite yelled at him to stop, but he couldn't. His pounding heart, his thrumming nerves, his quickened breath combined into two words screaming in his head.

Save her. Save her. Save her.

He slid into the first compartment, and it slammed shut before the Elite could reach it. Jake opened the next, every second seeming like an eternity.

Save her. Save her. Save her.

The next compartment opened and shut behind him.

The beating words transformed.

My fault. My fault. My fault.

At last, the cell of the door slid away at his touch. Shiloh lay crumbled on the floor of the cell, face down. And all Jake saw was red, spilled over the white. So much blood. Grim bent over Shiloh, shaking her, but she didn't stir.

"No! No! No! *Please*!" Grim pleaded, his voice a desperate wail. The shriek of a tortured man. Grim looked up as Jake flung himself toward Shiloh.

"Help her!" Grim cried.

Jake landed on his knees at Shiloh's side, grabbing her shoulder to turn her over. *Please, please, please.*

She moved like a viper striking, from stillness to attack in the space of a heartbeat. She pressed the sharp tip of the broken plastic, stained with only a little of her blood, against the side of Jake's neck—right on the spot where his own pulse fluttered. Her lips, only an inch from his, curled into a deadly smile.

"I missed my carotid artery," she hissed, "but I swear to fuck, I won't miss yours."

❦

"Hurry!" Nic yelled as they crested the top of the hill. Ali and Wallace drifted several yards behind, Ali coaxing Wallace on, a shine of sweat creeping on both their faces. The gunshots sang through the forest.

"Keep going, Eris!" Nic said, when the girl faltered on the other side of the hill.

"Look!" Eris stabbed a finger to the east, the opposite side of the crest. Nic paused at her side. She saw them, a half dozen Elite sprinting up that side of the hill.

Nic looked around—going back would lead them back to their mothers, forward would lead them into the Elite. She glanced to the north, where another slope climbed even higher in the woods. She pushed Eris in that direction.

"Go!"

Eris pulled her brother and sister along. Nic handed Ezra to Becca, who clung to him, even though he was half her size. "Take him for just a minute. I'll catch up."

Becca bravely nodded and trotted after the other children, her movements awkward as she held her brother. Nic looked back to where Wallace and Ali were cresting the hills, and then back to the Elite. They were a quarter of the way up already. They would catch them at this rate. Only a thick tree line at the ridge partially hid Nic and the others from view, but they'd be close enough to fire before too long.

Think, Nic, think.

"You have to leave me," Wallace said.

Nic spun toward him. "No!"

"I'm slowing you down too much," Wallace said, pulling away from Ali and leaning heavily on his walking stick. "They will catch us."

"Wallace, they'll kill you!" Ali said, but he was panting with the effort it had taken to get the man up the hill.

Wallace pulled a pistol from his hip, one Nic had never seen him draw. "Look at me, boy. I'm dying anyway, but at least this way, I can take a few of them bastards out with me." He winked his good eye, a semi-toothless grin forming on his face.

"No!" Nic snapped, balling her fists until her nails dug into the scabs on her palm. "That isn't an option! I'm not leaving you."

"You gotta, girl. You ain't got a choice."

"Wallace—" Ali protested weakly, but he glanced past Nic to where the Elite climbed.

The enemy was halfway up now. A few more yards and they'd be close enough to shoot.

Wallace patted Ali's cheek. "You're a good one, Chuckles. Stay silly, ya hear me? The world needs the light you bring."

Ali swallowed thickly, then nodded and swung toward Nic. "Let's go," he said, grabbing Nic's wrist and pulling her toward the slope where the kids had just run.

"No!" Nic dragged her heels. "I can't leave him." She'd left her mom, but she couldn't do this. Wallace was weak and defenseless, without any cover here. Her mother had trusted her to protect them. If she left him here, she was abandoning him to his death. "I won't!"

Ali grabbed both her shoulders and shook her hard. "Nic, get your ass up the hill before I throw you over my shoulder."

The fierceness in his gaze, so unlike the boy she knew, startled Nic. She looked at Wallace, then at the Elite. What choice did they have? If Wallace stayed with them, the Elite would catch them all. With his sacrifice, they stood a chance. And it was not an unwilling sacrifice.

"Go, girl!" Wallace said, throwing her one more cheeky smile.

Nic ran, Ali at her heels. They grappled with tree roots and trunks, pushing their toes into soft dirt and leaves. Soon they were back with the children. Ali swept Ezra into his arms, and Nic grabbed Naia's hand, and they all forged onward—running at times, scrambling at others.

Up and up and up.

Behind her, gunshots rang, but Wallace's voice yelled louder.

"Yes, come closer, bastards!"

A gunshot. Then two.

Up and up and up.

"Boom!" Wallace laughed as more gunshots rang out.

Up and up and up.

"Just like that, you—"

A gunshot, and then Wallace's voice didn't come again.

Beside her, Ali let out a sob, but he never faltered. Nic blinked away the blurring of tears. Shiloh and Luca and Wallace. There wasn't time for grief. Not now.

Up and up and up.

At last, the slope evened out. The trees gave way to another cropping of rocks, poking out from the forest floor like teeth. The Qadir children weaved around them and then froze. Beyond the rocks, there was nothing. Only a sheer drop of a cliff.

"No, no, no," Ali murmured as he realized what Nic had. There was nowhere else to go but back, and that wasn't an option. Back was where Elite were, where Wallace was already dead.

Nic looked over at Ali. He sucked in a deep breath, set Ezra down on the ground, and swung his rifle off his back. His shoulders formed an unrelenting line.

They could run no longer. All that was left to do was fight.

Nic pulled Ezra and Becca forward, toward the cluster of rocks closest to the cliff, that formed three walls. "All of you get in here."

The Qadirs huddled close, Eris reaching out to grab Becca, too. Becca hugged Ezra to her. He had stopped crying too; even as a toddler, he knew to be quiet.

"Whatever you hear," Nic said, "whatever happens, you all stay here."

Five brave little heads nodded.

When Nic returned to Ali, he had already propped his rifle on a rock at the edge of the hill. He lay on his belly, his eye trained on the sight, watching for the first Elite to come into view.

Nic settled down beside him, lifting her handgun. She could see nothing down the thick trees of the slope. Yet. But they'd be coming soon. A strange sense of peace settled over her skin, easing her breath, slowing her heart.

She'd likely die here. They only had so many bullets, so many chances before the Elite came. But she wouldn't be taken alive. She wouldn't let them put her back in a cage. She'd put a bullet in her own head first.

She looked over to Ali, and their eyes met. This silly, insane boy. There was something about the way he looked at her now, like he was gazing into the deepest parts of her soul. Like in that moment, despite the chaos, despite the surety of their own deaths, Nic was *all* he could see.

"Nic, I—" he started, but then made a sound like the words were stuck in this throat.

"What?" she asked, feeling strangely breathless.

But a rustle of trees told them it was already too late. Ali turned back to his scope, steadied his breath, and fired.

FIFTY-SIX

"Get up," Shiloh growled to Jake.

And he smiled.

He fucking smiled.

Or at least Shiloh *thought* he did. A flash of upturned lips quickly schooled into submission. She heard the Vault's door open once more—the Elite—and knew her time to wonder was over.

Keeping the point of the former spoon pressed to where Jake's artery pulsed, Shiloh grabbed his too-tight collar and pulled them both to their feet. From around Jake's shoulder, she could see the Elite freeze in the doorway.

"Luca, get behind me," she hissed.

She couldn't see the look on Luca's face, but she imagined he looked like he might kill her. When he'd realized what she was about to do with the spoon, he'd lunged toward her, shouting her name. She'd kept her hand wrapped around the spoon's handle, so only the very tip would pierce the muscle of her neck. Blood trickled down toward the hollow of her throat, but there would be no lasting damage. Still, it must have looked convincing because the howl that came from Luca's mouth reminded Shiloh of when he'd been tortured.

And Jake had come running, just as Shiloh thought he would. Right into her trap.

She kept Jake between herself, Luca, and the Elite. "Take a step closer," she said to the Elite, "and I'll kill him."

Shiloh didn't know if it was a bluff. She didn't know if she could kill Jake. Looking at him now—the plains of the face she had memorized—she didn't know if she could drive the point into his thrumming pulse. But she could do this. She could upturn Beck's carefully laid gameboard. She could make them believe she was capable of anything.

"Hands where I can see them," Shiloh ordered.

The Elite hesitated, his fingers too close to the gun that hung on his hip.

"I'm sure you'll love explaining to Councilor Osgood how his son is dead because of you." Shiloh applied pressure against Jake's flesh, ever so slightly. He flinched as the shank broke skin, and a bead of red slipped down his neck.

The Elite put his hands up in the air.

"Now walk backward and open the doors," Shiloh said.

The Elite didn't hesitate. #308, the white numbers on his chest read. He stepped out of the doorway, and when it tried to close, it suddenly jerked open. The other Elite, sitting at the controls, must have been holding it open. Which meant they were also likely calling for reinforcements.

"Hurry up," Shiloh growled, shoving Jake forward, her hand still coiled in his shirt. Jake's gaze felt heavy against her cheek, but she didn't look at him. She didn't know what she might find there. She thought about turning him around to walk, but she had a better angle at his throat from the front.

They stumbled out of the cell, and Shiloh glanced over her shoulder. Luca followed close, bent over from the effort. One arm cradled his ribs; the other reached forward to clasp her shoulder. For balance, or to assure him she was there. Shiloh didn't know which.

They stayed like that, all in a line, until they stepped into the lobby where the other Elite—this one #013—still stood by the computer. Shiloh nodded her head to the metal doors that closed in the computer room.

"Open that one, too."

#013 hit a button, and the doors groaned open, revealing the hallway that ended in the elevator. Shiloh wasn't sure where her plan went once they got to the elevator. But one step at a time.

"Drop your weapons on the floor," Shiloh said to the Elite, "and step away from them."

The Elite exchanged a glance.

Shiloh put a little more force behind the shank, slicing into Jake's neck. He flinched again.

"Stop froqing around!" Jake barked. "And do it."

He, too, must see something within Shiloh, must believe this more than a bluff. The Elite pulled their guns from their sides and dropped them onto the ground. They took two large steps back.

"Shiloh," Jake said, his voice low, breath on her ear. Her nerves pricked at the noise. Her eyes flicked toward him, only for a second. For a brief moment, she'd let her guard down. And that was all it took.

"Shiloh, look out!" Luca barked.

Shiloh snapped her head toward the two Elite in time to see #013 snatch a smaller gun from behind his back and aim at Jake's back. Shiloh shoved Jake down and flung herself sideways, even as Luca dove in the other direction. The tranquilizing bullet soared over their head and pinged against the metal doors.

Shiloh rolled toward the computer desk and wedged herself between the walk and the thick beam of the desk's leg. Gunshots exploded on the other side, grinding into the metal but not penetrating.

Froq!

She tried to glance around the corner, to see where Luca had gone, but she jerked back when a bullet flew past her head. If the

Elite walked closer, they'd have the right angle to put a bullet in her skull.

Something skidded across the floor and beneath the desk to where Shiloh sat. A gun. Shiloh snatched it up. Luca must not be dead if he'd managed to kick the gun over to her. Taking a breath, she leaned around her cover, found the first Elite, and fired two shots. The first pinged off his breastplate, but the second slammed through the lower plate of his visor. He crumpled to the floor.

Shiloh flung herself back, expecting more gunshots, but none came. Feet pounded against metal, and when Shiloh glanced out, she caught sight of the other Elite running down the hallway to the elevator. The double doors sealed shut behind him.

Shiloh rolled out from her hiding place. Jake sat, looking dazed, with his back near the wall next to the exit. But fine. Jake was fine. Shiloh let out a breath and found Luca next, crammed beneath a different desk.

"You okay?" Shiloh asked, as Luca crawled out on his belly.

He nodded.

Shiloh turned back to the desk, searching for the button that #013 had used to open the doors. There. She brought her palm down on it, but at the same second, an alarm screamed through the room, loud enough it stabbed into her ears.

"Prisoner escape. Commence lockdown."

Shiloh glanced over her shoulder, at the doors that didn't move. And there, beside the door, Jake stood with his hand over a large button. Above it, a sign read:

IN CASE OF PRISONER ESCAPE, HIT THIS BUTTON. DOORS WILL NOT OPEN UNTIL SOMEONE OF LEVEL IV CLEARANCE HAS DEACTIVATED ALARM.

No!

Shiloh slapped her hand down on the button on the desk, again and again and again. But the doors remained closed.

Shiloh swung to face Jake, strangling the butt of her gun. The small sliver of hope Shiloh carried within her—hope that Jake had been performing a role—blew apart in her chest. To say what Beck would want him to say in front of cameras was one thing—to prevent Shiloh and Luca from escaping was another thing completely. The fissures in her heart cracked open, burst like ice shattering. And it hurt.

It fucking hurts.

A scream built up in her throat from the pain, but she swallowed it. She lifted her gun and pointed it at his chest. "Open the door."

Jake held up his hands. "I can't."

Shiloh's hand trembled. She squeezed both her hands onto the handle of the gun to stabilize herself. "Open it!"

"I *can't*!" He took a step toward her. "Shiloh—"

She released the scream that had been building up within her. It tore from her lips as she pulled the trigger and the tranquilizing bullet slammed into Jake's chest. The cry finally ended as Jake collided with the ground. Shiloh wanted to fall to her knees with him, wanted to sob and pound on the ground as everything within her broke into smaller and smaller pieces. She forced herself to remain upright, pressed her hands—one still holding the gun—against her face, and echoed one sob. Just one.

She would survive this grief if she measured it out in small doses. Maybe...

Bang!

Something hard slammed against the exit doors. Shiloh jumped, dropping her hands. Unintelligible voices yelled as they, too, found themselves unable to open it. The reinforcements had arrived.

"Shiloh," Luca said, bracing himself against the desk, "we have to find a way out of here. There has to be a second door. The Elite wouldn't lock themselves in here with an escaped prisoner."

Shiloh spun around, searching. Luca did the same, circling the desks, pushing against the monitors in case they moved. A soft groan caught Shiloh's ear. She looked at the two bodies slumped on the floor. Jake was still unconscious, but the Elite—a finger twitched.

Shiloh raced to his side, rolling him over. Bloody shards of glass framed his face where his visor once was. #308 was young—young enough that the stubble along his jaw grew in sparse patches. That same jaw hung at an odd angle where her bullet had gone through.

"You're lucky to be alive," Shiloh said, her voice stunningly cold and unfeeling, even to her own ears. The gun clicked as Shiloh switched it from tranq to kill. She set the muzzle of the gun between the Elite's eyes. "Tell us where the second exit is."

A muffled sound came through the hole of his mouth. He pointed a finger toward the desk. Beneath the desk.

"Check," Shiloh told Luca.

Luca bent low to the ground and then kicked at something beneath. When he moved, a rectangle large enough for someone to crawl through lay on the wall.

"This better not lead to a trap," Shiloh said, "or I'll come back here, and my second bullet will have much better aim."

#308 shook his head frantically. She let his head drop. She took the Elite's gun which had fallen from his hand, and then, for good measure, snatched his radio and clipped it to her shirt. When she searched the pouch at his side, she pulled out a small black sphere the size of an egg. A single stripe of red ran all the way around it. Her lips twitched. That would be useful. Shiloh slid it into a pocket, then got up.

"Take this." She thrust the other gun into Luca's hand. "Let's go."

Luca grunted as he landed on his belly. He struggled to get his lengthy form through the hole, whereas Shiloh slipped in much easier. The space opened up into a dimly lit hallway, narrow but with enough room to stand. A red button was poised above the opening in the wall, a similar one to the button Jake had pushed. Shiloh hit it with the butt of her gun, and the opening slammed shut.

Luca glimpsed down the length of the hallway. Farther down, it turned into stairs. "Where do you think it leads?"

"Let's find out," Shiloh replied.

🔥

Ali's aim sang true.

As soon as an Elite came into view between the trees, Ali placed a bullet through an Elite's visor. One, two, three. Nic watched him in awe. But when Ali felled one Elite, another took its place, more than the half dozen Nic had initially counted. Soon, the Elite came two at a time, and Nic fired, keeping herself pressed against the boulder so the return fire cracked over her head.

Maybe, Nic thought, maybe they'd survive.

And then her gun clicked empty, and she had no more. Not another clip, nothing in the pack on her back.

"I'm out," Nic said. "How many more do you have?"

A bead of sweat slipped out of Ali's beanie and down the side of his face. "Maybe five."

Nic swallowed as he took another shot, striking one Elite. She could count at least five more, and those were just those she could see. She slid down the rock, her back falling against it. She shut her eyes, the same peace thrumming through her heart.

"Ali," she said, as he lined up his next shot, "save a bullet for me."

"*What?*"

"Don't let them take me. I can't let them put me back in the cage."

More gunshots. From all directions now.

Please, anything but a cage.

"Nic, look!" Ali said, and something like hope coated his voice.

Nic turned to peek over the rock. Gunshots were coming from more than one direction. The Elites were turning, looking back down the slope they'd come from. Then they began to fall. One by one.

It was over quicker than Nic could reason. The Elite fell, and then Nic saw them walking up the hill. Mom and Fatima and Brooks and Paul and others coming behind them.

Nic's head sank against the cool rock, tears of relief streaking down her face. She was alive. They were all alive. Ali laughed, long and hard, and grabbed Nic in a tight embrace. And nothing... not anything in her entire life... had felt as good as Ali's arms did in that moment.

Shiloh had to help Luca up the several flights of stairs that the hallway led to, one arm looped underneath his arm. His other hand clutched the rail. She had to pause several times to let him catch his breath. At last, they made it to another door. Shiloh creaked it open carefully, half-expecting the Elite to be waiting on the other side. But the wide expanse before her was empty. The towering pillars and the sound of falling water told her where they were.

The lobby of the Unity Center.

Shiloh creeped out cautiously, gun held out before her. The quiet in the lobby felt unnatural. Was it due to the weekend? Had everyone been evacuated when the alarms went off in the Vault?

It didn't matter. Shiloh didn't trust it. If anything, security guards were likely lurking.

"Keep close to the walls, in the shadows," Shiloh whispered to Luca behind her.

"Whatever you say, Princess," he replied, using the wall to hold himself up.

Good. The return of his snark must indicate he was beginning to feel better. She sprinted between the shadows of each pillar, half-dragging Luca with her. She pressed her back against each pillar and carefully peeked out, Luca copying beside her, until they were sure it was safe to try for the next one. They went as swiftly as possible, Shiloh certain that a camera would catch their movement and send Elite running.

She leaned around one more pillar and caught a glimpse of her and Luca's face in the mirrors of the Unity Fountain. She nodded to Luca and prepared to sprint.

"Shiloh Haven!"

Shiloh froze, pressing her back against the pillar, as the voice reverberated. Beside her, Luca wrapped his hand around her wrist. She leaned around the pillar again, cautiously. Around the bend of the fountain, she could make out the reflection of a line of Elite. She didn't have to see which one lead them to know that voice.

#111.

"Haven girl," she said, "why don't you come out from where you're hiding and save us all a lot of unnecessary work?"

Shiloh gritted her teeth, tightened her hold on the gun.

Luca squeezed Shiloh's wrist, two quick squeezes to get her attention. He motioned with his gun, and Shiloh followed his line of vision. In the shadows near the next pillar, a glowing sign read Exit. The door below it blared a warning:

Emergency exit. Alarm will sound.

A door, an escape out of this building, only ten feet away. Sure, Shiloh and Luca would be outside, but then the alarm would go off and lead the Elite right to her. It made little difference whether they died here or out in the sunshine.

Unless...

"Haaaven girl!" cooed #111, her voice closer now.

Shiloh stuck her hand deep into her pocket, rolling the sphere between her thumb and forefinger.

"Luca," she said softly. "I think I figured out what role I play in this fairytale."

Luca looked at her like she'd lost her mind. "And what's that, Princess?"

"I'm not the princess," Shiloh said, activating the Sphere in her pocket. "I'm the dragon."

She sprang from behind the pillar and threw the sphere. It landed in the fountain—that fucking fountain with its mirrors and message of conformity—with a splash. The Elites rushed back, sprinting for cover.

"The name is Shiloh Sanders, bitch!" Shiloh called, and then she grabbed Luca's wrist and yanked him toward the door.

The alarm screeched as they flung themselves outside. But it didn't matter because the door had barely swung shut, and Luca and Shiloh had barely taken cover, when the air ignited with fire.

FIFTY-SEVEN

When they finally came to a stop, Nic collapsed to the forest floor between Paul and Mom, clinging to both their hands. She might have been too old for hand holding, but she refused to let go. The Sparrows hadn't dared stop for several hours, until they were miles away from the last place the Elite had seen them. The going had been quicker, with more adults now to pull children onto their backs. But as everyone took a seat amongst the trees, the weight of those missing pressed into Nic's chest.

Shiloh and Luca and Wallace.

They'd found Wallace with a bullet through his heart, a ghost of a smile still on his face. They couldn't take his body with them, but Ali and Brooks had tucked Wallace at the base of a tree, folded his arms over his chest, closed his eyes, both cloudy and unseeing now. There'd been no time for anything other than brief good-byes, before they'd left him in his grave beneath the leaves and sky.

And as for the others—

"What are we going to do about Shiloh?" Val said through hard puffs of breaths, clutching her side as she marched toward where Sawyer sat on a log.

The leader of ROGUE turned the radio she held over in her hand, staring down at it.

"We have to do *something*," Val growled, when Sawyer didn't immediately answer. "And soon!"

Because every second that passed was a second more likely that Shiloh was dead.

"What do you want us to do?" Mick asked. "We don't even know if she's alive—"

"She's alive," Sawyer said, swaying as she got to her feet. "I know she is. She remains Arcadia's best way to get to me."

Val pinned Sawyer with a glare, her lips curling into a snarl. Nic forced herself to release Mom and Paul and stood, setting a hand on Val's shoulder.

"What about Luca?" Ali asked, twisting the strap of his rifle around his hands. "If he was with Shiloh, do you think they would have killed him?"

Sawyer didn't reply, but her silence was answer enough. Ali's face crumpled; his shoulders slumped. Brooks wrapped an arm around his body, pulling him close, whispering something in his ear. Nic's heart broke for him, and she almost went to him, but Val's voice held her in place.

"If Shiloh's alive, then we *need* to save her."

"I intend to," Sawyer said.

Nic blinked in surprise.

"How?" Paul asked. "Tell us the plan, and we'll go willingly."

A few heads bobbed. Shiloh was one of them now, always had been since the day she was born. Everyone here would risk it all for her.

Sawyer's hand tightened on the radio. "I offer Arcadia the deal they offered me. My life for Shiloh's."

Nic sucked in a breath. Everyone began speaking at once. Yelling and arguing. Only the children sat in silence, Becca and Ezra leaning into Charlie, the Qadirs leaning into Fatima, looking only somewhat awake.

"Shut *up*," Sawyer hissed, "all of you!"

Everyone fell silent, blinking at Sawyer. Her dark eyes had narrowed, her chin tightened into a harsh line.

"I am not arguing with any of you on this," Sawyer said. "Not this time."

"We all love Shiloh," Brooks said, taking a step toward Sawyer with her hands held out so as not to spook her away, "but you can't trade yourself. We need you."

Sawyer shook her head. "You don't need me. You've never needed me. All of you are leaders." She looked at Brooks and Amelia and Paul, and then her gaze shifted to rest heavily on Nic. "*Every* single one of you. There is nothing I have done in the last twelve years that one of you could not manage."

"You've kept us united," Paul said. "You've been convincing all the groups to rise again. To fight back."

Sawyer scoffed. "A great job I've done of that. Lots of factions still want to hide and do nothing. I got The Family killed with the plan to bomb the Cleansing, and almost blew up my own niece in the process."

Nic winced and looked down at her feet, the familiar ache in her chest rising as she remembered The Family. Her Family. The ones she'd lost.

"You convinced Imminent Reign to plant the flyers in Pittsburg," Paul pointed out.

"I didn't do that. Nic did that," Sawyer said, gesturing toward Nic with the radio.

"Me?" Nic asked, both eyebrows shooting up. She hadn't done anything.

"I told them what happened to you. About what the Elite did to you, to one of our own."

A cool sweat broke across Nic's neck. For a second, she only saw white. Boots kicking into Nic's ribs, electric pain rippling through her skin. She was screaming.

And then Val touched her hand, bringing her back to herself.

"Truth is dangerous, true," Sawyer said. "But our stories... those are even more powerful."

Nic swallowed. She'd never thought about it before. She'd wanted only to forget. To lock away what had happened in its own cage and build thicker and thicker walls until she couldn't feel it anymore. But that wasn't working. It only served to break her apart at the seams.

But what if she was brave enough to face it? To examine the broken bits of herself? Could something good come from it? Could she take what the Elite had done and use it against them?

Maybe.

Just maybe.

Sawyer looked at all of them again, her face wholly unguarded. For the first time, Nic peered past the leader's mask to the woman beneath. A woman who loved them all. A woman who'd done her best. A woman who would do anything for them. A woman who was tired.

"ROGUE doesn't need me," Sawyer said softly. "It certainly doesn't need what I'll become if I lose Shiloh again. It needs all of *you*. And it needs *Shiloh*."

Nic's throat hurt. Val crossed her arms over her chest. Silence crackled between them, electric with the power of this heady moment. Everyone looked at one another, and then back at Sawyer.

Brooks tugged at her own braids, shaking her head. "Okay," she relented, "okay."

Sawyer's lips twitched, even as she blinked away tears. She pulled the radio off her belt, prepared to trade her life for Shiloh's.

Love makes us, Nic thought. *And it destroys us.*

The most powerful thing on Earth.

◈

"You blew up the fucking capital building," Luca said, not for the first time. He sat on an overturned bucket in the abandoned cellar they'd stumbled upon several blocks away from the Unity Center. By the thick layers of dust and cobwebs, not to mention the burned-out hulk that was the rest of the building, they could tell it had been a long time since anyone had been here.

He scrubbed his palm over his face, looking like he was in shock. At least, he didn't look so bad. The swelling had gone down in his face, and he seemed like his breath wasn't as painful anymore. "I mean you—"

"Blew up the capital building," Shiloh finished for him, from where she sat cross-legged on top of an old, dusty desk frowning down at the Elite's radio. Or at least, what had been the Elite's radio. Using scraps of metal and some old tools she'd found in the basement, she'd torn it open and wires dangled everywhere. "To be fair, I didn't exactly blow up the *entire* building."

Just that fountain. Good riddance.

Chaos had rained in the city as flames burst through the domed roof of the capital building, all emergency services dedicated to putting it out and rescuing the people who may have been within before the fire spread. In that chaos, Shiloh and Luca had been temporarily forgotten, long enough for them to get to shelter. Where they went from here, Shiloh had no idea. Hence the radio...

Shiloh tried to remember when she'd pulled apart the ROGUE radio, trying to figure out what her mother had done to make them different. In theory, if she could remember enough about it, Shiloh could make this Elite radio into a ROGUE radio. Then maybe she could get a message to Sawyer and the Sparrows—or whoever had survived.

Shiloh shook the thought from her head. *They're not dead. None of them are dead.* She *refused* to think anything else.

"Seriously, Shiloh," Luca said, "that was incredible. We'd be dead if not for you."

The warmth in his voice was odd coming from him. It made

her skin itch in discomfort. She deflected it back. "Well, if you hadn't gotten me the gun, we'd have both died."

"The gun?"

"Yeah, the one you kicked to me."

He was quiet for so long that Shiloh glanced up from the work.

"Right," he said, smirking. "You're welcome."

Shiloh rolled her eyes and went back to her work.

The silence that fell between them was no better than the noise. Even though Shiloh tried to focus only on the puzzle of tangled wires and machinery before her, images kept creeping in. All of Jake, only Jake.

Had he survived the blast? Probably. He'd been all the way in the Vault. The explosion wouldn't have reached it. And she shouldn't care, she reminded herself. And yet, she did. The very thought of Jake made her eyes burn.

She blinked rapidly, but Luca must have seen because he began to say, "Shiloh, about Osgood—"

"If you tell me I told you so," Shiloh said, through her teeth, not looking up, "I'm going to shoot you."

"I wasn't going to. I was...um..." He rubbed at the back of his neck. "Are you okay?"

No, no she wasn't. Her chest was still hemorrhaging. Any moment, she'd bleed out on the floor. But she said, "I'm fine. Why wouldn't I be fine?"

"Shi—"

"Just let me focus so I can fix this before the Elite find us, okay?" she snapped.

He sighed. "Okay."

An hour later, Shiloh tightened the screws to seal the cover back on the radio. She flipped it on and turned the dial through channel after channel. No voices of Elite popped through, but no voices of ROGUE either.

"Did it work?" Luca asked.

"There's only one way to find out."

❧

Before Sawyer's fingers pressed the radio, it crackled to life, a voice popping through. Masculine, speaking in gibberish. Sawyer cocked her head at it, listening. Out of the corner of her eye, Val saw Charlie pull a pad of paper and a pencil from a blood-soaked pocket, scribbling furiously.

Ali's head popped up. "That's... that's..." He leaped to his feet, jumping up and down, his face lighting up with a smile. "That's Luca's voice. I'm sure of it! It's—"

"Shhh," Nic hissed, and Ali fell instantly quiet so Charlie could hear the rest.

As soon as the voice on the radio ended, Charlie let out his own whoop. "It's them, it's them, it's them, it's them!" In his arms, the littlest boy whined. Charlie patted his back, shushing him. "I'm sorry, sweet boy. But it's them. Luca and Shiloh. They were taken by the Elite to the Capital, but they escaped."

"They escaped?" Sawyer repeated, sounding winded.

Val's brain tried to wrap itself around what this meant. Her chest had been cracking open for so long that it took a moment to let down her defenses—to understand and believe what was being said.

"She's alive?" Val repeated, her voice weak.

Charlie looked at her, beaming a smile, his eyes wet behind his glasses. "Yes!"

Light exploded amongst the darkness of her chest. Nic let out a laugh beside Val, throwing her arms around her.

"How—" Sawyer muttered, as those around them broke into murmurs of excitement. Paul was thanking God, and Ali was dancing, and the children were clapping, and Brooks sank to the earth with her face in her hands.

If the Elite were anywhere near, their merriment would bring them right to them, but Val didn't care.

"What—" Sawyer tried again. "How—"

"She's Starchild," Val said, manic laughter bursting from her lungs. "That's how!"

Sawyer sagged against the tree, pressing the radio against her forehead. Tears slipped down her face, catching the rapidly fading daylight.

"There's more though," Charlie said, looking at his pad of paper. "They're still in the capital. Hiding. They need help getting out and back to us."

"Can you do that?" Val demanded, looking to Sawyer. "Can you get her back?"

"Yeah," Sawyer said, laughing through her tears. "Yeah, I can get them home."

FIFTY-EIGHT

The network of ROGUE ran deeper than Shiloh could imagine, or at least it had a lot of allies ready to take a risk when Sawyer called. It took a ride in a dump truck and a sail across Lake Michigan hidden in a crate of the hull of a ship, but Shiloh and Luca made it out of the capital alive.

When the boat anchored near an abandoned cove for the night, Shiloh and Luca snuck off, as they'd been instructed. They splashed into the cool, dark water and swam for the shore. A hand waited for Shiloh as she pushed out of the water, a hand large enough to swallow hers whole, yanking her out and pulling her into strong arms.

"I swear to God I am never letting you out of my sight again," Paul murmured against her ear. "You've shaved ten years off all our lives."

"Sorry," Shiloh replied, pulling away. She took a step back into the soft mud of the shoreline and two sets of arms collided with her.

"I'm going to froqing murder you," Val growled into Shiloh's ear.

"She won't," Nic reassured.

"The froq I won't."

Shiloh clung to both of them, relishing the surety of these two girls, whom she loved, who loved her. It held back the pain in her chest that threatened to consume her. Over their shoulders, she saw Ali stumbling toward Luca. The two brothers embraced, slapping backs and laughing. Brooks crashed into them both with a force that made Luca cry out in pain.

Somehow, Sawyer had gotten all of them there, all the way to Michigan. Yet another trick up her sleeve. Amelia and Fatima, Mick and Charlie, must have remained somewhere else to keep the children safe. Shiloh knew from the messages they'd receive that everyone had made it—except Wallace. Sweet, old Wallace. Luca hadn't spoken for a long time after they'd received that news, a cloud descending over them.

But the rest were here. Shiloh's family was here.

Sawyer stood a few feet away, a soft smile on her lips as she watched Shiloh and Nic and Val. Shiloh stepped out of Nic and Val's embrace and flung herself at Sawyer with a force that nearly bowled her over.

With only one arm, Sawyer still managed to hug Shiloh tighter than she'd ever been hugged. And she didn't know why it was this —this hug from this person—that broke Shiloh open. But the tears crashed past the dam she'd held, the cracks in her heart she'd slapped Band-Aids on bled anew, soaking their bandages. She buried her face into the crook of Sawyer's neck. Breathing in the scent of pinecones, Shiloh sobbed.

"Sh, sh, it's okay now," Sawyer said, running her hand up and down Shiloh's spine. "You're safe."

"It-it's not th-that," Shiloh said. She knew everyone else must be turning to watch. She tried to suck in air to slow her breathing and stop her chattering teeth. But the grief demanded to be felt, acknowledged, bled out.

"Then what is it?" Sawyer asked softly.

Shiloh hated the words. She spat them off her tongue just to get them out of her mouth. "You were r-right... about Jake."

Every muscle in Sawyer's body tensed for a second before she released a sigh. She soothed a hand through Shiloh's hair. "Oh, honey, I'm so sorry. I didn't want to be. I really didn't want to be."

⚶

A knock came at the door to the Osgoods' Chicago condo. Jake, who lay face down on the couch in the living room, wanted to tell whoever it was to *froq off and go away*. He wanted to tell the whole world to froq off and leave him alone. He wanted to scrub his brain raw and clean until he could forget how he'd watched Shiloh shatter before him, beneath the nail he'd driven in himself.

I broke her heart.

I broke her heart.

I broke—

KNOCK, KNOCK, KNOCK!

Footsteps sounded as the guard, who'd been sitting in the camera room off the main hallway, stepped out to answer the door. Jake hauled himself upright as he heard the lock click. His entire body ached, but otherwise, he was unharmed. Being in the Vault had protected him from the blast that had gone off several stories above his head. He'd seen the carnage Shiloh had wrought. Shattered glass and broken pillars. The whole fountain, destroyed.

Now that made Jake almost want to smile. Almost.

Of course, the media had stated the explosion had been some freak accident. Jake was fuzzy on the details of the exact lie the Council had spun, but it seemed ludicrous. He hoped people didn't believe it.

"Advocate Andreou," the guard said, and Jake stiffened at the name, "I'm afraid Councilor Osgood is not here today."

"I'm aware," Reese replied. "He knew I was in the city and sent me to check on his son."

Jake could only guess what all his father knew—what Beck had told him. But Samuel at least must have known Jake was in the Unity Center when the bomb went off to send Advocate Andreou along. Mom had called Jake, panicked when she hadn't been able to get ahold of him a few hours after the explosion, but Jake had reassured her he'd only been napping and hadn't heard his phone. He absolutely *hadn't* been in the building.

"Would you like me to get your jacket?" the guard asked.

"No, thank you."

Jake climbed to his feet as Stefani's mother entered the room, her hands tucked into a long grey raincoat. It must have been pouring outside because the fabric shone with moisture, and now that he thought about it, he could hear rain pounding against the rooftop. He hadn't noticed it before.

"Good evening, Advocate Andreou," Jake greeted.

"For the last time," she said, with her sweet, unassuming smile, "you can call me Reese."

It was a subtle reminder of when Jake had last seen her, sitting around the table of those who should be considered her enemies. Did she know what had happened down in the Vault? Did she believe, like Shiloh, that he'd taken the side of the Council? Jake hadn't even told Stefani what had happened, just replied to her frantic text of *'Are you dead????"* with 'Yes' and ignored all the ones that came after. Jake wasn't ready to face Stefani's reaction to what he'd done. He was afraid she'd hate him too.

"How are you?" Reese asked, as she took a hand from her pocket and offered it.

"I'm fine," he said.

Physically, at least, he thought.

He reached his own hand forward, and when she grasped his hand, paper crinkled between them. She pressed the paper into his palm. Keeping his hand partially curled, he read the message on the small slip of paper.

She's safe, was all it read. Two words that flooded him with so much relief his legs nearly buckled beneath the weight of it.

Somehow, Shiloh had found her way back to ROGUE. She was alive and safe, and for now, that was all that mattered.

"May I?" Reese asked, gesturing to a nearby cart set with crystal tumblers of alcohol.

"Help yourself."

She strolled over to the cart and poured a deep amber liquid into a glass. Jake slipped the note into his pocket. Later, he'd tear it into a million pieces and flush it down the toilet. Reese swirled the liquid but didn't bring it to her lips, her sweet mask unwavering as she looked around the room. She approached the mantel at the front of the room. A hologram fire burned within the white marble fireplace.

"Is this new?" Reese asked, pointing to a scaled replica of an eighteenth-century ship. It'd sat there for as long as Jake could remember. He'd gotten in trouble once as a boy for trying to play with it.

Jake took the bait, approaching her. Did she know that, if they faced the fireplace, they were the farthest they could be from the cameras?

"I don't think so," Jake said.

"Hm," Reese said, studying it for a moment.

In the silence, Jake ran a finger across his throat, at the scabbed cut beside his pulse where Shiloh had pressed the sharp tip. The fierce, unrelenting fire in her eyes, the thunder in her voice, had been intoxicating. He'd never seen something so breathtaking.

"I know what you did down there," Reese whispered. She lifted her glass, hiding even the movement of her lips. "I was warned that you might betray my secret."

Jake tensed, unsure what to say. He didn't know how to explain what he'd done and why he'd done it. That he'd been watched. That he'd had to play it right. That, when the shooting started, as he'd scrambled to cover, he'd made sure to kick the

Elite's fallen gun in the direction Shiloh had fled. And that button he'd hit to seal Shiloh in? He'd known as soon as he looked at Shiloh that action had shattered her trust in him. From where she stood, she couldn't have heard the boots of the Elite coming from the elevator, but Jake had. He hadn't hit the button to keep Shiloh in; he'd done it to keep the Elite *out*.

He didn't regret a single choice he'd made, but he regretted the ruin it left behind.

Reese took one small sip of her drink and went on. "But I don't think you're going to betray me. I think you're trying to do exactly what you told Scalpel you were going to do. I think you're trying to regain the trust of the Council to get close to them. I think... I think you were put into an impossible situation, and you played it the best way you could. Am I wrong?"

The rain on the windows pounded even harder, sounding like footsteps marching, soldiers going to war. Jake set a hand on the mantle, a casual gesture, but it'd hide the movement of his lips from all but Reese.

"No," Jake said. "I promise, my allegiances haven't changed."

She granted him a small smile, and Jake saw it—an opportunity.

"Can you get a message to her?" Jake asked, his words almost soundless. "So, I can explain what happened?"

Reese reached up and ran a light finger down the sail of the ship. "I could. But do you really want me to do that?"

"Why wouldn't I?"

"Because the best way to make your enemies believe you are on their side is to make your allies believe it, too."

Jake turned this idea over in his head, looking at it from all angles. And he hated that she was right. Scalpel and Shiloh and everyone associated with them would now believe Jake had caved into the promise of being a Councilor. That he had turned his back on them.

"How would Beck even know what ROGUE thinks?" Jake asked.

Reese lifted a single shoulder in a shrug. "She might not. But we must always assume our enemies know more than we think. It would be foolish not to."

It *would* be foolish. The last time Jake had sent a message, Beck had somehow anticipated that move. She'd known when she asked Jake to stay in the capital a few more days that Shiloh would soon be in reach. Jake didn't know how, but he knew he'd played right into Beck's hands... and nearly gotten Shiloh killed in the process.

The memory of Sawyer's words hissed through Jake's head: *You've done nothing but put Shiloh in danger from the moment you entered her life.*

And of course, Sawyer had been right.

Now, Jake had a choice. He could take another risk to send a message and repair what had been broken in the Vault. But if the message fell into the wrong hands—if Beck anticipated Jake's action—he could blow up any chance of destroying Arcadia. Of ensuring Shiloh remained free—because so long as the Council ruled, Shiloh would never be safe.

Glass slid down Jake's throat as he swallowed, remembering the look on Shiloh's face when she saw his hand on that button. The tear that had slipped down her cheek in the Vault. "She'll hate me."

Reese nodded. "Yes, she probably will. For a time."

Jake's eyes fluttered shut, and Shiloh was there in the darkness, just as she always was. The victory of her smile, the universe of her eyes, the serenity of her touch. But the image morphed to the memory of her fingers caressing across another man's—Grim's—forehead. And Jake could picture it so clearly: the future Shiloh might have if Arcadia fell. A life she deserved.

A life that might not be with Jake.

Maybe it'd be better... if she hates me.

Jake slid a hand through his hair, yanking at the ends. Maybe, this time he'd pull hard enough that all his hair would fall out. The rain had softened on the roof, no longer sounding like marching feet, transitioning into something more like sobs. And it took all of Jake's will not to join the sound with cries of his own.

"Jake," Reese said gently, looking around his arm to see his face. "Do you want me to send that message?"

His heart aching, he replied, "No."

FIFTY-NINE

"I just don't understand," Val murmured, sitting between Shiloh and Nic near the small fire the Sparrows had built along the riverbank.

The rise and fall of breaths sang a steady lullaby in the camp. Besides the girls, only Brooks remained awake, circling the camp, her boots not even making noise in the leaves. The trees above them swayed in a gentle night breeze, and in between the branches, Shiloh could glimpse the stars. A dozen of them blinked back, like scattered diamonds on onyx silk.

Jake's voice whispered in Shiloh's ears. *You're an entire universe.*

Shut up, she hissed to the invisible Jake. *Just shut up.*

Earlier, Luca had told the story of the Vault, so Shiloh didn't have to. Everyone had sat around the fire as he told them everything, and Shiloh had forced herself to remain stone as she watched anger and hatred settle over her family's faces. Only Val and Nic had appeared to refrain, and even now, confusion and hurt warred over their expressions. Shiloh understood. He'd been their friend, even if Val might not admit it, and Jake had betrayed them, too.

"I was so sure he loved you," Val said. She picked up a stick that rested near the flames and stabbed one of the smoldering logs. It hissed and sparked.

Shiloh tightened her fingers around the book in her lap—her father's journal. Sawyer had retrieved it from beneath Shiloh's mattress at the camp in northern Minnesota before they fled. She didn't have to flip to the last page to see those words Jake had written.

Forever.

"Maybe he does love me," Shiloh said. "But if loving me means betraying ROGUE, it's not a love I want."

Nic blinked rapidly, her eyes wide and glossy. "And you're sure —you're *really* sure it wasn't an act?"

Shiloh sighed. She wished. Oh, how she wished! Even now, some particle of her being clung to the hope that was what it had been. But that particle needed to die because that button—that froqing button! Distanced from what had happened, she could make sense of everything else. But that button she couldn't understand. That had been unforgiveable.

And besides, if it had been a misunderstanding, Jake knew how to contact ROGUE and explain. But he hadn't.

"I'm sure," Shiloh said. She pinched the bridge of her nose until the tears went away. Enough. She'd cried enough.

When the waves of emotion ebbed, Shiloh opened the journal to the very back page. She took out the slip of notepaper. Jake's handwriting, the promises. *You're still stuck with me.* Her heart lurched, the memory of his love flooding her with warmth. She wanted to cut out the part of her that loved him, that wanted him to love her. She wanted to root it out and burn it up. She couldn't; it went too deep. Maybe, she'd never be fully rid of him.

But she *could* try.

She crumbled the notebook paper—Jake's words, his broken promises, all her hopes and dreams—in her fist and held it out over the flame. Her hand shook as the fissures in her chest pleaded.

"Shiloh," Nic said softly. Val set a hand on Shiloh's back.

Shiloh let go.

The paper fell into the embers. With new fuel, the sparks turned into a flame. In moments, Jake's promises were nothing but ash.

Nic rested her hand on Shiloh's shoulder, as Val wrapped both arms around Shiloh. The silence hovered between them as the three girls, sisters by everything except blood, stared at the flame.

"What happens now?" Val said.

Shiloh knew what she meant. Val's entire life had been upended. The life before this one hadn't been what she'd wanted, but it had been the only one she knew. Now, all that was left was uncertainty.

Shiloh was uncertain, too. Jake had been the center of her orbit, her goal, her focus. But Shiloh fought for so much more than that. For her freedom. For her parents and Hope. For the Haven girls she had left behind. For the family she had found in the Sparrows. For a different world. A better world.

There were many types of love, and they were all worth fighting for.

But the next step remained unclear. Sawyer had gotten word tonight of riots in New York, spurred by the fliers of Councilor Bennett that had been left there. The riots would surely be quenched—little fires put out. But it proved people were willing to fight, if given enough of a reason. If only all of ROGUE was willing to push back, to come out of hiding and go to war. So many factions were waiting, ready, but so many more needed to be convinced that there was more to life than survival. And if the sister of Elaine Sanders couldn't convince them, maybe her daughter could.

Maybe. Just maybe.

Whatever that next step looked like, the path Shiloh walked remained clear.

"We keep lighting matches," Shiloh said, "and hope one burns the world down."

"Well," Val said, her lips twisting into a smirk. "I've always liked to play with fire."

❧

Jake knocked on Stefani's door, keeping one hand behind his back. Stefani answered a heartbeat later and leaned against the door-knob. Jake had seen her every day in the week since he'd returned from Chicago, since the day he'd purposefully shattered his heart into a million pieces. Still, the differences between the girl Stefani had been a few weeks ago and the girl she was now landed like a punch in the gut.

She wore her uniform exactly as she was supposed to, no longer tied above her naval. The streaks of color in her hair had faded, leaving behind only bleached strands, the color of bone mixing with her auburn. And though Stefani smiled, it didn't reach her eyes.

"Jakey-boy," she greeted, then paused, taking him in. "Is that a gun behind your back, or are you happy to see me?"

Jake left his hand behind his back. "Can I come in?"

Stefani opened the door wider, letting Jake slide in. As per usual, she slammed the door in the guard's face and signaled her music player to blast some Codex-approved pop.

Maybe Jake should be doing this with more fanfare or make some speech, but instead, he simply pulled his hand from behind his back and held the gift out to her. "These are for you."

Both of Stefani's eyebrows shot into her hairline. She held her hands up, away from his offering like it might be poisonous to touch. "You got me... flowers? Metal ones?"

The bouquet between them weighed heavily in Jake's hands. Metal flowers of various shapes and petals weaved together to form a batch of wildflowers, bound together by a slim metal bow.

"They're not from me," Jake said.

She frowned.

Jake pushed them closer to her. "Read the note."

Stefani took the metal bouquet hesitantly, fitting it into the crook of her arm so she could look at the tag tied into the bunches. Her eyes widened and then grew damp. Jake swallowed because he knew what those words said.

Flowers wilt.
love doesn't.
I hate you always.
Val

"Sometimes," Stefani murmured quietly, "we said I hate you because we couldn't say the truth when there were people who could overhear."

Jake nodded, shifting his weight from heel to toe. Perhaps he should leave, give Stefani privacy. Or maybe he should hug her, wipe the tears from her cheeks. Because, froq, how he knew her pain. It matched his perfectly, a pain that writhed in his chest, demanding to be felt at every moment. With every breath. Haunting him with the truth.

I love Shiloh.

And I betrayed her.

And now... she hates me.

Stefani sniffed and swatted at the lines of mascara on her cheeks. "H-how?" she asked.

"I thought maybe Val's things were still in her room, since they sent her to a Reform Home," Jake explained, "so I went to talk to her roommates. A little bit of charming, and... well—most of Val's things were thrown into the trash bin by a school official, but a roommate lied and said the bouquet was hers. She said she imagined Val made it for someone special, and if I knew who it was, I should give it to them. It just so happens that I know who Val hated more than anyone."

One more tear glistened down Stefani's cheek, falling from her chin. "Thank you," she said softly.

Jake shrugged, unsure what to say. Words felt meaningless in the weight of this moment. Two girls—who loved each other with the strength and the undying nature of metal flowers—had been kept apart by nothing short of cruelty. No words could make up for that.

Jake's phone rang, saving them both. Jake glanced at his wrist, and his heart lurched at the name. He cast Stefani a look, and she quickly twirled her wrist to turn down the music. He sucked in a breath and answered the phone.

"Hello, this is Jake Osgood."

"Jake, this is Councilor Bennett."

Please, Jake's heart begged. *Please.*

Jake hope there could only be one reason Bennett was calling, surely. But was Bennett the sort to offer up rejection phone calls? Serenity Jameson had felt the need to call Jake earlier this morning to give him the courtesy of saying she'd chosen a different candidate.

"Councilor Bennett, it is so good to hear from you," Jake said. "How are you?"

At the sound of Bennett's name, Stefani made a wild gesture, twirling the metal bouquet through the air. She mouthed enthusiastically, "Did you get it?"

Jake ran a finger across his throat and mouthed *Shut up*. She threw him a crude gesture.

"I'm well. Thank you for asking," Bennett replied. His voice seemed strained, tired. "I wanted to call you personally to tell you—"

Please, please, please.

"That I have selected you as my summer intern."

"Really? That's fantastic! Thank you so much!" He forced exuberance into his voice.

Stefani threw both her arms into the air and mouthed, *You froqing did it!*

He had done it, hadn't he? Jake barely heard the pleasantries he and Bennett exchanged before he hung up. He should be dancing, he should be pumping his fist into the sky. His plan had worked. The information he needed to destroy Arcadia would soon be within his grasp. But instead, Jake's chest felt hollow and empty. A cavernous, echoing pit.

He stared at his phone, running his finger up and down the thin edge.

"Oi, Jake-boy, why so glum?" Stefani asked, cocking her head. "If that bottom lip goes any further, you're gonna trip on it. You should be celebrating! You did it!"

"At what cost, Stef?" Jake asked, sinking into Stefani's desk chair. It replayed before him. The look on Shiloh's face as love turned to mistrust and then to heartbreak. Her scream of torment that had been the last thing he'd heard before he lost consciousness.

Stefani's smile fell. She was silent for a long moment, then: "She'll understand one day, Jake."

"Maybe," Jake said, but he thought of the way Grim's head had rested in Shiloh's lap. By the time he could be free enough to explain everything to her, would she have moved on?

In the end, it didn't matter, because Jake would still burn down the world for her. He'd do whatever it took for Shiloh to live a free and happy life. Even if that life wasn't with him. Even if she stopped loving him. And maybe Shiloh should. She'd always deserved more than the son of a Councilor, tainted by the evil of the generations before him. The very thought of it threatened to tear Jake asunder, break his already fractured heart, but he knew—whatever fate existed for Shiloh and himself—one thing would remain unchanged.

Jake's heart was hers. Forever.

And she could break it. Over and over and over.

Stefani brushed a hand against Jake's shoulder as she passed him, a touch that expressed sympathy and understanding. Comfort and grace. Maybe she, too, found words useless right now. She walked to the table beside her bed and lovingly placed the metal bouquet in a rainbow-hued vase sitting there, straightening it this way and that. She then picked up a glistening pink lighter she kept beside her bed—one Jake knew Stefani sometimes used to heat a silver of metal to unlock her tracker. A lighter that meant freedom. She prepared to light the potted candle beside the vase.

It struck Jake what else Bennett's offer meant. In a few weeks' time, he'd graduate. And then immediately after, he'd be headed to the Capital. Alone. He sucked in a breath, taking in Stefani, the girl he'd once despised, who'd helped him through all of this, who understood what it was like to love and lose in Arcadia better than anyone else.

His friend.

"I'm going to miss you." The words were out of Jake's mouth before he could think it through.

Stefani spun around toward him like a ballerina twirling, one hand splaying against her chest, her red fingernail chipped and overgrown. The other hand still clutched the lighter.

"You *are*?" she cooed dramatically.

"Yeah, yeah." Jake rolled his eyes. "Don't let it go to your head."

"I mean, this is an honor, Jakey-wakey!" She bounced onto the center of her bed, landing on her knees. "To be missed by you."

"Forget it," Jake said, spinning the desk chair around so he turned his back to her. "I take it back."

"You can't take it back." She must have begun bouncing because her mattress squeaked beneath her. "I mean, I could always tell Serenity Jameson I respectfully decline her offer. As good as we got along in the interview, how can I give up the opportunity for Jakey-boy Osgood to *miss* me?"

"For froq's sake! Can't you ever—*Wait!*" Jake stopped, his breath hitching as her words sank in. He spun the chair around to face her. "What did you say?"

Stefani pushed her bare feet into her bed and stood. "You are looking at the summer intern for Councilor Jameson." She curtsied.

"B-but you didn't apply?"

"Of course, I did," Stefani said, bouncing on her toes, the springs whining. "I just didn't tell you."

"You didn't have an interview."

"I didn't have an *in-person* interview. But oddly enough, one of the applicants, who *did* have an interview, got an email saying their interview had been canceled, and there was suddenly a gaping hole in the schedule. And I may have, conveniently, called Serenity Jameson's personal number and told her how terribly sad I was I didn't get a chance to be interviewed. And if she had something change to let me know. And what do you know? Someone didn't show up to interview."

Stefani swept a low bow, like she'd achieved her greatest performance. Hope blossomed in Jake's chest like the first rays of sun breaking through a long, dark night. *Stefani froqing Andreou!*

"You're coming with me?" Jake asked.

She grinned, and for the first time, it reached her eyes. They danced with a million colors, all tinted with mischief. "Uncovering dirty little secrets is what I do best."

A laugh bubbled out of Jake's throat. Relief, profound relief, poured through him. It propelled him to his feet and, before he could stop himself, he'd flung himself toward the bed and tackled Stefani in a hug. They both landed on the bed with an *oomph*.

"Get off me, you heathen," she said, shoving him away. "Who knows where you've been?" But she was laughing.

Jake flopped onto his back. Stefani sat up beside him. "Thank you, Stef."

"Of course, prighead." Stefani snatched the pillow from beneath his head and slapped him across the face with it. "You didn't think I'd let you steal all the glory."

"I don't want glory," Jake said. "I just want *her*."

The hole in his chest ached as it widened.

I just want her.

Her.

Only ever her.

Shiloh had become an impossible dream, a distant universe Jake didn't belong to, a flickering flame that remained his only hope in the darkness. And he was a foolish dreamer, an idiot, maybe even a little selfish. But some part of him couldn't let go. Not yet.

Stefani's smile twisted into something a little sadder. She looked down at the lighter she still held in one hand. "I know, Jake. Believe me, I know."

And she did. Of course, she did.

She stretched out her empty hand toward him. "Partners?"

Jake sat up. Partners in crime with Stefani Andreou? Peace and harmony, he was in trouble. And that was exactly where he wanted to be.

Despite everything, a crooked grin took over Jake's face as he shook Stefani's hand. "Partners."

Grinning wickedly, Stefani flicked the lighter on with her other hand. The flame glowed between them—red and orange and blue and white.

But don't you know? Jake thought. *Dissent is gasoline. And a single spark can set the world on fire.*

"Good," Stefani said, the fire dancing in her eyes. "Now, let's go get our girls back."

Acknowledgments

The words "Thank you" seem too small to express my gratitude to these amazing people, but these words are all I have, so here goes nothing.

THANK YOU TO...

- My husband, for listening to my frustration, putting up with my stupid TikToks, and always supporting me as I shoot for the stars. I love you forever.
- My son, Atticus, who was with me since the first book released (you just looked like a tadpole at the time— you're much cuter now). Thank you for only *occasionally* smashing my keyboard and destroying my papers. I hope if I teach you anything, it's that, sometimes, it can be scary to be yourself in this world. Be yourself, anyway. BE BRAVE, my sweet boy!
- My besties, Molly and Audj, for being first-readers and cheering me on every step of the way. Thank you for the 10,012x you've pulled me out of the self-doubt spiral, and the million more times you will in the future.
- Jaime, for being my beta, my artist's eye, my dopamine dealer, and my biggest hype woman. Your love for this series has not only brought so many new readers, but also kept me typing long into the night. Thank you for always making me believe in myself again.
- Brooklin, for being my reminder that every hard moment in writing this series is worth it, just to know

you love my story. Thank you for the fanart. I have loved every piece!

- My editors: Derek, this book could not have happened without you—both your skills and your friendship. Kelsey, you have a magic way with words and made this book more beautiful with your touch.
- My proofreaders: Serys, thank goodness for Booktok. I am so grateful for your friendship. Thank you for your ever-kind feedback and your sensitivity. Kristen and Audrey, thank you for lending me your fresh eyes.
- My Fearless Writers. You all make me brave.
- Every single person who read and loved HERESY. You are my dream come true. Your words and love for these characters has been my inspiration these last two years. Always remember: No matter what the world says, who you are is perfect. So BE YOU. Love who you love, believe what you believe, and empower others to do the same. BE A HERETIC!

And last but not least, a round of applause to myself. Holy fuck, I did it again.

Can I take a nap now?

About the Author

C. A. Campbell hails from Kansas City (The Missouri side, if you please), where she shares her writing space with her husband, three ridiculous dogs, and her rambunctious toddler. As well as being an author, she works as a family nurse practitioner and nursing professor. When she's not working, she can be found (likely, in her pajamas) spending time with family, listening to a true crime podcast, or listening to an audiobook at 2x speed.

For updates on The Heretics Saga, subscribe to C. A. Campbell's newsletter via her website or follow her on social media.

Website: www.cacampbellwriter.com
Contact information can be located on the website.

instagram.com/cacampbellwriter

tiktok.com/cacampbellwriter7

CPSIA information can be obtained
at www.ICGtesting.com
Printed in the USA
LVHW032118181022
731001LV00003B/19

9 781735 376424